Praise for *New York Times* bestselling author

Lori Foster

"Storytelling at its best!
Lori Foster should be on everyone's auto-buy list."
—#1 *New York Times* bestselling author
Sherrilyn Kenyon on *No Limits*

"Foster's writing satisfies all appetites with plenty
of searing sexual tension and page-turning action
in this steamy, edgy, and surprisingly tender novel."
—*Publishers Weekly* on *Getting Rowdy*

"Foster hits every note (or power chord)
of the true alpha male hero."
—*Publishers Weekly* on *Bare It All*

"A sexy, believable roller coaster
of action and romance."
—*Kirkus Reviews* on *Run the Risk*

"Bestseller Foster...has an amazing ability to capture
a man's emotions and lust with sizzling sex scenes
and meld it with a strong woman's point of view."
—*Publishers Weekly* on *A Perfect Storm*

"Foster rounds out her searing trilogy with a story that
tilts toward the sizzling and sexy side of the genre."
—*RT Book Reviews* on *Savor the Danger*

"The fast-paced thriller keeps these well-developed
characters moving...Foster's series will continue to
garner fans with this exciting installment."
—*Publishers Weekly* on *Trace of Fever*

"Steamy, edgy, and taut."
—*Library Journal* on *When You Dare*

Dear Reader,

I'm beyond thrilled to return to the world of MMA—
mixed martial arts—in my new Ultimate series.
No Limits is Cannon's story—you might recognize him
from my previous Love Undercover series. And while
you'll see a few familiar faces from that series making
cameos here, you'll also meet all-new characters who
I hope you'll love!

Anyone who follows me on Facebook and Twitter
knows that I'm a big UFC fan. Love the sport, respect
the fighters, and I'm always intrigued by how such
big, capable, lethal and motivated guys can not only fit
romance into their training and travel schedules, but
are also loving husbands and fathers.

The Ultimate series is not about fighting. It's about
fighters, aka alpha heroes. It's about romance. It's
about love.

I hope you enjoy *No Limits!* Feel free to let me know.
You can always reach me via social media, or email me
using the links on my website at www.lorifoster.com.
And if you missed *Hard Knocks,* the prequel novella
introducing the Ultimate series, it's available now
wherever ebooks are sold.

Happy reading!

Lori Foster

LORI FOSTER

NO LIMITS

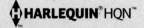

Recycling programs
for this product may
not exist in your area.

ISBN-13: 978-0-373-77904-8

NO LIMITS

Copyright © 2014 by Lori Foster

All rights reserved. Except for use in any review, the reproduction or
utilization of this work in whole or in part in any form by any electronic,
mechanical or other means, now known or hereinafter invented, including
xerography, photocopying and recording, or in any information storage
or retrieval system, is forbidden without the written permission of the
publisher, Harlequin HQN, 225 Duncan Mill Road, Don Mills, Ontario
M3B 3K9, Canada.

This is a work of fiction. Names, characters, places and incidents are
either the product of the author's imagination or are used fictitiously,
and any resemblance to actual persons, living or dead, business
establishments, events or locales is entirely coincidental.

This edition published by arrangement with Harlequin Books S.A.

For questions and comments about the quality of this book,
please contact us at CustomerService@Harlequin.com.

® and TM are trademarks of Harlequin Enterprises Limited or its
corporate affiliates. Trademarks indicated with ® are registered in the
United States Patent and Trademark Office, the Canadian Intellectual
Property Office and in other countries.

Printed in U.S.A.

www.Harlequin.com

Many, many thanks to the following people
who answered questions on police procedure
or business start-ups! You all rock:

Rick Peach, Valia Lind, Rosebud Lewis, Janel Klews,
Susan Moore, Ruth Hernandez-Alequin

CHAPTER ONE

COILED TIGHT WITH TENSION, Cannon sat in the leather chair and faced the lawyer's desk with loaded impatience. From head to toe, his battered body ached, but at present his mind focused on less-physical issues. After finally landing back in the States, he'd planned to spend the day in the hot tub, and the night in bed—with enough female company to help him forget how close he'd come to losing his last fight.

Three days ago he'd taken on the biggest challenge of his career, his most publicized bout on the main card for the Supreme Battle Championship—in Japan with a packed house and a lot of expectation from the organization.

Though he'd taken plenty of hits himself, he'd been beating his opponent on points…and then he'd fucked up.

After catching a kick to the liver, he'd lost his air, bent double in excruciating pain, and was going down. Only pure instinct had helped him throw one last punch when his opponent had charged in for the kill.

That punch had landed dead center on the Pit Bull's glass jaw. Lights out.

He'd struggled to stand upright while the other man came back around, and the fight had ended with him as the winner. But damn, it had been close, and being the winner didn't negate the hits and kicks he'd absorbed. He needed some R & R.

However, all his plans for taking it easy had gone awry when he'd gotten summoned back to Warfield, Ohio. It was a three-hour drive, and usually when he made the trip, he visited friends first thing.

This time, though, he waited around as a stuffy lawyer flipped through paperwork and a female assistant gave him the eye.

"Ah, here we are," the lawyer said, rattling his damn papers and looking at Cannon over the top of his reading glasses. "I'm sorry for the delay. Since I had expected you yesterday, you've taken me off guard."

The rebuke was wasted on Cannon. "Like I said, I was out of the country." Shifting, he tried not to flinch from his many aches.

"Japan, yes?"

Unwilling to encourage more chitchat, he gave a single nod.

Again sorting papers, the lawyer said, "You're a fighter? Isn't that right?"

"Yes."

"The SBC?"

"Yeah." Hell, he had the fight club logo on his T-shirt. He sat forward, his forearms on his thighs. He had no idea what this was about, but he wanted to get to it. "Look, how much longer is this going to take?"

Frank Whitaker divided papers into three stacks. "I only need a moment to get organized."

Organized with what? Cannon knew this had something to do with Tipton Sweeny, a local pawnshop owner who'd recently passed away. "If I hadn't been out of the country, I would have attended the funeral." And maybe seen Yvette, Tipton's granddaughter.

Just thinking about her stoked up his tension.

Without looking away from his papers, the fifty-something, overweight lawyer said, "I'm sure everyone understands."

Cannon had only known Tipton as a local business owner, a staple in the community he loved. His granddaughter, Yvette, attended school with Cannon's sister. That was where any real relationship ended.

Except that Yvette had always flirted with him, he'd always avoided her...right up until the day he'd kissed her, the day he'd wanted to go on kissing her and more—after helping to rescue her from perverted thugs.

Shit, shit, shit.

He didn't want to think about that, about her. So much time had passed, and still she had the ability to blow his composure.

How was she? Still in California apparently, or she'd be the one here dealing with...whatever had to be dealt with. "Didn't Tipton have other relatives?"

"Yes, I'm sure he did."

So how the hell was Cannon involved?

Cannon watched the assistant glide in, leading with her big breasts. A wave of perfume drifted with her. She handed more documents to the disorganized suit and then, smiling at Cannon, moved close enough to brush her thigh against his. Smiling down at him, she touched his knee. "Would you like a cola? Coffee?"

Trying not to be too obvious, he moved out of her reach. With women, he always stayed cool.

Except for that time with Yvette.

"Water would be nice. Thanks."

"Of course." She shifted her hand to his shoulder, stroked, felt his muscle beneath the soft cotton of his faded T-shirt and then trailed off. "I'll get it right now."

Being a guy, and therefore not immune to a come-on, Cannon looked her over more closely as she left. She had one of those supercurvy figures that got enhanced with a cinched suit, skirt and soft blouse. High-heeled pumps showed off her sexy calves. Big breasts, full hips, twisted-up pale blond hair. She wore her sexuality out there, almost bludgeoning him with her interest, her sly looks and the occasional lick of her shiny red lips.

Women hit on him, no big deal. But never in a lawyer's office under these circumstances.

Was she doing the lawyer? Were her blatant comeons to make Whitaker jealous? Cannon eyed the older man, wondering if he'd even noticed the dozen different ways his assistant had already made her interest known.

Not that he was cynical or anything. And not that he was biting.

At least…he didn't think he was. Still, when she came back in and leaned down farther than necessary to hand him the glass of ice water and napkin, Cannon went ahead and checked out her cleavage. Her skin looked soft, but that overpowering perfume assaulted his nostrils until he looked away.

The lawyer stacked his papers and took off his glasses. "Thank you, Mindi. I'll let you know if we need anything else."

Accepting the abrupt dismissal, she nodded. "I'll be at my desk." Behind the lawyer, Mindi paused in the doorway, made a show of looking Cannon over from shoulders to knees, her sultry gaze lingering on his crotch. She gave another slow lick of her lips and…yeah, okay, he was maybe a little interested.

Hell, he'd been so involved in training, traveling for the fight and then the fight itself, he'd suffered self-imposed celibacy for too long.

But for right now, Cannon gave his full attention back

to Whitaker. What could the man possibly need from him that took so damn many papers and notes?

Finally, somber in his preparedness, the lawyer folded his hands together and stared directly at Cannon. "You have inherited property and funds from Mr. Sweeny."

Whoa. A surge of fear brought Cannon forward. His heart thumped heavily in his chest. "Did something happen to Yvette?"

Bushy brows coming together, the lawyer slid his glasses back on, sifted through the goddamned papers and shook his head. "You're talking about Ms. Sweeny, the granddaughter?"

"Yes."

"She has inherited, as well."

Relief sent oxygen back into his lungs. Jesus. Cannon pinched the bridge of his bruised nose, annoyed by his over-the-top reaction. But then, with Yvette, it had always been that way.

The lawyer went on. "And in fact, Mr. Sweeny has evenly divided his assets between the two of you."

No way. "Between Yvette and me?"

"Yes."

Blank, Cannon sat on the edge of his seat and tried to sort it out—without success. "I don't get it. Why would he do that?"

"He left you a letter." The lawyer handed over an envelope. "I trust it will explain what I can't. But what I can explain is that Mr. Sweeny came to me three years ago with very detailed instructions on the distribution of his assets in the event of his demise. He revisited once a year to amend and further clarify as his financial status fluctuated. I saw him for the last time two months ago when his health started to decline."

"He had a stroke?"

The lawyer nodded, hesitated, then again folded his hands on the desk and dropped the officious attitude. "Tipton had become a friend. He was alone and I'd just lost my wife…." Whitaker shrugged.

"I'm sorry."

He tilted his chin to acknowledge that. "Tipton's blood pressure was high and he knew he wasn't well. He seemed to dismiss the first stroke, but the next was worse and the third worse still. That's when he finally closed up the pawnshop."

So he hadn't closed up shop three years ago, after the vicious attacks, as Cannon had always assumed.

"He was being treated, seeing the specialist on a regular basis, but he figured it was only a matter of time…."

Seeing the sadness on the lawyer's face sent guilt clawing through Cannon. Damn it, he should have gone to visit Tipton more. He'd known about the first stroke, but not the two after that—and then he'd been in Japan when Tipton's body gave up the fight. "Yvette was with him?"

Shaking his head, Whitaker said, "He didn't want to burden her." A measure of easiness showed on his face as he collected his thoughts. "I gather all of you shared an experience. Tipton never shared the details, but I assume it was something life altering?" He didn't wait for Cannon to give details. "His granddaughter moved away because of it and Tipton didn't want a sense of responsibility to bring her back, not, he said, when he knew her trips home were still difficult for her. He wanted her to return on her own terms, not out of a sense of obligation."

Bombarded with uncomfortable emotions, Cannon got up to pace the small office. Yeah, he imagined Yvette struggled anytime she had to be in town. No girl should ever have to suffer what she had. There were times when the memory of it hit him like a wild haymaker, leaving him dazed, angry, in a cold sweat.

And he wasn't the one who'd been threatened in the worst possible way.

Remembering softened his voice. "She didn't know Tipton was sick?"

"Like you, she knew of the first stroke. But Tipton felt strongly about carrying his burden alone." Chagrined, the lawyer shook his head and said, "No, I'm afraid that's not precise. He wanted you to share his burden. He said you could handle it." The lawyer gestured at the letter. "It's in there."

A burden? More confused than ever, Cannon tapped the letter to his thigh. "So what are the rest of those papers?"

"Deeds, bank statements, debts to be paid, retirement funds." He shook two sets of keys out of a padded envelope. "Responsibilities."

Chewing his upper lip, Cannon stared at the papers— and had the god-awful urge to hand back the letter. His plate was full, and then some. He could handle it, that wasn't the problem.

It was Yvette.

Could he handle her, the way she affected him?

More to the point, could he resist her now if she needed him? Just thinking about her, hearing her name, had his muscles tightening in that familiar way. "You said *deeds?*"

"One for the house, one for the business."

"The pawnshop?"

"Yes."

"The last I'd heard," Cannon admitted, "he was going

to sell it." After what had happened, he'd expected Tipton to sell the house as well, but he'd stayed put.

"No. He continued to work until the health issues forced him to retire. Said it was cathartic for him to stay busy. He also redecorated the house." The lawyer shrugged. "It was home to him."

Home. Cannon nodded in understanding. His mother had felt the same, refusing to budge from her house, the neighborhood, even after they'd lost his dad to extortionists.

Her insistence on staying put was Cannon's number one reason for learning to fight. He'd lost his dad, so he had been determined to protect his mother and sister. And he had—until his mother had passed away with cancer. Now it was just him and his sister, and…whatever it was Tipton had embroiled him in.

More than a little intrigued, Cannon asked, "So now what?"

"You sign a few papers and take ownership alongside Ms. Sweeny. Fifty-fifty. The two of you can decide to stay put, sell or one can buy out the other."

Cannon shook his head. "Have you seen Yvette?" He couldn't imagine her wanting the house, but even if she did, where would she get the funds? She'd be…twenty-three now. Still young for such responsibilities.

But finally old enough…for him.

"She was in yesterday."

Had Yvette expected him to be there, as well? Looked forward to it?

Or maybe dreaded it?

He hated the thought that seeing him might dredge up a past better forgotten.

Whitaker turned the papers, placed an ink pen on

top and pushed them toward Cannon. "If you wouldn't mind?"

He wasn't about to sign anything until he'd read it all and figured it out.

The lawyer sighed, pushed back his chair and stood. "Read Tipton's letter. I'm sure it'll all make sense then."

"You know what's in it?"

Whitaker looked away. "No, of course I don't. Tipton gave it to me sealed."

Suspicions rose.

Clearing his throat, the lawyer met his gaze. "I know...*knew* Tipton. He had a strong mind right up to the end. He knew what he was doing, what he wanted."

And he wanted something from Cannon.

Coming around his desk, the lawyer clasped his shoulder. "I'll give you a few minutes." And with that he stepped out of the office, closing the door behind him.

Walking over to a window, Cannon leaned a shoulder on the wall and studied the envelope. It was sealed, all right, closed with tape wrapped completely around it. He tore off one end of the envelope. With a sense of foreboding, he pulled out two neatly typed, folded papers. Opening them, he skimmed over the type to see Tipton's signature at the bottom.

Going back to the first page, he began to read. Each word made his heart beat heavier with trepidation—and anticipation.

Yes, Tipton knew what he wanted. He'd spelled it all out in great detail. One particular paragraph really got to Cannon.

This is her home, Cannon. No matter what, she should be here. She always trusted you and you were always there, such a good boy.

Despite the enormity of what Tipton wanted, a touch of humor curved Cannon's mouth. Being that he was twenty-six, only a grandpa would call him a boy.

I know it's a lot to ask, especially after you already risked your life for us. But she's too cautious now, too guarded. If you'll agree, I know you can free her from the nightmares so she can be her carefree, happy self again.

Did Tipton mean literal nightmares? Or just the nasty memories of being attacked, threatened with the worst a woman could suffer?

No, he didn't want to think about that now; it still enraged him, the helplessness, the fear he'd felt while being an unwilling spectator to the cruelty.

What a grandfather considered guarded could just be maturity. Just how free did he want Yvette to be?

The lawyer walked back in. Cannon ignored him as he finished reading.

If it's necessary, if your life is now too busy or if she won't agree, go ahead and sell both places with a clear conscience. But selling will require emptying the house—and that will bring about different problems for her.

What did that mean? What type of problems came with finalizing a sale?

In my heart, I know she'll be happier here in Ohio, in Warfield, than she could ever be in California. Whatever you decide, Cannon, please don't tell her

about this letter. Not yet. And please know, regard-
less, you will always have my deepest gratitude.
Sincerely,
Tipton Sweeny

Familiar feelings stirred up, feelings he'd long ago
tamped down and then forgotten. Or tried to forget. God
knew he'd done his best to demolish them, to sweat them
out in the gym, fight them out in the ring.

Screw them away with willing women.

But, damn it all, every sensation Yvette inspired was
still there, rooted deep.

Taut with anticipation, he asked, "Where's Yvette
now?"

"I'm not sure," the lawyer said. He stood behind his
desk, but didn't take his seat. "She took a set of keys, so
perhaps she's at the house."

Disquiet kicked Cannon in the gut, adding to the aches
and pains left over from his recent fight. Would Yvette
go there alone? He shrugged off the urge to race to her
rescue.

Again.

He'd done that once—and then she'd walked away.

Moved away.

Across the country to California.

He tugged at his ear, uncomfortable with the latent
resentment. Yvette was *not* the one that got away. She
wasn't a missed opportunity. She was only a girl he'd gotten to know better under extreme, dire circumstances. A
girl he'd wanted, but had been too noble to touch…much.

But she had gotten under his skin, and even after three
long years, he wanted her still.

Fuck it. He'd walked through one fight after another
to make himself a prime contender for the belt, but re-

sisting the lure of finally having Yvette was a fight he knew he couldn't win.

He faced Whitaker with barely banked anticipation. "Where do I sign?"

YVETTE STOOD IN the doorway of her grandfather's house. Yesterday, after the long drive back from California, she'd chosen to put aside the visit. Instead she'd gone to see the lawyer, and then checked into a hotel and tried to get some sleep. Impossible. The heaviness of what awaited her had her tossing and turning all night.

It wasn't just a fear of being in the house. No, it was a fear of seeing Cannon Colter again, losing herself in his appeal, relapsing back to that young, love-struck, vulnerable girl who'd let him play the hero without a single ounce of pride.

Her grandfather wanted her to stay in Ohio. Returning for his funeral had been difficult enough. But to live here?

She'd finally learned to conceal her cowardice and, more recently, to accept the limits of her romantic capability. Being anywhere near Cannon threatened her resolve on both counts.

For now, for however long it took to sort out her obligations to her grandfather, she really had no choice. She would be in Warfield.

Pushing aside the nerve-jangling fear, she stepped into the house and closed the door behind her. The click of it sounded so final that her heart missed a beat.

Until she looked around. Then her pulse sped up.

Sunlight spilled in through open drapes, brightening the interior, showcasing the many changes. From the carpet to the paint on the walls, even the lamps on the end tables, everything was different. Her grandfather had redecorated with used items, probably from the pawn-shop, but he'd pulled it all together.

For her.

Through a mist of tears she took in the remodel. God, she missed him so much already.

Forcing one foot in front of the other, ignoring the murky unease making a slow crawl up her spine, she went through the living room to the dining room and around to the kitchen. Familiar appliances filled the walls, but cheery new wallpaper and bright scatter rugs transformed even this room.

Flipping on lights as she went, she explored the house and all the changes. Although everything seemed different, the empty house still held the scent of her grandfather's Old Spice aftershave.

Just as it held the memory of Cannon's kiss.

Even while weepy from her loss, a tidal wave of warmth invaded her limbs whenever she thought of him. She again felt his protective touch, remembered the hot taste of his kiss. She'd built some elaborate fantasies around that brief moment in time. But now she wasn't sure if even Cannon could make a difference to her wounded psyche. Knowing that wouldn't stop her from wanting him, and that scared her more than anything else could.

Shame quickly followed, because she'd just lost her beloved grandpa, the one relative who hadn't given up on her, who'd taken her in after her parents' deaths and made her world better. She had to keep him and his wishes uppermost in her mind.

When she saw her room, fresh tears welled up. New bedding and drapes made it look different, but all of her more personal belongings were just as she'd left them.

She touched a hair ribbon on the dresser, an ancient carnival doll he'd won for her.

Slowly, she sat on the edge of the bed.

Cannon had missed the meeting at the lawyer's office.

For over three long years she'd honed her fixation on him, using it to help her get through trying times, using the example of him to hopefully become a better person. He was everything she wasn't, everything a good person should be. Generous, protective and caring. He had an athlete's body, a fighter's strength and an angel's heart—all wrapped up in gorgeous good looks. Every girl in the neighborhood had wanted him.

After months of ignoring her childish flirting, he'd come to her rescue when she'd needed him most. And afterward, he'd felt pity for the pathetic girl she'd been.

He'd finally seen her—but as a victim.

Well, she was stronger now, and she'd prove it, to him and herself.

She watched every SBC fight, soaked up every mention of him on the internet and in numerous interviews. To the general public Cannon had been dubbed "the Saint," in part due to his philanthropic attitude and always calm demeanor. Nothing and no one ever rocked his foundation of composure.

Insiders, however, claimed the nickname had more to do with his gentle treatment of women. He stayed too busy to engage in long-term romantic relationships. While he kept things brief, most of the ladies he knew became his friends without resentment, having nothing but good things to say about him.

Yvette could attest to his gentle concern and careful consideration. Difficult as she knew it'd be for her, she hoped he still claimed her as a friend, too.

It was necessary to see him, the sooner the better. But

first… She'd learned that expending energy helped her to overcome her reservations. Before facing Cannon, she'd do what she could to shake off her nervousness and the uneasiness of being back in Ohio.

With that goal in mind, she emptied her suitcases and, doing her best to block the foul memories of what had happened in this very house, prepared for a night out.

Cannon would no doubt go to Rowdy's bar, where he used to work. She'd find him there, and she'd show him that she wasn't a frightened little girl anymore. She wasn't pathetic. And she wouldn't fawn over him. She'd convince him that she was a different person now.

And then maybe she'd be able to convince herself, too.

THE SECOND CANNON got his signature on all the papers, the lawyer stood and grabbed up an overflowing brief-case. "I'm sorry, but I'm running late for court. I hope you understand."

"Sure." He had no reason to hang around for small talk, especially when he had so much to think about.

"Tipton was a good man." Friendly, sincere, Whitaker shook his hand. "If you need anything more, anything at all, please call Mindi and she can put you through."

"Thanks." With everything now in a big padded envelope, Cannon followed him to the door.

Before he could head out with the lawyer, Mindi reappeared. "You're not rushing off, are you?"

That Whitaker took note, and then ignored his assistant to continue on his way, left Cannon wondering even more about their relationship.

Her body language, the way she looked at him and her tilt of her lips all invited him to stay. But if she and the lawyer were involved…yeah, he had no interest in getting mired in that sinkhole.

"Sorry. I have a dozen things to do yet today."

Pretending to pout, she came closer. "But we have the office to ourselves." Deliberately crowding his space, she reached around him and turned the lock on the front door. "Did I tell you that I'm a huge fan?"

Her breasts brushed against his chest; he could feel her breath on his throat. "Appreciate that. Thanks." He kept his hands at his sides and tried not to breathe too deeply of her perfume. "Maybe another time, though."

She teased a fingertip up and down her cleavage, and, damn it, he looked.

Encouraged, she moved that teasing finger to his chest, up and over his collarbone to twine an arm around his neck.

Temptation pulled at him. He glanced back and saw no one outside the office. After reading Tipton's letter, he felt strung so tight that release would be welcome.

"He won't be back," Mindi said. Boldly she leaned into him…and stroked his crotch. "Don't worry about him."

God, he needed the distraction. And his body liked her touch well enough.

But his head wasn't in it.

He got the definite vibe that she and the lawyer had a thing. Plus he figured Yvette would have dealt with Mindi, too, might even have to deal with her again. He would never do anything to make this new transition harder on her than it'd already be.

And then there was the fact that he hoped to finally have Yvette… Yeah, to his brain, cozying up with Mindi seemed like a very bad idea. "Sorry, honey, but I'm just not up for it."

"Fibber," Mindi whispered. Her eyes grew heavy, her breathing shallower as she stroked him. "You are most definitely up."

Her twist of his words only marginally amused him. "Let's just say parts of me have no sense." Especially with her small hand expertly working him. "But the rest of me is shot, I swear." *The rest of me,* he admitted to himself, *wants Yvette, and only Yvette.*

She pressed her lower body against his thigh. "I'd only need ten minutes."

"Ah, now what fun would that be?" Gently, because he hated to insult any woman, Cannon tried to ease her back. "I'm sure you deserve more than ten minutes."

"Later," she whispered while nuzzling his neck, "when you have more time, you can make it up to me."

Her sharp little teeth grazed his throat. Damn it, he was started to feel molested. "Listen—"

She opened her mouth on him and Cannon knew he had to get control of things before she added a hickey to his other many bruises. Catching her shoulders, he physically moved her away, saying with firm insistence, "Not today."

Hurt overshadowed her lust, and she turned away from him. Hands to her face, she gave a nervous laugh. "Wow, this is embarrassing."

Even annoyed, Cannon sympathized with her. "Don't be embarrassed. I'm flattered."

She shook her head. "And not at all interested."

Stepping up behind her, he cupped her shoulders. "You had your hands on me, so you know that's not true." She'd felt his semierection. His dick liked her just fine. "But my last fight took it out of me, I just got into town and now I have a load of legal responsibilities to take care of."

"That's all it is?" She looked at him with hope. "Seriously?"

Not about to commit himself, he shrugged. "All I

know is that it's not happening now." Ready to make his getaway, he turned and unlocked the door. He got as far as his truck when she called to him.

Looking back, he saw her poised in the doorway.

"I'll take a rain check then, give you some time to get settled, but I'm not giving up."

He couldn't help but grin at her. Since he doubted they ran in the same circles, he wasn't worried about seeing her again. With a salute, he got behind the wheel, started the engine and drove away from the building.

No matter how many times it happened, it was still a nice thing to be wanted. Didn't matter that part of the appeal was his status in the SBC.

One thought led to another, and he had to wonder, would Yvette be as impressed? Even before he'd been picked up by the elite fight organization, she'd looked at him with idol worship, as if he had the answer to every question.

But that was years ago. For all he knew she could be engaged, even married now. He pictured her as he re-membered her: young and innocent. Just coming into her own. Shapely and sweet.

Ripe.

Unsettled with conflicting emotions, Cannon drove by Tipton's house, but when he knocked, no one answered. He had a key, but it didn't seem right to go in before talking to Yvette. He went by the pawnshop next, but it remained locked up, dark and empty. Like him, Yvette had probably found a motel room.

He'd track her down soon enough, and then they could get reacquainted all over again.

Damn, but he could hardly wait.

CHAPTER TWO

SHE'D BEEN GONE for hours. After making a very brief stop at the pawnshop, disappointed to see the shape it was in, Yvette had shopped for basic groceries she knew she'd need. After that, she'd bought a few new security devices, preparing the best she could for her stay at the house.

Anxiety still churned inside her, but it didn't matter. She had outgrown that embarrassingly timid girl who'd allowed herself to be a sniveling victim.

Never again.

She concentrated on presenting herself as a proper, poised woman, using that facade to hide the truth. So many dreams had died, but no one else needed to know that.

Preparing to see Cannon, she made herself as polished as possible and then set off.

Because of the mid-August heat wave, she wore a white tank top with her skinny jeans and sandals. She'd pulled her freshly washed hair in a high ponytail that hung down between her shoulder blades.

On the walkway outside Rowdy's bar, she hesitated. Judging by the noise alone, the place was packed. Being in such a crowded atmosphere would help keep her attraction under wraps. She had to see him, but she wanted to do it without embarrassing herself in any way.

A trio of men stepped out, gave her double takes and

leered. She heard "Well, hello," and "Hot damn," along with a low whistle from the third guy.

Yvette made a point of not encouraging that sort of thing—really *any* sort of thing—with men, so she merely nodded and stepped inside. The place looked exactly as she remembered it, with people laughing, a small crowd dancing to the jukebox, every stool lining the bar taken up with a body.

More men checked her out and, wondering if she looked as out of place as she felt, she smoothed her palms over her thighs. Only on very rare occasions had she ever visited bars. Rowdy's bar was different than most, friendlier, a part of the community she still loved and missed, but it left her self-conscious all the same.

Rowdy himself worked the bar tonight, and when she saw a flash of red hair, Yvette knew he had his wife by his side. She heard him laugh about something his wife said and she smiled with them.

Cannon used to work here, right up until his fighting career took off. She knew that whenever he came to the area, he stopped in to visit, so she hoped to find him here tonight. And if not, then surely someone could tell her where he'd be.

Before people started to wonder if she'd gotten lost, she began searching the room, making her way past the front tables, the dance floor—and finally she found Cannon back by the pool tables in the company of men and women alike.

As if her senses had been starved for him, a dozen emotions made her muscles weak. He looked even better than she remembered. In an otherwise dim room, fluorescent lamps over the pool table added blue highlights to his dark, unruly hair, still a little too long, curling on the ends. As he bent to take a shot, his T-shirt stretched over those impossibly wide and strong shoulders. Muscles flexed, making her stomach flutter in an expected way.

That particular reaction to Cannon was nothing new.

A woman was draped over him, whispering in his ear, and he grinned, his blue eyes bright. The lady kissed his jaw and stepped back.

Taking the shot, Cannon sank three pool balls.

Yvette had never learned to play pool, but given how the others reacted, that must've been a good shot.

Laughing, two of Cannon's male friends handed over bills and the women lined up for hugs. Part of the bet, maybe?

Or just because they all wanted an excuse to touch him? She'd bet on the latter.

Watching it all, Yvette noted the five-o'clock shadow and a few colorful bruises that darkened his handsome face. He'd always had a lean, strong build, but now he was positively shredded, his muscles bulkier and more defined, not an ounce of extra weight on his large frame.

Thinking of the number of fights he'd had in such a short time, she smiled. It was a running joke in the SBC that if a fight became available, if another fighter got sick or injured and had to drop out, Cannon was always there, ready to jump in. Drew Black, the owner of the SBC, loved it—especially since, so far, Cannon always won.

He'd had a few close calls, but every time he managed to pull it off. That last bout… It still amazed her how he'd finished the fight before it finished him.

Shifting inside the doorway and taking up an unoccupied spot against the shadowy wall, she studied him for a while, content to refamiliarize herself with how he moved and how his lips formed that particular cocky smile. Not that she'd ever really forgotten. He drew people like flies to honey, and occupied the entire room with his presence.

Thinking of the antics her grandfather had pulled, her brows twitched together. Cannon already had so much on his plate. He was out of town more than in, and he traveled all over the world.

He had to be wondering how he'd find the time to take on even more. Shortly, Yvette would relieve his mind. She knew her grandfather had always felt seriously indebted to Cannon. But this was not the way to repay him. As a fan favorite in the sport, he made a considerable amount of money with each fight. Endorsements were lining up for his approval. He'd been in a few commercials, done some commentating. He didn't need her grandfather's meager inheritance.

He'd earned it, she would never dispute that, but he shouldn't have to maneuver through the quagmire of responsibilities her grandfather had unloaded on him.

Though she wished it could be otherwise, she'd stay around only long enough to sell both properties, give Cannon his share and then move on.

But before she did that, she wanted him to know that she would no longer chase after him like a lost puppy begging for affection—especially when she couldn't do anything about it even if she got his attention.

Which she knew she wouldn't. Other than that one sympathy-inspired moment after the threat had been removed, he'd made his disinterest well-known.

Little by little, Cannon cleared the table. With only the cue ball and two others remaining, he chalked his stick, walked around for a better position, bent for a shot—and froze when his attention zeroed in on her body.

Yvette held her breath, especially when that electric blue gaze deliberately tracked up in minute detail, from her thighs to her stomach, her breasts—and finally her face.

Their gazes locked.

Her heartbeat rocked into overtime when, with an arrested expression, he slowly straightened to his impressive height. No smile, just those intense blue eyes consuming her.

Breathless from his potent stare, Yvette lifted a hand to wiggle her fingers in a small wave.

Suddenly he went into motion. Saying something to the guy next to him, Cannon handed him the pool stick. The other men—some of them fighters by the looks of them—jokingly protested. One of the women, smiling too widely, grabbed his arm with playful arguments.

After a whisper in her ear and a kiss to her cheek, Cannon disengaged from her. He pulled a roll of bills out of his pocket, tossed them on the table to appease everyone and walked away.

Knowing she'd caused a scene, heat rushed into Yvette's face. She could feel everyone staring at her now; in order to cope, she kept her gaze only on Cannon. Breathing harder, she tracked his stride around the tables, around human bottlenecks and displaced chairs on a path to reach her.

God, she thought she'd remembered, but the powerful way he affected her felt entirely new. She bit her bottom lip hard, fighting the urge to flee—or launch herself at him.

And suddenly it was too late to do either. Cannon reached her, still saying nothing as his attention moved over her again, this time with more familiarity. The reality of him was so much better than the memory—his height, how his wide shoulders blocked out the view of the rest of the room…sometimes the rest of the world.

She saw how deepened breathing swelled his chest, the loose-limbed way he held his long muscular arms, the intent way he watched her.

Being this near to him wrecked her poise. The silence made her more jittery still, so she licked her lips and whispered, "Cannon..."

One corner of his mouth curled as he touched her cheek, smoothed his fingertips along her jaw. Then, as if it happened all the time, he drew her into his chest and hugged her right off her feet.

HE COULDN'T STOP looking at her. Damn, he'd remembered her as pretty, but she'd matured into killer good looks—and didn't seem to know it. An angel's face paired with that trim but curvy figure, and yeah, he was pretty sure every guy in the place had already started fantasizing.

Too bad, because none of them would touch her.

If he'd had any doubts about wanting her, they were put to rest in a big way. Instead of three years, it felt like a decade he'd been waiting on her. Yes, he wanted her. He would have her, too.

The only question was how soon.

A few weeks ago she'd lost her grandfather, and she probably needed time to acclimate to being home around the unpleasant memories. He'd love to segue right from *hello* to *hell, yeah,* but he also enjoyed just looking at her and talking with her.

Sipping her Coke, Yvette stole a peek at him. Feathery lashes framed those big green eyes he remembered so well—eyes that used to watch him with innocent infatuation, but now seemed wary. She sat straight, proper. Spoke carefully. Avoided his direct gaze.

As Tipton had said, she was guarded.

She wore makeup, but not a lot. Even in a ponytail, her long dark hair made him think of it spilled loose on his pillows, or gliding over his chest.

Or his thighs.

And her clothes, while casual, covered such a sweet body it left him visually undressing her.

Repeatedly.

Knowing he had to get a grip, he asked, "Are you hungry?"

She shook her head. "But please go ahead and eat if you want."

"I'm good." Arms folded on the top of the booth, he smiled. "I can't get over how much you've changed."

That pleased her, he could tell. "It's been almost three and a half years."

Long enough for her to put the past behind her? To put *him* behind her? No, he wouldn't let her. "I'm so damn sorry about Tipton."

"Thank you." She set the drink aside, then nervously drew her finger through the damp ring the glass had left on the booth top. "I wanted to talk to you about that. About—"

"Hey, Saint." Two guys sidled up to the table. "Can we get a pic?"

Cannon forced his gaze away from Yvette. "Sure." He would never alienate a fan, but damn, the timing could be better. Yvette had been screwing up her courage to say something. Now he had to wonder what.

Stepping out of the booth, he bent a little to put himself more in line with the shorter guys, and with a double thumbs-up, smiled as a plump lady used her cell phone to snap a few photos.

That only seemed to unleash other fans, and before he knew it, he was posing with men and women alike. Some wanted to hug him, some wanted him in a fighter's stance, a few just wanted him to mug for the camera. Before he could get a handle on things, he'd taken around twenty photos and signed more than a dozen autographs.

Yvette watched it all with a look of fascinated indulgence. When there seemed to be a lull, he reseated himself. "Sorry about that."

"You're popular, I understand." Her long glossy ponytail spilled over her shoulder when she tipped her head to study him. "I watch the fights."

That pleased him more than it should have. "Yeah? What do you think?"

"You're pretty amazing."

He held back his grin. "I do my best."

That earned a short laugh. "Humble, too." Shaking her head, she teased, "No wonder they call you the Saint."

He'd rarely heard her laugh before, and hearing it now did funny things to him. It was nice. Rich. Husky.

A turn-on.

"It's a dumb fight name, but I don't have much say in it."

"Would you rather something else?"

Sure he would, but admitting it would sound juvenile. "Doesn't matter. What they call me isn't as important as whether or not they remember me."

"Being memorable is accomplished by putting on a good fight. And you always do." She leaned in a little, teasing him. "That's not just my biased opinion either. I've heard the same from the commentators, read it in articles and heard other fans say it."

"Yeah? When was this?" Had she attended a fight?

"I live in Cali. Last year you were only three hours away, so I made the trip."

"*Only* three hours, huh?" Damn it, why hadn't she told him? "I got a knockout in the first round of that fight."

"Everyone was on their feet screaming. Pretty exciting." She grinned. "A guy behind me spilled his beer down my back."

Cannon winced. "Idiot."

"I forgave him since he was cheering for you."

In his experience, most women who attended live fights either came on the make, or with a boyfriend. He didn't like either possibility for Yvette. "So who went to the fight with you?"

She shook her head. "Just me."

She'd gone alone? For some reason, that broke his heart. "What fun is that?"

A dimple appeared in her right cheek. "You got a first-round knockout. Believe me, it was fun."

"I wish you'd told me you were there." He'd thought about trying to look her up, but California wasn't a small state, and there'd been so much to do prefight.

Besides, she'd been the one who'd walked away....

As if she'd read his thoughts, she straightened, her shoulders back. "I couldn't be that bold. You were busy. It wouldn't have been right to bother you."

He didn't want her so uptight with him. Once, long ago, she hadn't been. "It would've been nice to see you." But carving more than a few minutes out of his jammed schedule would have been dicey.

A flash went off behind them, and Yvette turned to see a woman taking another picture. Unlike with other women, the intrusion didn't seem to annoy her, and the attention didn't seem to excite her.

Remaining poised, she said, "Maybe I should get going. There are a lot of people hoping for your time."

"I'd rather you didn't." No way did he want things to end so quickly. "It's easier for me to fend them off if you stay."

"You want to fend them off?"

"I like my downtime same as any other guy." Especially with her so near.

"Does that happen everywhere you go?"

The popularity inherent in the sport occasionally made him uncomfortable. This was one of those times. "More so the past year, but yeah, I sometimes get recognized."

Amusement had her lips twitching. "And you just take it in stride." Reaching into her purse, she located her phone and lifted it out. "Mind if I take one, too? I'll add it to my Facebook."

A good excuse to make his move. "Only if you're in it with me." Sliding out of his seat and over to her side of the booth, he deliberately took up space so that they sat touching. He put one arm over her narrow shoulders, keeping her close, and took the phone from her. "My reach is longer."

Yvette went very still, almost frozen, as he leaned in, near enough to feel the supple curves of her body, the scented warmth she radiated.

Stretching the phone out in front of them, he said, "Tell me when you're ready."

Gathering herself, she lifted her lips in a practiced smile, said, "Go," and then held her breath.

Sexual awareness slowly uncoiled inside him. Her long ponytail teased the skin of his arm, her sweet little body tucked in against his.

It was as if the years had never happened—except that now she was more mature and plenty old enough for his interest.

And yet, something held him back. Maybe her new reserve.

After snapping a few photos, Cannon handed her back

her phone—and stayed put. He'd go slow, but he wouldn't retreat.

He wanted to nuzzle her neck, drink in the light fragrance of her shampoo and the warmer scent of her skin. If she was any other woman, he'd whisper a suggestion or two in her ear. But this was Yvette, and they had a lot to talk about.

"So."

She concentrated on adding the photo to her Facebook page, along with the location of Rowdy's bar. "What?"

I want to get you naked. "How come you went to the fight alone?" Leaving his arm around her, Cannon idly let his fingertips tease the warm sleek skin of her shoulder. "Boyfriend isn't into Mixed Martial Arts?"

After peeking up at him, she said, "If I had a boyfriend, would I be sitting here like this with you?" Satisfied that she'd labeled the picture properly, she tucked her phone away in her purse.

"Why not?" He pressed his thigh to hers. "We're friends."

She seemed preoccupied with reading the front of his T-shirt. After a shaky indrawn breath, she looked away. "I don't have a boyfriend—but if I did, I doubt he'd like me getting so close to you."

"No boyfriend." He ran his hand down her ponytail and found her hair every bit as silky as he remembered. Expanding lust made his voice lower and huskier. "California guys are blind?"

"I had been dating, but…" She rearranged her purse, her drink, looked around as if seeking a distraction.

Cannon had a feeling she kept busy just to avoid answering. "But what?"

She folded her hands together on the tabletop. "We split up a little before I bought the ticket."

For reasons he didn't want to explore too much, he was glad to know she wasn't with anyone else. He gave her ponytail a gentle tug. "I'm sorry."

"It's okay. Things hadn't been going well anyway, so I'm glad I didn't waste the experience with him."

He liked how she put that, as if seeing him fight had been special.

"My best friend wanted to go, but she couldn't get off work. So I went alone." She lifted her narrow shoulders. "No big deal."

"Cheap seats?"

"What?" Confusion brought her gaze back to his.

He'd remembered her eyes as a striking green, but he'd forgotten how it made him feel when she looked right at him. She had that absorbed, heated look a woman got while straining toward an orgasm.

Damn. He blew out a careful breath, determined to get his lust under wraps. "At the venue. How far were you from the action?"

"Oh." Once again fascinated with the logo on his shirt, she murmured, "Club seats. They weren't too bad."

Without even thinking about it, Cannon continued to play with her hair. "I could have gotten you floor seats if you'd let me know."

"It wouldn't be right to ask you for a favor like that! And besides, the floor seats didn't appeal to me."

"How come?" Most everyone he knew coveted the limited vantage point.

"It looked like they had their own party going on. No one was really watching the fights. The guys were all going back and forth for drinks and the women were all flirting."

True enough. The ladies often showed up dressed for

a club atmosphere and hopeful of hooking up. "I take it you didn't plan to flirt?"

She shot him a guilty look that he didn't understand. "I never do."

"Never, huh?" That'd be a shame. He remembered her as being really good at it. He settled his hand on her shoulder again. "Why stop now?"

"Because it was wrong!" As if she hadn't meant to say that, she turned her face away. Even in the dim light of the bar, Cannon could see the blush on her cheeks. Seconds ticked by before she spoke again, this time quieter, more composed. "I know I used to be a terrible flirt."

That was so opposite of what he'd been thinking, he smiled. "Nothing terrible about it." She'd just gotten out of high school—though at the time he hadn't realized that she'd fallen behind and was older than most graduates. "Everyone flirts at that age."

Shaking her head, she denied that. Nervously, she pulled her ponytail over her shoulder so she could play with a lock of hair, winding it repeatedly around two fingers. "I was bad, always eyeing you like I did."

"Hey." Squeezing her shoulder, he hugged her a little. "I liked it."

Her soft lips tweaked to the side. "You did not. You avoided me when you could, and when you couldn't, you were careful not to be too familiar. I understand why now. But back then..."

Gently, he touched her chin, lifting her face so she met his gaze. "You're one of the prettiest, sexiest women I've ever met. Of course I liked it when you looked at me." But he'd thought her too young, and he'd been so determined to make it in MMA that, as she'd said, he'd avoided her.

She sounded strained when she whispered, "Thank you."

Watching her fingers stroke in and around her hair made him think about her fingers on him—teasing him the same way.

He wondered what she was thinking, if her mind had wandered into the same sexual arena as his.

"I don't want to make excuses."

"About?"

"How I...came on to you. It's just that after so many years of uncertainty, I'd finally finished school and was able to get a little independent. Not that I was planning to leave Grandpa."

"I know." She'd been very dedicated to Tipton, and vice versa.

Her gaze shifted away. "I loved him so much."

"He loved you a lot, too."

Her lips pursed, then curved with banked happiness. "He used to get after me for flirting. He said I was inviting trouble."

At the time, Cannon had considered *her* the trouble. "I'd always assumed you were just eighteen." Later, before leaving, she'd told him she was almost twenty.

As if that embarrassed her all over again, her pleasure faded. "It's not that I was dumb or that I screwed off in school."

"I know that." Because her parents had died when she was thirteen, she'd spent the rest of that school year grieving and got held back. Then for the year after that, different relatives shuffled her around from state to state, no one wanting to keep her.

Until she'd landed with Tipton Sweeny. But again, she'd missed so much schooling....

"I felt dumb," she admitted. "Most of the kids knew I was older. Especially the boys."

Cannon could imagine how they'd hit on her. With the way she looked, she'd have been every high school boy's wet dream.

She tugged at that lock of hair a little more before flipping it back behind her shoulder and putting both hands on the tabletop.

She did that often, catching herself and slipping back behind that mask of poise.

"You were so different," she said. "I guess that's why I always felt safe teasing you."

Safe. An odd word to use. "If it's any consolation, I had to concentrate real hard to resist you."

Biting back a laugh, she nudged him. "You are such a fibber."

"It's true." And now, being older, she was even more appealing. And he no longer had to resist.

Maybe gathering her thoughts, she sat silent for a moment. Tipton wanted him to be there for her, to make things easier, so Cannon waited patiently, giving her time—strangely content just to be with her.

When she looked at him this time, she kept her gaze deliberately direct. "After that, I proved what a coward I am." Loathing sounded in her tone. "That was even worse than the infantile flirting."

He was here for Tipton, Cannon reminded himself. But Tipton was far from his mind as his fingertips grazed her jaw, his thumb smoothing over her downy cheek. "That's not true."

Shying away from his touch, she leaned forward, her forearms on the table, her head dropping. "The rest of you were strong and brave and all I did was fall apart."

Laughing, she covered her face. "God, it still humiliates me to remember it."

"Listen to me, Yvette." He cupped his hand around her nape, his voice low, intimate. "You were young and afraid. No one would blame you for that. But you didn't get hysterical. You didn't escalate things. So you shed a few tears. So what? Hell, I was shaking I was so pissed off."

Twisting, she faced him—and in the process she managed to move away a few inches. "You shook with anger, I shook with fear." For a brief moment, her eyes closed. "I remember that day like it just happened. Those men breaking into the pawnshop, threatening me and hurting Grandpa, abusing that woman…"

"Shh." Cannon remembered it all in detail, too. If he lived to be one hundred, he would never forget. How much worse must it be for her? "They'll spend the rest of their lives rotting in prison."

"Thank God."

"Yeah." The cops had been after the sick fucks for a while. They were known for underground porn, forcing women into sexual situations and taping it for their own twisted thrills. They'd used the pawnshop to make one of their videos, gaining Yvette's and Tipton's compliance by dousing them in kerosene and threatening to set them on fire. Not because they needed the location, but because that had been part of the thrill for them.

Yvette worried that she'd been a coward; he marveled that she was still able to smile so easily.

"They'll never hurt anyone else," she swore softly.

"No." The two who had survived would die in prison. "They're gone for good." Before being caught, they'd twice gone after Yvette, breaking into Tipton's house with a twofold agenda in mind.

They had wanted to rape Yvette, using her in the porn video.

And they'd wanted to trap the cops who'd been after them.

She clenched her hands on the tabletop. "I want to see the lieutenant while I'm here in Ohio."

"I'm sure she'd like that." Cannon remained friends with the lieutenant and the detectives who had intervened that day. It was that friendship that had taken him to Tipton's house at the same time as the detectives. He'd been a part of it all, experiencing firsthand the helplessness and fear as the thugs repeatedly explained their plans to kill the cops and use Yvette.

Luckily, they'd been outmaneuvered and things had backfired on the bastards in a big way. Cannon had gotten in on that action, too, and the attack had ended with one of them dead and the other two arrested—but not before Yvette had suffered a living nightmare. No, she hadn't been raped, but she had been groped, threatened, terrorized and forced to watch the torment of others.

What Cannon remembered most about that day was how badly he'd wanted to protect her. He had avoided getting involved with her, but when he'd seen her so defenseless, when he'd felt her stark fear, it had all become very personal for him.

And somehow, through the passing of three long years, it remained personal. His hand curled into a fist.

Leaning into him, Yvette ducked her head and covered his hand with her own. "I'm sorry. I shouldn't have brought it up."

"We were both thinking about it." He turned his palm over to twine his fingers with hers. "We haven't really talked since then. Better to just get it out in the open."

And then hopefully they could put it to rest. He didn't want the ugliness always between them.

He wanted, eventually, to be more to her than a reminder of a living nightmare.

"Actually, that's why I'm here." Carefully, she disengaged from him, straightened, sat *properly*.

"Here, in Ohio?"

She shook her head. "I assumed you'd be here, at Rowdy's." Determination squared her shoulders. "I want you to know that I'm different now. I won't get in your way. I won't be a pest."

Cannon frowned. "I never said—"

"I can take care of everything, so you don't need to be involved."

He didn't understand her. Worse, he didn't understand himself. "What if I want to be involved?"

That stymied her.

Her lips parted but no words came out. She sank her teeth into her bottom lip, and before he could think better of it, he cupped her face in his palm, used his thumb to rub that lush lip.

Her breath came a little faster.

Time to redirect, or he'd be kissing her right here in the booth—and that was something better started in a more private place. "We have a lot to talk about, I know. But you look exhausted. How long have you been in town?"

"I was here for the funeral two weeks ago, but then had to fly back to Cali to take care of some things."

"That's a lot of traveling. When did your flight get in?"

"I got here yesterday." She sat very still until he removed his hand. "But I didn't fly in this time. I drove."

No way. "From California?"

"There's no telling how long it'll take to get things settled, so I brought a lot of my stuff and my car. It wasn't a problem. I enjoy driving."

"And sleeping in hotels?"

"Sometimes."

No wonder she looked so tired. "How long did it take you?"

"Longer than it should have, but I could only drive so many hours without getting sleepy. I stopped twice to rent a room for the night." And then with a cheeky grin, she added, "I'm not a hotshot fighter, so no fancy hotels for me."

He had no idea what she did for a living, who she lived with in California, or if the travel had cut into her budget. But they could cover all that later.

He was about to recommend they call it a night, thinking he could take her to her hotel room and, being noble, make a date to see her in the morning.

She spoke before he could make the suggestion. "You look a little tired yourself. I know you just got back from Japan."

"I'm sorry I missed the funeral."

"Grandpa would have understood." She studied his face.

"Pay no attention to the bruises. They look worse than they are."

"If you say so." Her gaze went to his jaw, and then to his chin.

Her intimate inspection almost consumed him before her eyes shifted away.

"The fights seem different on TV. Less violent. I'm really glad I was able to see one live, but I don't know that I'll be going again anytime soon."

"It's a charged atmosphere," he agreed. "The music, the lights. Everyone is pretty hyped."

"I liked all that, actually. And it gave me a good reason to wear my SBC T-shirt." She nudged him with her shoulder. "Don't let this go to your head, but the T-shirt has you on it."

He liked it when she relaxed enough to be familiar. "Which shirt?" No matter what she wore, guys would have noticed her. But he liked that she'd worn him.

"The one with you in a fighting stance."

He remembered the sponsor for that shirt—one of his first. Did that mean she'd been paying attention to his career all along?

"What?" she asked when he couldn't contain the smile.

"I was just imagining you in the shirt...with me all over your chest."

Dismissing any real interest on his part, she laughed.

She'd gotten good at deflecting attention, treating it as a joke. "Seriously, I'm flattered." And, damn it, more than a little turned on, even though she seemed oblivious to it.

"Let me tell you, it wasn't real flattering when the guy dumped his beer down my back." Eyes bright, smiling, she leaned in as if to share a secret. "I had to drive home like that. I was so afraid I'd get pulled over for something, and the cop would think I was smashed based on the smell of beer alone."

The urge to kiss her pulled at him—but she settled back in her seat.

"You didn't stick around to meet any of the fighters?"

"No. There was such a huge, noisy crowd, and I had a three-hour drive, so it seemed smarter to just go home."

Several men emerged from playing pool and headed toward them. "Well, you're about to meet some now."

She looked up in surprise—and transformed.

CHAPTER THREE

AS CANNON WATCHED, Yvette forced an expression of polite regard, adjusted her posture and smoothed her hair. To make a good impression? With his group of friends, she shouldn't have bothered. With her looks and bod, she only needed to sit there and they would all swarm to her, talk her up, and if he didn't set some boundaries, they'd probably hit on her, too.

Standing again, his body blocking her, Cannon asked, "So who won?"

Armie Jacobson, a good friend and partner of sorts who'd taken over the day-to-day running of the rec center Cannon had founded after Cannon had signed on with the SBC, took a dramatic bow. "That'd be yours truly."

"I should have guessed." Armie was good at everything he did—which included drawing women. "I think you owe me for bowing out."

Armie's dark gaze, a contrast to his very fair hair, jumped to Yvette with appreciation.

And now it begins, Cannon thought.

Moving around Cannon, Armie murmured, "I'd say you've been rewarded enough for that." He extended his hand to Yvette. "Cannon won't introduce us because I'm better at seduction than he is."

Cannon snorted, but as Yvette took Armie's hand, he said, "Yvette Sweeny, meet Armie Jacobson."

"It's nice to meet you, Mr. Jacobson."

At the formality, Armie's brow went up. He held her hand gently. "Pleasure's all mine. You have to drop the *mister,* though. Just call me Armie—or something more wicked."

"Wicked?"

"Yeah, like stud, or stallion, or—"

Cannon shoved him. "Stop being an ass."

The handshake broken, Armie righted himself with a grumble. "Why they call you Saint I'll never understand."

"Because I have to be a saint to put up with you."

"Yeah, maybe." Armie grinned. "We'll see you at the rec center tomorrow?"

"I'll be there." Cannon pointed back and forth from Armie to himself. "Plan to spar."

Groaning, Armie grabbed his chest as if wounded and turned to Yvette. "You see, darlin', that means I'm about to get an old-fashioned ass-whoopin'."

Yvette laughed at him.

"Not funny!" And then, his voice still too smooth, Armie said, "You should come by and visit us. Pretty the place up a little—and maybe soften old Saint so he'll go easy on me."

Her gaze shot over to Cannon's as if she expected him to protest. But hell, he liked the idea. "Yeah, you should. I can show you around."

"I was there…once."

Ignoring all the others, Cannon nodded. "I remember." It was the night she'd come to tell him goodbye before she'd moved across the country.

The night she'd left him.

Or so it had felt, even though they'd never really been an item.

Because he had dodged her at every turn.

"If it's been a while," Armie told her, "it's different now. Our boy here has brought us a lot of sponsorships."

Denver used that opening to draw her attention. "Everyone wants a piece of Cannon."

"Mostly women," Miles joked, and Stack backed him up on that. A few bawdy jokes followed.

Yvette greeted the comments with indulgence, treating the big rough fighters like unruly schoolboys.

Denver eased closer to her—something Cannon didn't miss. With one hand on the booth seat behind her shoulder, he beamed down at her. "So you're into fighters, huh?"

"I enjoy the sport," she explained with diplomacy. "But Cannon's the only fighter I know."

In some ways, Cannon decided, he'd be the *only* fighter she knew.

Though he surely caught the significance of what she'd said, Denver didn't retreat. "We need to remedy that."

"Thank you. I'd enjoy learning more." She looked to Cannon for introductions.

While chatting her up, the guys had openly flattered her, but she didn't reciprocate except to be cordial, so Cannon gave in.

He started with Denver, since that bum stood closest to her, and worked his way around to the others. Each one of them assessed her for possibilities, mostly because he never got that involved with women—so *usually* he didn't mind. But this was Yvette, and that made a huge difference.

He'd need to set them straight, and soon.

Armie, the dick, watched it all with keen eyes, as if he already understood that Cannon wanted her to himself.

Then again, he and Armie knew each other well enough that they rarely had to spell shit out.

Each man showered her with compliments, come-ons and good-natured ribbing. He knew exactly what they were thinking.

Because he was thinking it, too.

Yvette was just too hot. Her eyes were striking, her lush mouth a turn-on. And that soft, restrained laugh… it stroked over him.

Only now she was laughing with other guys—guys who didn't need much encouragement to horn in.

Without showing a single sign of awareness for their over-the-top flattery, Yvette spoke with each of them.

Denver even took Cannon's seat beside her. Stack sat across from her. In one way or another, each man angled in close to her until she was surrounded by big, muscled fighters.

Didn't seem to bother her, though.

Armie, the only one hanging back now, elbowed Cannon. "You've been holding out."

"She's a friend." Who would be more soon as he could arrange it.

"No shit? Can I be her friend, too?"

"No."

Armie laughed.

Folding his arms over his chest, Cannon continued to watch her while schooling Armie. "She's not your type."

"Meaning she's nice instead of nasty?"

"Very nice." Cannon eyed him. "Aren't you supposed to be meeting a girl later tonight?"

"Yeah." He checked his watch. "In fact, I'm already late."

Armie was not known for his consideration toward the fairer sex—except maybe in bed. "Figure she'll wait?"

He shrugged. "If she doesn't, she doesn't."

There were times when Cannon didn't understand his friend. More often than not Armie seemed to work at driving "nice" women away.

Speaking loud enough for them all to hear, Cannon said, "Time for you guys to hit the road."

Stack leaned in toward Yvette. "He means he wants you all to himself."

"Selfish," Miles added. "That's Cannon."

"At least when it comes to the pretty girls," Armie explained. "Otherwise, he's a 'saint,' don't you know."

As Denver stood, he said, "Right now, I can't say I blame him."

The way she gazed up at them from her seat made her eyes look even bigger and more innocent. She lowered her lashes—and they all looked ready to fall at her feet.

Cannon shook his head.

Not understanding just how smitten they all were, Yvette teased, "Are all fighters so outrageous?"

That started another round of jokes, but as they wrapped it up, Armie said with a teasing lilt, "'Bye, Yvette."

She grinned. "'Bye."

When the last guy had walked away, Cannon reseated himself beside her. "There you go. You're now well acquainted with the warped psyche of fighters."

"I'd call them colorful, not warped."

"That's because you're a nice person."

Far too serious, she shrugged. "I try to be." Before he could question her on that, she said, "Do they fight professionally? I don't recognize any of them."

"At different levels, yeah. Armie's good. He could be competing with the SBC if he really pursued it. But he's also great with kids and he loves coaching, so he runs the rec center for me around fights in smaller, more local organizations."

"He has a lot of interesting tattoos."

"Not as many as some of the fighters." Armie's tats were mostly on his forearms, with one in the middle of his shoulder blades. "He's into the art, though."

"Do they have special meaning?"

"He's never said." In general, guys didn't talk about *special meanings* with each other. Smiling, he told her, "The woman he's seeing now has more ink than him, along with a lot of jewelry."

Yvette tipped her head in that curious way. "You mean like a belly button ring?"

Cannon tugged at his ear. Yeah, the girl had that— and more. She hadn't been shy about sharing the various body parts she'd pierced. Armie swore it was hot, but it hadn't appealed to Cannon.

Rather than go into all that, he said, "Denver's already with the SBC, but he's between fights right now."

"He's the one with the longer brown hair, right?"

"Yeah, that's him. He has to put it in a ponytail when he fights."

"Does he wear contacts?"

Ah, so she had noticed. Most women commented on Denver's predatory gaze, usually to Denver himself. Cannon appreciated that Yvette hadn't reacted as others had. "No, that's his natural eye color."

Her phone made a sound; she glanced at it while saying, "He has the eyes of a wild animal."

"So I've heard." Cannon would admit the color was different, sort of a bright golden-brown.

She frowned at the phone before tucking it away.

"Anything important?"

"No," she said too quickly and without conviction. When she didn't elaborate, Cannon let it go.

For now.

"Miles is good, too. He's making a name for himself. And Stack is getting there. He helps Armie at the rec center a couple times a week."

As if looking for a change in subject, she asked, "How's the rec center doing?"

"Great. Busy. Come by tomorrow and see for yourself."

She nodded, started to say something and instead had to cover a yawn. "Sorry. It's been a long day."

They'd indulged in a lot of chitchat and numerous interruptions. It all felt so surface, when being with her wasn't. He took her hand. "You look good, Yvette."

"For someone who's driven cross-country?" She smiled. "Thank you. Of course you know you look amazing. You were always incredibly fit, but now..."

"Now what?"

Squeezing his hand, she pulled away and glanced around the bar. "Every woman in here is stealing looks at you."

He doubted that was true, and even if it was, he didn't care. "The men are all watching you."

She smoothed her ponytail. "Probably wondering how they can come and get a picture with you."

More like wondering how they could get her in bed. But saying so might be pushing things too much. "How long will you be in town?"

"However long it takes." She caught her bottom lip in her teeth, visibly collected herself and finally lifted her gaze to his. "I want you to know I'll take care of everything."

Following along wasn't easy when lust kept getting in his way. "Everything?"

"All the legal stuff." Nervousness rushed her into a long explanation. "I can only imagine how busy you are now with your fight career and the rec center and everything you do for the community. You have your sister and your friends and all that training and travel. I want you to know that you don't have to worry about anything."

He'd already told her he wanted to be involved. No reason to beat it into the ground. She'd find out soon enough when he didn't back off.

"I plan to talk to a Realtor tomorrow so I can get the properties listed right away. Hopefully we'll get a quick sale. In the meantime I'll take care of—"

"You want to sell?"

The question took her off guard before she recovered and said, "Of course." She drew in a careful breath. "I can't really pay you otherwise."

"Pay me for what?"

"Your half of the inheritance."

Damn. He didn't want it, any of it. But Tipton had trusted him to discourage her from selling. Her grandfather wanted her to stay in Warfield, to claim it as her home. And now, after seeing her again, Cannon wanted the same.

They needed to talk. In no way did he feel entitled to her inheritance; the only thing he'd take from her was her time, her attention.

Her sexual interest.

Yeah, he wanted that. More so by the second.

He started to reach for her hand again, and a woman leaned down, twining her arms around his neck. "There you are. I wondered where you'd gotten off to."

Well, hell. He'd totally forgotten that he'd made alternate plans.

Earlier in the evening, thinking he wouldn't see Yvette until tomorrow, and being on edge, he'd made a semi-agreement to hook up.

But once he'd seen Yvette, he'd forgotten all about the woman now latched on to him. He had to figure out a way to get rid of her without too much insult, because no way in hell was he letting Yvette walk away until they got a few things settled.

YVETTE LOOKED AT the beautiful woman pressing herself up against Cannon's solid shoulder, one hand on his chest, the other in his hair, and she wanted to flee. Unfortunately, short of crawling over or under the booth table, Cannon had her trapped in her seat.

The other woman was chic and polished in a way Yvette could never be. Wavy, light brown hair, a sheer blouse and high heels only made her more attractive— and left Yvette feeling underdressed, out of place and far too intrusive. She'd come to the bar to give Cannon a message, to release him from any obligations, and instead she'd just...enjoyed him.

When so many others wanted his time and attention, her actions reeked of selfishness, making her stomach burn. Cannon had just gotten into town, but not only had she dragged him away from his friends, she'd apparently interrupted his romantic plans.

Envy stiffened her smile, making her feel clumsy and too obvious about the way she took in the circumstances.

As he stood, Cannon said, "Sorry..." as if trying to remember the woman's name.

"Mary," she supplied with a laugh, tightly hugging his arm, running her fingers over his solid biceps.

Damn, but Yvette envied her that. More than once tonight she'd wanted to do the same. Cannon had a body that begged to be touched. She wanted to explore all those bulging muscles and hard planes.

A lesson in frustration, for sure.

"Right, Mary." Even standing, he stayed near the bench seat so Yvette couldn't slide out. "Yeah, I'm sorry, but my plans have changed."

Yvette stared. Oh, no. No way would she let him cancel on her account. She wanted him to see her as a better person now, not a continued bother.

Determination got her moving, and she deliberately slipped toward the end of the seat. "I really should get going."

"Oh, good," Mary said. "I was afraid you two were together."

"We're not," Yvette assured her.

At the same time, Cannon said, "We are," while he continued to block her retreat.

Both women stared at him, Mary with dismay, Yvette with disbelief.

"Yvette and I are old friends." Not in the least bothered by her denial, Cannon pried Mary from his body. "I haven't seen her in years."

"Friends?" Mary asked hopefully.

"Actually—"

"Yes, only friends." Yvette managed to say it with friendly insistence, but it wasn't her best effort. To Cannon, she said, "We'll have plenty of time to catch up." She wanted away from the uncomfortable situation, but his big body remained in the way. "You don't need to—"

"I want to." With one hand on her shoulder, he kept her in place. "We have too much to talk about." And before Yvette could refuse him again, he said to Mary, "I'm sure you understand."

Starting to look annoyed, Mary propped her hands on her hips. "No, I'm not sure I do."

Oh, God, after being at the center of one of the biggest scenes the town had ever known, she hated causing them, and she especially hated feeling guilty. "Really, Cannon," she insisted, "it's fine."

He ignored Yvette's protest and, being blunt, said to Mary, "I'm sorry, but I was just about to take off with Yvette." And then, all but dismissing Mary, he asked Yvette, "Where are you staying?"

Feeling ridiculous, Yvette avoided looking at Mary. "I'm at the house."

Cannon's brows went up. "By yourself?"

Oh, now that stung. She lifted her chin. "Why not? It's my house now." She wasn't a child who needed adult supervision. And if memories intruded, well, she'd deal with them.

"Part mine," Cannon gently corrected, and then, "I only asked because I planned to stay there, too."

That unexpected announcement had her jaw loosening. "You do?" Not once had she considered that possibility. It didn't even make sense. "You have a house already."

In negligent response, he rolled a shoulder. "Rissy lives there now. I gave it to her. A couple of months ago she brought in a roommate."

"I'm sure your sister would still love to see you!"

At her raised voice, Cannon's mouth curled into a crooked grin. "Yeah, she will. But she went to Japan with me and she's still there, stretching it out into a vacation. I doubt her roommate, who's female—" and also in Japan, but Yvette didn't need to know that "—would

appreciate me moving in on her." It was just a small fab-
rication, and Cannon didn't mind fudging things a little
to get what he wanted.

Instead of leaving, Mary stuck close, making Yvette
more flustered.

"Cannon," she began, unsure what else to say.

"Yvette," he replied, copying her tone and fixing his
will on her. "I'm staying at the house."

Mary finally spoke up. "Oh, my God." She pointed a
manicured finger at Yvette. *"You're that woman."*

Oh, no. Heat swelled up from Yvette's churning stomach to her chest and finally settled in her face, making
her light-headed. No, no, *no.* The urge to flee sent her
heart stuttering.

"Mary," Cannon said, "why don't we talk over here?"
He tried to lead her away.

She resisted. "You're that woman who was raped, the
one who was almost set on fire."

"I wasn't raped," Yvette squeaked, her voice far too
weak.

"Those men… It was in all the local news and everyone was talking about it." Mary shrugged off Cannon's
hand when he again tried to draw her away. "They made
you watch when they brutalized that other woman. You
watched them videotape it!" She splayed a hand over her
chest. "Oh, you poor thing."

"That's enough," Cannon said in a low voice.

But Mary wasn't done. Yvette couldn't tell if she was
titillated or truly sympathetic.

Either was awful.

In a scandalized whisper, Mary asked, "Did they really douse you in kerosene and threaten to burn you
alive?"

Memories crept in, bring with them old feelings of

panic. Although her thoughts bounced about wildly in a frantic search, Yvette couldn't come up with a single appropriate reply to give.

"Excuse me." Avery, Rowdy's wife, insinuated herself into Mary's line of vision. "I'm so sorry to interrupt, but, Cannon, Rowdy wants to talk to you. He's in the break room. Oh, and, Yvette, he'd love to see you, too." With that, she turned to Mary, moving her petite body so close that Mary had no choice but to back up a few spaces. "Before he was famous," Avery explained with false enthusiasm, "Cannon used to work here. He's like family still. I'm sure you understand."

Mary protested that no, she did *not* understand at all, but Cannon had already drawn Yvette out of the booth seat. Keeping a firm hold on her upper arm, he grabbed up her purse and propelled her forward.

In a shocked daze, she allowed it, stumbling along on wooden legs.

Bodies crowded the bar, but Yvette barely noticed. By rote, she kept her chin up even as Mary's words reverberated in her thoughts over and over again. Somehow they seemed twice as damning when spoken aloud. She had stood by and watched another woman brutalized. The reality of that squeezed all the air from her lungs.

As they left the main floor for a private hallway, the din of conversation, music and laughter faded into the periphery. Cannon leaned closer, his warm breath brushing the sensitive whorls of her ear when he whispered, "Almost there."

The concern in his tone kick-started her pride. Swallowing hard, she blinked several times and cleared away the fog of shame.

She'd been a victim, she reminded herself. Realistically she knew it, but that had nothing to do with the mélange of emotions that sometimes bombarded her, with disgrace always at the forefront.

"In here," Cannon said, drawing her through a doorway into a private room that housed a long table surrounded by chairs, a coffeepot and paper cups, lockers and a few vending machines.

He hooked a chair with his foot and drew it out from the table. "Want something to drink?"

Knowing he expected her to sit, she instead squared off with him. Not in anger, but in determination.

"You don't need to pamper me." Not anymore. Not ever again. "I'm fine."

That drew him around, eyes narrowed and jaw hard. "Bullshit."

Hearing him curse like that shocked her, but it was nothing compared to the inferno in his eyes. If she'd changed, well, apparently so had he.

He stepped closer, tall, powerful. Indomitable. "You don't have to do this, Yvette." He searched her face. "Not with me."

A little panicky, she said, "I don't know what you mean," even as she attempted to get her mask of contentment back in place.

The edge of his fist touched under her chin, lifting her face so that she couldn't avoid his probing scrutiny. So many sensations erupted: nervousness, excitement, need. She nibbled her bottom lip and literally felt it when his gaze transferred to her mouth.

Hotly, he stared, then inhaled a slow, deep breath— and stepped back. "That woman upset you."

"That woman?" Derision choked her. "You had a date with her and you don't remember her name?"

The accusation gathered his dark brows together. "Mary or something. Who cares? And it wasn't a date."

"Sounded like a date to me."

"Then you haven't gotten around much in the past three years." He indicated the chair. "Let's talk."

She'd had enough talk for one night. Now she just wanted to escape...all of it—Mary's taunting insight, Cannon's seductive caring, the exposure of old wounds. But fleeing would be cowardly, and by God, she would not regress.

Dropping her purse onto the long table, she sat. Mulish. Annoyed.

And, damn it, amusement replaced discontent as Cannon took his own seat. "Am I holding you up from something important?"

"No."

He nodded to her phone sticking out of her purse. "Someone contacted you earlier. Someone male?"

She thought about lying, but no, he deserved better from her. "That was nothing...important." Sitting forward to convince him, she said, "I want to go to the house and catch some sleep. It's been a long trip and this is all—" *unbearable* "—uncomfortable."

"Which was my point." The opposite of her, he slouched back in his seat. He continued to study her until, very softly, he said, "I'm sorry."

Now, why did that make her heart trip and her eyes burn? "For what?"

"Bad timing?" While collecting his thoughts, he looked down at nothing in particular. "I hooked up with Mary before I knew you'd be here." His gaze swung back up to snare hers. "But now that you are here, I—"

Her forced laugh cut him off. "You don't owe me anything."

"It's not about owing." His right hand worked, closing into an imposing fist, then relaxing again. "We have a whole lot to straighten out."

"We could talk tomorrow."

"Count on it. But tonight—"

Rowdy stepped in, a cola in each hand. Clearly he and Cannon had caught up earlier, given the relaxed way they greeted each other.

"Better?" Rowdy asked.

"Much. Thanks." He accepted the cola. "For this, too."

Rowdy set the other drink in front of her. "Yvette Sweeny, right?"

"Um, yes. Hi." For a moment there, her tongue got stuck. Rowdy Yates was just so…much. Of everything. No way would she have forgotten him, but… "I'm surprised you remember."

The words no sooner left her than she winced. Of course he remembered. As Mary had said, details of the entire ordeal had played out in the news. She'd refused all interviews, but she knew her face had appeared plenty of times.

His attention, friendly as it might be, didn't help to calm the stampeding of her pulse. "You're not at all forgettable."

Nodding, she said in apology, "Of course you're right."

One brow lifted and he grinned.

Oh, God, worse and worse. Yvette tried a glance at Cannon, but if anything, he looked more amused than Rowdy. "I meant because of the trial and everything. I sometimes forget how many times they plastered my pathetic face in the news."

"That's not how he meant it," Cannon chided.

Rowdy's mellow gaze warmed. "No, it isn't." Luckily, he let that go as he turned to Cannon. "Make use of the bar however you want."

Wondering what that meant, Yvette watched Cannon, but he just nodded. "Thanks."

"I'll let you get back to your private chat in just a second. But first, a lot of people are calling in, asking if you're really here. Word is spreading. I suspect we'll be mobbed very shortly."

"Damn." Cannon stretched out his long legs and shook his head. "Sorry about that."

"It's not a problem for me. We like the business." After a glance at Yvette, Rowdy said, "I'm assuming you plan to cut out for the night?"

"Yeah, sorry."

"No worries. I understand."

Well, she didn't. Again, she wanted to protest, but with Rowdy standing between them it would be rude to interrupt.

"How would you feel about announcing a night that you'll be around? Say in a week or two? That'll give you time to settle in, and hopefully keep people from crowding you in the meantime."

"A week or two?" Her appalled tone blew her cool, polite facade. "You're staying that long?"

"Yeah, I am." The heated stare Cannon leveled on her held too many meanings for her to decipher. "At least."

Happiness bloomed—but she denied it. Okay, so it'd be fantastic to see him more. It was still unexpected. She had assumed he'd make it a couple of days at most—long enough for her to explain that she'd handle everything, then send him his check once things were settled. He'd said his sister still had the family home here, and she knew he visited often, but from what she'd understood, his life was now in Harmony, Kentucky. "What about your training?"

"I just finished a fight, so unless the SBC says differently, I'll wind it down some." His eyes darkened. "Besides, I have weights I can set up in the basement."

"The… What basement?"

"Our basement."

Oh, good Lord. Now he considered her grandfather's house *theirs?* Sure, technically it was, but she hadn't expected him to assert his rights beyond wanting a quick sale of the properties.

Every question she had sounded rude, so Yvette clammed up.

Apparently that suited the men just fine.

"I could throw out some promotion, make a big deal of it." Rowdy propped a hip on the table. "Think you'd be in for autographs and photos?"

"Sure. Whatever you want. Maybe I could even work that night, like I used to."

Rowdy laughed. "I wouldn't ask you to do that."

"I'm offering. It'd be fun." He glanced around the break room. "To be honest, I miss the place."

"Simpler times?"

"Something like that."

With both men looking at her, Yvette almost squirmed. Were they insinuating that she'd complicated things? Ha! She did her utmost to make it easier on Cannon. He was the one being difficult.

Clapping him on the shoulder, Rowdy said, "If you have the time, come by tomorrow. We can talk more then. And hey, if you need help with anything, let me know."

"Will do."

The second Rowdy left the room, Yvette surged to her feet. Cannon didn't. If anything, he lounged back more, his indolent posture reminding her of a lean, muscular jungle cat.

Just waiting for an opportunity to pounce.

Wound too tight, beyond weary, she rubbed at her temple to fend off an approaching headache.

"Loosen your hair," Cannon suggested, but the way he said it made it sound sexual instead of sensible.

"It's okay." She dropped her hand, then went straight to her top concern. "You really intend to stay at the house?"

Folding his hands behind his head, he nodded. "Yup."

Keeping her attention on his face instead of his awesome physique proved impossible. That particular position put outstanding biceps on display and pulled his soft cotton T-shirt taut over the solid surface of his chest and rigid abs.

Just looking at him made her breathe deeper. But then, thinking about him did that to her, too. Being in close, personal proximity with him, seeing his easy smile and modest attitude, was enough to keep her flushed with sexual curiosity.

God, the man was fine. Wide, solid shoulders, narrow hips and his... She swallowed hard and skipped her gaze past his lap to his long, solid legs.

Stop, she ordered herself. Only a masochist would continue teasing herself when she couldn't do a damn thing about it.

Reminded of her deficiency, Yvette snatched up her purse and shrugged the strap over her shoulder. "All right, then. I guess I'll see you there."

All kinds of suspicious, Cannon sat forward. "You're still going there, too?"

Ah, so he'd hoped to find an altruistic way to spare her from staying at the big, bad house where all her trauma had occurred.

Her lip almost curled—with self-derision. "Yes, I

am." He'd see that she didn't need to be saved. "Is that a problem?"

Maybe now *he'd* bow out.

Instead he unfolded that long, tall body until he stood over her. Too close. So close that she felt the heat radiating off him.

He kept doing that, getting in her space in an intimate way. Making her heart race. Making her want things she couldn't have.

He touched her chin. "Not for me."

Oh. The way he said that, as if he expected it to be a problem for her.... And it would be. A torturous, frustrating problem—one she'd deal with on her own. "There are three bedrooms and two baths, so it should be fine."

With probing intensity, his gaze moved over her face. "If you say so."

Discretion being the better part of valor, she decided to retreat.

Catching her arm before she'd taken a single step, Cannon used his thumb to caress her skin. "It'll be just the two of us, alone there together."

"Well, I hope so." She hadn't even considered the alternative, but maybe she should have. Unpleasant possibilities had her glaring. "You don't plan to move anyone else in, do you? Mary or some other woman?"

He laughed before catching himself. "No." Showing no signs of offense, he caught her other arm, too. "Just you and me."

The way he stared at her mouth prompted her to lick her lips.

Bad idea, given the flare in his blue eyes.

"I'll, ah, give you privacy." It took all her conviction not to lean into him, to resist the lure of his nearness. "If that's what you're worried about."

"Not even close."

The rough velvet words weakened her resolve. "Then—"

"My worry is a man and woman alone with beds nearby." He drew her up to her tiptoes. "Unless that's what you want."

She couldn't think. "What?" she whispered.

His breath teased over her lips. "Us, together." His voice went deeper, rougher. "Making use of the beds."

When she only stared at him, she saw the smile in his eyes—seconds before his mouth touched the corner of hers.

"Sex," he breathed.

"Oh." He wanted to have sex with her. "You're coming on to me?"

Wry humor kicked up the corner of his mouth. "Seriously? You can't tell? I must be losing my touch."

No, his touch was dead-on, heating her with sizzling awareness. "But you just sent Mary away!"

As if she should have understood, he said, "You aren't Mary."

The surprise bubbled out as a small laugh. Appalled at herself, Yvette put a hand to his chest. She meant to lever herself away, but instead, the solid muscles had her curling her fingers against him. "No," she said with apology. "I'm not."

His thumbs started that wicked caressing again. "I'm glad."

Only because he didn't understand the major difference: Mary could accommodate him, but she could not.

Knowing she had to be fair, Yvette tried to explain. "You might want to rethink things. With Mary, I mean. See...I don't..." Was there a polite way to put it? No, there wasn't. "Do that."

Comical confusion showed in his expression.

And no wonder. She sounded so absurd. "That is, I'm not... I can't..."

"Can't?"

"Won't?"

He searched her face. "Pick one."

She blew out a breath. "Don't." Now she pushed away from him, but landing back on her own feet without support left her shaky. "I don't." Gesturing, she explained, "Do that."

Dubious, his gaze roamed over her from head to toes and back again. "You don't have sex?"

"No." And now, with him so near and so...focused, she had more regrets than ever.

"You're not a virgin."

She sputtered over the accusing way he said that. "No, but that was then, and now..." She rubbed her brow. "Sorry if I'm confusing you. But I don't do any of that anymore. I mean dating or sex or anything. So anyway, you see, there's no problem." Her smile fell flat. More discussion was not going to make any of this better. Knowing that, she backed up one step, then another. "I'm going to head out now."

Discontent furrowed his brows, making his blue eyes incendiary. "You're going to say that and then just book?"

Definitely. Inching toward the door, she nodded. "I'm exhausted." To give credence to that excuse, she staged a huge yawn. "I need some sleep. You probably do, too."

He didn't move.

"So...I'll see you there. Whenever. Don't hurry on my account, though." She backed through the doorway. "I think Mary is still waiting for you."

The frown got darker. "Forget Mary."

"Okay, sure." She continued inching away. "You have a key to get in, right?"

Muscled arms crossed over his chest and he looked down his nose at her. "Yeah."

"Okay, then I'll leave the door braces off."

"Door braces?"

"Added security. You know…those bars that… Never mind. I'll show you. Later." She cleared her throat. "When you're there. Though probably not until tomorrow because I'm going straight to bed—"

"I'm coming now." He started toward her.

"You don't have to!" More than anything she wanted to avoid another confrontation until she had her wits collected and could speak without sounding like an idiot. She could accomplish that by being in her room with the door closed before he showed up. Tomorrow morning… well, she'd get up early as usual, maybe go for a jog to clear her head and help collect her thoughts.

She hadn't expected him to want to pick up where they'd left off.

Three years had passed!

But since he did, and since she couldn't, she'd have to figure out a way to explain it all to him without actually baring her soul.

Still retreating, she almost bumped into someone, looked over her shoulder and apologized to Rowdy's wife.

"Don't mind me," Avery said, her arms laden with dirty glasses after clearing tables. She continued on as if it was a normal night.

As if Yvette weren't backing away from a superhunk who inexplicably wanted sexual involvement with her.

The night ranked right up there as one of the least normal she'd had—since moving away.

CHAPTER FOUR

CANNON WAS ON her by the time she looked away from Avery.

Green eyes flared wide when she realized he intended to leave with her—as in, right beside her with his hand curled around the nape of her neck beneath her long ponytail.

Unaccountably provoked, he whispered, "Let's go," but her feet remained glued to the floor.

Lacing her fingers together, she blinked up at him. "You don't have to do this."

He flexed his neck to relieve the knotted muscles there. "This?"

"Dogging my heels."

That pissed him off.

Until she clarified, "Protecting me."

No, maybe he didn't. But he wanted to. Bad. Hell, he was half-hard and all he'd gotten from her so far were denials, rejections and hilarity at his interest.

And that far-fetched tale about her not having sex. He urged her forward, and she reluctantly gave in.

"This is pointless."

Determined to prove her wrong on that score, he kept them both walking.

She dug in, saying, "I'm not going to cheat you."

Even in the crowded, noisy bar, a few people looked

up—including Mary, who stood among a small crowd of men.

Steering Yvette to the side, Cannon said, "Keep it down, will you."

Appalled, she looked around, more upset than she should have been. She lifted her chin and squared her shoulders, and that implacable mask of poise fell into place.

Now, in a much softer tone, she said, "I'm sorry, but I want you to know. Soon as I sell everything, I'll send you your half. You don't have to hang around. I'm sure you have other, more important things to do."

He wanted to do her, and that was as important as it got. She might not realize it, but the more she tried to run him off, the more determined he was to stay. "Understand something, Yvette."

A little wary, she asked, "What?"

Smiling to soften his inflexible tone, he leaned closer. "I'm not going anywhere."

Huffing, she gave in, no longer fighting him as they headed across the floor, but still stiff-necked under his hand.

Good thing he had a healthy ego. He sensed she wanted to avoid something, but he wasn't convinced that it was him. There was something more going on.

He planned to find out what.

"This is ridiculous," she muttered.

"We'll talk when we get home." They were almost to the door when a heavy hand landed on his shoulder.

Senses prickling, Cannon turned—then ducked out of reach as someone threw a wild haymaker.

Tucking Yvette back behind him, he said, "What the hell?"

Sour beer breath blasted his face when a man swayed toward him and shouted, *"You insulted 'er."*

Looking beyond the idiot slurring his words, Cannon saw Mary watching, her hand over her mouth in dismay. Shit. He hated drama over women. "No insult intended."

The guy wouldn't let it go. "You thin' you're such a hotshot?"

Sighing, Cannon felt the fascinated gazes of the crowd. The guy challenging him was big and muscular—but not a real match by any stretch. It'd be manslaughter if he took him on. "Look," Cannon said, "why don't you let me call you a cab?"

"Fuck you!" He poked at Cannon's chest. "You were shitty to 'er."

Cannon caught his hand, jerked him forward then around and put him in a headlock. It'd be so easy to put the guy to sleep...but that didn't seem fair. He looked up at Mary. "Happy now?"

She gasped. "I didn't know he'd come after you!"

Without much effort, Cannon contained the wild flailing of the man he held and said to her, "You didn't put him up to it?"

"No! I would never do that."

He wasn't sure if he believed her or not, but it didn't really change anything anyway. "You know him?"

Miserable, she nodded. "He's a...friend."

"Then see that he gets home." Cannon released the man—then had to push him back when the idiot reached for him again. Pointing at him, Cannon said, "No more."

Too drunk to listen, the guy tucked down and charged. *Shit, shit, shit.* Pulling the punch as much as he could, Cannon struck him with a straight right jab—and watched him sink, boneless, to the floor.

Stepping to the front of the crowd, Rowdy watched the drunk stir. "Sorry, I got here quick as I could."

"It happened fast."

"Bar fights usually do."

That had Cannon snorting. There'd been no fight to it.

"Thanks for going easy on him."

"No problem."

Shaking his head, Rowdy said, "You are freakishly calm."

With a shrug, Cannon said, "Not always, but I'm not going to get bent over a drunk." He turned—and didn't see Yvette. He searched the room.

"She's gone," Rowdy told him. "Lit out the second you got preoccupied."

Now, *that* riled him. Only half under his breath, he muttered, *"Fuck."*

The drunken idiot groaned. Together, Cannon and Rowdy helped him to his feet.

"All of you," Rowdy said to the small group. "Time to go." They grumbled, but followed Rowdy as he started toward the door. As if they weren't escorting a bloody-nosed patron and his cronies to the curb, Rowdy asked, "You plan to move in on her?"

In more ways than one. Shrugging, Cannon held the door open as the small group departed with their buddy. "I told you, half of everything is mine."

The last man, on his way out, handed Rowdy some cash to cover their tab. "Sorry about that."

"If it happens again, he's banned from returning."

That caused more grousing, but a second later they were all gone.

Still by the door, Rowdy rested back on the wall. He stared toward Mary, who'd already moved on to a different tableful of men. "She's trouble."

"You could have warned me earlier."

"You're a big boy." When Ella the waitress came by, Rowdy handed the money to her. "Besides, she's only trouble when she finds an idiot to help her dole it out."

Ella took a minute to bounce her gaze back and forth between them before sighing dramatically. "Y'all are going to cause a riot if you just stand there looking so mouthwateringly scrumptious." She patted each of them on the chest and headed off for the cash register.

Cannon grinned after her. He and Ella had hit it off right from the start back when he'd first worked at Rowdy's. She teased, but never, not once, had she honestly come on to him. He was willing to bet the same was true for her treatment of Rowdy.

"So you plan to claim your inheritance, huh?"

Only half listening, Cannon nodded. "For now anyway." If he refused it, how could he cozy up to Yvette?

"What does she think of that?"

"Don't know yet." Should he still go to the house? Yvette had been clear on her preferences. She didn't want him there.

"You get challenged a lot?"

"That wasn't a challenge. That was just drunken stupidity."

"I guess other guys have enough self-preservation not to go there, huh?"

Cannon shrugged. "Maybe I'm just a nice guy." And maybe Yvette truly didn't need him anymore—

Laughing, Rowdy nudged him. "Yeah, you're nice enough. So here's some well-meaning advice—when in doubt, go with your gut."

"Meaning?"

"You want to go to her. I can see it. Hell, everyone in here can see it."

That prompted Cannon to look around, and he found the room ripe with speculation. He drew in a deep breath…and caved.

With new determination, he pushed off the wall. "Yeah." He'd go to her, and if she was already in bed—probably avoiding him—well, then, at least he'd be there, close by. And in the morning he'd catch her for a nice long chat, and more. "Thanks."

"Cannon?"

He paused.

"Go easy on her, too, okay? I think she's probably more fragile than she's letting on."

Damn it, since he'd always trusted Rowdy's insight, a new urgency gripped him. "See you tomorrow."

Turbulent thoughts pushed him to drive too fast. When he reached the house, he found it lit up like Christmas with every outdoor light on. It was by far the most illuminated house on the block. Bright lamps decorated either side of the front door and over the driveway, and floodlights shone over each side of the yard.

Yvette had parked in the driveway, so he pulled in behind her. If she had thoughts of leaving before him in the morning, he'd know, because she'd need him to move his car.

He felt manipulative, but what the hell. For now, it worked.

He tried the doorknob, found it locked, and dug out the key to get in. Would she be curled up on the couch watching TV? Maybe in the shower? Or would she be tucked into bed? Each visual was nice, but he preferred the shower scene.

Unfortunately, when he stepped in, silence greeted him. So she had turned in? Hard to tell with so many lights on, but yeah, one glance down the hallway and he saw her closed bedroom door.

Disappointed, he dropped his overnight bag and looked around. The house was different, but how he felt about it wasn't. The open dining room drew his gaze. It took only a nanosecond for him to recall exactly how Yvette had looked caught up against the thug's body—and how her helplessness had turned him inside out. Thinking of how differently that day could have gone stirred his rage anew.

Yvette might not need him to be here with her now, but *he* needed it.

Doing his best to block the black thoughts, he roamed the house, first going down the hall to the room he'd use. Not her grandfather's room, but the spare room—the one closest to Yvette. He set his overnight bag beside the bed and emptied his pockets on the nightstand. The bed was only a twin, but he'd manage.

Turning to the wall, he thought of Yvette on the other side. Did she sleep on her side, snuggled into her pillow? Or on her back, her legs open and relaxed? Heat crept up the back of his neck; he placed his palm on the wall, thought of touching her and had to fight the urge to knock on her door.

Leaving his shoes by the bed, he made no sound as he reentered the hall. At Yvette's door he paused to listen, but it was so quiet that he imagined her holding her breath. Hard as it might be, he wouldn't disturb her.

Not tonight.

Instead he went into the kitchen, where a low light shone over the stove. If she kept this up, the electric bill would be through the roof. But he wouldn't complain.

Not with the proof of her difficulty there on the kitchen table.

Dead bolts, bars for the doors and alarms filled the tabletop. Seeing a few empty packages, he went to the window over the sink and found a narrow bar wedged into place, giving the lock a little backup on the off chance someone tried to get in. He checked the other windows and found the same. Striding to the basement door, he located the lock bar wedged under the doorknob, ensuring no one could sneak in—as they had three years ago.

She'd taken security measures to extremes. For her peace of mind, he could make a few more improvements.

And he'd stick close. For the foreseeable future, he'd protect her, whether she liked it or not.

WEARING ONLY JEANS, not yet shaved or showered, Cannon stood in the middle of the kitchen the next morning and cursed. Where the hell was she?

If he'd had any doubts about her dodging him, they were now confirmed.

The coffeepot remained half-full, and her car was still in the driveway. But her open bedroom door and the empty house told him she'd taken off.

On foot?

To where?

He'd be more concerned except for the note she'd left in front of the coffeepot that read, "Help yourself," signed with a feminine, curly *Y.*

At only a few minutes after 7:00 a.m., morning sunshine poured in the kitchen window, spilling warm amber light over the counter and floor. Today would be a scorcher.

He always woke early, usually to work out, often to jog.

After a near-sleepless night where he'd pondered a dozen different scenarios, he'd planned a confrontation with Yvette. He'd expected to be there in the kitchen, alert and ready to sort out the confusion, when she emerged from her bed.

Still edgy with carnal need, he'd imagined catching her half-awake, maybe in a nightgown, her hair tumbled, her defenses down, warm and drowsy, sensual and sweet...

Instead she'd gotten up before dawn, made coffee for him and then skipped out.

The idea that she might be running from him ramped up the raw, basic urge to claim her. Filled with the predatory need to chase—and catch—her, he paced the floor, cursing himself for not getting her phone number. But he hadn't expected her to bolt last night, and he sure as hell hadn't expected to find the house empty this morning.

Maybe where it concerned Yvette Sweeny, he should stop making assumptions and come up with a strategy instead.

Where to start? Confused ideas clamored in his brain, impossible to sort out. Drawn by the scent, he decided a little coffee wouldn't hurt. He wasn't a caffeine junkie, and in fact avoided it while training. But it was one of those small treats he allowed himself between preparing for fights.

One taste and he groaned. Perfection. Strong enough without being bitter.

If Yvette ever returned, he'd thank her for it.

While waiting for her, he finished his mug off and poured another. Eight o'clock came and went. Frustration mounting, Cannon went about checking all facets of security concerning the house. He wanted to know what was needed before he made some calls.

As he'd already noticed, the lighting was over-the-top, so he would suggest motion sensors. With the occasional stray cat or critter, they could be bothersome, but it was better than lighting up the whole neighborhood.

Before the sun set again, he'd install the additional dead bolts for her. Trotting down the basement steps, he checked out the window that had been used to break in so long ago. It was now secured with a metal grate that locked from the inside. Barefoot, Cannon crossed the cold concrete floor and touched the sturdy bars.

Anger intruded, settling in his gut like molten lead. In pure reaction, he curled his hands into powerful fists. If he could fight the past, he would. If he could go back and somehow do it all differently, the miserable fucks would never make it to prison.

Instead Yvette had to deal with the memories, same as he did. If he lived to be a hundred, it would still enrage him to think about it.

She could deny it all she wanted, but he knew it'd be the same for Yvette. Or worse. Much worse.

Trying to ease the strain, Cannon rolled his shoulders and looked around the open area of the basement. Without analyzing his decision, he configured a floor plan in his mind, knowing right where he'd put each piece of workout equipment. The overhead beams could easily support a heavy bag if he used the right hardware.

Back upstairs, he gave Armie a call. The phone rang six times before his friend answered with rushing breath. "You're late."

"And you sound winded."

"I'm working out my frustrations."

Huh. Did that mean the lady hadn't waited for him after all? Ready to rib him, Cannon said, "I take it you didn't get laid?"

"Actually, smart-ass, I had a three-way."

"Yeah?" Nothing new for Armie. Sounding as serious as he could, Cannon asked, "What's the other guy's name?"

"Funny—not." He could hear Armie guzzling water before he explained, "This time it was Beth and her friend Carly."

Ah, so Beth with the many piercings and tats had not only waited, she'd brought along added enticement. He already knew it wasn't Armie's first ménage, but if he'd just indulged, why was he frustrated?

"Actually," Armie said, "they asked about you."

Him? He had to wonder how that conversation had gone—and when. But he said only, "Of course they did."

"I told them no-go. Said you were a virgin."

Cannon couldn't help but laugh. "Bullshit."

"Okay, I told them you were a lousy lay. Whatever. They settled for me."

Glad that Armie knew him well enough not to bother trying to draw him into an orgy, he said, "Gee, thanks."

"So is there a reason for this call? 'Cause you're interrupting my routine."

Cannon grinned. Didn't matter how late Armie stayed out at night—sometimes all night—he still hit the rec center bright and early, and always jumped right into his workout. He was fanatical about staying in shape, about being healthy.

And about getting laid.

"Yeah, sorry. Just wanted you to know that I won't make it in for a few more hours."

"Dodging me? Damn, Cannon, I know I scare the average man, but you don't need to worry." Tone going suggestive, Armie asked, "Or is that sweet little thing you drooled over last night keeping you otherwise occupied?"

"Yeah, but not the way you mean." Hard to sleep with Yvette when he couldn't get her to stay in one place long enough to even kiss her. Maybe next time he saw her, he'd take care of that right off, then figure out the rest. "Got any free time this week?"

"Changing the subject, huh? Must mean you struck out in a big way, you poor bastard."

"Are you busy or not?"

With new humor, Armie said, "I have a date every night, but I can rearrange things. What's up?"

Cannon shook his head at the ready accommodation; Armie canceled dates as easily as he got them. "I want to set up some workout equipment."

"Sticking around awhile, huh?"

"I think so." But either way, he'd make himself at home here so that Yvette couldn't easily boot him out.

With forced indifference, Armie said, "I thought your little sister turned the downstairs into a separate area for her roomie."

Since Armie had helped him expand the outdated bath for that very reason, he already knew the answer. Was he interested in the roommate? Cannon had met her on a few occasions, each brief, so all he really remembered was medium blond hair, dark eyes and a cute bod.

Yeah, Armie was probably interested.

But that'd put him too close to Merissa, and Cannon didn't like that idea, so he issued another warning, this one more direct. "I don't want you messing around with the roommate."

Armie snorted. "Don't sweat it. She's not my type."

"What type is that?"

"Same as your sister—a *nice* girl."

Cannon laughed at how Armie inferred being "nice" made a female unacceptable. In the case of his sister, he was glad. It'd be way too uncomfortable to think about Armie, with his over-the-top sexuality, anywhere near his little sis. "Rissy's got her own life going on and I see no reason to move in on her." He took a breath and admitted, "I'm staying with Yvette."

Silence—and then, "That was fast."

"Again, not the way you're thinking."

"Damn, man, I'm thinking she's hot, you're male and you're arranging a lot of alone time with her. Don't tell me it's so you can hold her hand and watch old movies, because I just might puke."

"It's complicated, that's all." Cannon took a minute to explain the situation to Armie.

"Fuck," Armie said with feeling. "I thought she was the girl, but I wasn't sure. Must be rough for her."

"Not as much as you'd think." Or else Yvette did a great job hiding it. "Anyway, I plan to stay with her until the place sells—or until I'm sure she's comfortable being alone."

"Uh-huh."

At that mocking tone, Cannon's shoulders tightened. "What?"

"You're all noble and shit, I don't doubt it. That's just you. But you're also looking to get boned in the bargain, so just admit it."

If it was any woman other than Yvette, Cannon might have just agreed and let it go. But with Yvette, the protectiveness smothering him was far too powerful for him to joke about it with anyone, even his best friend. "Armie—"

"Give it a rest, buddy. I know what I know. After seeing her, I'd think it was weird if you didn't. But don't sweat it. I'll be all circumspect and shit whenever I'm around her."

Defensive as well as protective, he warned, "I don't want her hassled. By anyone."

"Noted." Armie moved right on past the topic, saving Cannon from more awkwardness. "How about you order in a pizza and I'll come by after work on Friday? That soon enough for you?"

"Yeah, sure." To be fair, he added, "Thanks. I owe you."

Armie snorted over that. "Maybe someday I'll collect. See you later."

After putting his phone back in his pocket, Cannon checked the time. Almost nine o'clock.

Where the hell was she?

He was not a man who got keyed up. In the SBC he was known for his cool head and meticulous manner. But now, dealing with Yvette, his impatience rivaled a swelling tide. He needed to expend energy somehow, either by taking off on his own jog, hitting something...or maybe indulging in a long, hot shower.

He didn't want to be gone when she returned, and he hadn't yet installed a heavy bag, so the shower won out.

Besides, it wouldn't hurt to be clean, shaved and dressed before she returned. Driven by thoughts of what he'd do and say to her, Cannon left the hall bathroom door open and kept his ears cocked as he let the warm water relieve some of his residual aches and pains from the last fight.

He'd just stepped out when the landline rang. Hastily wrapping a towel around his hips, he followed the sound and located the old-fashioned, curly corded phone on the wall in the kitchen. Huh. Skeptical that it'd really work, he picked it up on the fourth ring. "Hello?"

"Cannon? Oh, good. I was afraid you wouldn't answer."

The female voice sounded familiar, but he wasn't sure—

"It's Mindi, from Frank's office."

"Frank?"

"Mr. Whitaker."

Biting back the groan, Cannon dropped against the wall and forced some pleasantness into his greeting. "Morning, Mindi. How are you?"

"Working, so don't get all worried that I'm calling in my rain check."

Appreciating her humor, he smiled with her. "Sorry. I'm just slammed, that's all."

"You poor thing, having so much dumped on you. How is Tipton's granddaughter?"

Cannon frowned. "We're fine."

"Working through everything?"

He pushed away from the wall. "Did Whitaker ask you to call?"

Her laugh was meant to be teasing, but instead it annoyed him. "No, but I'm hoping I can be helpful. I've found someone who wants to buy the pawnshop."

A disturbing mix of regret and resolution glued Cannon to the spot. Through the restriction in his chest, he said, "Come again?"

Still sounding chipper and unfazed by his lack of enthusiastic reply, Mindi explained. "A buyer. For the pawnshop."

Carefully, giving himself time to think, he said, "I didn't know you were helping with that." He got his feet moving but couldn't pace far, not with the phone attached to the wall.

"Officially, we're not. But you know that Frank and Tipton were friends, so I've let others know that it's up for sale. I figured it was the least I could do."

So she called the lawyer by his first name. Interesting. Then again, it could mean nothing. Whitaker ran a small office and probably didn't go on formality. "I see."

"Is there a good time I can bring him by to check it out?"

Just then, Cannon heard a slight noise at the front door. Anticipation surged through him, obliterating everything else. "I'll talk to Yvette and get back to you."

Mindi was still thanking him when he hung up.

CHAPTER FIVE

AFTER SEEING HIS car still in the driveway, Yvette had to fight the urge to take off again. If her legs didn't feel like noodles and if sweat didn't soak her clothes, she might be tempted. But after the extended jog, she'd walked in the park, bought a coffee and donut, lingered, procrastinated and all in all been a complete coward.

Admitting it to herself didn't improve the fault.

With all her avoidance, she'd only managed to make things more difficult, because now she looked outright awful.

Trying not to make a sound, hoping she'd be able to sneak to her bedroom for a quick shower and change before seeing Cannon, she turned the doorknob, poked her head inside—and found him standing there.

Arms crossed over his bare chest. Legs naked. Hips and other...vital parts...barely concealed by a small white towel.

Good Lord. Her jaw loosened.

Her heart punched into her throat, and then dropped hard into her belly.

She stared without blinking.

Mouth quirking, Cannon said, "You may as well come on in. I'm not budging."

She did, quickly stepping in and closing the door behind her, then dropping back against it. "You're—" *naked* "—not dressed."

"Just got out of the shower."

It took a very deep breath before she could squeak out, "Oh." That breath had filled her head with the scent of masculine soap and warm male.

Her hungry gaze tracked down his body, taking it all in. Those sleek, hard shoulders. His wide chest half-hidden by muscular arms arrogantly folded. Down his solid rib cage and...mmm.

Those abs.

The bruises, a few of them really harsh, didn't detract from the perfection. A silky trail of dark hair bisected his body, teased around his navel and disappeared into the loosely wrapped towel.

There wasn't enough oxygen in the air to keep her properly ventilated.

"Yvette."

His voice had dropped an octave, drawing her gaze up to his. "Hmm?"

"They're just bruises."

He thought that was why she stared? Well, yeah, the bruises were ghastly. But she'd seen enough postfight photos to know it wasn't uncommon for a fighter to sport evidence of the battle.

The largest bruise was also the darkest, almost black in the middle, then fading into purple and lilac as it spread out over his ribs. Because it was a better excuse than the truth, she said, "You look like you should be—" *In bed.* Steering clear of that verbal trap, she amended, "Resting."

As if he knew her every thought, he smiled. "I can almost feel that stare, and I don't mind telling you, it's having an effect."

That made her look harder, and sure enough, the

tightly wrapped towel now showed things she'd be better off not seeing.

"Yvette," he said again, this time with gravelly insistence.

Realization of her rudeness hit and she pivoted fast to face the door. But...then what? She faced a closed door. Dumb, dumb, dumb.

"The back view is nice, too."

No way could she ignore that tempting admission. But when she looked over her shoulder at him, he still faced her. "I can't see the back."

"No." On a low laugh, he nodded at her rear end. "I meant yours."

Slapping her hands over her butt, she turned away again. If nothing else, it hid her burning face and kept her from visually molesting him.

And, darn it, now *she* became the recipient of a hot stare. "This isn't at all proper."

"I remember a time," he said, closer to her, "when you weren't all that worried about being proper."

She'd been young and foolish. "I shouldn't have stared and I'm sorry."

"Don't be. I'm not."

Knowing she had to get hold of herself and the situation, she staged a friendly expression and cautiously turned back to him. Utilizing Herculean effort, she kept her attention above his sternum. "It's hardly my fault with you standing there, flaunting yourself like that."

"I don't *flaunt*." He made a rude sound of denial. "I'm just standing here."

Looking as he did, that was enough. "You aren't decently dressed."

"I'd just gotten out of the shower when the phone rang."

"Well." He'd offered her the perfect excuse for fleeing. "I'll just let you finish getting ready—"

Before she could take a single step, he moved, and she got caught up watching the muscles in his bared body flex as he closed the small amount of space left between them.

She was hot, sweaty and suddenly mute.

When he reached out, she flattened against the door and almost squawked, it so surprised her.

"You're afraid of me?"

Her turn to scoff. "No, never."

Cannon paused for only a second before nodding with satisfaction. "Good." Gently catching her hand, he tugged her forward and started toward the kitchen.

Going along without complaint, Yvette tried to collect herself, but couldn't.

He was right—the back view was freaking *awesome*.

Long muscles moved with each step he took. Water glistened on his shoulders. His still-wet hair sent a trickle down the deep furrow of his spine.

And that little damp towel... How she envied it. Wrapped around his hips, it hugged his butt, showcasing the tight muscles there.

A big bubble of heat popped inside her, flushing her whole body. "Mmm, what are we doing?"

"Going into the kitchen."

"Why?"

"We need to talk." He looked over that boulder shoulder at her. "And I don't want you sneaking off again."

"I didn't sneak." *Liar.* "I just went for my morning jog."

"For more than two hours?" Pulling out two vinyl-covered chairs from her grandfather's refurbished kitchen table, he gestured for her to sit.

Since her legs were quivering from exhaustion, ready to give out anyway, she dropped down.

"I didn't know you jogged." His bright blue gaze moved over her, probably seeing her perspiration-soaked clothes and shiny, flushed skin. "Need something to drink?"

She needed him to get some pants on before she fainted. "No, I'm fine." Determined to be as blasé as him, she unhooked the belted purse from around her waist, removing the empty water bottle from the loop that held it, putting that and her cell phone on the tabletop.

Cannon gave her a long look, turned to the refrigerator and took out an icy bottle of water. He unscrewed the cap and set it in front of her. "You're pretty wilted. Drink up."

Wilted—what a nice way to put it. Reminded of how wretched she looked, she started to stand. "I need a shower."

A hand on her shoulder pressed her back. His tone even and cool, Cannon said, "Let's talk first."

He literally loomed over her with all that naked flesh up close and personal. She was eye level with a small brown nipple, with the sparse dark hair on his chest. She could smell his soap and something more. Something hot and sexy and all male.

Curling her hands into fists, she resisted the powerful urge to touch him. But that didn't stop her from looking— at his throat, over his collarbone, those sculpted pecs…

"You're doing it again."

"What?" she breathed in a strangled whisper.

His other hand flattened on the table beside her, caging her in. "Eating me up with those pretty green eyes."

She'd prefer to eat him up with her teeth, her tongue…. "Put on more clothes and I won't stare!"

Contentment showed in his eyes. "I will."

Thank God.

"After we talk."

Trying to find her backbone, she straightened in the chair and put a hand to his chest—his hot, hard, naked chest—to lever him back a few inches. "You're acting too familiar, Cannon." She had to concentrate hard to keep her fingers from caressing. "Like we're involved or something."

The second she touched him, he went still, then his eyes narrowed and his jaw flexed. "We've been involved for over three long years." Too serious, he covered her hand with his, keeping it trapped against his body. His chest hair tickled her palm and made breathing harder still. "It doesn't matter how long it's been or how far away you were. There's something between us."

Choking off a groan, she offered a compromise. "Tell you what." Infusing a dose of reason into her tone, she said, "Get dressed while I shower and then we'll—"

"Not happening."

Why did he always have to sound so controlled and collected? "Does another fifteen minutes really matter?"

"Does since you've been avoiding me. Given half a chance, you might take off again."

"Cannon…" She really, really needed him to back up enough to let her unclench. "You can't expect me to do this with you naked!"

Finally he stepped away, glanced down at himself, then tightened both the towel and his mouth. "Everything is covered."

"Actually…" *Stop eating him with your eyes.* "There's still a whole lot of *you* showing."

His mouth didn't smile, but, damn it, she could tell he enjoyed her extreme reaction.

When he continued to watch her, she shifted her feet,

tried crossing her arms, but there was no way to hide. "I am a miserable mess," she muttered with embarrassment.

"No," he asserted, "you aren't." He dragged a chair over close to her and seated himself.

In. A. Towel.

With his knees almost touching hers, he looked at her legs, at her snug shorts and her damp, fitted tank top. "If you want the truth—"

"I'm not sure I do," she said in a hurry.

"I can't stop picturing you without the shirt and shorts."

His blunt admission left her blank. "Naked in running shoes?"

His mouth quirked. "Okay, you can maybe lose the shoes, too." His focus now on her chest, he continued. "And you know, I'm betting that sports bra didn't do enough to stop some sexy bouncing."

"Cannon," she groaned, raising her arms to wrap around herself.

He caught her wrists, keeping her still. "It bothers me, thinking about all the guys who probably saw you jogging by and immediately started imagining more."

Her heart tried to punch out of her chest. "No one—"

"Because that's what I'm doing."

Though her mouth opened, nothing more came out. It took her three hard heartbeats before she thought to say, "Well, just stop it!"

"I'll try." Releasing her, he said softly, "If you'll stay and talk to me."

"But…"

"It won't take long."

"Neither would my shower," she grumbled, starting to feel put out by his pushy manner.

"Maybe. But with the way you keep dodging me, I don't trust it."

That made her eyes narrow. "You mean you don't trust *me*."

Shrugging, he rested his elbows on his thighs and let his hands hang loosely between his knees. "Close enough."

The insult should have taken precedence, but for a second there it looked as if he might lose the towel, and that annihilated every other thought. She held her breath, but no, it stayed put.

"Yvette."

"You are so badly bruised." She wanted to touch him, to somehow make his ribs better. He'd taken a vicious kick in the fight and almost lost. But somehow he'd managed to throw that one last punch—which had been enough. "Does it hurt?"

"Not much, so don't change the subject."

When she took in his determined expression, it shook her. Never had she wanted him to see her as anything but self-assured, mature and poised. Her best bet now would be to get the talking over with so she could go make herself presentable. "All right. Let's hear it."

Instead of launching into his all-important talk, he breathed deeper, zeroed in on her mouth and whispered, "First things first."

Yvette had no idea what he meant by that—until he came forward and put his mouth right to hers. Barely there. Lightly touching. Tentative.

She froze, her breath suspended and her body taut. Only her heartbeat seemed to function as it leaped into overtime.

When he didn't pull away, her eyes sank shut. Sharing

breath with him, drowning beneath a rush of intimacy, she made a small sound.

He reciprocated by touching his tongue against her, moving softly over her lips, tracing the seam where she held them closed.

In a dark, husky voice, he whispered, "Open up for me, honey."

The sexy command made her gasp—which was just the opportunity he wanted.

Still going slow and easy, he teased his way in as if savoring the experience.

She forgot she was a wreck, forgot this could lead nowhere, forgot...*everything.*

With a soft growl, he adjusted for a better fit. His mouth nudged hers open more. One of his hands caught her ponytail, tilting her head back. The other opened on the small of her back, urging her to the edge of the seat. He brought her into the solid cradle of his big body, surrounding her in so many ways. Without deliberate decision, she slipped her hands up to his shoulders, and, oh, God, he felt incredible, as good as she'd always imagined.

Every nerve ending jumped in awareness.

It had been so long since she'd been kissed, especially since she'd been kissed like this.

The last time was three years ago—with Cannon.

She forgot about her appalling state of sweat and wrinkled clothes, the wind-tangled ponytail he held.

He sank his tongue in, tasting her deeper, hotter. His hand left her back to settle boldly on her bare thigh just above her knee, his strong fingers wrapping around her, encircling her leg.

When he slid that hand upward to the edge of her shorts, she finally regained her wits.

She shoved back so fast she almost toppled the chair.

For a split second, they stared at each other, his gaze smoldering, hers—though he probably didn't realize it—full of regret. They both breathed too fast.

Shooting to her feet, Yvette got as far as the kitchen doorway before Cannon caught her.

His strong fingers held her shoulders, their heavy breathing the only sound in the room. After several tense moments, he deliberately loosened his hold and eased her back into his chest. She might have thought he had calmed, except that she felt his furious heartbeat against her shoulder blades.

"Don't run from me," he said low, his mouth touching her ear. "Swear to God, Yvette, it only makes me want to chase you."

If he could actually catch her, she'd have no problem with that. But she knew what he didn't, so she'd have to be the one to stop. "This was a mistake."

"Felt like a hell of a lot more to me."

Not leaning against him took every ounce of her willpower. "I'll shower and change and then we'll talk all you want." Now that she realized how combustible things could be, she knew they needed to clear the air. She needed him to understand that nothing would come of it.

She might even have to admit she was broken.

By small degrees, his hands opened from her shoulders and he took a step back. Time ticked by, and finally he said, "I'm sorry."

"Don't be." Knowing she wouldn't be able to handle it if he stayed in that damn towel, she asked, "Just…get dressed, okay?"

"If you promise not to keep me waiting."

A negotiation? So she had to bargain to get him clothed? The irony of it hit her: most women would be trying to steal his towel, not urging him to put on clothes.

When she'd found out what her grandfather had done, not once had she imagined this scene as a consequence. Other than Cannon's one moment of weakness during the darkest time of her life, he'd kept a safe, and platonic, distance away. She'd expected more of the same.

Logic had told her that Cannon, now a superstar with many demands on his time and his choice of women, would make a quick agreement to let her take care of business. For the sake of her wounded heart, she had counted on his only involvement being that of signing papers and then accepting what was his.

Instead he'd moved in with her—for how long?—and used his body to taunt her, to tempt her into wanting things she already knew she couldn't have.

With one sharp nod, she said, "Give me fifteen minutes."

NONE OF THAT had gone quite as he'd planned.

Well, parts had. Like her melting.

Like the taste of her.

The softness of her skin and the way her hair smelled.

Her impact on him was the same as three years ago when he'd first kissed her. She'd started an itch that had never gone away, and instead had grown to nearly consume him. Now he didn't have the excuse of consoling her, of trying to distract her from harsh reality.

No, he just wanted her. Bad.

But she shied away like a virgin. Or worse, like a woman injured. And for some damn reason, that made him act like a damned Neanderthal when he'd never been that heavy-handed with women.

Her reaction to him tortured him, making him want her sexually all the more, but also wanting her in other, less familiar ways.

Ways he didn't yet want to name. Hell, they'd only been reunited for a day. Less, considering she'd spent much of that time avoiding him.

When the phone she'd left on the table made a noise, he glanced at it.

A Facebook alert. Nosy and not giving a shit, he read the screen.

Facebook 1 min ago
Heath: Who the fuck are you posing with?

Hmm. A comment on the picture he'd taken with her? He wanted to know, but didn't want to invade her privacy enough to check the phone for more details.

To keep from tempting himself further, he went down the hall and into the bedroom across from hers. He opened his overnight bag and dug out fresh clothes. Shoving his feet into his favorite pair of worn jeans, Cannon cursed himself.

He had a boner no woman could miss. Especially not a woman so skittish and uncertain—a woman who'd devoured him with her gaze.

Carefully, he eased up the zipper while ordering his body to calm the hell down. Knowing she was so close, he had marginal success with that.

He was sitting on the side of the bed, tying his sneakers, when her bedroom door opened.

True to her word, she'd showered and changed in record time. At the open bedroom doorway, she peeked in at him, saw he was dressed and let out a tense breath.

If it were anyone other than Yvette, it'd be amusing how his exposed chest and legs had thrown her. He couldn't recall any other woman demanding that he get dressed. Hell, if she watched the fights as she claimed, she often saw him in nothing more than shorts.

Of course, that wasn't so up close and personal. That wasn't near enough to sense his lust and feel his need.

Unlike her, he'd wanted to drop the damn towel, get her hands on him, maybe skin her out of those damp duds she'd worn so he could reveal the heated body beneath....

"Cannon?"

She'd changed out of the sexy running shorts and into faded skinny jeans and replaced her sports bra and tank top with a red halter. Her feet were bare, her hair wet, her face clean of makeup and still he had a hell of a time getting his dick to behave.

Holding her gaze, he stood. "Feel better?"

"Yes." Her hand trembled as she tucked her wet hair behind her ears.

The urge to strip her naked pulsed inside him. He kept his distance, working to get those crazy, overwhelming urges under control. "Have you eaten?"

"A donut in the park."

His mood softened, going from pure red-hot lust to something even more uncomfortable, something like tenderness. "Was that so you could stay away longer?"

Shifting, she curled her toes against the carpet. "I run to help unwind. Whenever I start to get too keyed up, I can sweat off the tension." She glanced down the hall, one shoulder rolling. "This morning took a little longer than usual."

Since he did the same, he understood. He walked to where she stood, resisting the instinct to touch her. "Next time you want to run, let me know. I'll go with you."

Her gaze shot up to his.

She looked so horrified that he lifted a brow. He'd thought it was being home, in this house, that bothered her. But maybe not. "Or am I the reason you were wired?"

Disgruntled, she started down the hall. "You were part of it, yes."

Watching the restrained swish of her sexy ass, he followed her into the kitchen. She was wired again—or still—so he let that go for now. "A donut is hardly breakfast. Are you hungry?"

"A little."

"After we work out a few things, we could go by Rowdy's for lunch."

She reseated herself in the same chair she'd had earlier. "I don't want to intrude."

What the hell did that mean? "You're not." How could she intrude when he wanted to spend every available moment with her? And thinking that, he took his phone from his pocket. "Before I forget, what's your number? I don't like not being able to reach you."

Lifting her chin, she asked, "Do I get your number, too, then?"

"Yeah."

"Oh." Clearly that surprised her. "I just assumed... I mean, you're famous now. I didn't think you'd want your number out there."

He slanted her a sideways look. "Yeah, don't post it on Facebook or anything like that."

"I wouldn't!"

A perfect segue.

Sitting across from her, he kept a little distance between them this time. Otherwise he wasn't sure he'd be able to keep his hands to himself.

That one kiss... It shouldn't have been a big deal, but he'd completely lost himself. He'd meant to make it a small taste, to tease her, to appease his curiosity.

Instead he'd teased himself, and his curiosity was now at a fever pitch.

With little involvement on her part, he'd forgotten everything except Yvette, her taste, her touch, the comfort of having her close.

Unsettling, to be sure.

Everything she did, every facial expression, each small gesture, seemed specifically designed to turn him on. He knew it wasn't deliberate.

And that only made it more disturbing.

"Speaking of Facebook..."

She frowned. "Were we?"

"Who's Heath?"

She did a double take. "How do you—"

No reason to lie about it. "An alert popped up on your phone."

Scowling, she snatched the phone off the table, tapped the screen a few times, quickly read and then went still with disquieting resolve.

"Yvette?"

That false smile slid back into place, leading the way toward feigned composure. She inhaled, blew it out as if gearing up. "He's no one. A guy I dated for a little while."

Bullshit. "He's the one you said you broke up with before going to the fight?"

She shook her head. "No, that was someone else."

Jealousy prickled, damn it. So she got around. He'd figured as much. Just looking at her, even with her not trying to look her best, he knew guys would flock to her.

Hoping to make light of it, he said, "Left a lot of broken hearts behind, huh?"

"No. No one's heart was involved." She chewed her bottom lip, then launched into more explanations. "I broke things off with Heath long before Grandpa passed. It wasn't working out."

"How so?"

That stalled her again.

Making him a little nuts, she nibbled her lip again in what he now recognized as nervousness. Cannon couldn't stop himself from reaching out, smoothing with his thumb, freeing that soft flesh from the sharp bite of her teeth.

As his fingers cradled her face and his thumb drifted over her mouth, she went perfectly still, her eyes wary. Against his fingers, her cheek warmed.

Sliding his hand back into her damp hair, he relished the warmth and silkiness of her neck. "You can tell me anything, you know that, right?"

Her forced laugh bothered him more than her uncertainty. "There's nothing to tell." She caught his wrist. "And really, Cannon, I keep telling you I'm not that scared, clingy kid anymore."

"I'm glad." They sat like that for several heartbeats, his hand curved around her nape, her slender fingers holding his thick wrist. With one more caress, he retreated. "But if anything comes up, I'm here."

"Here, in the house."

Here, in her life—whether she wanted to accept that yet or not. "Since we're sharing the house for now, we should keep each other up on plans, don't you think? If we head off to different places, I'll tell you when to expect me back." That way, she wouldn't be spooked when she heard him coming in.

"You aren't accountable to me."

Damn it, why did she insist on fighting him over every little detail? "It's considerate," he told her. "I'd expect you to do the same."

As she thought about it, she licked her lips—and he had to swallow back a groan. Damn, but he wanted to kiss that mouth again, taste her deeper, longer.

All over.

He rubbed at the back of his neck. "Your buddy, Heath."

"Not my buddy." She set the phone on the table—facedown. "What about him?"

"He wasn't thrilled to see you in a picture with me."

She shrugged as if that didn't matter. "He's tried to get back with me a few times."

The understated way she explained that told more than she meant it to. Apparently old Heath was still hung up on her. Not that Cannon could blame him. "You're not interested?"

She huffed a short laugh. "No. Definitely not."

Unwilling to let it go, Cannon shifted. "He seemed angry."

"I think he misunderstood the picture—"

"No, he didn't."

Her widened eyes locked with his. She started to reply, but appeared to have run out of words.

Cannon didn't mind explaining it to her. "Guys have a sixth sense about stuff like this. Poor old Heath knows what I want, and he's not happy about it."

"What you...?" She cleared her throat, frowned. "Don't be ridiculous." Then, worrying a little, her voice small and hesitant, she asked, "What is it you want?"

"You."

As if the one-word statement had grabbed her, she pressed back in the chair and locked her hands on the seat at either side of her hips.

"I kissed you, Yvette. Not a friendly, token peck either." And she'd kissed him back with enthusiasm—until she'd caught herself. He narrowed his eyes, determined to make her accept the truth. "My tongue was in your mouth, and we both liked it."

More heat stained her cheeks; a pulse went wild in her pale throat.

Interesting. "You had to know."

Worse than denying it, she said, "It doesn't matter."

The hell it didn't.

Intrigued by her reaction but not overly concerned, Cannon tipped his head to study her. One way or another, he'd win her over. For the foreseeable future he'd be under the same roof with her, in close proximity. Anything and everything could happen.

He'd see to it.

Eventually he'd find that girl who had adored him, the one who'd wanted him enough to rely on him, to trust him completely.

But for now, he hoped to wade through her denials without scaring her off. "It matters to me."

"Cannon, please." She pressed fingertips to her temples. "You're throwing too much at me at one time."

True. She'd just lost her grandfather. Moved from California. Inherited a house and a business.

On top of all that, he'd moved in on her. To the world he could claim friendly, caring motives. The need to protect her from fear, from ugly memories, definitely existed.

But being honest with himself, he had to admit his intent centered mostly on getting her in bed. If he weren't so raw with needing her, if it didn't feel as if he'd suffered three years of heavy foreplay, he might have backed off, given her some space.

But he couldn't.

He could, however, slow things down and give her a

little more breathing room. "Let's start with exchanging info." After she got comfortable with having him around, then they could move on to exchanging more. A lot more. "If anything comes up with the legality of the property, we'll need to be able to find each other, right?"

"What would come up?"

No time like the present. He only hoped he could steer her in the right direction. "Mindi Jarrett called."

With a barely perceptible glitter, her eyes went from wary to antagonistic. "Who?"

Jealousy sounded in the tight query. Nice. He hated suffering alone. "The lawyer's assistant."

"Oh." For a brief second, her thick lashes swept down as she closed her eyes. When she opened them again, she muttered, "Sorry."

Hiding his chuckle wasn't easy. "She has an offer for us."

"An offer for...?"

"The pawnshop. I didn't ask how much. She wanted me to come meet her but I told her I'd talk to you and we'd both go. I'm supposed to call her back."

She pushed out of the chair to pace. "I didn't expect an offer so quickly. I've only driven by there once. I don't really know what it's worth or..."

"Or if you want to sell?"

She flagged a hand in the air. "We have to sell."

Maybe. Leaning back against the table, Cannon crossed his ankles and watched her nervous stride around the small kitchen. "What is it you do?"

"Do?"

"For a living."

"Oh, right." She went to the sink—as far from him as she could get without actually leaving the room. Leaning back in a pose similar to his own, she said, "I'm an eBay vendor." Without him asking, she explained. "I learned a lot working at the pawnshop, and eBay seemed like an easy way to use what I know. I take things from other people and auction them with a commission paid to me. But I also buy stuff at yard and estate sales, and overstock items to resell."

"You make a living doing that?"

"I wasn't getting rich, but I was able to live on my own and save for a rainy day." Restless, she pushed off from the sink to pace again. "My friend Vanity works with me. We can both do any of the work, but mostly I take care of acquiring and listing the stuff with photos, and she mails off or delivers it after the sale. In fact, she'll continue to do that with my remaining stock in California."

"Vanity?" Unusual name for a girl.

Yvette nodded while tracking the perimeter of the kitchen, much like a caged pet. Her long stride drew his gaze repeatedly to her legs and her bare feet. Her vibrating energy was another new facet that he enjoyed.

"Vanity Baker. She's gorgeous—you'd like her."

"You're gorgeous." *And I more than like you.*

A smile teased her mouth. "Thank you, but Vanity is different. She's a stereotypical California surfer. Tall, toned and tanned, with really long blond hair and…well, she's stacked. She could be a living Barbie doll except that she despises anything pink."

Not getting the reference, Cannon asked, "Pink?"

"Yeah, you know. Barbie has a pink car, a pink scooter, a pink house with pink furniture and so on." She wrinkled her nose. "Everything is a Pepto-Bismol shade of pink."

"Never realized."

She cast him a look. "Your sister wasn't into Barbie?"

"I don't know. Maybe." He wanted her to understand something. "However pretty you think your friend is—"

"She's beyond pretty, believe me. Men stop and stare."

He shook his head. "They do that to you, too, Yvette."

"Not really." Parking at the sink again, she locked her hands together and flipped back her hair. "I guess you'd just have to meet Vanity to see what I mean."

With no plans to head to Cali any time soon, he dismissed that possibility. "Let's get back to your phone number." The second he said it, her phone chimed with a text message.

They stared at each other.

Making no move to check the message, Yvette said, "Are you ready?" and she gave him her number.

After saving her in his contacts, he glanced at her phone. "Want me to put my number in for you?"

That got her feet moving. "No, I can do it." She snatched up the phone, read the message, then clicked over to a new screen. "Okay, what is it?"

While reciting the number, Cannon moved closer. When she finished, he tipped up her chin. "Now. About tonight."

Her gaze dropped to his mouth, then his chest, down to his abs and beyond. "Tonight?"

Keep it up, he thought, *and I won't last past the next five minutes.*

CHAPTER SIX

WITHOUT REALIZING IT, Yvette went up on her tiptoes, drawn to Cannon, swaying in closer to his appeal.

The rough edge of his thumb teased under her chin, then up to her bottom lip again. He made a low sound of encouragement. "You're begging to be kissed."

That deep, affected tone stroked over her—until she realized what he'd said. Her heels landed back on the linoleum floor with jarring impact. "I— What?"

His sexy mouth quirked at her confusion. "Mindi called, remember? Did you want to meet with her tonight?"

Humiliation hit her like a dash of icy water. Good grief, she'd sent so many mixed signals, the poor guy was going to crash before she got her head on straight. "Right, sorry."

"On second thought…" He scooped her in close and took her mouth in a warm, blessedly brief kiss. "I like your idea better."

How could she resist so much temptation?

She could, because she had no choice. "Cannon—"

He shushed her with another, longer kiss.

With him moving at Mach speed, she couldn't think clearly, especially when her bones turned to butter and his scent left her dizzy and he tasted *so* damn good.

Looping his arms loosely around her waist, he eased

up but kept her against him. "You want some time, don't you?"

An eternity, but grateful for the reprieve, she only nodded.

"I'll try, all right?" His next kiss landed on her forehead. "Won't be easy, though."

She'd always known that Cannon was rock solid and sexier than any guy should be. But she hadn't realized that being a fighter would ramp up his already considerable confidence and hone his appeal, both emotional and physical. "I could tell you about hard."

"That should be my line." He nudged into her. "Any more kissing and I'll have a full-fledged boner."

What she felt wasn't full-fledged?

"Again," he added.

Right. Of course she'd noticed earlier. Impossible to ignore, really, though she'd tried.

His amusement kicked up another notch. "Looking at me like that isn't helping."

Realizing that she'd been staring at him while thinking about his erection, Yvette tried to wiggle out of his arms.

Cannon didn't let her.

"Settle down." He drew her in closer, one hand between her shoulder blades, the other just above her behind. "We have a lot of ground to cover yet, and to be honest, I prefer to settle it just like this." He nuzzled against her temple, sending gooseflesh up and down her arms. "Okay?"

"Do I get a say in it?"

"Sure." He tilted her back, his expression serious. "I'm listening."

What could she say? *I don't want to start something*

I can't finish? That'd lead to more questions, and she didn't have enough answers.

Without meaning to, she smoothed her hands over his chest. There were so many wonderful places to touch him, each more enticing than the other. "I need to know how we're going to work this."

"This, meaning us?"

"This, meaning both of us here in this house together." She tipped her head to judge his reaction. "I'm fine with us being considerate. It's true that I'm still a little jumpy over being here and I'd appreciate knowing when to expect you, or when...when I might be here alone."

"Ditto."

Right. Surely Cannon didn't expect her to believe that being in the house disturbed him. He was so much stronger than her. "But I don't want to step on your toes."

"I don't know what that means, honey."

His use of endearments kept throwing her. "It means that you're back in town and plenty of women want your attention. This is rightfully your home—"

"Yvette—"

"—and if you're staying here, it's inevitable that you might want to bring home...company." Just saying it made her stomach sick. "When you do, you should feel comfortable about it."

His hands moved up to her face, holding her steady for his uncompromising stare. "Let's get something clear up front."

He had such big hands that he left her feeling tiny. It wasn't an entirely unpleasant feeling, not with Cannon. "Okay."

"I don't want you dragging in other dudes."

Wait, what? That was so far from what she'd expected that she went blank.

He gave a soft growl, kissed her hard and fast and finally freed her to run a hand over his dark hair. "Are you planning to see other guys?"

Other guys meaning men besides him? "I'm not seeing *anyone*."

His blue eyes went flinty. "We'll be living together, so you'll be seeing me."

Not the way he implied. "Sharing the same house is not—"

"Sharing the same bed? We'll see."

Her mouth opened, but no protest emerged.

"Still." He chewed the corner of his mouth while forming his reply. "It could be uncomfortable for both of us, don't you think?"

With no idea what he meant, she shook her head in confusion.

"You with someone else, me with someone else. Not cool, right?"

Shoot, it wasn't as if she wanted to see him with another woman! "It could be uncomfortable, yes." His insistence started to wear on her. "But what about Mary?"

"Forget her."

"There will be other women—"

"Forget them, too." He drew a slow breath. "I've made it as plain as I can, honey. I don't mind giving you some time, but you need to understand the facts. The only woman I'm interested in right now is you."

That was so blatant, so bold, she fell back a step. Elation tried to burst free, but she stomped it into submission and took a stance instead. "Since when?"

"The truth?" He leaned in close, angling his body down to hers, nose to nose, aggressive and annoyed. "Since you walked out on me three fucking years ago."

ARMIE WATCHED AS Cannon and his lady walked into the rec center. Trouble in paradise, he thought, noting the difference in how they both held themselves today.

Funny.

Yesterday Cannon had been so territorial that he'd half expected him to start shoving the other guys out the door. Course, that just made Stack and Denver and Miles more interested.

Grabbing up a towel to mop the sweat from his face, Armie winced. His cheek hurt like a son of a bitch and his swollen lip still smarted. He prodded the cut inside his mouth with his tongue before saying to Denver, "Finish up and then have them spar. I'll be back in a few minutes."

Denver followed the direction of his gaze and grinned. With his long brown hair half out of the tie, he looked more like a barbarian than a good instructor for kids. "Cannon looks a little out of sorts, doesn't he?"

"Yeah." Armie slung the towel around his neck. "Think I'll see what I can do to tweak his bad mood."

"You have a death wish," Denver said on a laugh before turning back to the youths he instructed, showing them the proper way to kick a heavy bag.

Stepping off the mats, dressed only in athletic shorts, Armie walked up front to meet his friend.

Yvette—such a doll—looked at him and grimaced. "Ouch. Are you okay?"

"Fine." He glanced at Cannon. "'Bout damn time, man. You're only four hours late."

Rather than reply to the jibe, Cannon looked him over, taking in every bruise. He lifted a brow in query.

"I'm so sorry." Yvette raised a dainty hand. "It's my fault."

Ignoring Cannon's curiosity, Armie turned his attention to her. "What is?"

"Cannon being late."

Trying not to grin, Armie asked, "Yeah, how so?"

Cannon gave him a shove. "Not what you're thinking."

With his whole body bludgeoned, Armie almost groaned. But never in front of a lady. He sucked it up and laughed at Cannon. "What was I thinking?"

Cannon glanced at Yvette, and, damn, he looked hungry.

Okay, so maybe he hadn't tapped that yet. Poor bastard.

Either unaware of the undercurrent or adequately pretending, Yvette explained. "I went jogging this morning without realizing that Cannon wanted to talk with me. He waited for me to return and it put us behind."

Huh. Armie eyed his friend. "Why didn't you just jog with her?"

"She didn't tell me she was leaving."

Yvette flushed, more over being ratted out than from embarrassment. "I didn't, at that time, realize that we'd be checking in with each other."

Oh, man. This was hilarious. "So let me get this straight."

Shifting, Cannon said low, "Fuck you, Armie."

Unfazed, Armie said, "You and Cannon are...what?"

Appearing unsure of how to answer, Yvette deferred to Cannon.

Tight-lipped, Cannon shared with him the brunt of his disgruntlement. "You don't have enough bruises? Looking to get a few more?"

"Nope. Idle curiosity, that's all."

Cannon appeared ill at ease, but only for a second. He was not a man who suffered insecurities of any kind. He turned to Yvette. "You want to look around, check out the place? Break room is through that back door. Johns are back there, too. Looks as though Denver is teaching a class. You can watch that for a few minutes if you want. I'll join you soon."

Armie smirked. "Yeah, take in all the sights while Cannon vents his bad mood."

She tilted her head, studied each of them and, given her serene smile, must have decided they were joking. "Take your time."

Little did she know that fighters often joked with their fists. And seriously, Armie wouldn't shy away from a little one-on-one practice with Cannon, but he really wasn't up for it if he could avoid it without losing face.

Yvette was barely out of hearing distance when Cannon said, "What the hell happened to you?"

Pretending not to understand, Armie asked, "What?"

"Someone—maybe a small crowd by the looks of it—beat the shit out of you."

Giving up, on at least that small bit, Armie admitted, "There were four of them."

Disbelief narrowed Cannon's eyes. "Only four, huh?"

"I got blindsided by the first one. Before I realized it, they were on me."

"I hope you sent them limping away."

"Pretty much." But not before taking a good dose of punishment, which maybe he'd had coming. "Now let's talk about you."

Cannon shook his head. "I'm not done with you yet." He crossed his arms over his chest. "Who and why?"

Damn it, he didn't want to get into this. He *couldn't* get into it. "I was snooping, if you have to know."

"Snooping where?"

Near your house. "Let's just say I suspected a lady

was being used by a scumbag prick who isn't good enough for her."

Snorting, Cannon said, "Using, as in the way you use—"

"Hey, *I'm* always up front about avoiding monogamy." Bragging a little, he added, "And we both know the ladies use me in return."

Since he couldn't deny that, Cannon said only, "Go on."

"This lady is different."

One of Cannon's brows went up. "Meaning?"

Yeah, dumbass. Explain that one. Armie took a minute to swab his face again with the towel. "You know what I'm saying."

"She's a nice girl?"

Real nice. The nicest. Too damn nice to get used. "Something like that."

The other brow joined the first as Cannon studied him. "Since when do you concern yourself over nice girls?"

"Hey, I don't sleep with them, but doesn't mean I want them abused."

Cannon kept staring at him.

"What, damn it?"

"I'm trying to picture you as a white knight, but the image isn't coming together. Too much rust in the metal."

"Fuck you." Disgruntled over the interruption, Armie huffed. "You want to hear it or not?"

"I'm all ears."

Lying asshole. He was all grins and harassment. "So I was doing some surveillance—"

"Alone?"

He worked his jaw. "Interrupt one more time and I swear to God—"

Cannon gestured for him to continue.

"I was *alone,* checking up on things, and I guess the bastard saw me. Only instead of facing me man to man, he sent his buddies after me. One of them hit me in the back of the head hard enough that I fucking saw stars and—"

Cannon grabbed his ear, using it to twist him so he could investigate.

"Goddamn it, Cannon." Flinching, Armie tensed all over. His head still felt like it might fracture into pieces and his temples pulsed. "Lighten up."

"Stop whining." Cannon searched through his hair, pressed, whistled low and let him go. "You sure you don't have a concussion?"

"I might after you manhandling me!" Smoothing his hair back over the massive goose egg, Armie grimaced again. "I don't know what they hit me with, but it left me stunned long enough for them to knock me to the ground." Amid a bunch of heavy boots and bad intentions.

"They didn't kill you," Cannon said, "so I assume you caught your wind?"

More like instincts had taken over and he'd done what had to be done to survive. Muscle memory could often be a lifesaver. "Yeah. I kicked out a knee." That guy would be limping for a good long while. "Nutted the other fuck."

"Good for you."

"The third nearly stove in my ribs before I caught his foot and got him down on the ground with me." And then Armie had made him regret the error of his ways.

Remembering brought him a little satisfaction. He cracked his aching knuckles.

"Give me some names."

Oh, shit, Cannon sounded calmly furious—which boded well for no one. "Let it go. It's my business."

That perked him up. "Personal?" And then with more disbelief, "Over a *woman?*"

Armie gave him a dead stare. "Yeah, imagine that."

Shaking his head, Cannon said, "Can't."

The antagonism cracked, and Armie ended up laughing. Seriously, he did not get that involved, had no interest in a *relationship* and avoided nice ladies as though they had thorns. "Yeah, me either. Let's just say I felt like busting some heads and almost got caught up in more than I could handle."

"Four against one sucks."

"It wasn't that bad."

Cannon did that damned annoying quiet perusal of his, dragging it out until Armie felt like stomping away.

Finally he said, "I wouldn't mind busting some heads, too."

Dressed and showered after his workout, headed for the front door, Stack heard Cannon and paused beside them. "Whose heads are we busting?"

Cannon nodded at Armie. "The ones that did that to him."

Snorting, Stack said, "I think it was his last dating duo that put an ass-whooping on him." With deliberate provocation, he asked Armie, "You tell Cannon about the lady's whip?"

"Whip?"

Armie rolled his eyes. "I already told you that was just a prop."

Cannon turned from Armie to Stack. "Let's hear it."

"The night of your fight we had a party here to watch. Armie left with a couple of women who seemed more into each other than him."

"Appearances are obviously deceiving," Armie said with smug satisfaction.

"The one chick had a whip in her belt." Stack grinned hugely. "Kinky."

"Only seems kinky the first time," Armie told him, totally deadpan.

Cannon turned back to Armie. "The two you mentioned?"

"Yeah, so? They liked it enough they returned for an encore."

"You didn't tell me about the whip."

"Because it didn't mean anything. It was like… I don't know. Jewelry or something."

Stack laughed. "Says the man who's now beat all to hell and back."

Cannon narrowed his eyes. "He says four guys did that to him."

Damn it! "Big mouth. Did I say to announce it?" Armie didn't need his private business spread around.

Stack whistled low. "No shit? Well, hell, man, if we're retaliating, count me in."

"There you go," Cannon offered.

"Four against three? Since when do we gang up on idiots? It'd be a slaughter, and none of us wants that, so forget it." Searching out Yvette with his gaze, Armie found her in the back, fingers laced together, attention rapt as she listened to Denver explaining something to her. The kids, ranging in age from ten to sixteen, studied her wide-eyed. "Enough about me. What's wrong with you?"

As Cannon stared at her, he started breathing deeper. "Nothing."

"Yeah, right." It was all Armie could do not to laugh. "You look like you're going to jump her bones any second."

To Armie's surprise, Cannon growled, locked his

hands together behind his neck and paced off toward the reception desk.

Wow. Armie and Stack shared a look.

Knowing Stack was on his way out, Armie said, "I got it."

"Go easy on him."

"That's not what he needs." After Stack nodded and left, Armie went after Cannon. "That bad, huh?"

"Fucking unreal."

Seeing how his friend vibrated with constrained menace, he commiserated. "You did without before the fight, didn't you?"

Cannon didn't have to answer. Armie knew how obsessed he got when prepping for a fight, especially the past few weeks. Despite the urban legend of athletes abstaining, most of the guys he knew never turned down sex. Hell, propositioned by the right woman, he'd be knocking boots the night before, using sex to shake off the jitters that came with a big fight.

But not Cannon. He was too damn selective from the get-go, and when in training he got downright picky. He turned away far more women than he laid.

In that, they were total opposites. It took a very rare woman for Armie to deny himself.

It took an even rarer woman for him to want to defend her honor. *Stupid, stupid, stupid.*

Rather than go down that road and maybe tweak Cannon's interest again, Armie distracted him. "Thinking that way almost cost Gage the girl."

"Harper?"

"Yeah." Everyone knew the two of them were an item—though God knew Gage had nearly screwed it up. Armie grinned, remembering. "They were here the night of the fights, too, but they were so busy dancing around each other they missed more than they saw." He leaned in, eyebrows bobbing. "Gage dragged her off to the office and they didn't emerge until after your fight had ended. Harper had the look of a well-laid lady, and she agreed to move in with him, so Gage must've made us proud."

Cannon eased up enough to smile. "Good for them."

"Yeah," Armie agreed, but added, "if you're into that whole commitment thing."

"They are."

He agreed again. "Speaking of commitment…" He focused on Yvette. "I think Denver's going to show her a move."

Cannon jerked around so fast, Armie almost got hit with an elbow.

Apparently uncaring that sweat covered Denver's chest, Yvette allowed him to maneuver her into a standing rear naked choke. He put one arm under her chin with his hand on his opposite arm above his elbow, his other hand at the back of her head—in the right position to apply pressure.

Yvette automatically wrapped her hands over the beefy forearm around her neck. "Wow," Armie said, "I can't believe she's—"

Snarling, Cannon strode off.

"Damn." Seeing the set of Cannon's shoulders, Armie chased after him.

When he reached his side, he said, "You know you're going to make an ass of yourself, right?"

Cannon kept walking without replying.

"Might make an ass of her, too."

He turned on Armie so fast, Armie stepped back.

"Just saying." He held up his hands. "Denver won't

hurt her—you know that. No reason to go all King Kong and shit."

At that precise moment, they both heard Yvette laughing. They looked up to see Denver sprawled dramatically on the ground while Yvette held his fingers twisted.

"It's not even a real hold," Cannon complained.

Armie couldn't stop grinning. The kids, all of them needy in one way or another, snickered and elbowed each other and all in all had a good time at the absurd display.

Denver pretended to be in agony, which was pretty ridiculous given Yvette now barely held his pinky. She, too, kept laughing, her long hair spilling forward, a very sweet ass on display as she bent toward Denver's supine form.

One of the boys jumped up, helping to haul Denver back to his feet so he could try the escape. As carefully as he had with Yvette, Denver put the kid in the choke.

Cannon's long exhalation brought Armie back around.

"You, my man, are in a very bad way."

"Yeah," Cannon agreed. "I am."

"So go get laid already."

It shocked him stupid when Cannon said, "Working on it," and then with frustration, "but she needs some time."

"Why?"

He rocked a shoulder. "She just lost her grandfather, moved, hasn't seen me in years."

For the women Armie knew, none of that would matter. Sex would be the cure, the relief, the escape, always. But he could tell Yvette was a different kind of lady.

Different from what he preferred.

Different to how Cannon felt about her.

She was the kind Armie avoided. "All right. So give her some time." At Cannon's scowl, he asked, "Or is that a problem?"

"She has some guy who keeps calling her."

Competition? Things were getting interesting. "Who?" He'd put his money on Cannon every time.

"She says her ex."

Maybe not so interesting. "He's around?"

Shaking his head, Cannon said, "In California."

Armie just stared at him.

Cannon stared back.

Yeah, now would be a really shitty time to laugh. Might even get him decked. So instead Armie cleared his throat. "If he's that far away, I don't see how—"

"I don't want her attention divided." Cannon opened and closed his fists in frustration. Voice going low, almost tortured, he said, "I want her one hundred percent focused on me."

"Can I offer a suggestion?"

Cannon stewed, worked his jaw and finally said with deceptive calm, "Let's hear it."

"First, bring it down a notch. Dude, you are seriously heaving like a caveman and it's just not like you. It's making me uneasy, and you don't want to fuck me. I can only imagine how the little lady feels."

Hands again locking into massive fists, Cannon stewed some more.

Biting back a fat grin, Armie gave some—what he considered sound—advice. "Second, why not use the time she needs to win her over? You're in the same house, right? So there'll be a lot of alone time. Rein yourself in, take advantage of proximity and she'll be the one sinking. Then you can just go down with her instead of drowning alone."

"Your metaphors are getting more confusing by the minute."

Armie rubbed his chin and tried to clarify. "It's old-

school, I know, but you might try seducing her. You'll
have time and opportunity. That's all I'm saying."

Cannon transferred his gaze back to the lady. She was
busy oohing over a kid's barely there biceps, then listening intently as one of the older boys told her a joke. She
laughed, ruffled his hair, and Cannon clenched all over.

"I like her," Armie stated. He clapped Cannon on the
back. "Get it together, do your thing, be your usual irresistible self and like all the other ladies, she'll be begging for it in no time."

"God, I hope so," Cannon told him quietly. "Because
I'm not sure how long I can wait."

He walked off to collect Yvette, so he didn't see
Armie's surprise.

Huh. Cannon rarely talked about sex. The most the
bastard ever did was smile when asked. So Yvette was
unique.

Nice.

He'd spread the word around. It wouldn't stop any of
the guys from egging Cannon on when they could, but
they'd also go out of their way to assist whenever and
wherever possible.

Having Cannon back in town for an extended time
would be even more rewarding than he'd first assumed.

Now, if he could just resolve his own issues…

CHAPTER SEVEN

WHILE YVETTE TOOK in all the improvements at the rec center, Cannon went over things in his head.

I can't, I'm sorry.

Over and over, Cannon heard those softly whispered words. He didn't buy it. Can't? What the hell did that mean? She could. She most definitely would.

With him.

But as Armie had suggested, he probably needed to cool it just a bit before he spooked her too much.

They'd agreed—her with relief, him under duress— to discuss her odd statement more later. She claimed to be overwhelmed with all the changes. He could buy that.

But when she kissed him, the way she looked at him, he knew they were on the same page.

For some reason, she didn't want to be. For some reason, she wanted to deny them both.

Twice more her ex had contacted her. Once again in text, once by a call that she let go to voice mail. The idea that she might be hung up on some other man made him more than a little nuts.

Hell, he didn't like seeing Denver touch her, even in jest. He definitely didn't want to stew on some bozo she cared about getting busy with her.

Turning his head toward his shoulder, Cannon cracked his neck. So much strain had crawled in that his muscles were knotting.

Before coming to the rec center, they'd stopped by
Rowdy's for lunch. Luckily, it was a lighter crowd and
the women were mostly moms with their kids, or women
with their boyfriends. Yvette had relaxed, chatting with
Rowdy and Avery, praising them on the bar, answering
questions about her life in California.

He wanted to get her alone, but for now, with her
hands-off policy, being out and about was safer.

"This place was great when I saw it last, but now it's
amazing."

"Thanks." He, too, looked around, trying to see it as
she would. Most of the fighters came in the morning
and early evening, which left the afternoon free for the
neighborhood kids and the after-school crowd. "Armie's
made a lot of improvements."

She lightly elbowed him. "Don't be modest. He said
most of the equipment came from endorsements you got."

True enough, but not the point. "He puts the stuff to
good use."

They headed for the break room together. On the way
they passed Armie, who greeted a high school boy who'd
just come in, dressed for a workout. "What's he doing
now?"

"He works with some of the wrestlers to help them
with their techniques and to show them how wrestling
can be put to good use in the SBC."

"Is it the same as grappling?"

"In some ways. Taking a shot, sprawling to avoid one.
Doing a switch or running a half, switching to a double
leg. A crotch lift, or a suplex…" When she gave him a
blank look, he smiled. "Sorry."

"It's interesting—when I understand."

"Wrestling is a great tool to bring to MMA. But the
point of wrestling is to get your opponent on his back. A

lot of wrestlers naturally panic when that happens. But for real competition in the SBC, being on your back is just another offensive position. There are a lot of submissions that can be done from your back." Being casual, Cannon smoothed her hair, then tucked it back behind her ear. He felt the stillness that settled over her, but pretended not to. "Armie works with the guys to show them how to transition wrestling moves into MMA skills."

She cleared her throat, took a breath and focused again on Armie. "How many hours a day does he spend here?"

"More than he should." As they stepped into the break room, Cannon put a hand to the small of her back and even that, the touch of his palm to her, through clothes, he felt everywhere. "He likes the kids a lot."

"Funny." She took a seat. "He said the same about you."

"Yeah." If he could, Cannon knew he would save every single child in the neighborhood. Save them from poverty, from neglect, from abuse.

From the bullies who gravitated to gangs and the bastards who peddled drugs.

He wasn't a superhero, so instead, he did what he could. Luckily, guys like Armie carried more than a full load of responsibility. Denver, Stack, Miles, Gage…they all lent a hand.

Cannon got them both a Coke. "You were pretty good with the boys."

"I love kids." She took a sip, turned the can, traced a finger through the condensation. "When I was in school, I used to think about being a teacher."

"Yeah?" He settled back in his seat, content to watch her.

"After everything that happened, though…"

He didn't press her, didn't try to fill the silence. The

drone of voices, of strikes against the heavy bag and music from a CD, drifted in around them.

Her gaze shied away from his. He didn't mind. He enjoyed just looking at her.

Quietly, she explained, "What happened changed my plans a lot."

True. But she was here now. With any luck, she'd stay. "The important thing is that you don't let it change you."

She gave a mirthless laugh that she quickly stifled.

Again, Cannon just waited.

"What will your routine be while you're here?"

Avoidance? He'd let her get away with that—for now.

He shrugged. His routine would accommodate hers, but she probably didn't want to hear that. "I was thinking I'd visit tonight with the guys." Visiting being their excuse to scope out the neighborhood, to make sure everything remained right and tight in their own little corner of the world.

"I thought you said you usually jog really early in the morning."

"Twice a day, every day. It's part of what I do to stay in shape. But I won't be that late." And in case she thought to dodge him again, he added, "And I'm always an early riser, no matter how late I stay up."

Denver walked in, saw them and stalled. "Hey. Sorry." He started to backpedal.

"It's fine," Cannon told him. "We won't be much longer."

Still, Denver crept around as if he was afraid of waking the dead. Carrying a white towel, he wore snug shorts and nothing else. Sweat dampened his chest and his long hair. The activity had left his face flushed. He inched quietly toward the water machine.

Cannon met Yvette's gaze, and they both grinned.

He and Denver shared a similar height, but Denver had twenty pounds on him, making him a heavyweight instead of a light heavyweight. "I was just telling Yvette that we'll get together tonight."

Relaxing a little now that he'd been included, Denver nodded. "Sounds good to me. Say nine or so? Meet out front of Rowdy's?"

"That works. Ask around and see who wants to join us."

"Gage is out." Denver upended a bottle of water and guzzled down half of it. When he finished, he mopped his face with the towel again. "He and Harper are burning up the sheets at his place. Making up for lost time or something, Harper told me."

Cannon noticed how Yvette tried not to stare. But again and again, her gaze went over Denver. He didn't see the heat of interest in her eyes, just the gawking of a woman surprised to be near a mostly naked man with muscles pumped from a workout.

He supposed if a woman stood in front of him dressed the same, it'd distract him, too.

"Sounds like Harper."

"They're so nauseating about it, you'd think they were newlyweds."

To Yvette, Cannon explained, "Gage was supposed to fight in Japan, too, but he took an elbow to the eye in practice and after too damn many stitches he was medically ineligible to participate."

"Wow," Yvette said with sympathy. "What a letdown that had to have been for him."

"Sounds like Harper is helping him get over it."

"That she is." Denver drew out a chair and straddled it, bracing his arms along the back, the water bottle held loosely in one hand, the towel flung over his shoulder.

"He'll fight again and he knows it. But I'm going to miss their verbal sparring."

"They set sparks off each other," Cannon told her. "Pretty damn amusing most of the time."

"So, uh…" Denver again drank from the bottle, finishing it off. "Cherry is in Japan with Merissa?"

Damn it. He didn't want Yvette to know his house was empty, making it the perfect place for him to stay. Too late now, though. But before he gave it all away, he shot Denver a look. "Why are you asking?"

"No reason."

"Try again."

Going oddly defensive, Denver grumbled, "Just curious, okay?"

Yvette looked back and forth between them.

"Cherry lives with my sister," Cannon reminded him quietly.

"Yeah, no shit. It's not a secret."

"No, but if you're sniffing around Cherry, then it becomes my business."

Denver pushed back his chair. "It was a simple question, Saint. No reason to get all pissy about it."

Cannon stood, too. Damn it, Denver wanted to hook up with Cherry. He scowled. "Have you hit on her yet?"

"Cherry isn't your sister, so back off."

"This brings us full circle, since Cherry is living with my sister."

"So what, man? It's not like I plan to stage a damned *orgy* with your sister as the audience."

Hearing the word *orgy* in the same sentence with his sister made Cannon rigid from his eyebrows down to his ankles. "You—"

Suddenly Armie was there, hauled in by Yvette.

Both Denver and Cannon stared at them.

"Yeah," Armie said, patting Yvette's hand on his arm. "I was fetched to referee so you two big dopes wouldn't maim each other in front of the lady."

Yvette looked uneasy but determined.

Forcing himself to relax, Cannon looked at Yvette. "You thought we'd come to blows?"

She tugged unobtrusively at the hand Armie continued to hold in the crook of his arm. "I wasn't sure."

Seeing Yvette's unease, Cannon transferred his gaze to Armie. "You can let her go now."

Grinning, Armie did just that, but then said, "You," pointing at Denver, "keep your romantic pursuits to yourself."

Cannon started to speak, but Armie pointed at him next.

"And you. Christ, man, your sister isn't a baby." Before Cannon could reply, he said, "And Denver isn't Chester the Molester."

"Thank you," Denver said in a ridiculously snooty voice.

"No, but I know him. I know all of you."

"So?" Denver asked.

"So I know how you think—and I know what you want."

Yvette's foot began to tap. "What? What does he want?"

Her tone didn't bode well for anyone. "Let's just say it isn't romance."

"So?"

"So women like to be romanced."

Rolling her eyes, Yvette said, "Some do. Some don't. Maybe Cherry would enjoy—" a red flush rose up her face, but she finished with "—whatever it is Denver has planned."

"Jesus," Denver said. "Does everyone think I'm planning perverted shit or what?"

"Nothing wrong with a little perversion," Armie cut in. "But the main thing here is that Denver is a trustworthy guy. Hell, Cannon, I'd think you'd like having someone like him hanging around the place, given two girls live there all alone."

"Women," Yvette interjected into the tense room.

All eyes went to her.

Her foot stopped tapping and she said again, "They're women, not girls."

"Thank you, Gloria Steinem." Armie skewered each of the guys with his scowl. "Is my work here done?"

"I wasn't going to maim him," Cannon told Yvette.

Denver snorted. "No, he definitely wasn't."

Their gazes clashed again.

"I'm not quite as radical as Gloria," Yvette said a little loud and way too fast, and her efforts to distract became perfectly clear to one and all. "But they are women, not girls."

Dropping his head, Armie laughed.

Yvette propped her hands on her hips. "Well, how would you like it if I called you guys boys?"

"Doesn't matter to me," Denver said.

Cannon shrugged. "Who cares?"

"See?" Armie told her. "No biggie."

"Yeah, well, everyone knows guys are dense." Irritation had her pivoting around and stalking out of the break room.

"I think she's getting away," Armie told Cannon, staring after her.

"I drove," Cannon explained. "She won't get far." And then to Denver, "Armie's right. I don't have any personal objections against you."

Denver threw up his hands. "Great. So I'm cleared for landing?"

"Not entirely, no."

Armie barked a laugh, but Denver groused.

"Go after Cherry if you want—but only if you're serious about her."

"How the hell would I know if I was serious when we haven't even had a private conversation yet?"

"You know what I mean." Cannon wanted no misunderstandings. "She's living with Rissy, so if you're just looking to get laid, look elsewhere. Cherry's off the list for one-night stands."

Denver gave a careless lift of one shoulder that didn't fool anyone. "I'm okay with that if she is."

"Like Yvette said," Armie chimed in, "Cherry might only want one night with him."

Now they were just baiting him. Cannon didn't give them the satisfaction of reacting to that. "Just keep things respectable around my sister."

Denver wanted to protest again, but Cannon turned on Armie. "My turn now."

Armie tried to make a strategic retreat. "Sorry, dude. Gotta get back to—"

Cannon stepped around in front of him, blocking him with his body.

"Fine," Armie groused, and then, "What?"

"You tell me."

"No idea what you're talking about."

"The hell you don't. Something's going on, and I have a feeling it might have something to do with my sister and Cherry living alone."

Armie stared him in the eye. "That was just random concern."

"You are so full of it."

Eyes narrowed, Armie leaned into him. "Why don't you change into some shorts and we can work it out on the mat?"

Both men were surprised when Yvette suddenly returned and somehow wiggled between them. Cannon's only complaint with her tactic was that she faced Armie.

"He can't, sorry," Yvette said, a little breathlessly given that Cannon touched all along her back.

"No?" Armie didn't back up at all, so Cannon had no doubt they did a little touching around front, too. "Why not?"

Yvette squared her shoulders. "He has to drive me to the pawnshop."

"Aw, now, doll, you're stealing my thunder."

Gently, hands flat to Armie's bare chest, Yvette backed him off. "Not now, okay?"

Cannon stared down at the top of her head. "Yvette?"

Without glancing back at him, she asked, "Hmm?"

"Are you *protecting* me?" And with exaggerated disdain, "From *Armie?*"

Cannon knew she couldn't miss the fat smiles Armie and Denver wore, but she had no clue she'd literally gained the attention of the entire gym until she turned and found everyone watching.

Her face went hot. "No," she whispered low. "Of course not."

"It's unnecessary, you know."

She went all prim and proper. "Well, of course two grown men wouldn't get into an actual altercation over something so silly."

"Yeah," Armie said. "So silly."

Rolling his eyes, Cannon put an arm around her shoulders and anchored her close as he spoke to Armie. "You going with us tonight?"

Armie nodded. "Hell, yeah."

"Good." He gave a smile that was only partly friendly. "We'll finish our conversation then." Taking Yvette with him, he headed out.

"Oh, God," she said, seeing everyone still staring at her. "It's like walking the gauntlet."

"Smile," Cannon advised. "It'll confuse them."

To his surprise, she did. She even waved.

And every guy in the place waved back.

THEY REACHED THE pawnshop only twenty minutes later. With every mile they passed, Yvette's uneasiness grew. A vicious crime had overshadowed all her wonderful memories of working with her grandpa there, and she hated that.

Was it possible to reclaim the good memories? To use them to snuff out the ugliness that had taken place at the hands of madmen?

"You okay?"

Cannon was such a rock that in comparison she felt like a complete wuss.

So she lied.

"Of course." Her smile might not have been as bright as she intended, but she got it out there. "Can I ask you something?"

"Anything." After he pulled up to the curb and put his truck in Park, he turned to face her.

His close scrutiny, ripe with sympathy, only made her feel more agitated. "You guys weren't really angry, were you?"

"Armie and me? No, course not." Smiling at her question, he got out and walked around the hood of the truck.

Yvette opened her door. "And you and Denver?"

Because his truck sat so high off the ground, he helped

her out—and then lingered, his hands on her waist, his body blocking her sight of the pawnshop, near enough to be a buffer from the darkness that tried to creep in.

"We disagree on occasion, but you don't have to worry about us actually coming to blows. Not in anger anyway. Hell, we fight for a living. We spar almost daily. Believe me, we know the difference between sport and life."

"It seemed so…angry."

"Just men being men."

"Or fighters being fighters?"

"Maybe. But keep in mind that professional athletes, in MMA especially, are extremely disciplined. We can blow off steam on occasion without letting things get out of control."

"I'll try to remember that."

His mouth twitched into a smile. "It was cute how you tried to take charge of things."

Things being big, muscular, capable men. Groaning, she covered her face. How silly she must have looked.

Cannon chuckled and hugged her into his chest. "You sure got everyone's attention."

She thought again of all those men staring at her, and swatted at Cannon. "Stop." But she, too, grinned.

Smile fading, Cannon tipped up her chin. "Want me to go in first?"

She shook her head. "No, it's fine." Somehow she'd make it so.

After a deep breath, she stepped around him and faced the squat building. Blinds kept her from seeing through the dark, dirty windows that used to be lit with neon signs and proud displays. Without her grandfather's weekly upkeep, dry weeds grew up in clumps along the foundation where the front walk had cracked away.

Leaves and garbage had gathered in the corners of the door, carried by the wind, sealed by the rain.

So many times she'd come here after school, and one of her first jobs was always to sweep the walk. Her grandpa had insisted on everything being well organized, including her. He'd given her boundaries and purpose.

And so much love.

She didn't realize how long she'd been standing there until Cannon's hands rested on her shoulders and he leaned down to press his mouth to her temple.

Not rushing her. Just offering understanding.

With the keys already in her hand, she began unlocking the door. She appreciated how close Cannon stayed at her back, following her in so that she didn't have to face the musky interior alone. Without air-conditioning, every breath that filled her lungs was thick and hot and stifling.

She flipped on the overhead lights. Everything looked so...stark.

The empty shelves and cabinets. The bare floors. The paint-chipped walls.

As Cannon pushed the door open wider to let in the humid breeze, Yvette walked to a metal shelf that used to hold coin collections. Next she turned to the glass cases that her grandpa had used as a reception area. It was barren now, but she could still picture how gold and silver watches and a variety of jewelry had glinted from the overhead fluorescent lights.

That was when it hit her, the warmth occupying places she hadn't known were still so empty.

Heart beating fast in exuberance, she turned a circle, taking in the dimensions of the big front room. She wanted to fill it again. She wanted to bring this building—and the good memories—back to life.

"Over there," she said, "is where they set up their video camera."

Rather than crowd her, Cannon propped a shoulder against the wall. "I know."

Of course he did. He'd learned every detail of what they'd done. But something inside her urged out the words, as if saying them again would somehow take them away. "The woman was drugged when they came in. We were just closing up. They pulled out their guns, drew down the blinds."

Though he held silent, his presence alone gave her the security she needed to relive the past.

That awful day had been only the start of her nightmare. After she and her grandpa had been doused in kerosene, they'd had no choice but to helplessly watch the rape of the doped-up woman, all while wondering what would happen to them next. She'd never seen her grandpa so helpless and so afraid. For her.

But when the three men had finished with their sick game, they'd packed up to go—after warning Yvette and Tipton about what would happen if they called the police.

They hadn't called, but Cannon had noticed things amiss. He was like that, always so vigilant when it came to his neighborhood and the small-business owners he cared so much about. He'd brought two friends, both detectives, to the shop and found Yvette and Tipton.

The memory was so vivid, Yvette wrapped her arms around herself.

Pushing off from the wall, Cannon approached. "I sometimes wonder if they'd have come after you at the house if I hadn't interfered."

Still studying the interior and layout, Yvette said, "You could never interfere, and yes, they would have come after me anyway. I knew it all along, though I tried to tell myself they wouldn't. I tried to believe it had ended. But I knew." Talking about it sent a shiver up her spine despite the suffocating heat. "I think they'd always planned to come back for me."

And they had. She'd been assaulted at the pawnshop, then again in her home. Both times, Cannon had done his utmost to protect her. "If it wasn't for you, I'd have been raped that day at home. I know that, too."

There wasn't a sufficient way to ever thank him, but her grandpa had tried. Looking up at Cannon now, Yvette asked, "Do you want to sell?"

"No."

Hope tightened her throat. "Are you sure? Because, Cannon, I owe you—"

"You don't." He cupped her face, his brows drawn in earnestness. "Don't talk like that."

But she knew the truth whether he'd accept it or not. "I'll sell in a heartbeat if that's what you want. We can call Whitaker's office and—"

"What do you want?"

Such a loaded question. She could tell him that she wanted to be whole again, that she wanted to *feel*, to experience that special, hot culmination of sexual involvement.

That she wanted to be a woman again.

But that would be laying too much on him. And, as other men had done, he'd take it as a challenge to "fix" her. She couldn't bear to go down that road again.

Not with Cannon.

His thumbs brushed along her jaw. "Tell me the truth, Yvette."

She loved it when he touched her like this, when she felt his strength mixed with gentleness. It was a hot, macho, potent combination, and no one ever had possessed the same ability to make her feel so many things.

Wrapping her hands over his wrists, she looked up at him. "I want to give you everything you're supposed to have."

His gaze dropped to her mouth. "What if I'm supposed to have you?"

Her breath caught. "Cannon," she chided.

Pleasure showed in his blue eyes. "Yvette."

She cleared her throat, determined to do the right thing. "My grandfather wanted me to repay you."

"Your grandfather wanted you to be happy," he said when she prepared to argue. "You know it as well as I do, so don't go there. Instead be honest with me. Tell me what would make you happy."

She couldn't, not about everything.

"Yvette." He used his thumbs to turn up her face. "If every option was open to you, what would you most want to do? Right here, right now." He kept her caught in his gaze. "Tell me the truth."

Possibilities teased her and she smiled uncertainly. "I...I'd want to reopen the shop."

His smile eased into place, too. "Yeah? Would it still be a pawnshop?"

"Or an upscale resale shop." Enthusiasm expanded. "Grandpa taught me a lot, and I used what I learned for my online business, but also to buy things I knew I could sell for a profit. I have a lot of stock, stuff that I could set up in here. And it's the right time of year for me to buy more from yard sales."

Cannon pressed a firm, quick kiss to her mouth. "I like it."

Carried away with the idea, and that tantalizing kiss, she breathed faster. "In no time I could have this place looking as good as it used to. I could maybe even get Vanity to come out for a visit to help get everything set up."

"Count on me to pitch in. And some of the other guys, too."

Whoa. Grinning like an excited kid on Christmas morning, she shook her head. "I can't impose on them. Or you." She spun away, seeing everything with new eyes. The reality of what had happened here remained, but the promise of what she could do nudged the ugly memories into the corner of her mind. "I'll enjoy digging in and rearranging things."

"You know Tipton put stuff in storage, too. You might already have a lot."

"That's right!" She went back to the glass case, thinking of how it'd look after she gave it a good washing. The floor looked a little rough, but scrubbing, waxing and adding some colorful rugs might fix that.

"Do you know everything that'll have to be done?"

"Things might be a little different here than they were in California, but I should be able to get everything squared away within a month or two."

"So we're keeping the shop."

We. That one word seemed to carry so much meaning. Yvette tried to calm the sudden stampeding of her heart. Keeping her back to Cannon, she said with forced lightness, "I promise to buy you out as soon as I can."

"Or we could stay partners."

How had he gotten so close without making a sound? She turned and he was right there, toe to toe with her.

"Not that I'd tell you how to do things. But I wouldn't mind taking part when I can."

"That's what you want?" She could handle it, maybe run the place but give him a percentage of profits—

"I thought you'd have it figured out by now." His mouth settled on hers again, longer this time, deeper and hotter until clear thought became impossible.

Reluctantly he ended the kiss, but kept her face turned up to his. "I like the shop, and the house is nice. But most of all I want you." As if that was no big deal, he smiled. "I'm going to keep telling you until you believe it."

And until she wanted him back?

Yvette shook her head. They both knew that had happened more than three long years ago.

CHAPTER EIGHT

TOMORROW, CANNON DECIDED, he would call Mindi to tell her they were keeping the pawnshop. Tonight he wanted to make sure things were settled with Yvette.

After he'd declared himself again at the pawnshop she'd gone so quiet that it worried him even though he tried not to let it.

He'd told her several times now, always with the same result. She did want him. He was sure of it. Eventually he'd win her over.

After picking up dinner, they'd ridden home in relative silence. Yvette used her phone to look up necessary numbers and locations to get things rolling on the shop. She made two calls and added notes to the calendar on her phone.

As he listened to her putting down roots, digging in with the intent of sticking around, a sense of peace settled over him. He wanted her to move back home for good, he realized.

If he'd had any doubts about her being happy here, listening to her now put them to rest.

Her grandfather was right. This was where she belonged.

Instead of eating the loaded burgers—a treat for him—at the table, they'd both sat on the couch and watched TV.

Yvette surprised him with her appetite. For such a

small woman, he'd expected her to pick at a salad, not wolf down a burger, fries and chocolate malt.

Looking at her now, curled up at the other end of the couch, her feet tucked up beside her, a throw pillow in her lap, he wanted her more than ever.

She nibbled on her last fry and he wanted her.

She sucked at the straw in her drink and his muscles tightened.

But he could bide his time and, as Armie suggested, maybe put some effort into seducing her. That thought made him smile.

She glanced his way. "What?"

Cannon shook his head. "Just thinking."

About seduction.

It had become a lost art. Even before making it in the SBC, women hadn't been a hardship for him. Now, more often than not, women came easily to him.

But not Yvette.

She frowned at him askance, and with reluctance took her attention back to the TV.

"When do you want to check out the stock Tipton left behind?"

She took another long drink of her malt, finishing it off, then stood to gather up their empty wrappers. "I wouldn't mind checking it out right away, just so I know what I have to work with. Maybe sometime tomorrow." On her way into the kitchen she added, "I'll call Vanity soon, too."

Jumping right in. He liked her enthusiasm, especially since the more enmeshed she got, the better the odds of her staying on for good.

Cannon turned off the television and strode into the kitchen behind her. "I'll go with you."

She paused in the middle of putting the trash in the bin beneath the sink. "Okay."

A message beeped on her phone. Without looking at him, she went back to where she'd left it on the end table, glanced at the message and put down the phone without replying.

Her boyfriend again? Ex-boyfriend, he reminded himself.

"Everything okay?"

Looking a little guilty, she gave a bright but false smile. "Sure."

When she started around him for the kitchen again, Cannon stopped her. Seduction, he reminded himself, and he leaned closer, spoke lower. "So what do you have planned tonight?"

"Tonight?"

He touched her hair, smoothing it, then let his fingertips trail over her shoulder and down her arm. "Remember, I'm heading out soon to meet the guys."

Second ticked by, then she shook herself. "Catching up with old friends?"

That, and more. But he only nodded. "I'll be gone awhile." He put both hands on her waist and pulled her closer. "You plan to just stay in?" Hopefully she'd think about him, miss him a little.

She waffled. "I'm not sure yet."

Not the answer he'd been expecting. Where did she think to go? Not back to Rowdy's bar. Did she have other friends in town?

Or was she nervous about being home alone? Maybe he should cancel his plans and stick around. "If you'd rather—"

"I'd rather not be a bother. Go. Have fun." Phone in hand, she darted around him as if seeking escape.

Once more, he trailed her into the kitchen. Luckily the house wasn't large since Yvette seemed determined to make him chase her.

She'd set her phone on the table as she removed the garbage bag from the can. Damned if another message didn't come in.

Yvette ignored it, so he tried to, as well. "You have some friends you're going to reconnect with?"

"Not really. After I moved away, I didn't stay in touch with anyone here." She tied the bag shut and shook out another to replace it.

Was she deliberately elusive? "Then where would you go tonight?"

"I don't know." Dusting off her hands, she steered clear of his gaze. "I could maybe take in a movie or something."

He should definitely cancel tonight. He'd never hear the end of it from the guys, but still, the idea of her sitting in a movie theater alone—

Her phone rang.

They stared at each other until it stopped.

Cannon cocked a brow.

Hefting the bag, she forged out of the kitchen.

He stopped her with a hand on her arm. "I'll run it out to the garage."

She didn't let go. In a tone far too surly, she growled, "I'm more than capable of taking out the trash."

Withdrawing his hands, Cannon held them up in supplication. "My apologies."

Blowing out a frustrated breath, she looked away. After three beats of silence, she regained her calm demeanor. "It's not a big deal, that's all I'm saying."

"Fine. Then let me do it."

Indecision had her scowling again before she thrust the bag at him. "Fine. Knock yourself out."

"Phrasing, honey. Never tell a fighter to get knocked out." He stole a quick kiss off her mulish mouth, then whistled on his way to the garage. The things that got her prickly amused him, and the way she reacted each and every time to his kiss made him want to rush things despite his good intentions.

Rush them more than he already was, because seriously, he'd come on like a steamroller and he knew it. He should probably apologize—and explain that it was likely to happen again.

The can in the garage was already filled with the empty packages from her additional locks, reminding him of how difficult this would all be for her. He stomped the trash down in the can, dropped in the bag, replaced the lid and headed back in.

He found Yvette leaning against the counter, her phone in hand as she read a message.

"Who keeps calling?"

She actually jumped, then frowned in accusation. "When you said you'd run it out, I didn't know you meant literally."

Taking in every nuance of her expression, Cannon saw not only the fractious temper but the worry, too. "I didn't run. You're just distracted." He moved closer. "I'd really like to know what's wrong."

Her phone beeped again.

Yvette bit her lip. "He says he's coming to visit."

Uneasiness prickled beneath Cannon's skin. "He who?"

"Heath."

Heath, her ex. "When?"

"I don't know. It might just be a threat." She sighed, then made a decision. "He's a little obsessive."

"About you?"

"About everything. It's part of his personality. He wants to keep going over stuff and I don't, so I've been ignoring him."

"His phone calls?"

"And his texts and email and Facebook messages. That's probably why he says he's coming here. To get me to talk to him. I doubt he means it. He's just hoping I'll cave and reply."

"He makes you nervous?"

She shook her head hard. "I'm not afraid of him."

"Okay." She was so defensive about not being fearful anymore. "Take it easy."

"I just…" She set the phone aside and rubbed her temples. "I don't want to rehash the past. We've already done that several times. It's over whether he accepts it or not."

"Hey." Cannon took her hands away, replacing them with his own. "I'm not going to let anyone hurt you."

She laughed, leaned in against him and gave him a tight hug.

Folding his arms around her, Cannon tried not to get turned on. She wanted affection, not an erection.

It was nice, having her initiate contact this time. Hopefully, like him, she'd begun to feel comfortable, as if the three years apart had never happened.

He'd feel better about things if he knew exactly what was going on between her and her ex. "Why'd you split from him?"

She shifted against him, but didn't move away. "I broke things off with Heath for the same reason I can't start anything with you."

"We're not starting anything," he gently explained. "We're picking up where we left off."

On a soft groan, she put her forehead to his chest and stared down at…well, maybe his fly, but more likely her own feet.

In a barely there whisper, she said, "That'd be ground zero, then, because there was never anything between us."

No way could he let her slide on that; there'd been almost too much for him to comprehend until he'd seen her again and it had all came rushing back. "I know you've been through a lot, but—"

"Cannon," she whispered, interrupting him. "Will you please do something for me?"

In such a short time, he was beginning to think he'd do anything for her. "Sure."

When she leaned back and looked up at him, she wore a sincere smile. "Promise?"

God, what this one woman did to him. "Yeah."

"Please, go see your friends. Go and have fun. And don't worry about me. Just…just pretend I'm any other woman. Not the woman who was threatened and hurt. Not the girl who cried and let herself be a victim." He started to speak and she put a finger to his mouth.

And even that turned him on.

"Don't associate every thought of me with the past, okay? Can you do that for me?"

Why didn't she ask for something easy—like the moon?

Holding her waist, he lifted her up to sit on the counter. She grabbed for his shoulders to steady herself, and he stepped between her legs, then slid his hands down to her slim hips and snugged her up close, groin to groin, breasts to chest. "I'll go. And I'll try not to worry. But, honey, no way can I think of you as any other woman. Like it or not, you're special to me."

She got that "aww" look in her eyes again.

Seduction, he had to keep reminding himself. Maybe with Yvette it came more naturally than he'd realized, because she sure as hell looked seduced.

"Will you promise me something, too?"

"All right."

"Promise you'll tell me if Heath becomes a problem."

"I can handle him."

Acknowledging that with a nod, he said, "Promise me anyway."

"All right."

"I'll keep my phone on me. Call me if anything spooks you."

She touched his throat, his collarbone. "How about I'll call you if I actually think there's a threat? After I call the police. Will that work?"

Meaning she often got spooked and wasn't confident about her instincts anymore. "I could be late. Midnight, maybe one."

She faked a yawn. "I'll long be in bed by then."

Cannon could tell she was up to something, he just didn't know what.

"You could let me know when you get in, though. Just so I don't hear things and think—"

He took her mouth, far from brief, far from as much as he wanted. "I'll let you know."

Slightly dazed, she stared at his mouth, then shook herself. "You should probably quit doing that."

He gave her the truth. "I don't know if I can."

Her smile flickered into place, and she surprised him by saying softy, "I shouldn't be, but I'm sort of glad."

His heart leaped. To hell with leaving. If she was willing—

Pressing against his chest, she said, "Now go."

Damn. Cannon didn't tell her that she was shoving him out the door an hour earlier than necessary. She claimed there couldn't be anything between them, but she'd gone all soft and willing from a simple kiss. He wanted time to think, and she looked as if she wanted some privacy of her own.

He set her back on her feet and went down the hall to change. When he came back out, she was at the kitchen table with papers spread out.

"Your grandfather's stuff?"

She nodded. "I didn't find what I needed with what the lawyer gave us, but I remembered that Grandpa always kept the paperwork in the hutch."

Over her shoulder, Cannon saw the wrinkled yellow receipts and a few torn pages.

"It's not as orderly as usual, but I can sort it out. He has three different storage units. It could take some time to go through everything and get it inventoried."

"Sounds like an outing." He could go with her, stop to pick up the things he needed for the house security, maybe a few more groceries, too. It'd be a full day, especially if he got everything installed.

"I thought of something." Smiling, she turned, saw him in his jeans, a black T-shirt in his hand, and she stalled.

Enjoying the way her face went rosy and she breathed deeper, Cannon took his time pulling on the shirt.

When he finished, her chin went up. "I like to jog early."

"Yeah, me, too."

She waved a hand at his body. "But you're coming off a long trip and you're going to be out late, so—"

"No worries. I can handle it."

She leveled a frown of concern on him. "You're still bruised and recovering from that last fight and—"

No way did he want her to list his injuries, to mention how he'd screwed up, or how he'd damn near lost. "It's no big deal."

"But if I'm up before you tomorrow I don't want to wake you."

"What time do you usually take off?"

She pursed her mouth. "Six?"

"You don't know?" Or was she making up a time in hopes of putting him off?

"Six."

"Good. Six it is. I'm usually up by five-thirty anyway." True, he'd looked forward to sleeping in during his visit, but for Yvette, he could handle a little less sleep. "Anything else?"

"Well…" She blew out a breath. "There is one other thing."

"Okay."

Another breath, and she blurted, "I do like it."

Now, why was she blushing? "It?"

"That…that I'm special to you." She rushed on. "I know it's for horrible reasons, that what happened has kind of tied us together, but…I'm still glad to have you as a friend."

Friend, hell. He'd disabuse her of that notion very soon. But not right now, when he was on his way out. "Me, too." As naturally as he could manage, he went to her and kissed her goodbye. "Don't leave without me in the morning."

"If you're sure…"

"I'm positive." More so every minute that he spent with her.

And if he didn't go now, he wouldn't go at all, so he turned on his heel and walked out.

THE MINUTES, THE HOURS, dragged by at a snail's pace until Yvette couldn't bear her own company anymore. She'd tried TV. Tried stuffing her face with popcorn, and then later chocolate. But being alone in the big empty house had her hearing things that weren't there. She needed to take off for a while, to *do* something to keep her brain occupied.

She wasn't dumb enough to jog alone this time of night, and as she'd told Cannon, she didn't have any friends around. The idea of sitting at the movies by herself didn't appeal to her at all, so instead she decided to rent a DVD. She pushed her feet into sandals and shrugged on a button-up shirt over her T-shirt. Within a single minute she was out the door, locking up securely behind herself.

It was only sensible, she told herself, for a woman alone to be skittish while out and about after dark, never mind that tall streetlights kept the area well lit. After driving toward the small commercial area, she searched for the rental shop she remembered, but it had been replaced with a secondhand clothing store. She drove on, past Rowdy's bar until, farther down the road, she found a video store.

She parked at the curb, got out and locked her car door, then kept her keys tight in her hand. She knew exactly where to find the mace in her purse, and made a point of scanning her surroundings as she crossed the street and went into the slightly run-down shop.

Uneasiness throbbed beneath her skin, but she told

herself to ignore it. If she ever wanted to get over the past, she had to push herself past ridiculous fears.

To give herself a moment to figure out the layout, she studied the interior. There seemed to be only men inside, five of them, not counting the clerk. Dusty racks held dated DVDs sectioned off by genre in the front of the shop. Lights surrounded a back door that led into another room, but Yvette made a beeline for the action flicks to her left.

Unfortunately, two men loitered there, talking to each other. It wasn't until she got nearer to them that she wondered if they were making a drug deal, given the close, quiet conversation combined with their shifting gazes.

Looking for something to catch her interest, Yvette pretended to ignore them as she perused the shelves. They got quiet, watching her in such a calculated way that she could actually feel their smarmy attention moving over her. Growing nervousness made her hands clammy.

Anxious to be on her way, she snatched up an older Tom Cruise movie and headed to the register. The clerk was younger, his shaved head tattooed, but it was the way he smiled at her that made her want to mace him.

Get it together, she told herself. *You're in a public place. The front door is open. People are on the street—*

"Anything else?" he asked with sneering suggestion.

She jumped at the sound of his deep voice. "No, thank you." As quickly as possible she finished up. It wasn't until he handed her the movie that she saw the stack of returned DVDs behind him.

Sex videos.

Porn.

She jerked around to stare at that damned lit door in the back of the room.

How could she have been so stupid?

Seeing her realization, the two men leered at her.

She snapped around to leave, and ran face-first into a tall, hard body. The guy caught her arm to steady her. "Hey now. Easy."

She looked up into deep brown eyes and wanted to melt. "Armie."

The shock on his face might have amused her at any other time. "Yvette?" Still holding her arm, he glared around the room, mean mugging all the other customers.

Everyone turned away.

Voice lowered, he asked, "What the hell are you doing in here?"

She held up Tom Cruise—and saw the tremor in her hand.

His mouth flattened with disapproval. "You shouldn't be in here."

"I didn't realize…"

He looked over his own shoulder, then back at her. "Cannon is going to have a cow."

She almost choked on her laugh. Seriously, Cannon was the very least of her concerns. Freeing herself from Armie's hold, feeling plenty brave now with his presence, Yvette relaxed her knotted muscles. "So what are *you* doing here?"

"Buying porn."

Now she did choke. "No, I meant…" She rolled her eyes. Armie was one of those sexually outrageous guys that no woman could take seriously, but that every woman probably felt safe with. "I thought you were with Cannon tonight."

"Yeah, I am. He stopped to visit with some, ah…" He rubbed the back of his head, making his already spiky blond hair messier. "Some local people, so I came on ahead to do my business." Clearly trying to distract her, he gave a shameful grin. "I'm entertaining a lady tomorrow who goes wild with a few visuals."

Yvette crossed her arms and tapped her foot, and damned if Armie didn't squirm. "So," she said, squinting. "Cannon is visiting some women?"

"Not the way you're saying it, no. I mean, he *could* visit them that way because they're all kinds of willing, you know. But he's been dodging them for years."

Sort of the way he'd dodged her years ago? "Who are they?"

Now that he'd partially fessed up, he jumped in with both feet. "Topless dancers. Used to work at Rowdy's bar before he bought it. Rowdy got rid of the pole, and all but one of the gals moved on to another place so they could keep the tips they made from working their wares."

Wow. Yvette had no words. Just...wow. Why was Cannon visiting with them if he wasn't interested? She seriously doubted they discussed the weather.

Finally, when Armie said, "There are five of them," she found her tongue.

Five? "Wonderful. I'm sure they appreciate his attention." She made a move around Armie and he, the jerk, fell into step with her.

"Ready to go, huh? No more shopping to do? Got everything you...need?"

Yvette didn't answer, but that only encouraged him.

"You check out the back room? No? It's a sight. They have toys hanging from the ceiling."

Sheer surprise tripped her up and she stopped to stare up at him. "Toys?"

"Yeah, you know. Different-size vibrators, some clamps, a variety of dil—"

"No!" She started walking again, a little faster this time. "Just hush."

Grinning, he said, "Okay. But I'll walk you out."

Glad for the company after getting shaken, she still said, "Aren't you forgetting your porn?"

"It's not going anywhere."

Yvette could hear the snicker in his every word. She sighed.

"They have plenty to choose from."

"I wouldn't know. I went only as far as the action section."

"Oh, they have action. Naked action. Threesome action. Discipline-and-bondage action. Backdoor action. Doctor-and-nurse action. Every kind of action you could think of."

He couldn't know about her past. About the animals that had forced her to watch as they'd videotaped a drugged woman. The sick cretins who had threatened her—

"It's not all like that, you know."

Okay, given the gentleness of his tone, maybe he did know. She must've been obvious without meaning to be. Yvette wasn't sure what to say so she looked away.

He dipped his head into her line of vision. "Sometimes," he continued, now all teasing and silly, his eyebrows bopping, "it's just dirty fun."

"Armie."

Satisfied that he had her attention again, he straightened. "Yeah, doll?"

"This is my car."

His grin was so big that he almost made her grin, too. "Can't make you blush, huh?"

Cannon made her blush all the time. She gave another sigh. "Not over something so silly."

"So maybe I need to try harder."

She unlocked her car door. "And why would you want to do that?"

Going super serious, he stared down at her and spoke in a quiet, sincere voice. "Because Cannon cares about you, and he's like a brother to me, so that means I care, too."

Now she blushed.

And Armie loved it. "There you go," he said softly. "Cannon will be along any second now if you want to wait."

"No." The very last thing she wanted to do was butt in on his night out with his friends. She touched Armie's arm. "You don't have to mention to him that I—"

"Was shopping for a movie in the legendary local porn shop? Yeah," he said on a laugh, "I most definitely do. Fact, I can't wait."

She glared, but that only amused Armie more. "Butt-head."

The insult sent his brows high. "Don't know why I'm surprised at the name-calling," he muttered as he watched her get into her car. "I mean, after catching you in the dirty-video store, nothing should be a shock, right?"

"Goodbye, Armie."

He grinned. "'Bye, Yvette."

The way he said that, all sugary and teasing and full of wickedness, well, Yvette could see why the naughty ladies loved him.

But she'd be willing to bet the not-so-naughty ladies were drawn, as well. Just not her.

She'd already fallen for Cannon.

And given what Cannon had said earlier, and what Armie had just confirmed, she needed to level with him.

It was bad enough that she had to be miserable.

No reason to make Cannon that way, too.

CHAPTER NINE

AFTER WHAT ARMIE told him, Cannon cut his evening short. It was still late, but not as late as he'd figured on. He'd lasted only an hour more and then couldn't take it.

The guys laughed at him when he separated from them, but he didn't mind. With their warped senses of humor, they found a lot of twisted shit hilarious. They continued on through the neighborhood and he cut back across a few empty lots to where he'd parked his truck.

The drive home took him past the pawnshop, and that was when he saw the guy go running away from the front door. He'd have parked and given chase, but the flare of a fire stopped him.

Keeping an eye out for an ambush, he approached and saw the fire was a bucket of trash set up close to the front door. Probably just vandalism, but, damn, what lousy timing since Yvette had just decided to reopen it. He snuffed it before any damage was done, and then, knowing Rowdy would still be working at the bar, he called him.

Ella answered, meaning Avery must've been on a break. When she laid the phone down to get Rowdy, Cannon could hear the noise of the boisterous crowd in the background. A packed room. Cannon hated to bother him.

Half a minute later, Rowdy answered with an intuitive, "What's wrong?"

"Maybe nothing." Pacing alongside his truck, keeping an eye on some youths across the street, he told Rowdy what had happened. "I just convinced Yvette to reopen the place, but with a damn fire… I don't know. I don't want her spooked."

"First off, I'll give Logan a call and let him know, just so he can have some officers keep an eye out. You might want to put some cameras up, maybe an alarm or two."

"Yeah. I was going to do it to the house anyway, so might as well include the shop." Which meant Yvette would definitely know about the fire. "Hell."

"Second thing," Rowdy said, easily interpreting his curse, "she's not made of china."

"No, she's not," Cannon agreed. "It's actually surprised me, how strong she is. But the threat of a fire has to hit her differently."

"You were there, too, threatened same as Yvette, and you aren't spooked by a bucket of old rags. Don't assume she would be either. Tell her about it first thing," Rowdy advised. "Let her decide whether it's worth it to battle some vandalism or if she'd rather leave the headaches behind."

It was whether or not she'd leave *him* behind that Cannon was worried about. He wanted a chance to get to know her again, in every way imaginable.

He wanted a chance to fulfill that particular fantasy.

"One more thing," Rowdy said.

"Yeah?"

"If she's not with you, does that mean she's alone? Because much as I assume it was just vandalism, I can't discount the past."

"Same here," Cannon admitted, and that was the crux of his concern. "In all the time that she's been gone, no one has bothered the shop. I know because I check on it every so often when I'm in town."

"Ditto," Rowdy said.

It didn't surprise Cannon that Rowdy had kept an eye out. His streak of protectiveness ran bone deep. "I'm heading there now."

"If I don't hear from you, I'll assume everything is fine."

"Yeah. And, Rowdy? Thanks." Cannon put the phone away as he jogged around the hood of the truck and got in. He was less than ten minutes from the house, but the drive felt like an hour.

When he pulled into the driveway, everything looked secure, with enough light to guide a ship. Some of the apprehension let up, but he'd feel better once he saw Yvette.

Assuming she'd be in bed, he quietly opened the door and stepped in without a sound.

"Hey."

His gaze zeroed in on her. Blue light from the muted television washed over her where she sat curled on the couch in a white camisole and striped cotton pajama pants, her hair braided over one shoulder.

"Hey." He closed and locked the door. "I thought you were going to be in bed."

One bare shoulder lifted. "If you're not too tired, I thought maybe we could..." The words fell off and she looked away.

His cock twitched in anticipation of what she'd say. "I'm not at all tired." In fact, he was suddenly so wired he knew he wouldn't be able to sleep.

Breath left her in a melancholy sigh. "This is... awkward for me."

Making sure not to charge her, Cannon joined her on the couch. "It's just me. No reason to feel awkward."

As he sat beside her the cushion dipped, rolling her hip nearer to him.

Trying for subtlety, he leaned closer to fill himself with her scent, a stirring combo of shampoo, lotion and Yvette—warm and sweet and so fucking sexy.

Her pajama pants were striped in candy colors, long and loose, almost covering her small feet where she had them tucked up next to her. But her camisole… Lord.

The white stretchy material hugged her breasts and showed her nipples as small shadows. Not touching her was impossible, but he steered his hands to her shoulders. "You're okay?"

She nodded. "I mean, I am. But I'm not."

He had no clue what she was saying, but he had to kiss her. Right now. He tried to resist, and lost. Leaning in, he touched his mouth to hers, barely there, relishing the moment—

Yvette slid her arms tight around his neck and pulled him closer.

An irresistible invitation.

Turning his head, he nudged her lips open, took her mouth with his tongue, and, God, she tasted good. He pressed her back into the couch, one hand curved around her nape, the other sliding down to the curve of her waist. The insubstantial cover of that soft camisole made it easy for him to get his hand underneath and onto softer skin.

He stroked upward, and Yvette pulled back. "Wow, I'm sorry." Trembling, she sank into the corner of the couch…away from him. Eyes wide, her fingers touched her mouth.

"Yvette?"

She shook her head. "I shouldn't have done that."

Cannon reined himself in. Discomfort took precedence over modesty, so, ignoring her stare, he adjusted himself in his jeans. With that done, he sat back, one arm along the top of the couch almost touching her. "Okay. Let's talk."

"That's what I wanted to do. I mean, that's why I waited up."

So not for sex. Damn. "Armie told me what happened."

"What? Oh, no." Dismissing his assumption, she shook her head. "He told me he would. That's not what I want to talk about."

"It didn't upset you?"

"I felt like an idiot for not realizing what kind of video store it was, and sure, once I did realize it made me uncomfortable. There were male customers in there and they stared at me. But I was about to leave when Armie showed up."

Since he still sported wood, he wasn't in the mood to tease her as Armie had done. "You watched your movie?"

Frowning, she said, "It's not porn."

He smiled. "I know."

"Oh." She nodded. "I watched most of it. I heard you coming in, though, and turned off the sound." Saying that, she picked up the remote, paused the movie and then turned off the set. "There's something else I want to talk about."

The sudden buzzing of his phone sounded obscenely loud. "Damn. Sorry." Retrieving it from his pocket, he checked the caller ID. "It's Mindi." Before she could ask, he said, "The assistant who works with Whitaker."

"I remember." Twisting to see the clock on the wall, Yvette made note of the time and raised a brow.

Assuming her only reason for calling this late would be an invite, Cannon put a hand on Yvette's thigh to keep her close and answered the call.

"I was just about to hang up," she said. "Am I calling too late?"

"It's okay. I meant to get hold of you anyway."

"Do tell."

Determined to keep it brief, he said, "We're keeping both properties."

"Both?"

"The house and the pawnshop. Appreciate that you were willing to help us, but tell your buyer we're not interested."

"But…" Mindi floundered before annoyance took over. "How is that even possible? Everything in the pawnshop is gone."

"Yvette has inventory from her old job." Cannon met Yvette's killing glare with a wink. "And apparently Tipton has stuff he'd put away, too."

Mindi went silent, then muttered, "I didn't realize."

"Yeah, apparently he filled several storage units." When she said nothing to that, Cannon added, "Thanks again," and started to hang up.

"Wait." He felt her hesitation before she finally said, "If you're going to go through everything…" She paused for effect. "I'd be happy to lend you a hand."

Yeah, he'd just bet she would. Her hand, her mouth… "No, it's not a problem, but thanks."

"Really, Cannon, if you need anything, anything at all, let me know."

Cannon rubbed his thumb in small circles over Yvette's thigh. "Will do. Take care, Mindi." He put the phone on the coffee table. "She wanted to offer up her assistance."

Yvette snorted. "Yeah, right. She wanted to offer up herself, you mean."

"You're a fantasy for me. You know you always have been."

Twice Cannon started to speak, but with her looking at him so earnestly, he had no idea what to say. He settled on, "So far I don't see the problem."

He'd happily be her fantasy, because she was his.

"It's true," she said as if he hadn't spoken, "that being away for three years didn't change that. How I feel is the same, but now I'm different."

"Older, more mature." No longer off-limits.

"True, but also, I can't…"

He waited, saw her struggling with herself, and prompted her. "You can't what?"

She looked so damned grave, it bugged him.

"Here." He scooped her up and onto his lap, then held her there when she automatically started to scramble off. "You're not comfortable?"

"I am."

"I scare you?"

"I already told you that you didn't."

"Then let me hear what it is you can't do."

She went still, but remained stiff.

Cannon kept his arms loosely looped around her when what he really wanted to do was bring her close, as close as she could get. "It bothers you for me to hold you?"

"It does, but not for the reason you think."

Smoothing his hand over her hair and then down her braid, he asked, "How does it bother you?"

"It makes me want you even more."

He'd never had a problem with patience before. But now, with Yvette, figuring her out wore on him. He wanted to race to the finish line so they could move on to more physical things.

Like sex.

Opening his hand on the small of her back, he rubbed, soothing her. "But you can't...why?"

Relenting, she got as close as he wanted her, curling into him, her head tucked under his chin against his chest. In a tormented whisper, she explained, "I can't... finish."

With no idea what that meant, Cannon kept quiet.

She toyed with the cotton of his T-shirt, her nervous fingers plucking at the material and then smoothing it. "Something in me is broken. When I have sex, I mean."

It felt like a fist landed in his gut. Cannon forgot to breathe as he took apart what she said. In his mind he ran through one absurd scenario after another and still didn't quite get it.

He tried to tip up her face but she huddled in close, hiding, a little desperate.

To reassure her, he kissed the top of her head and tamped down a surge of jealousy. "I want to understand, okay? So I'm going to ask some questions. That all right?"

She nodded.

"Don't be embarrassed with me, okay?"

Her laugh was raw, devoid of humor. "Of course I'm embarrassed. It's an embarrassing problem."

He hugged her tighter, his arms around her slender body. He couldn't think of a delicate way to put it, so he just asked. "You're saying you can't come?"

He heard the catch of her breath, felt the way she lowered her face more. "Yes, that's what I saying."

"During sex?"

A nod.

So she'd been with some selfish bozo? So what? That wasn't him. Hell, he loved pushing ladies over the edge, feeling them clench, hearing the sounds they made, how they breathed and cried out and the way they moved.

With Yvette, yeah, he could get hard again just thinking about something that hot.

And talk about hot... He lowered his mouth to her temple. "What about by yourself?"

A long, tense pause and then... "No."

Damn. Visualizing her trying—

Her small fist caught him in his bruised ribs. "Stop it, Cannon."

Hiding his wince, he said, "Can't." Though she resisted, he framed her face, brought it up and kissed her again, a killer kiss that left them both breathless. And, damn it, she didn't respond like a woman with issues. She gave back, took and enjoyed. Maybe not as much as he did, but given how much he wanted her, that'd be a stretch for anyone.

When he let up, he kept her there, looking at him. "You could get off before?"

Heat rushed into her face, making her green eyes more vivid. "Before I left here? Yes."

Which meant before she was so badly abused by the scum who'd assaulted her, showing her things no young lady should ever have to see. "But since then?"

She bit her lip and shook her head.

Sorting things out in his head, he reminded her, "You like kissing me."

Gently, her fingers touched his mouth. "Kissing isn't a problem for me. Neither is touching. I enjoy it." Her gaze lifted to his. "Far more so with you."

Cannon was acutely aware of her firm bottom on his lap, how her breasts pressed against that thin camisole, her scent and her warmth. It was the oddest thing to be having this conversation. He had to think that once they got together, it'd all be fine. He'd obliterate her concerns with red-hot pleasure.

But he wanted her to know that he took her worries seriously, that it wasn't only sex he wanted, so he held back and listened.

"That's what I wanted to explain to you." Her fingertips went from his lips to his jaw, rasping over his beard shadow. "When I can't...can't react the way I should, I don't want you to think that reflects on you."

She couldn't be serious. "So if I get mine and you don't get yours, it wouldn't be my fault?" By sheer force of will, he kept the disbelief from his expression. "That's what you're saying?"

"I'm saying I can't seem to do...that, no matter what. So you wouldn't be to blame. There's just something broken in me."

"Yvette—"

"You need to understand up front, so you won't be disappointed."

So she'd made up her mind that they would be together? Knowing she'd climax, because he'd ensure it, he said, "You could never disappoint me."

"So far I've disappointed every guy I've ever been with."

Yeah, not something he wanted to think about. "You already told me I'm different."

Her smile was sad and fleeting. "And because of that, I'd still enjoy being close to you, being...with you. So if you want—" she stared him in the eyes "—I'm willing."

Willing? But not anxious. She hoped to be a sacrifice. Screw that.

"What I don't want," she continued, "is for you to think if you try hard enough, if you're patient enough, it'll make a difference. I'm sorry, but I can't go through that again. It makes it even more frustrating."

The words sank in. *I can't go through that again.* "Spell that one out for me."

With two fingers she anxiously toyed with a loose lock of hair that had escaped her braid. "I dated guys who were cocky enough to think they only had to finesse things a little more and I'd miraculously launch into a screaming climax."

He stiffened. "How many guys are we talking about?"

Defensively, she said, "I was trying to find one that'd work!"

He laughed, but he sure as hell wasn't amused.

Insulted, Yvette started to push off his lap.

Immediately he regretted his reaction. "I'm sorry." He held on, and when she continued to shove at him, he said again, "I'm sorry! Swear."

An inch from his face, she snarled, "It is *not* funny."

"No, it's not." He ran his hands up and down her arms in apology. "That was more a sound of jealousy than humor anyway."

"Jealousy? Get real." Still irked, she poked at his chest. "You're the one who was with five women earlier."

His brow went up. "Not *with* them. Don't say it like that. I was just talking to them. Don't confuse me with Armie."

At that she did a double take. In an appalled whisper, she asked, "Five? Seriously? I mean, I know he's out there, but—"

"I was exaggerating."

Somewhat disappointed, she said, "Oh."

"Back on track now, okay?" He eased her against him, arranged her the way he wanted with her snuggled close.

And she went along with it, her head in the curve of his shoulder, her long legs draped over the side of his thigh.

"You tried with these other guys, but it didn't work out?"

"We had sex. It was…okay. But I didn't…"

"Come." He couldn't imagine what it'd be like to go through the motions but never find release. "Did you tell them about your past?"

"No. I've never discussed that with anyone."

"Not even Heath?"

"He knows only the basics, what was in the news. He knows that you saved me. But that's it." She released a sigh. "I've never been comfortable talking about it with others."

Only him. He hugged her for that. "So they thought… what?"

"One guy said I wasn't trying hard enough."

What an idiot.

"Another assumed I wasn't sexually attracted to him. He decided I must be into women instead." Her hand tightened in his shirt. "A couple didn't care enough to worry about it."

Damn, but hearing that felt like another punch. He didn't resent her for seeking pleasure. She was young, healthy, beautiful. But now that she was back, now that he was with her again, he wanted her only with him, and vice versa. "Even though you don't come, you enjoy sex overall?"

"To a point. But it does get frustrating." She tilted back to see him. "Heath said I should at least fake it, pretend for his sake, but I couldn't do that."

Jesus. "Heath is a fucking idiot." No, he didn't want her faking anything. He wanted the real deal, and he'd get it.

No doubts at all.

"In his defense, he was patient for a very long time. And he tried, far more than the other guys did." She wrinkled her nose. "It's just—"

Cannon put his fingers over her mouth. God almighty, the last thing he wanted to hear was sex stories about her and Heath. "Did he—did any guy—know he was on a tryout?"

"I don't know what you mean."

Time for more plain speaking. "You said you were trying to find a guy that'd make it work."

She rolled in her lips. "God, that sounds so awful, doesn't it?"

No, it sounded desperate. "All women are different, honey. Some get off easy, some don't. Some like things slow, some rough. Maybe you just haven't found your way yet."

She listened, her eyes wide, her cheeks warm.

Had anyone bothered to really figure out what Yvette liked? Did she even know? If she immediately assumed she had a problem, maybe she'd focused so much on that, she'd inhibited herself.

"I know you didn't discuss the past, but did you tell any guy up front that you had difficulty getting to the big finale?"

Her neck stiffened and she ducked back against him, unwilling to meet his gaze. "It wasn't exactly a conversation starter. When exactly do you think I'd have brought that up?"

"Right after he came and you didn't."

Her laugh held no humor. "No. That would have sounded too much like blame."

Because it would have been, the selfish pricks. A man should always ensure a woman's pleasure first. Cannon brushed his thumb over her warm cheek, thinking of what he'd do and how he'd do it once he got her under him—

She wrapped her fingers around his wrist and drew his hand down. "Understand, Cannon. Sometimes guys are selfish, but not always. Others have been patient, and they have tried."

Others were not him, and as Yvette had said, he was her fantasy. That had to count for something.

How she'd viewed him had always counted for a lot with him. When Yvette looked at him with her big green eyes, he felt about twelve feet tall, and invincible, too.

He wondered about foreplay, about oral sex, if she'd experimented with different positions.

Or had she simply accepted the belief that tragedy had forever altered her?

Not wanting a blow-by-blow report on past lovers, he made up his mind to do his own experimenting with her. He'd discover what she liked and didn't like, slowly, patiently, methodically, and in the process he'd win her over.

With that decided, he kissed her forehead, the bridge of her nose, down to her mouth. "Here's what we'll do."

CHAPTER TEN

YVETTE LISTENED TO Cannon's plans—plans that included staying with her, dating her, enjoying her; kissing and touching and making each other crazy.

But no sex.

She marveled that once again he'd surprised her.

"I don't understand," she said. "I thought you wanted…"

"Damn right. But I'm not a selfish person."

"I already know that."

"Then you should know that I don't want to do things I'll enjoy a hell of a lot more than you will."

Did that mean he'd get his enjoyment elsewhere? With a woman who'd be less trouble?

"You like kissing me," he said. "I think you'll like me touching you, too, but not tonight. We're both tired. We'll ease into the touching."

"You're touching me now," she felt compelled to point out.

His mouth lifted in a cocky smile. "No, I meant naked touching. On your breasts and nipples, your ass and between your legs."

Her jaw loosened. Such blatant speaking…well, it spiked her temp and set her heart racing. "I, ah, see."

The grin turned wolfish, and he brought his face close to hers so that she felt his warm breath when he whispered, "I promise you'll love it when I touch you."

She believed him. But… "Won't that just frustrate us both?"

"Yeah." His mouth moved over hers, his tongue touched, teased, withdrew. "It's going to be like freshman year all over again."

She'd spent her freshman year dying for him, and he'd barely noticed her. "You actually think that's going to be enough?"

Another kiss, a little deeper, definitely hotter. He eased up, but only to her throat, where he murmured against her skin, "I like being with you." Then he opened his mouth, sucked gently, made her toes curl tight.

"For…" Yvette swallowed. When Cannon did that— oh, and that—to her, it made talking difficult. She sank her fingers into his dark hair. "For how long?"

"I'll let you know if I start to crack." His damp mouth moved over her, leaving a tingling trail from her throat to her collarbone, to the sensitive hollow of her shoulder. "Do you always taste this good?"

She let her head drop back. "I don't know."

"I bet you do." He took a gentle love bite of her shoulder muscle, making her gasp as he soothed it with his hot tongue. "I bet you're this sweet all over."

It took her a second to piece together what he'd said. Once she did, sensation spread out like a forest fire. *"Cannon."*

"Yvette." He kissed her chin, her nose and her mouth again. Standing, he caught her hands. "Know what I want to do?"

Her knees felt like noodles, and she held on to him for balance. "You haven't been shy about telling me!"

Laughing, he hauled her up and over his shoulder, then started down the hall.

From her ignominious position, she watched the muscles shift in his tight tush. "Cannon!"

"Maybe a little touching," he said as his hand moved over her behind.

The thin cotton material of her pajama pants did nothing to blunt the heat of his palm or his exploring fingertips, especially when he traced the outline of her thong panties.

"Nice," he whispered, and he kissed her hip.

Bracing her hands against his back, Yvette said, "What are we doing?"

He veered into her bedroom. "Calling it a night, so don't get excited."

Too late. She'd gotten excited with his first kiss. "I see." Disappointment welled up, but she kept it to herself.

One-handed he pulled back her comforter, deposited her gently against the sheets, then sat on the side of the mattress.

For a stunned moment she just lay there, but as he bent to untie his sneakers she scampered into a sitting position.

"Cannon?" she said again, this time with confusion.

Toeing off each shoe and pulling off his socks, he set them next to her nightstand. "I'm going to sleep with you, okay?" Not waiting for her to deny him, he reached back and pulled his shirt up and over his head. He dropped it over a chair.

Yvette stared. As a fighter, he was so physically fit and downright perfect that it was no wonder a slow burn started in her belly.

Especially when his hands went to the fly of his jeans.

She felt like she should have done something—moved, spoke. Encouraged.

All she managed was some heavy breathing.

Shoving his jeans down, but leaving on his dark blue boxers, he smiled at her. "Just sleeping."

Right. There'd be no "just" to it, not with a man like Cannon.

She was still sitting there speechless when he said, "Scoot over."

In his boxers.

All that gorgeous flesh showing. Those ripped muscles. And his scent…

She scooted.

He stretched out facing her, one arm behind his head, the other touching her face. "So how do you sleep?"

"Alone."

"Not tonight. Or tomorrow. Or…I guess however long you let me stay."

Forever. No, she couldn't say that. Eventually he'd want what she couldn't give. When it sunk in that she wasn't very fun in the sack, then he'd be done. But until then… "Usually on my side."

"Left or right?"

Her heart beat too fast and her mouth felt dry, but she wasn't a dummy. She wasn't about to pass up the best offer of her lifetime. As she'd told him, he was her fantasy.

And he wanted to sleep with her, to hold her all through the night.

"How about like this?" Slowly, Yvette lay back down, then curled up against him, her head in the crook of his arm, her hand resting protectively on his bruised ribs. And, oh, God, it felt right. "This okay?"

His voice went husky and deep. "Better than okay." He tugged her closer, kissed her head and stretched out his other arm to kill the light.

The darkness cocooned them, making it all seem more intimate.

Cannon trailed his fingertips up and down her bare arm. "I almost forgot to tell you. There was some attempted vandalism at the pawnshop."

She tried to lift up to see him, but he said, "Shh. No damage. Just a kid being an idiot. I ran him off."

Envisioning graffiti on the walls, she sighed. "I guess with it being empty, that's going to happen."

"Probably. So I was thinking our priority should be putting up more lights and maybe an alarm system."

Enjoying the novelty of conversation in bed while hugged up to Cannon's hard frame, she gave it a quick thought. "Grandpa left some money. We could use—"

"I've got it."

Comfortable as she was, she knew she had to take a stand. "If we're not using the cash left to us, then I'll have to insist on paying my half."

He stilled, but not for long. "I guess you have a point. We probably need to sit down and go over everything Tipton left. See what our options are."

"Thank you."

His hand continued to glide up and down her arm in a tender caress. "Yvette?"

"Hmm?"

"We're going to work this out. All of it. The house. The shop." He shifted, pulled her thigh up over his and settled in more comfortably. "Us."

It hit her then.

Cannon had come to her rescue in the past; he wanted to rescue her again. Old habits, it seemed, were hard to break.

She gave one small nod, whispered, "Okay," and did her best to hide the disappointment—with herself.

Apparently three years hadn't really changed anything after all.

AMAZING HOW QUICKLY you could get used to something. It had been only five days, but she and Cannon had quickly gotten into a steady routine.

They jogged together in the mornings, then often parted ways for the afternoon, although they sometimes met up for lunch at Rowdy's. He did his thing, she did hers, then they hooked up again in the evening.

And slept together every night.

She loved it. But so much closeness had her on the ragged edge. Maybe him, too. They'd both stayed as busy as possible during the day.

Cannon had worked on changing out some of the security features on the house and adding others to the pawnshop. Once that was done he and Armie had set up a minigym in the basement. His stamina was through the roof. He never seemed to tire, had boundless energy and was the most dedicated person she'd ever known. Other than treating himself a couple of times with fast food, he stuck to a healthy diet-and-exercise program, both at the rec center with the other guys and at home.

In fact, there were a few mornings when he'd already been out of bed and working up a sweat in the basement before she'd even awakened.

Though Cannon seemed to be handling things just fine, the novelty of it all kept her slightly off balance. Showering with Cannon in the house. Seeing him in his boxers in the morning when he left the bed. Watching him shave. Watching him sweat when he did a hard workout.

Each night they had dinner together, then relaxed in the evening with a movie or games on her Wii.

Until he led her off to bed.

To sleep.

Oh, he touched her. A lot. Kissed her, too.

But not the type of touching he'd hinted at.

Never before had she enjoyed this sort of comfortable but charged familiarity with a man. With Cannon around, making new memories, the old memories didn't have a chance of intruding.

A text sounded on her phone. She glanced at it, but it was Heath. Again. Cannon knew her ex was still bugging her and he didn't like it, but she'd told him she was handling it, and she would. Rather than text Heath back, Yvette just shoved the phone into her pocket and headed for the garage.

At five o'clock with the sun high overhead, not a cloud in sight, the heat was enough to keep most people indoors. In the garage it was even worse, so she wrestled up the old, heavy door in hopes of catching a stray breeze.

To help keep herself from going nuts, she'd worked her way through much of the stuff her grandpa had stored away. So far she'd inventoried the contents of two of the storage units and had only one more to go. She found a method to his organizational style, realizing that big, bulky things were in one unit, pricey items in another more expensive but also safer facility.

She couldn't wait to see what he'd put in the last.

But just an hour ago, several boxes had arrived from Vanity. Yvette wanted to know exactly what she had before she got set up, to ensure she didn't have to move things too many times. The boxes from Vanity were good-size, but she assumed they held numerous smaller items—jewelry, knickknacks, games, that sort of thing.

It was as she was opening boxes in the garage that she noticed the new folding ladder on the garage ceiling. Huh. She didn't remember ever seeing it before. A rope hung from the ladder, presumably to pull it down and give access to the garage attic. But she couldn't reach it.

She was standing there, staring up at it, when her phone rang. Again it was Heath.

Tired of the games, Yvette snatched up the phone and said by way of greeting, *"What?"*

Silence greeted her.

Fine. He wanted to pout? He could do it alone. "I'm hanging up now."

"No." Heath's voice, raw with appeal, called out to her. "Don't."

"You have to stop calling me, Heath."

"I can't."

His ragged breathing stole some of her anger. She had dated this man for months, she'd been as intimate with him as she was capable of being, so some level of compassion remained. "Are you okay?"

"Come home, Yvette."

Her shoulders sagged—in relief. Obviously he hadn't left California as he'd claimed, or he wouldn't want her to return there. She knew the nicest thing she could do for him was to make him understand that things were over. Gently, but with firm insistence, she said, "I can't."

Defeat left his tone, replaced with a surprising explosion of rage. *"Or you won't?"*

She was so tired of his anger, of his mood swinging from adoration to loathing. "Both. But, Heath, it doesn't matter." As calmly as she could, she laid it out for him. "Even if I was there, we weren't together anymore. We'll never be together again. Please believe me. It's over."

A chilling laugh sounded through the phone. "You can be such a fucking bitch sometimes."

"Heath—"

"Does your new boyfriend know that? Does he know what a lousy lay you are? Does he realize your heart is so fucking frozen that all you do is lie there and—"

Breathing hard, her compassion blown, Yvette disconnected the call. Shaking all over, she badly wanted to throw the phone, but what good would that do?

"What is it?"

At the sound of Cannon's voice, she screeched and jumped a foot. When she whipped around, Cannon stood there in the open garage door, his gaze far too astute.

"Dear God, you startled me."

He didn't move toward her. "That was Heath?"

Expelling a big breath, she nodded. "Yes. He was... unhappy." She almost snorted at herself. Such an understatement.

"How many people have your number?"

"Not many. You. Vanity." She made a face. "Heath."

"Let's get you a new phone and a new number."

Since he didn't come to her, she felt uncertain of his mood. Always, every single time, Cannon greeted her with soft kisses and smiles.

"I can just block him."

Suspicion brightened his blue eyes. "Then why haven't you?"

"He wasn't that nasty before."

"And you feel sorry for him?"

More like guilty—but not anymore. Sweat gathered between her breasts and at the small of her back. Loose hairs from her braid stuck to her temples.

Cannon was in much the same shape, his T-shirt sticking to his skin in several places, his glossy dark hair damp with sweat.

Setting the phone aside, Yvette plucked at her shirt, letting some air underneath. "Did you jog in this heat?"

His attention sharpened as he looked her over. "No." He peeled off his shirt and used it to swipe over his chest. "I usually shower at the rec center, but it was packed today, so I figured I'd shower here instead."

Despite Heath's recent attack, a smile tugged at her mouth. "More guys are showing up because you're there."

"Yeah." He strode closer, his gaze locked with hers. "Armie says I'm good for business. I think he signed up ten new guys today alone."

From what she understood, the more MMA devotees who signed up, the more programs they could offer to the at-risk kids in the neighborhood.

"That's nice."

Focused on her, he got closer.

She tried to pull her gaze away but couldn't. "Cannon…"

He stopped in front of her, looking all over her, especially at where her shirt stuck to her breasts. "It's hot as hell in here."

Staring up at him, suddenly breathless, she whispered, "No air circulation."

With a touch of awe, Cannon trailed his rough fingertips down her throat, back and forth over her upper chest, then teased down into her cleavage. "How can you look so fucking sexy even now?"

He rarely cursed in front of her, and hearing it now with that particular rasp in his voice shook her. "I don't. I'm a mess."

"No." He bent to open his mouth on her throat, his lips lingering against her heated, damp skin. One hand opened on her waist, then slowly, so damn slowly, moved under her shirt and up, until he covered her breast.

They both went still, Yvette breathing heavily, Cannon growling softly.

Sweltering hot, humid air hung heavily around them. Outside the garage, a bird chirped. Somewhere nearby a car door closed.

With his face still against her throat, Cannon moved his thumb up and over her nipple.

"Hope I'm not intruding," said an amused female voice.

Yvette tried to jerk away, but Cannon held her still for a heartbeat, then turned, tucking her behind him.

"Hey," he said to their visitor. "Wasn't expecting you."

Yvette peeked around Cannon's bare shoulder and saw the lawyer's assistant. Despite the heat wave, she had on full makeup, including bright red lips. Beneath a silky blue sleeveless blouse, tan tailored skirt and high-heeled sandals, she looked cool and chic.

And even with Yvette watching her, she ogled Cannon's naked upper body.

After a slow lick of her glossy lips, she murmured, "You've healed up nicely, though I can still see a few faded bruises."

Yvette's hair nearly stood on end. Had Mindi seen Cannon shirtless already? Had she—

"Should have seen it before," Cannon told her, alleviating Yvette's worry without even knowing it. "I was pretty colorful there for a while. But yeah, I heal quick." He cocked his head. "So what's up?"

"I'm sorry to just drop in, Cannon, but you didn't return my call."

Another call? Yvette stepped around in front of him.

Mindi slid her gaze over her, taking in all the sweat and dust with barely veiled disdain. "Ms. Sweeny."

Trying not to sound mean or territorial—no matter how she felt—Yvette said, "Ms. Jarrett."

Changing tactics, the woman put on a sympathetic face and crooned, "How are you, honey?"

The demeaning tone meant for the "poor little lost girl" cut right through Yvette, leaving a swatch of pain in its wake. "What do you mean?" Just how much of her past did the assistant know?

"You lost your grandfather, relocated... I'm sure it's been difficult."

Inner trembling settled, and the constriction left her lungs. So her facade of sympathy wasn't about the past, but the present. "We're fine, thank you." She stressed the word *we*.

Still with exaggerated pity, one hand to her chest, Mindi asked, "No bad moments?"

Indignation rising, Yvette stiffened. "Excuse me?"

"Being back here, in this house? I understand you suffered serious trauma."

Oh, God. Had Cannon told her everything? Her heart plummeted and sick betrayal rose up to burn her throat.

"I don't know the details, of course, but your grandfather hinted—"

"What? What did he tell you?" She refused to believe her grandfather had discussed anything with the woman.

"Oh, honey," she crooned. "I didn't mean to upset you."

Putting his hands on her shoulders, Cannon asked, "What can we do for you, Mindi?"

Nettled, Yvette couldn't miss how familiarly they addressed each other. She was Ms. Sweeny, but he was simply Cannon.

"We should talk." Mindi stepped just inside the garage, which left the sun behind her to make a glowing halo of her pale blond hair and her shapely figure.

Yvette disliked her more by the second, but not as much as she disliked the situation.

She would not be a weak person.

Raising her chin, she faced Mindi. "What is there to talk about? Has Mr. Whitaker sent you here for a reason?" *There,* she thought. *Deal with that.*

Mindi's smile hardened. "Frank knows I'm here, if that's what you mean." She turned to Cannon. "I didn't hear back from you."

"There's nothing more to talk about," Cannon said, his hands now massaging Yvette's shoulders. "We're staying."

Mindi fanned a hand in front of her face, trying to stir the heavy air. "But I explained that my friend had upped his offer."

"Doesn't change anything," Cannon said.

Another offer? That was news to Yvette. Just how many times had Mindi called him? Not that it mattered, Cannon was right about that. The longer she remained, the more she wanted it to be forever.

"You haven't heard the offer," Mindi said, now trailing her manicured fingertips over the many boxes stacked in the garage.

Yvette hid her hands behind her, until she realized that put them right over Cannon's fly. His only reaction was to tighten his hold on her shoulders.

Flushing, she pulled them around front again, curling her hands to hide her short fingernails. "I'm not selling."

Smiling, Cannon repeated, "We're not selling."

The sweet scent of Mindi's expensive perfume dissipated in the musty garage. "You realize that staying here, in this house, doesn't require you to keep the pawn-shop." As Mindi said that, she looked at Yvette. "You have a big career that leaves little time for unimportant distractions."

Getting the not-so-subtle message that *she* was an unimportant distraction, Yvette shimmered with anger. "I'll run the shop."

"And you can buy out Cannon?" Mindi lifted one box lid to peek inside, but bubble wrap hid the contents. "Because I know half of it was his."

"What it is," Cannon said firmly, stepping around Yvette to close the box again, "is none of your business."

Both women stared at him. It surprised Yvette that he could say something so insulting without any sign of anger. He'd sounded almost tender, as if he'd given the woman a compliment.

Of course she knew he had a reputation for making friends with every woman he met, but she'd never seen him in action before.

"True, of course." Mindi's mouth pursed and annoyance narrowed her eyes. "I'm sorry if I'm overstepping myself, but—"

"It's fine," Cannon cut in, then added, "as long as you stop now."

A palpable silence throbbed in the air.

Mindi smiled. "Yes, of course. I apologize." Instead of withdrawing, she took in the cluttered garage. "So what is all this?"

Knowing Mindi addressed Cannon didn't stop Yvette from answering. "It's inventory for the shop."

"Tipton's leavings?" She peered into the box closest to her. "Have you found anything interesting?"

"Much of this is from a business I had."

"Oh." She closed the box. "Have you gone through Tipton's storage units yet?"

Not liking her nosiness, or the familiar way she used her grandfather's name, Yvette stayed mum.

Cannon filled in the silence, saying vaguely, "One thing at a time."

"I see." She smiled at Cannon. "Well, I should be going now. If you change your mind—about anything— please let me know."

Cannon moved to her side and took her arm. "I'll walk you out."

Oh, now wait a minute! Yvette wanted to protest, but Cannon glanced over his shoulder at her. "Be right back."

CHAPTER ELEVEN

OF ALL THE... More than a little furious at being dismissed, Yvette went through the interior door into the house, but resisted the urge to slam it shut. She didn't want Mindi to know she was bothered.

Choosing not to wait for Cannon to finish his private talk, she went into her bedroom, locked the door, then into the bathroom for a cool shower.

He could talk to Mindi for as long as he wanted. She didn't care.

Or rather, she didn't want to care. Damn it.

Knowing she'd never look as elegant as Mindi, she didn't even try. After drying off, she put on lotion, took her long hair out of the braid and dressed in an oversize logo T-shirt and cutoff shorts.

When she left her room, she found Cannon in the kitchen cooking, also freshly showered and dressed in shorts and a T-shirt. They were both barefoot. But that was where the similarities ended.

Unlike her shirt that fell loose around her body, his fit his muscled torso to perfection.

Whereas her cutoffs resembled Daisy Dukes, his cargo shorts went down to his knees.

With the braid out, her hair hung in long ripples. He'd finger combed his wet, inky black hair, leaving it rumpled.

Given how smooth his jaw looked, he might have shaved.

As he chopped an onion, she watched the movement of muscles in his back and shoulders. It was seriously unfair that any man could look so good.

"Come on in," he said. "I'll have dinner ready in a few minutes."

Yvette headed to the fridge for a cola, but when she saw his big icy pitcher of sugarless tea, she chose that instead.

His good habits were contagious.

"Pour me one, too, will you?"

"Sure." Trying for a note of diplomacy, she asked, "So. What did you and Mindi have to talk about?"

"Told her I had to renege on her rain check, that's all." He used the edge of the butcher knife to push the onions off the cutting board and into a hot skillet with olive oil.

"Uh-huh." Giving herself a minute to think, she poured the tea, set his beside him and took a long drink of her own. "A rain check for what, exactly?" He'd told her he wouldn't see anyone else, so unless they had some important business to discuss that—

"Sex."

Choking, she put the back of her hand to her mouth and wheezed for air.

Cannon glanced her way. "You okay?"

Nodding hard, she gestured for him to continue.

"She hit on me at Whitaker's office when I first got home."

Finally able to get a strangled breath, she rasped, "At the *lawyer's* office?"

"Yeah. Whitaker had to take off for court, we were alone, she was interested and didn't mind saying so." He hitched one shoulder in disinterest. "I gave her a rain check, though, because, well, you know, I was pretty banged up, and the idea of Tipton leaving me half his stuff really threw me off stride. Then I met up with you again and…" His gaze dipped over her, sticking a moment on her thighs. "Not interested in Mindi."

Swelling with umbrage, Yvette plunked her glass down onto the table. "*She's* still interested."

He flashed her a grin. "Yeah, I know. She said so. Got all grabby and stuff right out there on the sidewalk."

Both hurt and furious, Yvette stared at him. Pride took over. "I hope you didn't turn her down on my account."

"You know I did."

Fighting herself more than Cannon, she said, "I told you I couldn't—"

"I remember what you said." He began to dice a tomato. "You offered to accommodate me."

Did he want her to do that? Now? And if so, why'd he sound so curt when bringing it up?

Her heart felt too heavy to stay in her chest. "Yes. But that was nearly a week ago."

"You've changed your mind?"

Resenting that she had to offer again, she lifted her chin. "No."

"Good, because I only want you."

Then why was he still waiting? "You're sure about that?"

He laughed. "Positive. So why would I mess around with Mindi?"

Maybe because Mindi didn't have any hang-ups?

"I wouldn't," he said, answering his own question. "But apparently she hasn't caught on to that yet, so now seemed like a good time to clear things up. I didn't see any reason to be cruel about it, especially after I let her think I might be willing. *Before you.*"

"So you explained it to her?"

He nodded. "She understands now."

Yeah, sure she did.

The silence stretched out until Yvette felt compelled to say something. "What can I do to help?"

"With Mindi? I took care of it."

She gnashed her teeth. "With dinner."

Barely suppressing his humor, Cannon quirked a smile. "Oh, right. Gotcha."

Damn it. It was too hot to cook and she was in no mood to be teased. "Forget it." She put her empty glass in the sink and would have walked out, but Cannon forestalled her temper by wrapping those strong arms around her and trapping her against the counter.

"You're killing me, you know that, right? These shorts... You could be lethal."

He pressed his hips in against her denim-covered behind.

"I want you nonstop. Only you." He nuzzled against the side of her neck, effectively melting her anger, if not her hurt. "Even when you're confused about things." A damp kiss. "Or jealous?"

"Cannon." Her willpower waned, but she got out the protest. "I'm mad."

"Don't be." He teased his nose behind her ear. "Damn, you always smell so good, even earlier when you were sweaty."

It took so little for him to turn her on. "I do not."

"I want to breathe you in all over."

Before she could get too excited over that, he gave her one of his gentle love bites on her shoulder muscle.

As usual, her toes curled and her belly did a somersault.

As if he knew, he opened a firm hand over her stomach, above the waistband of the hip-hugging shorts. Through the cotton of the T-shirt, she felt the heat of his palm. "Know what I want to do?"

She had an idea, but still asked, "What?"

"First I want to kiss away your mad, or your confusion or jealousy or whatever it is you're feeling."

All of the above, actually, and yes, him kissing it away seemed like a terrific idea. Eyes closed, she sighed. "And second?"

"I want to enjoy dinner with you."

Her eyes popped open again. She had been expecting something altogether different from him. "Dinner. Really? Oookay."

Smiling against her sensitive neck, he added, "And then…" His hand crept back up to her breast, this time outside her T-shirt. While cuddling and stroking, he said in a hushed, husky whisper, "I want to touch you some more. Like this, but without your shirt in the way."

The soft groan came of its own volition.

"Those itty-bitty shorts have me fantasizing all kinds of things."

Glad that he liked her shorts—because she knew she'd worn them specifically to get his mind back on her—she pressed back into him.

"Yeah. Like that."

His hand was big, hard, hot, and the way his palm rasped over her stiffened nipple made breathing difficult. "You want me to touch you, don't you?"

"I do, but—"

"Say you do, Yvette."

To encourage the right answer, he caught her nipple, tugging gently, rolling, so that her *"Yes"* came out as a quivering moan.

"There you go." His hand went down to her thigh. "It's

going to be really easy to get under the frayed hem of these barely there shorts." To prove his point, he edged his rough fingertips along her upper thigh, higher and higher until he slipped under the fringe—

"Cannon…" She wanted him, so much, but she didn't want to leave him disappointed when things didn't go as he hoped. "I'm not sure—"

"Just touching." Pulling her around to face him, Cannon took her mouth in a consuming kiss. One hand tangled in her hair, the other opened wide on her backside to keep her pressed tight to him. Against her mouth, he said, "I can handle it if you can."

It took two shuddering breaths before she was capable of answering. "Okay."

Satisfaction, and something more, grew bright in his mesmerizing gaze. She stared up at him, knowing it'd be agony to have his hands on her without ever actually reaching release. She wasn't at all certain she could bear it, but denying him—or herself—would only be worse.

At the interruption of a ringing phone, Yvette realized she'd left her cell out in the garage. She was both relieved at the delay and frustrated that she couldn't discover where the moment would lead.

When she stood there, Cannon brushed the backs of his knuckles over her cheek. "Want me to get it?"

She wanted him to go on touching and teasing her.

"No." She smoothed her hand over his chest, down his impressive abs, then got her feet moving even though her legs felt weak and she assumed it'd just be Heath pestering her again. "I'll be right back."

"Okay. I'll finish up our dinner."

Heated from the inside out, Yvette wondered at Cannon's new plan, and whether or not his detachment was part of that plan, or if he could really do this and remain so unaffected.

Because she couldn't.

Just as she reached the garage, the phone stopped ringing. Of course it was Heath again. His message went to voice mail. She listened to him rant about loving her while also cursing her for not loving him back. Relieved that he was on the opposite coast, she deleted the vile message and blocked his number.

Cannon had closed and locked the garage door so her packages were secure. Before she started going through everything again, she'd wrestle open the dusty window adjacent from the interior door so that the air could move a little. Maybe then it wouldn't be so bad.

She might also figure out how to pull down that ladder so she could check out the storage space up over the ceiling.

She got back in the kitchen in time to see Cannon drop angel-hair pasta atop the onions and olive oil, stir it all up and add fresh Parmesan cheese.

It smelled *heavenly.*

He watched her put her phone on the counter. "Heath again?"

No reason to bore him with the ugly details. "Yes, but I blocked him." Getting out plates and refilling their glasses, she set the table. And even that, the simple act of two place settings instead of one, filled her with emotion.

Taking her by surprise, Cannon stroked her backside, murmured, "Irresistible," then stepped around her to load up the plates. "What are you thinking about so seriously?"

Still on high alert from that casual caress and incredible compliment, she smiled at him. "I haven't done this since I moved away." She indicated the table. "Sitting down with someone for a home-cooked meal night after night."

He put diced tomatoes over the pasta. "Tipton was a good cook?"

"Country cooking." Very different from the healthy stuff Cannon preferred. "Most everything he fixed was a one-pot meal, with chicken and dumplings being his specialty."

A gentleman to the core, Cannon pulled out her chair. "He taught you to cook?"

"Yes." Yvette realized that having someone to talk to, especially about her grandpa, was as poignant as the cozy dinners together. "Stew, soup, sauerkraut and ribs, ham and cabbage." She grinned. "All stuff you don't eat."

"All stuff I love." He sat across from her, then stretched out his long legs so that his feet caged hers in. "Mom was a country cook, too. I took up running early in life just so she couldn't fatten me up."

"Bull." For as long as she'd known Cannon, he'd been a specimen. "I'm not believing that."

He smiled with her. "Bean soup and ham with corn bread was one of my favorites. I could finish off half the corn bread all on my own. Rissy would have a fit when she wanted seconds and it was gone."

"When do she and her roommate get home, by the way?"

He went still, making Yvette shake her head.

"What, you thought I wasn't paying attention? I realize you wanted to be here, so here you are. But you did have options."

"True enough." He watched her take a bite, then moan with pleasure. His eyes darkened. "Glad you like it."

"It's amazing."

As casually as he'd stroked her rear, he said, "You'll like me touching you, too."

Her turn to go still—only that didn't slow Cannon down at all.

"But if there's anything you don't like, I want you to tell me. Or if there's something you especially enjoy—"

Already overheated, she interrupted him. "We were talking about your sister."

"Safer subject, huh? Okay, I can work with that." Watching her intently, he ate another big bite before answering. "I could have gone to Rissy's, true, but it is her place now, not mine. I respect her privacy and with her and her roommate out of town it didn't seem right to just make myself at home."

"She wouldn't welcome you there?"

"Course she would."

"What about her roommate?"

"Cherry Peyton. I don't know her well, but she seems nice enough. Denver might be interested, remember?"

"Yes." Denver was definitely interested, from what she could tell.

Moving right on past that, Cannon added, "There's always the Colonial. I've stayed there before."

She gave a tight smile. "Mary expected to find you at a hotel." And if Yvette hadn't shown up at the bar that night, he'd have taken Mary back to his room with him.

"Forget Mary," he said. "Forget Mindi. I wanted to be here. With *you*."

Petty jealousy had never been her way. Because he was so special to her, Cannon deserved the truth. "I'm glad it worked out this way."

He picked up her hand and kissed her knuckles. "Now, if that's settled, let's eat. The sooner we get done, the sooner I can get my hands on you."

With the fork halfway to her mouth, she paused.

He glanced at the clock. "It's early. We'll have hours to play before bedtime. I'm already half-hard just thinking about it." He forked up another big bite of pasta.

Lust, apparently, didn't dent his appetite. But then, he stayed more active than any person she knew.

For her part, Yvette wanted to melt right off her seat. "You know I can't—"

"Climax?" More gently, he said, "It's okay. Touching, that's all we're going to do, remember?"

But why? Surely he'd want more than that. Just because she couldn't didn't mean he—

Then he finished by saying, "Tonight anyway. Eventually I'm going to want all of you."

Thinking about it, him over her, in her, sent a sweet clench of desire into every muscle. "Okay," she whispered.

Gaze playfully stern, he said, "But not tonight. Tonight is for touching only. Touching and kissing and going a little nuts." He drew in a slow breath. "So finish up. I've tortured myself enough already."

YVETTE HAD BEEN quiet through the rest of dinner and the cleanup afterward.

Maybe feeling nervous, as soon as the last dish was put away she'd gathered up dirty laundry and disappeared into the basement for an hour. Unwilling to rush her, he'd used the time to do other cleaning. When she'd heard the vacuum, she'd charged back up the steps.

It was kind of funny how she'd reacted. Even after he'd told her he was a neat freak and could damn well handle housework, she'd seemed put out. Reluctantly she'd put away the laundry and taken a seat, mostly so that he would sit, too.

As he joined her, her gaze went watchful and wary.

Did she expect him to jump her? To strip off her shirt and start pawing her? If so, he'd disappoint her by going so slow, she'd be the one asking him to take the shirt off her.

Eventually she'd ask for everything.

But as he'd told her, tonight would be a sweet torment. They'd both end up frustrated, but she'd get comfortable with him.

Eventually comfortable enough to let herself go.

She'd put her cell phone on the coffee table, so he did the same, then put his wallet and keys there, as well.

She went wide-eyed, maybe thinking he was going to stop. Hell of an idea, because he'd love to have her hands all over him, but not yet. His iron control, strong as it might be, had limits.

Facing her as he sat, one arm along the back of the couch so he could toy with her long hair, Cannon did his utmost to sound casual instead of primed. "Did I tell you that Rowdy and I agreed for me to work the bar on Saturday? He advertised it all week. Should be a big crush."

"Saturday?"

"Yeah." Twining his fingers in her hair, he used it to tug her closer. "You'll be there, right?"

Her lips parted and she breathed deeper. "I don't know."

Well, he did. She'd go with him, and they'd have a blast. It was important for her to understand the chemistry between them wasn't just sexual.

As he leaned down toward her, her thick, dark lashes lowered over her eyes. Big, beautiful, green eyes.

But then he found everything about her appealing.

Taking her mouth gently, he kissed her lower lip, then

her upper before aligning their mouths perfectly in a soft, hungry kiss.

It gratified him, encouraged him, when she melted against him.

Surely a woman who reacted so easily could be taken over the edge to the big O. With the right man.

Him.

"I want you there," he told her while kissing a path to her ear.

"Okay."

"I don't mind if other women flirt—"

She started to pull away but he kept her close.

"—as long as they understand the limits." He traced her ear with the tip of his tongue and felt her shiver. "Seeing you there with me will make others understand."

Her hands fisted in his shirt as she leaned into him. "Understand what?"

"That we're together." He kissed behind her ear, down to her nape. "The guys will be there, too. But they already know how it is."

"Other fighters?"

"Mmm," he answered while opening his mouth against her skin. "About that touching..."

Her breath caught. "Yes?"

He took her hand and carried it down to his erection. He was already engorged, throbbing. But giving himself time hadn't helped with his control.

No, it had only made him more urgent.

"You can go first."

Now she inhaled sharply. Her hand was small, her touch tentative as she traced along his length.

Dying just a little, Cannon encouraged her with murmured words of pleasure. She wrapped her fingers around him as much as she could through the material of his cargo shorts—then squeezed.

"Damn." He held himself still a moment until he gained control, then took her hand away. "Hang on a sec, honey."

She watched with smoky intensity while he pulled off his shirt and tossed it aside. "Let's try this again, above the waist this time."

Without hesitation she put both hands on him, stroking over his pecs to his shoulders, then back down again to silently examine each ab muscle. When she bent toward him, he froze, his heart hammering hard.

The first touch of her mouth tested his resolve. She brushed her lips gently over each fading bruise, rubbed her cheek against his chest hair, inhaled deeply, drinking in his scent.

Knotting a hand in her hair, Cannon said, "You should know, babe, everything you do to me, I get to repay in kind."

Her heated gaze lifted to his. While they stared at each other she brought both hands over his nipples, lightly dragged her nails over him, then bent again to flick with her tongue.

Jesus. He let her play a minute more, then abruptly said, "My turn." It wasn't easy to remember his plan with his heart trying to punch through his ribs, but he got it together.

"I like touching you."

"Yeah?" He went back to kissing her neck, down to the upper swells of her breasts.

"You told me to tell you what I like. I like that."

"What about this?" Carefully, he closed his teeth over her T-shirt–covered nipple, then pressed with his tongue, leaving the thin fabric damp.

Her hands clenched in his hair, and when he moved to the other breast, she led him to her, arched into him. Right before he kissed that nipple, he asked, "You like this, Yvette?"

"Yes."

"This?" he asked, sucking gently through the material, "Or this?" He plucked with his lips.

And then with his teeth.

Squirming, she gasped, *"Yes."*

He kept it up, using his mouth to tease one nipple, his fingers to roll the other until she whispered raggedly, "Cannon..."

"Tell me."

Instead she leaned away and nearly leveled him when she pulled off her shirt.

God almighty, she was so hot he didn't know how much more he could take.

Her soft, pink nipples were pulled tight, her pale breasts full and flushed. She breathed quickly, watching him, anxious.

Savoring the moment, Cannon put a hand to her narrow waist. Her skin was so silky, and incredibly warm. Those sinful shorts rode low on her hips. They barely covered more than panties would.

He stroked two fingers over her hip bone to her navel, getting hotter still when she wiggled. "Ticklish?"

"Yes."

He couldn't wait to see how she reacted when he stroked those same two fingers deep inside her.

"Come here." Sitting back, he lifted her over him so that she straddled his lap, facing him. Without their shorts, he could enter her like this. That thought tested his resolve, especially now that her open thighs rested directly over the ridge of his erection.

She moved against him, rolling her hips until he clasped them to keep her still.

Given the difficulty she'd admitted to, he'd expected her to be more reserved.

Instead she seemed starved for release, and that, too, fired his blood.

Covering both breasts with his hands, he kissed her again, long and deep, light and easy, using his tongue, his teeth, until they were both panting. At every second, he was aware of her, her reactions, gauging what she liked, what she loved, what turned her on the most.

"Cannon," she groaned. "My shirt is off now."

A hint? "Believe me, baby, I know." He played with her nipples the same way he teased her mouth, first lightly brushing, then insistently tugging.

Would she tell him what she wanted?

Hopeful, he took her mouth again in a deep eating kiss, all the while his hands moved over her, up and down the toned length of her narrow back, down to the gentle swell of her hips, from the top of her silken thighs to her knees and back up again.

Hooking one arm around her waist, the other under her hips, he arched her forward and trailed wet, hot kisses down her throat to the tops of her breasts.

With his tongue, he taunted her, getting close to her nipple, but never quite touching no matter how she shifted, trying to direct him.

"Cannon."

"Tell me."

He felt the urgency of her deep breaths, the indecision that held her back, until she cupped a small hand around his neck and drew him forward, saying raggedly, "I want your mouth on me."

"Where?" Enjoying her like this, he licked her throat.

"Here?" Down to her cleavage, where he dipped his tongue. "Like this?" Farther down, lightly touching his lips to her nipple. "Or right here?" And with that, he sucked her in.

She cried out, her hips pressing in to his abs, her runner's thighs squeezing him, her fingers so tight in his hair that it stung.

Taking advantage of her position up on her knees, her body taut, he locked her to him and drew on her until she was rhythmically riding against him.

Just like that, he thought, more convinced than ever that her only problem had been being with the wrong man.

Which meant any man other than him.

He switched to the other breast, kissing around her throbbing nipple, curling his tongue around her, pulling and licking before treating her to another long, leisurely suckle.

Her reaction was the hottest thing he'd ever experienced.

With her head tipped back, her long hair draped over his forearm and her breasts lifted higher. Open around his hips, her long, trim legs quivered. She gasped each breath, whimpering, moaning.

He loved seeing her like this, a little lost, a whole lot turned on.

She didn't have any problems, not with him.

Initially he'd thought to drag this out for hours, and then for days, until she was ready. But he'd never seen a woman more ready than Yvette was right now.

Even as he cautioned himself not to rush her, he opened the snap at the top of those itty-bitty cutoffs, then eased the zipper down so he could get his hand inside.

He cupped her over her panties and still felt the damp heat of her excitement.

Straightening, she went utterly motionless except for the bellowing of her deep breaths.

Ever so lightly, he touched her while still lazily drawing on her nipple.

Groaning, her nails bit into his shoulders and he looked up to see her head dropped forward, her eyes squeezed shut. Her dark hair fell around her face like a curtain.

She felt pressured, he realized, and was already worrying about "performing." He wanted her back to mindless pleasure, so he redirected her thoughts.

"Just touching," he whispered to her.

She gave a shaky nod, and said, "I don't know if I can stand this."

"I know it's difficult for you, but I love touching you, Yvette. Here," he said, licking her nipple. "And here." He pressed his fingers to her sex, able to feel her swollen lips through the slinky material of her panties.

Her hips rocked once, then stilled.

"Okay?"

"I…" She trembled as he delved a little deeper, tracing her vulva.

"For me," he urged her, plucking at her nipple with his lips. "Tell me it's okay."

Rather than speak, she nodded.

He withdrew his hand from the front of her shorts and instead slipped it underneath from the back, moving over her perfect ass.

She wore a thong.

Groaning, he drew her nipple deeper while exploring that smooth, firm flesh. As he'd told her, the high, loose legs of her cutoffs made it easy to get his hand inside. He eased her up and forward—and got his fingers on her slick, hot flesh.

Silky wet.

Swollen with need.

Leaving her nipples wet and tight, he took her mouth again, drugging them both with a devouring kiss while barely entering her with one finger. She tried pressing down against him, shifting, wanting more, but he outmaneuvered her each time. It wasn't easy to remember his purpose right now, not when he'd wanted her so long and she was so incredibly hot.

"Easy," he told her.

But she surprised him by kissing him again, then whispering, "You told me to tell you."

Curious how bold she'd be, he nodded. "Yes."

She stared into his eyes. "Then I want your fingers inside me. As deep as you can go."

Fuck. Control shot, Cannon put his head back against the couch and drew her forward. "Brace your hands on my shoulders."

Urgently, she did—which brought her up to her knees.

Holding her gaze, he parted her, tested her gently, then slowly worked two fingers into her.

Gasping, she leaned in, rubbing her face against his throat and squirming her hips. "God, Cannon, that feels…"

"Good?"

"So good."

He knew what would feel better, but, damn it, he was afraid of blowing the moment. Better to let her lead the way right now.

"Kiss me, honey."

She did, her fingers in his hair, her breasts rubbing against his chest, her body clamping down on his fingers, squeezing each time he withdrew, getting wetter each time he pressed them in again.

She was so tight, so hot.

He brushed his thumb up and found her little clitoris already distended, beaded tight. Teasing over her brought a funny little catch to her breathing. He felt the way she trembled, and he had to believe she was close.

He moved over and around that sensitive little bud again and again, slicking her own moisture over her, rasping, tormenting.

"Oh, God."

Now, he decided. It had to be now. "Will you trust me, Yvette?"

She kissed his shoulder, bit his chest. Her husky "Yes," followed by an urgent, *"Please,"* reassured him that everything would be fine.

"Good." Taking his hand from between her legs, he turned her to her back on the couch. "Then how about we lose the shorts?"

Her hair tumbled around her. Lust left her eyes dark and heavy, her lips soft and swollen from so much kissing. As he watched, tears glistened in her eyes, but she nodded.

Wasting no time, he dragged the shorts down and off her legs, leaving her in nothing more than a minuscule black thong. He wanted that off her, too, but first...

"This is for me," he reminded her. "So just relax." Then he leaned down and pressed his open mouth to the damp material between her legs.

CHAPTER TWELVE

SENSATION SO SHARP should have been painful. Instead it was a nearly unbearable pleasure. Already with Cannon she'd felt things she'd never felt before. Amazing things.

Scorching promises that pushed her nearer to something she wanted very badly.

It hovered close, rolling over her in ever greater waves, only to recede again.

"I need to taste you."

His long fingers hooked in the waistband of her panties and peeled them away and she didn't care. She wanted him to see her.

And, God, yes, she wanted his mouth on her.

She was almost desperate for that.

For the longest time he just looked at her—and that was fairly indescribable, too. An incandescent heat lit his vivid blue eyes. Every muscle in his torso looked more defined, much in the way she'd noticed during his fights when his blood pumped harder from exertion. His expression was so focused, so possessive, that he made her feel sexy when she'd always felt ruined instead.

Watching him, she whispered, "Cannon?"

He parted her legs so that he sat between them. His big, rough hands looked dark against her pale skin, feeling over her in a slow sweep that encompassed her shoulders, her breasts—where he lingered at her nipples—then her waist, down to her hips and to her inner thighs where he edged her legs wider still.

His nostrils flared. He breathed deeper.

Narrowing his eyes, he turned his hand against her, palm up. She felt him parting her, then the pressure of two thick fingers pushing in. That was enough, but then he did something, crooked his fingers a certain way and reached a spot—

"Ooh." Automatically her hips lifted up to that sizzling sensation.

His gaze flicked up to hers, probing, interested, then back to where his fingers worked her.

She shifted her legs, stunned at the climbing pressure inside her, the ache that grew tighter but was so very sweet. It couldn't be this easy. Not after so much disappointment. Not after—

"Stay with me, honey." And then, "You'll like this."

With building anticipation Yvette watched him bend down until his dark head was between her thighs, his breath hot, his mouth hotter.

He inhaled her scent, and groaned.

She couldn't get enough air to make a single sound.

Using his thumbs to open her, he licked boldly over her—*in her*—with his rough tongue.

Incredibly moved, both physically and emotionally, Yvette put her hands in his satiny black hair, stroking, encouraging.

He hooked his arms under her legs, anchoring her with his hands at her breasts, and continued to eat at her until she knew it would happen. Each thrust of his tongue told her so.

Especially since he followed each thrust with a flick up and over her clitoris. She caught herself anticipating that elusive touch, reaching for it, trying to follow with her hips. And every time it happened, she tightened more until she thought she might shatter.

She wanted to. So very much.

Eyes closed in concentration, absorbing every sensation to the fullest, she whispered his name, begging for what she hoped he could give.

"This," he growled. "Tell me if you like this." Instead of just teasing with his tongue, he closed his mouth around her clitoris, sucking gently.

The overload of stimulation drew her body taut. She twisted in reaction, but with the way he held her she couldn't move much.

"Please," she whispered, afraid that somehow the building urgency would escape her. She held him closer, blind with need. *Please, Cannon, please—*

"Easy, honey," he murmured.

She felt his jaw against her inner thighs, his fingers on her nipples, the heat of his mouth sucking. "Don't stop." She knew tears tracked down her cheeks, but she didn't care. "Please don't."

"No, I won't." He shifted so that he held her still with one hand splayed flat on her stomach, and with the other he stroked his fingers back into her, reaching for that same magical spot.

"Ah—" Tighter and tighter, coiling, clenching... *"Cannon."*

He made a rumbling sound of deep satisfaction, and the orgasm took her.

Aware only of the awesome release, she gave herself over to it, uncaring of how she moved or how loudly she cried out. Cannon stayed with her, relentless, taking from her until she had nothing left.

As the tension gradually uncoiled, it took her strength, leaving her limp on the couch.

When Cannon kissed her mouth, she got her eyes open. He was over her, between her legs, and with one look at him, she knew he hadn't come yet.

She wanted to touch him, but honestly, her limbs felt too heavy.

Appearing fascinated, he brushed the tears from her cheeks and smiled at her. "Hi."

Wow. She'd really done it. Or rather, he'd done it. A little bewildered, she stared at him. "I came."

Tenderness turned his smile up another hundred watts. "Yeah, I know." Teasing her, he said, "I heard."

In the moment, she didn't mind the teasing, not at all. She was too confused to care. "But...I don't understand."

"You're as perfect as I knew you'd be. And honest to God, babe, I feel like the best lover on earth now."

"You *are,*" she told him, meaning it.

He wasn't nearly so serious. "I hadn't planned to go so far today."

Since he hadn't yet gotten relief, she didn't think he'd gone far enough. "I am so glad you didn't stop."

"Me, too."

She could feel his erection throbbing against her, yet he made no move to enter her. In fact...she shifted her leg against him and felt material.

He still wore his shorts.

"Don't you want to get naked, too?"

He kissed her so gently that more tears tried to fill her eyes.

When her phone rang, Yvette said, "Ignore it."

"Planned to." His thumbs rubbed her temples as he continued to put butterfly kisses to her face. She felt cherished, which made it difficult to stop the emotional overflow.

A second later, his phone rang. He put his forehead to hers with a quiet curse.

Yvette tightened around him. "Ignore it, too."

"Yeah." He sat up, but immediately lifted her into his lap. "Time for bed."

Oh, good. "Okay." She grabbed for his shoulders as he stood. She wasn't a big person, but still, it awed her how he could carry her so easily. He might as well have been carrying a pillow. "You are so strong."

His smile went crooked. "True, but you can't judge me by this. You weigh nothing."

A hundred and twenty pounds was not "nothing," but she got his meaning.

He put her in the bed, stepped back and removed his shorts.

But not his boxers.

"Unfair. You still—"

Resolute, he reminded her, "Just touching."

Intrigued, she considered things. "You want me to do to you what you did to me?"

A mix of surprise and hunger froze him. He blew out a breath. Closed his eyes. Stood there, still and rigid, his hands clenching, until he seemed to have composed himself. "I want you to let me hold you while we sleep."

Oh, no way.

Thinking he only needed confirmation from her, she came up on an elbow. "Don't be silly. I want you." Nodding at his tented boxers, she said, "And you want me."

"Don't push me, Yvette. This is new for you and we're going to take it slow if it kills me."

"But—"

"Don't make it harder than it has to be, okay?"

He turned the light out and got into bed beside her.

Mired in conflicted thoughts, Yvette tried to decide what to do.

He took the decision from her, pulling her close so he could spoon her, one large hand cupped over her breast. After a perfunctory kiss to the top of her head he said, "Sleep."

Annoyance chipped away at her mellow mood, but she had no idea how to proceed. It seemed he'd made up his mind. Still, she tried. "I'm naked."

"Mmm." His hand cuddled her breast for only a second, but given how sensitive her nipples were now, it made her shudder. "I like you naked."

Calming her heart, she said reasonably, "But you're *not* naked."

"Me being naked wouldn't be a good thing."

She thought it'd be a very good thing. "Why?" So that he wouldn't understand, she clarified, "Why do we have to wait?"

He was quiet so long, doubts began to creep in. At the time she hadn't cared about much except that reaching the unattainable—that incredible orgasm.

But now…well, maybe she'd done something wrong. Been too enthusiastic or loud. Turned him off somehow. Maybe—

"Stop overanalyzing, honey. Sharing that with you was about as hot as it gets."

Relief had her slumping back against him. "Then—"

"Fact is, I want more than sex with you." He surrounded her, hugging her with his muscled arms, aligning his strong, hairy legs against the backs of hers. His scent and heat lulled her; the sweet way he kissed her shoulder made her eyes feel heavy. "How much more… that's something we'll work out. But I know it'll be better if we get there one step at a time."

Her hand over one of his, she traced his knuckles. It amazed her how a man so capable of a brutal one-punch knockout could be so unreservedly gentle when touching her. "I don't want you to be uncomfortable."

"Because I have a boner, you mean?"

She nodded.

"I can handle it."

She'd sort of like to see that—

He squeezed her. "Mind out of the gutter, babe."

Hearing his amusement made her grin, too. "Sorry."

"Go to sleep, and have sweet dreams."

While so much confusion plagued her brain, she didn't think she could, but with Cannon holding her, exhaustion won out. She closed her eyes and listened to his even, relaxed breaths, felt the heavy thumping of his strong heartbeat against her back. She realized she felt safe, protected. Not from anything specific, but in general terms.

Until she felt it now, with Cannon, she hadn't realized how unsafe she'd felt for so very long.

The sense of well-being allowed exhaustion to creep in. As she slipped into slumber, she did indeed dream of Cannon.

And neither of them thought about their phones.

CANNON FELT HER body sink against his, her breathing deepen as she fell asleep. Thank God. If she'd asked him even one more time to take her, he'd have crumbled. But as raw as he felt, as desperate as he was to get inside her, he knew he wouldn't be able to control himself.

She would deny it, but she needed gentleness, reassurance, a considerate lover.

At the moment, he wasn't capable of that.

Letting out a pent-up breath, he hugged her carefully, protectively.

What the hell had he been thinking?

He'd wanted to sweetly seduce her, to ease her into a sexual relationship.

Instead he'd lost his head and laid her out in front of him. Naked. While he'd still worn his shorts.

He'd gone down on her as if eating her on his couch was an everyday occurrence instead of a fantasy he'd assumed would never happen.

Squeezing his eyes shut, he thought of her sweet taste, how wet she'd gotten for him, how she'd lifted to the stroke of his tongue.

Her broken moans.

The tensing of her slim legs, the fisting of her hands. How her back had arched and her belly had sucked in.

The tears in her eyes after her release had dwindled away, leaving her soft and shaken and dazed.

How she'd looked at him with wonder…just the way she used to.

He gave her ten minutes to make sure she wouldn't awaken, then, knowing he wouldn't be able to sleep, he slipped from the bed, from her bedroom, and went to his own room to relieve himself. It didn't take him long, not with her scent still clinging to him.

When he rejoined her in the bed, less edgy but still in need of her, she shifted in her sleep, turning to face him, snuggling in against his chest.

It took him a very long time to get to sleep, but he'd never enjoyed a sleepless night more, or for a better reason.

MERISSA DIDN'T ALLOW herself time for doubt. *Any excuse in a storm.* Yes, she knew that wasn't how the saying went, but for her and her unique purpose, it worked.

She went up the steps two at a time because if she

hesitated at all she'd chicken out. For the tenth time she checked her watch. Only ten-thirty. Not really late. But just in case... When she reached the right door, she tapped softly. If he was in bed, well, then, no reason to wake him.

She'd barely lowered her hand before the door swung open, and there stood Armie. Flushed, with mussed hair. Shirtless. Barefoot. The button and fly of his jeans opened to reveal a happy trail.

Her heart stuttered and almost stopped.

Until she noticed the redhead draped over his shoulder.

As soon as she did notice, he shrugged the woman off, stepped over the threshold and closed the door behind him.

They stared at each other...and slowly a frown replaced the surprise in his dark brown eyes. "What the fuck, Rissy." He looked around her as if searching for someone. When he realized she was alone, he looked even more furious. "I thought you were Kelli."

Meaning he wouldn't have opened the door mostly naked if he'd known it was her? "Kelli?" She had a hard time keeping her gaze off his body.

"Yeah, she's Avril's friend and..." He looked appalled at himself, which fried his temper and left him brewing like a thundercloud—a thundercloud that had just been wallowing in carnal activity. *"What are you doing here?"*

At almost the same time, she asked, "Kelli *and* Avril?"

The door opened behind him and the redhead, grinning at her wickedly, asked, "Is she joining us or not?"

Merissa stumbled back.

Together, she and Armie both said, *"Not."*

The woman wore only Armie's shirt with mile-high

strappy sandals. Pouting, she reached around him for his fly, her hand dipping inside the open waistband. "Then where's Kelli?"

Armie caught her wrist and held her hand higher— still against his bare, taut skin.

Merissa's heart pounded in sick resentment. She licked her dry lips and started to come up with any excuse to leave. "So I, ah—"

From behind her, a woman said, "Here I am!"

She turned. A blonde. With more boob showing than she had covered. She carried a bottle of wine in one hand, her sandals in the other, and she looked ready to…party.

Eyes narrowed, jaw set, Armie pushed the door open and said to the women, "Wait inside. I'll be there in a minute."

The two women greeted each other with a lingering kiss. Armie watched without interrupting, and when they finally got out of the way, he pulled the door closed again.

Rissy had a difficult time breathing. Okay, sure, she'd heard about Armie's excesses just as she'd heard about his aversion to nice women. Maybe *nice* meant anyone who wouldn't accommodate his overblown sexual appetite.

For far too long he stared at the floor, then finally turned to her. "Why are you here?"

She no longer remembered her excuse. "You…? They…?"

He worked his jaw. "It's a threesome. No big deal. Don't faint."

Armie flaunted the fact that he was a sexual hedonist— and so many women loved that about him.

She wasn't one of them.

Finally finding her voice, she said, "I make no guarantees."

Eying her, he took a step forward. "Shit. You do look pale."

With embarrassment! "I can't believe you—"

Through the door, one woman yelled in a singsong voice, "Hurry up, Armie, or we'll start without you!"

Armie rubbed his mouth, then dropped his hand. "There you go. Seems I'm needed inside, so how about you get to the reason for this little unexpected visit."

No. This was a big mistake; no reason to make it worse with lame excuses. "Never mind." Hugging herself to ward off the chill of humiliation, she turned to go.

Armie caught her upper arm. "Oh, no, you don't." Very close behind her ear, he growled, "Don't leave me in suspense."

She felt the heat of his bare torso all along her back. Her height of five-eleven put him only an inch taller. But where she was thin, he had the bulk and muscle of a fighter.

When she remained mute, he didn't step away. He might have even smelled her hair.

"You shock me," she admitted in a mere breath of sound.

"Back atcha."

Merissa freed herself and turned to face him. "Is that a joke?"

Shaking his head, he tracked his gaze over her. Unlike his lady friends, she was fully dressed in jeans and a sleeveless baby-blue blouse.

Almost unwillingly, he grated, "Every fucking time I see you."

Her jaw loosened. "My God! You have *two* women waiting inside for you—"

"Probably not waiting anymore." His smile taunted her. "They're the impatient sort."

"—and still you flirt with me?"

His bare shoulders bunched. "I wasn't."

Oh. Her confidence suffered, but she faked it, flipping back her long hair and staring him in the eyes. "I thought—"

One big stride brought him chest to breasts with her. He radiated hot anger—and so much more. "You came to me, little girl."

She didn't quail, not from Armie. In a whisper, she asked, "Why are you mad?"

His gaze searched hers, and he jerked away with a curse, turning from her, his hands on his hips, his head dropped forward. Muscles twitched, locked. His chest repeatedly rose with slow, deep breaths.

Merissa stared at his long back, his sun-darkened skin in appealing contrast to his fair hair. The deep furrow of his spine bisected all that firm muscle and without even thinking about it, she followed it down to the paler skin of his taut backside displayed by the loosened, drooping jeans.

Catching herself, she pulled her gaze back up to the tattoo of a winged heart wrapped in barbed wire that rested between his shoulder blades. No color. Just stark black and…sad.

The tats on his arms were different—simple, colorful tribal designs that backed up his badass rep. She doubted they meant anything. But that heart…

He rubbed the back of his neck and muscles shifted everywhere, igniting a secret heat inside her.

"I'm sorry for dropping in," she said softly.

Over his shoulder, he scowled at her, then slowly faced her again.

"I was looking for Cannon, but obviously he's not here." She couldn't imagine her discriminating brother ever participating in a *ménage à trois*. If he did, no one would ever know about it—and it definitely wouldn't be with such extroverted women who might kiss and tell.

Armie's deep brown eyes watched her with a sizzling sort of menace, and she cleared her throat. "I tried calling him, but he didn't answer, and he's not at the hotel. I thought maybe—"

"He's with Yvette."

Why did Armie always keep her at a distance? And why, for the love of God, did that only make her want him more? "Yvette who?"

"Sweeny. You knew her, I think. She's—"

"I do!" Wow, she'd wondered if Yvette would ever return. A million questions went through her mind, but she settled on one in particular. "Why is Cannon with her?"

Armie cocked a brow.

"Oh." Wow again. Cannon and Yvette? Still? It had to have been…what? Three years. In rapid order, she went through the timeline, recalling how Yvette had always crushed on Cannon and how Cannon had helped to rescue her—and how he'd gone off to fight in the SBC and she'd gone off to live in California. "I see."

"I have company waiting, so Cannon can fill you in on everything, but he's at her family home with her. Living with her, actually."

The surprises kept coming. "Since when?"

"Since the get-go, far as I can tell." For the first time that night, Armie gave her a sincere smile. "She arrived and he moved in."

"That was fast."

"Slow, if you ask Cannon."

When Armie smiled, he was the most devastatingly handsome man she'd ever seen. "Slow?"

"Seems he's been waiting on her for a while."

The door opened yet again, and this time the redhead and blonde each wore only their panties.

"Oh, for the love of…" Merissa turned away, anxious to avoid any more embarrassment.

From behind her, she heard hushed words from Armie, whining words from the women, and thought about sticking her fingers in her ears. Instead she concentrated on her retreat.

She'd gotten down ten steps when Armie grabbed her again.

"Hold up, damn it."

"What?" she asked as she turned to face him.

Her temper apparently cooled his. He turned patronizing. "I'm walking you to your car."

"Ha! No way." She started off again.

He didn't argue, but damn him, he followed all the same. Mostly naked. Those worn, faded, open jeans riding low on his lean hips.

Using both hands, Merissa slammed open the wide double entry doors and stalked out into the humid evening air. Security lights warded off any imagined danger, except for the danger of Armie at her back.

Danger to her peace of mind. "Go away, Armie."

Mocking her, he asked, "Why are you so mad?"

"I'm not."

He snorted and tugged on a lock of her hair. "You have steam coming out your ass."

Gasping, she rounded on him. "I do not!"

He scrutinized her. "Maybe your ears, too. And just where the hell did you park?"

"Over there." She pointed to her little—and ancient—blue car.

Hands on his hips, Armie stared where she indicated. "In the dark. Away from the apartment building." His gaze slanted her way. "Just where the hell is your boy-friend?"

She shrugged. Didn't know and didn't really care. He was supposed to pick her up from the airport, but he hadn't shown. Which was fine by her. He wasn't her boyfriend so much as...convenient. Now that he wasn't so convenient, well, then, she had no reason to keep see-ing him.

Knowing she'd have to explain that to him, though, she said, "I'll hook up with him tomorrow."

Both brows lifted. "Hook up?"

"I don't mean that. I mean meet up." She shook her head at him. "Not all of us are oversexed apes."

"I'm not an ape."

She noticed he didn't deny the oversexed part. "Good-bye, Armie."

He followed her. Again. Still.

"You aren't worried that your lady friends will fin-ish without you?"

"If they do, I'll just get them started again. I'm good at that, you know. At revving the engine and—"

When she looked at him, he clammed up, then mut-tered, "Damn it."

"What?"

"I shouldn't talk like that to you."

"You talk like that to everyone."

Ignoring her interruption, he added with more heat, "You shouldn't *let* me. Hell, you shouldn't even be here."

Another smackdown. In every way imaginable he'd let her know she was unwelcome.

While trying to think of a suitable rejoinder, Merissa opened her car door and got in. Already the interior had gotten stuffy, so she rolled down the window, kicked on the engine and turned up the air.

Suddenly Armie was there, his hands braced on the top of the window frame as he leaned down, his face somber, his mood officious. "Don't ever do this again."

Why the sight of his underarms left her flustered, she didn't know, except that the way he stood and what he displayed emphasized his masculinity in a big way.

"Rissy?" he whispered, sounding pained.

She'd heard the nickname most of her life. It sounded very different coming from him, somehow more personal. Preparing herself for his impact, she met his gaze.

As she stared up at him, his face hardened. "Never again." He straightened. "Lock your doors," he ordered before walking away.

At the curb, he looked back with impatience.

Holding up her hands in apology, Merissa closed the window and hit the automatic locks that secured all doors.

He nodded and left.

And with every swaggering step he took, she wanted him more.

Stay away? She doubted she could.

CHAPTER THIRTEEN

JUST INSIDE THE BUILDING, Armie stood aside in the shadows and waited until Rissy's car went past. Jesus. Letting out a tight breath, he dropped back against the wall. His cock hurt and it had nothing to do with the two naked hotties carrying on without him in his apartment.

In fact, now that he'd seen Merissa, he had less than zero interest in either of them. He'd known she was coming home today, and that was the only reason he'd invited Avril over in the first place—as a distraction. It had been Avril's idea to mix things up and invite Kelli to join in. Hell, the more outrageous he got, the more some women vied to keep up.

But not Rissy. No, she'd looked equal parts appalled, disgusted and embarrassed. For him.

He slammed a hand against the wall.

Nice girls were off his list, and Rissy was nicer than most. Add that to the fact she was Cannon's sister and he had no damn business putting thoughts of her in his spank bank.

But he would anyway.

He'd rather jerk off thinking of her big blue eyes and her openmouthed surprised at finding him with his jeans open than be used up by the two nymphos.

Shit, shit, *shit*.

He looked up the stairs. The women wouldn't like it,

but lucky for him, he was enough of a prick that he'd send them packing anyway. Decided, he jogged up the steps.

For his peace of mind, he hoped Merissa kept her distance.

Because he sure as shit couldn't rely on his own control. Not with her.

Not when every damn day he wanted her more.

CANNON WOKE WITH a pounding head and his arms full of soft, warm woman. But not just any woman. Yvette.

Her scent did insane things to him; her warm breath on his chest affected him like a blow job.

He was already so hard that he hurt.

Luckily, she seemed dead to the world. She didn't even stir when he eased her to her back. Her eyelashes left shadows on her cheekbones. Barely parted lips begged for attention, and because he couldn't resist he leaned down for a butterfly kiss. Her long hair poured over her shoulders, making a stark contrast against her pale breasts. And those small pink nipples…

Damn, but he wanted to put his mouth on her, to suckle her softly until her nipples tightened and ached.

Until she woke wanting him as much as he wanted her.

When she made a sound in her sleep, his heart thumped heavily, his cock twitched.

But she only sighed and slept on.

Damn it, he had no business doing this, tormenting himself like a masochist. As quietly as possible, he left the bed, found his shorts on the floor and pulled them on. With one last lingering look at her body, then at her beautiful relaxed face, he snuck out of the room.

He was a fighter, damn it. He had control. He had willpower.

He understood motivation and staying the course despite discomfort to his body. He could and would do this—and in the end, he'd get the prize.

Yvette.

Twenty minutes later, anxious to run off the taut urges before facing her again, Cannon headed out the door. He wore shorts and running shoes, but he had his phone with him in case Yvette woke and called him before he got back.

He saw the writing on his dusty truck as soon as he reached the driveway. "Rissy was here."

Her typical M.O. He'd often found similar notes from her, always short and succinct, whenever he missed her visits. "Rissy was here." That was his cue to get in touch.

He smiled. So his sister was home. He checked his cell and sure enough, the call he hadn't answered last night was from her. He immediately called her back.

She answered on the third ring with an exaggerated groan. "Not all of us get up at the butt crack of dawn, Cannon."

"It's seven-thirty."

"Isn't that what I just said?"

Loving her a lot, he smiled. "You wrote on my truck."

"I wrote in your dust. Seriously, clean the thing."

He circled the truck and noticed footprints that couldn't belong to his sister. "Been busy."

"Yeah." Sounds of her sitting up filtered through the line. "I heard."

Looking around the area and finding nothing more suspicious than an elderly couple smooching on the porch across the street, he asked, "From who?"

Silence. A long, strain-filled silence.

"Rissy?"

"Fighter gossip. You know how the guys are."

He laughed. "You're nuts."

"So how about breakfast? You free?"

"Sure." He wanted to see her. "I can skip my jog."

"No, not now. Around ten?"

"That's damn near lunch, but sure. I'll pick you up."

"No, your truck only seats two and I want you to bring Yvette. Come home. I'll cook."

He paused, frowning. So she knew about Yvette, huh? Maybe the guys were gossiping like a bunch of old hens.

Rather than get into it over the phone, he said, "You just flew in from Japan. Instead of cooking, take the day off. My treat." They could spend the morning together and he could explain…what? That he'd manipulated a bad situation so he could take advantage?

She snorted. "Did you take a day off after you got home?"

Rubbing the back of his neck, Cannon walked around the house, checking every window, but saw nothing amiss. "That's a long story."

"And I can't wait to hear it. So are you taking a break? Can I cook an old-fashioned breakfast or do I need to make puke, puke, puke-wheat pancakes or something?"

Grinning at her antics, Cannon said, "I'd kill for some home fries and bacon."

"And drop biscuits and honey? Yum. I'm on it. Ten o'clock, okay? Don't be late."

He ended the call and clipped the phone to his waistband, but before he could take off, he felt eyes on him.

Turning, he found Yvette in the front doorway. When his gaze met hers she blushed bright red and looked down at her feet.

Morning sunshine poured over her, making her fair skin golden and showing reddish highlights in her dark hair. She wore only a shirt, leaving her beautiful legs on display. He knew for a fact she wasn't wearing a bra, and given how she tugged down the hem of the shirt, he guessed she'd left the panties behind, too.

Fuck the jog. A triathlon wouldn't diminish the lust-inspired need twisting through him.

Looking at her body, he headed back up the walk. "Morning."

Her bare feet shifted. "You were going without me?"

"You looked pretty zoned when I left the bed." When he reached her, he smoothed back her long hair. Her skin was sleep warm, her hair tangled, her eyes heavy—and his cock thickened with wanting her. "Sleep well?"

Nodding, she asked, "You?"

Barely a wink, but he lied. "Yeah." She wouldn't meet his gaze, and he knew it was embarrassment. He never should have rushed things. "I'll wait if you want to get ready."

She shook her head.

Only then did he realize how she held herself. Not just embarrassed, but defensive. Worried. Uncertain.

"Hey." He tipped up her chin. "What is it?"

"I want...I want to be totally up-front and honest. About everything."

"Yeah." He wanted that, too. Nudging her back inside and out of view of passersby, he agreed. "Always."

She shifted her weight from one hip to the other, drawing his attention to her legs again. Like a molten flashback, he remembered her tender thighs against his jaw, the heady taste of her, how she'd moved and the provoking sounds she'd made.

"That was so...unexpected."

"What was?"

"How you made me...come."

He got his gaze off her rack and onto her face in time to see her tongue slick over her bottom lip.

He barely contained a groan. Damn, he was on the ragged edge again. If she touched him just once, he'd go off like a Fourth of July celebration.

Since she was still fussing with the hem of the shirt, he took her hands in his and tried to sound reasonable instead of turned on. "What's on your mind, honey?"

In a sudden rush, she blurted, "I hope you believe me. I mean, you made it seem so easy that now I'm kind of embarrassed for making such a big deal of it." She breathed faster, her hands squeezing his. "But I swear, until last night, I couldn't... I hadn't..."

"We're good together," he told her with satisfaction. And he knew, even if she didn't, that once he got inside her it would be nothing short of mind-blowing.

"No." She shook her head. "It was you."

"It was *us.*"

"But I didn't do anything!" And with accusation, "You wouldn't let me."

He absolutely could not think about her reciprocating right now, not if he wanted to maintain any semblance of control. "I helped you along, true. It's called foreplay, and I loved it. But there was never anything wrong with you."

Pulling away, she hugged her arms around herself. "But don't you see, there was. *Is.* I...I don't know." She pivoted back to him. "I don't want you to think I exaggerated."

Now he was really lost. "What?"

"Don't think that I was somehow using my—" she searched for a word "—my issues, to use you. That I was only telling you things to get pity or to coerce you."

She thought he'd accuse her of making it up? "Yvette—"

"It's not a secret that I always wanted you," she continued in a rush. "Back then, back before—" she swallowed "—before what happened, I'd have done a lot to get your attention."

He reached for her, but she sidestepped him. "I wouldn't use the sympathy card, though, I swear. I would never make up something so pathetic or—"

"Stop it." Pushed too far, Cannon caught her shoulders and brought her around. "You think I'd accuse you of that?"

Her eyebrows lifted at his anger. "I don't know."

"Well, I wouldn't. Jesus, Yvette, I'm not an idiot."

"I never said—"

He kissed her, but only for a second because, damn it, he had a lot to say. "And you're not that manipulative."

Breath left her in a sigh and she touched his bare chest. "You can't know that, Cannon, because you don't really know me. You never did, but now, after so long, well, I've barely been home a week, so how could you?"

She was wrong. On some elemental level, he'd always known her. "I know women." Kissing her again, he backed her up to the wall, leaned into her and continued kissing her until her hands were clutching his shoulders and her mouth was moving under his, just as hungry.

He wedged one thigh between her legs, then lifted his head to suck in air because he'd just verified it.

No panties.

Slowly, dragging out the suspense, he slid his hands down to her hips, holding her still while he wedged in closer to her.

All but straddling his thigh, she stared up at him, her gaze smoky, her lips parted.

He fought it…and lost. Keeping her pinned to the wall, he reached beneath the loose shirt to find warm flesh. Bringing his hands up her body, he raised the shirt so that his hard abs were against her smooth belly, and, God, that was sweet.

"I know women," he repeated against her throat. "Groupies who come after all the fighters. Women who just want a good time. Women who hope to tie me down."

"I don't want to hear about them," she whispered, moving subtly, already aroused.

Knotting his hands in either side of the shirt, he pulled it up more until her breasts were bared.

"I know how to read women. I know how to read you. You're different from all the rest." He breathed hard, then bent to draw on one nipple.

Yvette reacted immediately, arching her back, sinking her hands into his hair. Going on basic carnal instinct more than good common sense, he hooked an arm under her ass and lifted her up.

She wrapped her legs around him.

This was no slow tease. He sucked at her breast, relishing her broken groans, how she twisted against him.

Bracing one hand on the wall by her head, he ground against her.

"Oh, God, oh, God, oh..." Her voice rose. *"Cannon."*

He was about to tear off his shorts and to hell with consequences when Yvette's phone rang.

The sound didn't entirely cut through the lust, but it did slow him down.

"No," she said, her tone pleading. "Cannon, please."

The phone stopped ringing.

He'd just about convinced himself to seal the deal when it started again.

Then again.

She groaned loudly.

"It must be important," he reasoned. "You blocked Heath, right?"

She looked near tears. "Yes."

Torn over what to do, he stepped away from the wall, still holding her, and went to the couch. He sat with her on his lap, facing him, and snagged the phone with one hand.

Using his thumb, he answered. "Hello?"

Silence, before an outraged woman demanded with a touch of panic, "Where's Yvette? Is she all right? Who is this?"

"She's right here," Cannon soothed. "She's fine." Very fine. "Who's calling?"

"I asked first."

So he had to play? "Cannon Colter."

"Oh."

She knew of him? "Your turn."

"Vanity Baker."

Ah, her friend from Cali. Wondering how much Yvette had told her, he said, "Nice to meet you, even if only via cell phone."

"The pleasure is all mine." She made a whistling sound, then said, "Is Yvette there listening?"

"Right here, yeah." About as close as a clothed woman could get.

"The thing is…I have news about her a-hole ex, so do me a favor and stick around, okay?"

Cannon liked her protectiveness, but not her timing.

Or maybe that was spot-on. too, considering he'd just told himself to move more cautiously, which sure as hell didn't include banging her against the wall with very little finesse.

"I'm not going anywhere," he told Vanity.

"Yeah? Good to know."

Yvette watched the exchange with minimal interest. Of course, she straddled his lap and was still breathing hard, so…he cupped her breast and watched her eyes sink shut.

She was every bit as turned on as him, evidenced by the way she kept squirming on his erection.

But, damn it, he didn't want to leave her fractured with need. With regret, he arranged her shirt so that it fully covered her again.

Yvette groaned again.

"So, Cannon," Vanity said. "My girl tells me you're some badass fighter or something."

He smiled. "Or something."

"You're also heroic, right?"

Yvette was starting to look suspicious, so Cannon suggested, "Why don't you just tell me what's on your mind, Vanity?"

"Let me talk to Yvette first."

"Hang on." He held the phone down against the couch. "It's your friend Vanity."

Yvette started to move off his lap, but he wasn't ready to let her go just yet. With a hand on her hip, he stayed her, then caressed. "I like holding you."

She bit her lip, took the phone from him and lifted it to her ear. "Hey, Vanity."

"Why didn't you answer last night?"

Since she'd accidentally just put the phone on speaker, Cannon heard Vanity loud and clear.

Blushing, Yvette said, "I was…"

"What? What were you doing? *O. M. G.* You did the nasty, didn't you?" She squealed. "Tell me. Details."

"Vanity—"

She gasped. "You're in bed with him now, aren't you? That's why he answered?" Another squeal. "Was it hot? Have you been converted? Are you now among the must-have-it crowd?"

Yvette looked so flustered that Cannon grinned. Clearly Vanity knew some of the details.

"His voice is dreamy," Vanity continued before Yvette could get a word in edgewise. "Tell me the bod matches."

Yvette rolled her eyes. "He's ripped."

She said, "Yes!" like a victory yell.

Rushing on, Yvette said, "But we aren't... We haven't..."

"Well, damn. Why not?"

"Mostly because you interrupted," Cannon said. "But I'll forgive you just this once."

Closing her eyes, Yvette said, "You're on speakerphone, Vanity."

Silence. Then in a scandalized whisper, "He was listening the whole time?"

"Yup."

"Well." Shaking off the awkwardness, Vanity said, "*C'est la vie.* I refuse to blush. In fact, jump his bones, I say. He sounds worth it."

"Vanity."

"That's her warning tone, Cannon, just so you know."

Cannon liked Vanity more by the moment. "Thanks."

"And now here's mine—be good to her."

"We already worked that out, didn't we?"

"Maybe. Yvette wouldn't let you near her if you weren't one of the good guys. Which is why old Heath got booted. But I meant sexually. She deserves—"

"Vanity!"

Fighting off a laugh, Cannon said, "Agreed."

"I might visit."

"You'd be more than welcome to stay with us."

"Us?" More silence, and then, "Yvette, you hussy. You moved in with him? Why haven't you called to tell me that?"

"We're sharing her grandfather's house," Cannon explained.

"Tell me there's only one bed, one shower—"

"I'm going to kill you when next I see you." Yvette snatched up the phone to take it off speaker.

Vanity said quickly, "Wait! I want Cannon to hear this."

"If it's advice—"

Vanity snorted. "If he needs it, then you should move on."

Though recent actions couldn't prove it, Cannon said, "I don't."

"Didn't think so. But anyhoo, I wanted to tell you about Heath."

Cannon sat a little straighter, one arm going around Yvette. He had a very bad feeling. "What about him?"

"He hopped a plane last night and, sadly, he's headed your way."

"No," Yvette said. "That's...nuts!"

"Which describes Heath perfectly. He posted on Facebook that he was going, then did a status update at the airport. And get this, he said he's going after what's his. In case that's not clear enough, he means you, toots."

"He means me," Yvette repeated, looking dumbfounded.

"Figuring time difference and flight times, I'm thinking he's probably already there. So you might want to keep an eye out. You remember what an ass he was before you left—"

"Thanks for telling me," Yvette interrupted as she scrambled off Cannon's lap.

Which made Cannon wonder just what Heath had done, and why Yvette didn't want him to know.

One hand in her hair, Yvette said, "I blocked him from my Facebook and from my phone, so I had no idea."

"He's seriously unhinged. I'll keep watch and if I see anything else I'll text you."

"Do me a favor," Cannon said. "If you see anything over-the-top, copy it and send it to me. I'll give you my contact info."

"Will you kick his ass?"

He had no idea what the right answer might be, so he said, "I'm not going to let anything happen to her."

Yvette propped her hands on her hips. "Stop it, both of you. I'm a big girl and I can take care of myself."

The silence following that statement only infuriated her more. She gave a low sound of frustration. "Vanity, thank you. Seriously. You know I love you."

Vanity made kissing sounds into the phone.

"But it might be best if we just ignore Heath—"

"Oh, hell, no. Tried that last time and look where it got us."

She scowled, probably because she realized Cannon would insist on knowing now.

Thanks to Vanity, he didn't even have to ask.

"He broke in," Vanity stated. "He rifled through your stuff. He's an unbalanced perv, Yvette, and you shouldn't forget it."

THEY DIDN'T GET to run, not after Vanity blabbed about Heath. But Cannon got in his exercise by following her around the house and grilling her in great detail.

He paced around her while she drank her coffee and ate a muffin, leaned against the sink as she brushed her teeth, didn't budge when she got out clean clothes, but at the shower, he relented and gave her some privacy.

When she emerged, dressed and slightly refreshed,

Cannon was on a laptop checking out everything he could find about Heath. "I can't see much since we aren't Facebook friends," he said, "but I connected with Vanity."

Which meant he could now see her photos, and he'd know just how gorgeous she was. "And?"

"And what?" He closed the laptop and stood, his gaze going over her in that heated way.

"Did you look at her photos?"

"I saw a few of you with her." Moving closer, he said, "Including one with you in a bikini."

That was what he'd noticed? Next to Vanity, she all but faded away, or so she thought. "Vanity was in a bikini, too."

He cupped her face and bent to her mouth for a soft kiss. "I'm sorry I rushed things again."

The sudden change in topic had her shaking her head. "What?"

"Earlier. Before Vanity called." Another kiss, this one a little longer but also restrained, as if he held himself in check. "I hope you're still hungry."

How did he mean that? "Umm…"

Smiling at her, he kissed her nose and stepped back. "My sister called this morning. She wants us over for breakfast."

Oh. Knowing he meant hungry for actual food instead of sex left her deflated, proof that Cannon had turned her life upside down.

"I'd enjoy that." She and Rissy had known each other through school, had been casual friends back then, but hadn't been close enough to stay in touch.

"Good. On the drive there, you can tell me more about Heath breaking in."

Within minutes they were on the road, but it'd be a

short trip so she got right to it. Hoping her private business could stay private, she wanted to finish up this discussion before they reached his sister's. "I'm not sure what else I can tell you, Cannon, but I'll try."

"You said you came home and the place was trashed. You had stuff missing."

"Not cash or anything valuable. All of my electronics were still where I'd left them, but someone had been going through my emails and my Facebook. My, um…" Knowing how Cannon would react, she decided to just get it said. "My panty drawer had been dumped."

His hands tightened on the wheel but he said nothing.

"I tend to buy matching bra and panties, so I realized some pieces were missing."

"He sounds sick and desperate."

That about covered it, which was why she refused to take his calls. "He gave everything back."

Incredulous, Cannon glanced at her. "Are you making excuses for him?"

"No! It's just…well, it was kind of pathetic. Desperate, like you said." And she had to admit, to herself if not to Cannon, she'd felt guilty for hurting him so much.

"I'm guessing he didn't do any time?"

"He was never arrested."

More squeezing of the steering wheel. "Why not?"

"I knew when I saw the mess that it was Heath. I was so furious that I called him and set him straight."

Cannon grunted at that, making his opinion of her tactics for handling it understood.

Defending *herself* and her decisions, she forged on. "He fessed up, apologized profusely, gave back my stuff and for the most part has left me alone."

"For the most part?"

She hated how the day had gone sour, especially when

it had started with that amazing kiss and the promise of more.

Against a wall.

Pinned there by Cannon's hot, hard body.

She got tingly all over again just thinking about how urgent he'd been. She wanted to have sex. She wanted to know it all.

And instead she was stuck talking about stupid Heath.

She needed the day to improve.

She needed…Cannon.

Distractedly wrapping two fingers in a long lock of hair, she tried to defuse his mood. "As you already know, he's started sending the occasional resentful text. I plan to ignore it. To ignore *him*. I hope you'll do the same."

Cannon pulled into the driveway of his family's modest house, now his sister's home, put the truck in Park and turned off the engine. The seconds ticked by in silence before he took out the keys and shifted toward her, his blue eyes impossibly bright in the morning sunshine.

"I'll think about it." He gently untangled her hair from her fingers, then lifted her hand to kiss her knuckles. "Unless he shows up here and tries to hassle you. Then all bets are off."

CHAPTER FOURTEEN

ARMIE COULDN'T BELIEVE he'd been summoned to Rissy's house. Damn and double damn, he didn't want to see her again. Not this soon.

No matter that he'd gotten to the gym early, that he'd lifted weights, done cardio and pounded the heavy bag until he'd been drenched with sweat, he hadn't yet recovered from that close encounter with her last night.

When he pulled up to the curb, he saw Cannon, Yvette and Rissy all standing beside Cannon's truck. Rissy wore shorts, so his attention snagged on her until he caught himself. Never mind that the temps were nudging upward of the mid-nineties. He knew why he was suddenly too hot, and it didn't have a damn thing to do with the weather.

When he got out, Yvette approached. "Hi."

"Hi, Yvette." He struggled not to look beyond her at Rissy. "What's up?"

Pinched with worry, she gestured to the truck. "Vandalism."

All four tires were flat.

Cannon crouched down by the back passenger tire. "Nails in all of them."

With a long whistle, he joined Cannon on his haunches. "You drive through a damned construction site?"

"Nope."

"Huh." The look Cannon gave him spoke volumes—he thought someone had fucked with his truck. Alarm took Armie back to his feet. "That happen here, or at Yvette's?"

"I'm guessing at home." Cannon stood, too. "If the nails were fresh, the tires wouldn't be flat already. But we got here for breakfast around ten, so…" He shrugged.

A couple of hours ago, then, since it was now high noon. "Still," Armie said. "I'm thinking it might be a good idea to load up on some security here."

Cannon strode over to the other side of the truck, away from the women.

That suited Armie perfectly. Fuck if he couldn't *feel* Rissy right there, only a few feet away. The more distance he put between them, the easier he'd breathe.

He looked at Yvette. "Mind grabbing me something cold to drink?"

Yvette said, "Oh, uh…" She glanced at Rissy.

He did not.

"They want privacy," Rissy said with a huff. "He knows better than to send me off on a made-up errand, but I guess he figures you're easier to dupe."

"Or just nicer," he heard himself say. Then he cursed under his breath.

From the other side of the truck, Cannon tried to play referee. "Play nice, Rissy."

She feigned innocent confusion, making an O of her mouth and batting her eyelashes in an exaggerated way. "But I thought you wanted Armie's help? And if I'm *nice,* won't that scare him into next week?"

"Rissy," Armie warned, with no effect at all.

"He's liable to scream in terror and run away, then how can he assist you?"

"Actually," Cannon said, saving his ass from saying

something he'd later regret, "I'm thirsty, too. So how about a couple of cold ones?"

"For you, sure." She hooked her arm through Yvette's and dragged the poor confused girl along with her.

Armie watched them walk away—until Cannon gave him a shove, half knocking him into the side of the truck.

He hadn't even noticed Cannon coming close again. "What the hell?"

"You were picturing another threesome, and shit like that just might get you killed."

Appalled, Armie straightened with knotted fists. "The hell I was! One is your sister." And never would he involve her in anything that sordid, not even in make-believe. When he thought about sex with Rissy—and yeah, he did—it was only the two of them. "The other is your girlfriend. I'll admit I'm a bastard, but I'm not that low."

Cannon considered him, then hitched his shoulders and rolled his head as if trying to loosen his coiled muscles. "Sorry."

Taking pity on him, Armie lightened his tone. "Actually, I was kind of amused at the differences. I mean, with Rissy so damned tall." So leggy. "And Yvette so petite. Other than the long dark hair, they're as mismatched as can be."

"Yeah." Cannon ran both hands through his hair and paced away.

Crossing his arms and leaning back on the truck, Armie read his agitation. "So what's really going on?"

"Her fucked-up boyfriend might be in town."

"No shit?"

"Her girlfriend called last night and said Heath had hopped a plane. He posted some nonsense on his Facebook about reclaiming what's his."

"You think he's already here?" He nodded at the tires. "You think he did this?"

"No idea, but I don't like it."

"What can I do to help? Besides giving you a ride today, I mean."

"Would you mind helping me put up that extra security here that you mentioned?"

Oh, hell, no. He swallowed. "Here?"

"Yeah." Cannon watched the door. "I don't want to alarm Rissy or Yvette, but I've got a bad feeling about things."

"Her ex is that bad?"

"Maybe. From what Yvette's told me, he's the stalker type. But I swear, it feels like more than that."

Rissy worked during the day. He could get Stack or Miles to cover things at the rec center and come by then so that he didn't have to butt heads with her.

So he didn't have to resist her.

"Yeah, sure. Glad to help out. You know that." Armie figured they could wrap it up in just a few hours. Surely he could keep it together that long.

"Hey, guys."

They both looked up to see a sleep-rumpled Cherry Peyton approach with two dewy cans of Coke. Her dark blond hair bounced as she walked and mascara was smudged under her brown eyes.

"Cherry." Now, there was a woman he could lust after, Armie thought. "Did we wake you?"

She wrinkled her nose. "Rissy did. Slamming cabinets and cursing you."

He drew back. "Me? What'd I do?" But yeah, he knew.

All teasing and flirting, she leaned in. "Now, Armie, what haven't you done?"

The grin slipped in on him. "You got me there." He took a Coke from her.

She handed the other to Cannon.

"Thanks." Cannon popped the tab. "Late night?"

Covering a jaw-stretching yawn, she nodded. "We got in late," she said around her hand. "Then I couldn't get to sleep. I tossed and turned and finally passed out this morning."

Charmed by her, Armie grinned. Yeah, he knew Denver was sweet on her so he wouldn't overstep. But he could have some fun all the same. "A drink might've helped."

"Tried that, actually, with a glass of wine."

"Then maybe it was a man you needed."

Cannon cautioned him with a scowl.

Laughing, Cherry smacked his arm, then admitted, "Maybe," before sauntering off again.

Her snug sleep shorts and a clingy tank top looked sexy enough to keep his thoughts occupied watching her walk.

As she disappeared through the front door, Cannon opened his mouth—and Armie said, "Save it. It's too late. I already have that fantasy locked away."

"Armie," he warned.

"Fuck off, Cannon." Without any real animosity, he said, "She's not your sister, not your girlfriend, and my imagination is not under your purview. I can damn well fantasize about her if I want to."

"Listen to you talking all fancy."

Armie froze, winced and turned to see Rissy standing there. Eyes narrowed. Arms crossed. One foot tapping.

Damn, she was hot. "Hey, Stretch. Way to sneak up on a guy."

After a burning glare, she dismissed him. "I have to take off," she said to Cannon.

"You're working today?"

"No, I don't start back until Monday, but I got a call from Steve. He was supposed to pick me up last night and was a no-show. Took Cherry and me an hour to catch a cab."

"Why didn't you call me?" Cannon asked.

"I did, remember? You didn't answer." Grinning, she waved away his automatic apology. "We made it home safe and sound, no biggie. Anyway, Steve just called. He said he's laid up. Something about getting jumped and beat up."

Wasn't easy, but Armie managed to keep his face blank, even when Cannon stared at him. Steve was a damned liar, but whatever.

Rissy didn't look real concerned over her boyfriend's plight, he noted. "You're going to go play nurse, huh? Sounds kinky."

Cannon shoved him again.

But Rissy forestalled her brother's temper by saying, "Actually, I'm mostly just going there to tell him we're over."

While Armie staggered, at least figuratively, Cannon asked, "Why? What happened?"

"Nothing, really. I just realized I didn't miss him while I was in Japan. I had more fun with Cherry than I would have if Steve had gone along. That's pretty telling, don't you think?"

Always the supportive big brother, Cannon said, "I think you're smart enough to know what you're doing."

She shrugged. "Hope so, because there aren't any other prospects currently on the horizon."

Armie worked his jaw. Was she hinting? For his benefit?

Ha. Not happening. He wasn't a dope. And she damn well knew how he felt about—

"I hate to run off." She fretted with her purse strap. "Do you still have a key?"

Cannon nodded. "Don't sweat it, hon. We're taking off anyway."

"Well, if you do need to go back in, Cherry will be here, but I think she might be going back to bed." She pointed at Armie. "Not a word out of you."

Forgetting what he'd been about to say, something to do with Cherry and a bed and not sleeping, Armie closed his mouth.

Keeping a cautious eye on him, Rissy slowly moved her gaze back to Cannon. "If you find yourself with extra free time, give me a call."

Cannon hugged her close. "Will do."

She leaned her head against him. "I like her, Cannon. Don't screw it up, okay?"

Laughing, Cannon mussed his sister's hair, kissed her forehead and let her go.

Armie made a point of not looking at her. Hell, he tried not to look at Cannon either. But Rissy had no sooner pulled away from the curb than Cannon stared him down.

Cannon was good at that, but then, so was Armie. "What?"

"Why the hell didn't you tell me it was Steve you fought with?"

Seeing no reason to deny it, Armie snorted. "There was no fight to it, that's why. He and his punk friends jumped me, got in a few licks and then ended up limping away. You heard Rissy. The wuss is still lazing in bed, no doubt milking it for her benefit." Disgruntled by the idea, he muttered, "Bastard is probably hoping to appeal to her softer side."

"What do you know of my sister's softer side?"

"Only that she hides it well." He clapped Cannon on the shoulder. "We going to call someone about the tires or what?"

"Roadside service is on the way. Soon as they get here we can take off. I just need you to drop Yvette and me off at home. We'll use her car to go to the rec center. Stack wants me to meet some of the new kids. As it is, I'm cutting it close."

"Let's get to it, then."

"Right." Folding his arms over his chest, Cannon went all stern and insistent. "Soon as you tell me what happened with Steve."

"I already did."

"Not by a long shot."

Knowing Cannon well enough to see he wouldn't let it go, Armie shrugged. Why not? He'd censor appropriately and if anything, Cannon would thank him. "I heard him shooting off his mouth, that's all."

His expression went dark. "About Rissy?"

Shaking his head, Armie said, "No." He'd have done more than knock him around for that. "About some other chick he's banging. As in, sleeping with while Rissy was in Japan."

Cannon's arms dropped. "He was cheating on her?"

Just the umbrage Armie had counted on. "Yeah, and from what he said, it's happened before. He went into a nauseating amount of detail about how the chick was desperate and easy—and finished off by saying with Merissa out of town, he had to take his pleasure where he could."

"So he did talk about her."

Rushing, Armie said, "You don't need to do anything."

"Because you already did?"

"Uh…" Yeah, that about covered it. But he didn't want to give the wrong impression. "You heard Rissy. He's already a beaten dog. Why dirty your hands finishing him off?"

Cannon seemed to be considering things. "They weren't really locked down."

"Don't defend him."

"Wouldn't." He looked at Armie. "I'm just saying, Rissy doesn't like to get too tight with anyone. They might have had an understanding, I'm not sure on that. But any guy who'd go bragging to his buddies is an asshole anyway."

"Exactly." He'd followed the putz, not trusting him after he'd also made a few jokes about getting the woman high and needing to stock up his supply before Merissa got home.

Unfortunately, Steve was a paranoid putz, so when he felt he was being followed, he'd reacted by having his buddies circle around on Armie.

"How bad did you hurt him?"

"Bad enough."

"Details."

"I might've broken his jaw, probably a finger or two. Possibly even his hand." Armie gave it some thought. "I wasn't exaggerating about him limping either, but his knee should be okay. Just sore for a few days."

"Jesus." Cannon choked on a laugh. "Anything else?"

Armie narrowed his eyes. How the hell could Cannon find any humor in this? "I landed a nut shot, so even if Rissy makes up with him, he won't be any use to her for a while."

That wiped away all signs of humor. "I don't want to think about that."

"You're a wuss, too."

"Says the guy without a sister." Cannon started moving stuff from his truck to Armie's SUV. "I have to say, though, you play the big brother well. Thanks for looking out for her."

Yeah...brotherly thoughts had never occupied his mind, not where Merissa Colter was concerned. "My pleasure."

"I'm wondering now, though, if we should tell her before she sees him."

"Naw." Rissy was smart. She'd see through Steve's bullshit, if she hadn't already. "If she suddenly makes up with him, then sure, we'll tell her." Or rather, Cannon could tell her. Because he'd be keeping his distance.

By the time they finished jawing and moving stuff to Armie's ride, roadside service showed up. While Cannon talked with them, Armie went inside to get Yvette.

He followed laughing female voices to the kitchen table. Yvette and Cherry sat together discussing fighters, and he listened in without a speck of remorse.

Still giggling, Cherry said, "Guys just crack me up."

"They do keep things interesting," Yvette agreed.

Now, what was that about? Armie listened, but apparently he'd missed the joke.

"It's too bad you couldn't have gone to Japan with us. We had a great time."

"I bet. I've only ever seen one live fight."

Armie was fairly certain Cannon would change that. If he knew his friend, and he did, Cannon would want her close by from now on.

"Hopefully Cannon will have some time off before he's offered another fight."

Yvette sat back in the chair, long legs crossed, one arm folded under her breasts, the other hand playing with the ends of her hair.

It was one of those feminine habits that Armie adored. Women like Yvette could be so damned sexy without even realizing it. He enjoyed seeing a woman fuss with her nails, reapply her lipstick, smooth a tight skirt... Course, he never saw any of that with Rissy and he was damn near blind with lust for her.

"Should be at least a few months," Yvette said, "but so far it never seems to work out that way for him."

"Rissy says he's quick to take every opportunity to fight."

"And he's a fan favorite." Yvette smiled. "He loves the sport. But then, so do I. I started watching because of Cannon, but now I'm hooked."

"I like the fighters, and their hot bodies," Cherry admitted with a grin. "But the actual sport confuses me. The weight classes, the rules, the moves. Sometimes it'll look as if a guy's losing and then somehow he wins. Or a guy who looks really tough isn't, and vice versa."

"It's more heart than physique." Yvette let out a dramatic sigh. "Luckily Cannon has both."

"Denver's body..." Cherry shivered. "He's pretty hot, don't you think?"

"Heck, they *all* are."

"I'm curious if they look that delicious all over."

"Probably. I haven't seen a dud in the bunch." As if in deep thought, Yvette rearranged her cold drink. "They all seem pretty nice, too. But Cannon is special."

Cherry teased her, saying, "You'd know, since you get the up-close-and-personal view."

"Maybe," Yvette teased back.

"I love Denver's shoulders. And his thighs."

Armie was about to laugh.

Then she added, "And Armie's arms. And Stack's chest. They're all so sexy."

Poor Denver. Not quite stealing the show yet. Though he'd have loved to listen in a little longer, Armie announced himself by tapping on the wall. "Knock, knock."

Both women swiveled around to stare at him, surprise quickly morphing into guilt.

He put on his wickedest grin. "Caught you gossiping, didn't I? And about superficial stuff like a guy's body." Putting a hand over his heart, he tsked. "I'm crushed. I thought women were more enlightened, caring only about feelings and shit like that."

Mortified heat bloomed in Cherry's face, turning her cheeks bright red.

Yvette shook a finger at him. "You have a bad habit of showing up at inopportune times."

"And here I thought my timing was perfect when I found you at the local po—"

"Armie!"

Grinning, he relented. Oh, he'd tease her about the porn store from now until eternity, might even buy her a few pornos for her birthday, but in front of others he'd curb it.

He liked to tease, but he didn't really want to embarrass her.

"Next thing," Armie teased, taking a different route, "you'll be telling me size does matter."

Regaining her aplomb, Cherry slowly rose from her seat. "Oh, I dunno. Like with boobs, bigger is better." She put her shoulders back, which made Armie's attention drop to her chest. "But I say it's more about how you use it."

"Yeah? Tell me more, and don't leave out any details."

With a strained smile, Yvette pushed back her chair and stood. "I'm going to see if Cannon needs any help."

So the casual flirting bothered her? Armie watched her leave the kitchen, unsure what he could say to put her more at ease.

He turned back to Cherry. "You want to see a fighter's physique up close and personal, huh?"

She faltered, her teasing used up. "Just how long were you snooping?"

"Long enough to hear about your curiosity. And I have a solution." Just to unsettle her, he touched the snap on his jeans.

Her reaction was priceless.

He couldn't wait to tell Denver about it.

"Relax." Touching her chin to close her mouth, he said, "I'm not planning to strip for you."

"Wow." She went limp with relief, but said, "Truthfully, I'm a little disappointed."

"Don't be." Cherry had wit, he'd give her that. Wit and guts, blond hair, big brown eyes and definitely a nice rack. No wonder Denver was smitten. "I have it on good authority that Denver would happily give you a show—and he's the best-hung one in the bunch." He winked and headed out.

Leaving Ms. Cherry Peyton speechless behind him.

When he glanced back, he saw her drop into her seat, eyes closed, one hand on her chest, the other fanning her face.

If she took the bait, Denver would owe him big time.

OVERALL, YVETTE FELT like the day had gotten back on track.

She liked Cannon's sister a lot. Not once did Rissy bring up the past, though of course she was aware of everything that had happened. Her brother had played a major role in her rescue after all. But Rissy was warm and welcoming, focused on the present instead of the past and openly anxious to get to know Yvette all over again.

They talked mostly about fighting. Cannon's sister knew nearly as much about it as Cannon himself. And since Yvette understood quite a bit, she'd enjoyed every word.

Amid his protests, Rissy gave insight into Cannon's home life. Though they'd all been laughing, Yvette had to admit he seemed like the quintessential big brother. Capable and protective and loving.

They'd all agreed to get together again soon.

After Armie took them to get her car, they headed to the rec center.

Along the way, Cannon seemed distracted, alternately watching the road and...touching her. Her hand, her knee.

Other, more tantalizing places.

He was attentive to her, but not as focused as usual.

She understood that he was concerned about the damage to his truck, and she prayed that Heath hadn't had anything to do with it. When she'd mentioned paying for the damage, just in case, Cannon flatly refused, then changed the subject.

"Did you enjoy yourself?"

"Your sister is terrific."

He smiled. "Yeah."

"I like Cherry, too."

"Apparently everyone does, especially Denver."

It'd be nice to have some girlfriends. "The three of us might go shopping later in the week."

"Sounds good." He checked the rearview mirror

again, then said, "We could invite everyone over one night, too, if you want."

Their own little party. "I'd enjoy that." In so many subtle ways, Cannon made her feel a part of his life.

He pulled up in front of the rec center. "We'll be here for a while. If you get bored or need to leave, let me know first, okay?"

"I won't." Then she rethought that. "As long as I'm not in the way…"

Leaning over, Cannon caught her nape and pulled her in for a lingering kiss. "You won't be."

On his way in, Stack knocked on the driver's window. "Get a room."

Grinning, Cannon said, "Ignore him. He's green with envy."

After they went in, Yvette put up with some teasing, but it was all good-natured and she didn't mind at all.

The guys were all so different in some ways, but so very much alike in others.

They enjoyed trying to make her blush.

As Cannon had said, they were at the rec center through dinner. Yvette relished getting to know more about Cannon's world. He was great with the kids. All the guys were, but Cannon was the best-known fighter there and the boys idolized him.

The crowd changed in the late afternoon, with older boys coming in, more men who paid for training, a few women. Cannon stayed busy with individual coaching first, then by leading a class. In between that he talked with fans, took photos, signed a few autographs and checked with her often, no matter how many times she assured him she was fine.

She loved watching him, seeing his strength mixed with gentleness. The fluid way his muscled body moved, whether he was demonstrating for the older boys or tussling with the younger. When he laughed, her heart beat harder and emotion swelled inside her.

She stood off to the side now, talking with the grandparents of two of the boys. They raved about Cannon, not just about how he'd influenced their son in a positive way but how he'd helped with their business, successfully and peacefully getting drug peddlers moved away from their corner.

She had no real rights, but pride nearly took away her breath.

She was lost in thoughts of Cannon, of his overwhelming presence, when from behind her a thick male voice whispered, "Hello, Yvette."

Shock sent tension down her spine, and she jerked around to see Heath standing there. He smiled, a sheepish, happy smile, not at all threatening—but damn him, she knew better.

He'd actually done it, actually followed her.

From California.

Reaching out, he touched her hair with near reverence, smoothing a long tendril behind her ear. "Cat got your tongue?"

The older couple moved away, giving them privacy, and when they did Heath enveloped her, hugging her despite her lack of welcome.

She had to get it together. Right now. "Heath." Hands on his shoulders, she levered herself away.

With obvious reluctance, he let her put distance between them.

Yvette took a step back. Heath Nordan in no way resembled a stalker creep. At six feet tall, his athletic body visible beneath an expensive polo shirt and pleated slacks, his dark hair neatly trimmed and his smile bright with welcome, he fit right in with the other men at the rec center.

Big, handsome, muscular. Happy.

To see her.

CHAPTER FIFTEEN

YVETTE SHOOK HER head to clear it. She didn't bother hiding her frustration. "What in the world are you doing here?"

As if it should have been obvious, he said, "I came to see you."

Oh, Lord. She refused to look back for Cannon. She knew if she did, if he met her gaze, he'd get dragged into her personal drama.

Yvette put a hand on Heath's arm, urging him toward the opposite side of the gym, and hopefully out of view of the fighters. "When did you get here?"

"Early this morning."

So he could have been the one to damage Cannon's tires. Petty destruction was certainly his speed.

Now some distance away, on the other side of the registration area, she again moved a few feet from him. "How'd you find me?"

He laughed, and the fact that his laugh sounded so normal, merely amused instead of insane, didn't reassure her.

"It wasn't hard." Again, he reached out to touch her, but Yvette dodged him, earning a slight frown. Showing his disappointment in her, he dropped his hand. "You're hanging out with a famous fighter, who hangs out here." He rolled one shoulder. "Didn't take a sleuth to figure out you'd be here."

But how did he know she'd be here *now?* The idea of him maybe watching her, following her, was so repugnant that she wasn't sure how to proceed.

"Say something," he told her, teasing, expectant.

She tried to smooth out her frown but couldn't, and that made him frown. "Heath—"

"Don't tell me to go."

Ah. There was that unbalanced voice she'd been waiting for. It reeked of demand and desperation, underlaid with simmering rage.

"That's what you have to do and you know it. You *have* to go."

He reached out again, and this time dodging him did her no good. He locked that big, hard hand on her upper arm and, oh, God, she felt it—his determination. His intent.

Too tight. Unbreakable.

He'd never before manhandled her. But then again, he'd had a series of nasty texts to build him up to this point.

With one small tug, he brought her closer so that she almost bumped into him. "I've missed you," he insisted, as if she should be thrilled to hear it. "I've missed *us.*"

Straining away, Yvette stated, "There is no us." She tried to wiggle free, but he only clamped down harder until she winced.

"Don't say that." His gaze went a little wild. "Don't ever say that. You know you don't mean it."

If she weren't in such a public place, she'd give in to the urge to fight. One yell and men would be there to help her, Cannon at the front.

She knew that, and knowing it helped calm her.

Right now, she mostly wanted to avoid a scene. She'd

been at the forefront of too much ugly news already. "Listen to me, Heath…"

"There you are." Wearing only boxing shorts and fingerless gloves, his blond hair spiky with sweat, Armie invaded their space.

Did the man live at the rec center?

He had his dark gaze zeroed in on Heath, and as he looked him over, his brows lifted.

"Armie," she said with relief. "Hi."

"Hi, Yvette," he said in that teasing way she'd already grown accustomed to. Still with one brow quirked, he mused, "You got a type, don't you, doll? Big, dark…" He shook his head. "For some reason, I expected him to be different. Softer, shorter. Dopier looking."

So Cannon had told Armie about Heath?

"Who are you?" Heath demanded. "Another boyfriend?"

"Naw. I'm just the guy who's going to break a few of your limbs if you don't turn her loose real quick."

Not a single ounce of animus could be heard in his tone. In fact, Armie might have been discussing the weather.

"You're not dating her?"

"Nope." He took a drink from his water bottle. "You have to the count of three, my man. One, two—"

To her surprise, Heath let her go.

As if he'd expected no less, Armie took another drink.

Yvette resisted the urge to rub her arm, unwilling to do anything that might set Armie off. Sidling closer to him, she said in a low voice, "Time for you to go, Heath."

"I came all this way to see you. I'm not leaving until we talk."

Armie looked at her. "You interested in talking to Slick? Or should I boot his ass to the curb?"

Damn it. Armie was spoiling for a fight, and that'd only draw the attention of everyone in the place.

"Take it easy, Armie. Please. I'd as soon avoid causing a scene if I can, okay?"

He laughed. "Now, honey, you gotta know I don't mind a scene."

Mouth tight, she said, "You might not, but I do."

"So I can't rough him up?"

Heath worked his jaw. "I'm allowed to be here. It's a public place."

"Not really, no," Armie told him.

Quickly, Yvette interrupted. "If you have something to say, Heath, say it and then get out." If Armie told him that Cannon owned the rec center, it just might become the victim of vandalism. She couldn't bear bringing more trouble to him.

She'd done enough of that already.

Heath bristled, Armie smirked at him and she racked her brain to find a way to defuse things without having Heath misconstrue her intentions.

Suddenly an arm slipped around her and Cannon's familiar heat enveloped her. In front of God and Heath and everyone else, he tipped up her chin and put his mouth to hers. He didn't prolong things, but neither was it a simple peck.

Against her parted lips, he asked, "Why wasn't I invited to this little party?"

On a silent groan, Yvette closed her eyes.

His breath touched her ear, and he said so softly only she could hear, "Have a little faith, honey."

Then, still with one arm cuddling her, he held out his hand to Heath. "I'm Cannon."

Eyes bright with hatred, Heath stared at him. "I know who you are."

Cannon didn't miss a beat. "Heath, right? How are you?"

Nonplussed, Heath looked at the proffered hand... and warily accepted it. There was no one-upmanship, no breaking grips or anything beyond a friendly greeting.

Cannon was cool personified.

"I'm fine." Heath's gaze went from Armie to Yvette to Cannon. He shoved his hands in his pockets. "Tired actually, after my trip. I'd like to talk to Yvette before I go back to my room to rest up."

Armie made a show of cracking his knuckles and neck. The caveman.

For only a split second, Cannon smiled at his friend. "I've got this, Armie. Why don't you go finish up the demonstration for me?"

"You never let me have any fun." Armie walked off with the same easy attitude he'd used to approach.

Anger swelling, Yvette eyed both men. Beyond wanting to avoid an ugly public confrontation, she didn't want Cannon fighting her battles.

"So." Staying relaxed, nonthreatening, Cannon shrugged. "She doesn't want to talk to you."

Heath stiffened anew. "You don't speak for her."

"Wouldn't even try," Cannon said. "She speaks for herself, and we both know she's been clear."

"More than clear," Yvette said. "Multiple times."

Unwilling to accept that, Heath leveled his most intimidating glare on her. "You've gotten awfully lippy."

Both men looked at her, Heath with anger, Cannon with support. "I'm fed up, Heath. How else can I say it? We're done and there's nothing else to talk about."

"You sure you want to take that tone?" He ignored Cannon and focused only at her. "After everything?"

When Cannon tightened, she put a hand on him to

let him know she could handle it. Sure, she was shaking. Mortified. Nervous. But she would not let Heath cow her. "I'll take whatever tone is necessary for you to understand."

Heath started to take a step closer and Cannon moved into his path. "No."

Around him, Heath said, "I know you better than anyone else. I know you better than *he* ever could. You might want to remember that."

Her lips felt stiff, her eyes burning. "You couldn't be more wrong."

"Yeah, right." His mocking gaze went to Cannon. "She tell you all about her hang-ups?"

"That's none of your business," Yvette said.

"Far as I can tell," Cannon added, "she's perfect."

Heath went red faced with rage—a rage he aimed at Yvette. *"So you're fucking him?"*

She flinched at his raised voice. If she looked, would everyone in the place be staring at them?

"Whoa." Cannon moved her behind him. "That's enough."

"Fuck you, too!"

As she'd seen him do before, Heath went from zero to eighty in the blink of an eye.

"Here's the thing," Cannon said, still calm with a quiet authority that unnerved Heath more than a shouting match ever could. "You're not going to talk to her alone. Not today, not ever. If you want to talk to her at all, it'll be when you're calm, and I'll be there. Even then, it's only if Yvette agrees. Right now, she doesn't."

"She never does!"

"With the way you're acting, can you blame her?" He let that sink in, then added, "I know you don't want to upset any of the other nice people who are here, many of them kids."

As if only then remembering the public locale, Heath's gaze scanned the room.

"We don't want anyone calling the cops, right? So how about you go cool down and think about things?"

Heath bunched and unbunched, but by some miracle he held himself in check.

"Where are you staying?" Cannon asked. "Nearby? Close enough that we can get together later and talk?"

Understanding why he asked, Yvette stayed quiet.

Suspicion increased Heath's color. "We?"

"You and me."

He looked beyond Cannon to where Yvette stood, arms crossed, her face hot.

Cannon stepped into his line of vision. "Look at me, Heath. Not her."

"I'm at the Colonial."

"I know where it is," Cannon said. "I've stayed there myself before when I visit town."

"You don't live here?"

"Not full-time." Cannon started edging him toward the front door. "You have a card or anything? I'll give you a call and we can arrange a time to sit down and settle this. What do you think?"

With pronounced longing, Heath looked back, trying to see her, but Cannon kept his attention with his hand on his shoulder. "Breakfast, maybe? Or lunch?"

Outmaneuvered, Heath nodded. "Sure, that'd be fine." He dug a card from his wallet and handed it over, but then planted his feet at the door. "Understand, though, I will talk with her." He looked back at Yvette again. "I gave you time. I tried to be understanding. You've dodged me long enough."

And with that, he slammed out.

Frozen to the spot, Yvette admired how well Cannon had handled that. Unlike her, he hadn't gotten distraught. He hadn't gotten physical either, as Armie had wanted to do.

Maybe it was Cannon's extreme ability that kept him from needing to react. He could handle whatever Heath did and knew it, so why get riled up about it?

When Cannon stayed at the door, making sure Heath actually drove away, she ducked around the corner and headed for the break room. With every step she felt eyes on her, everyone watching, everyone speculating.

Again.

Keeping her head up and her gaze straight ahead, she tried not to race away. Cannon deserved so much more than the trouble she brought him. He deserved more than a spectacle.

Damn it, she was working on it. No way would she let Heath ruin her progress.

DOING HIS BEST to hide his rage, Cannon watched Heath go to his car, noted the make and model, the plates, and waited until the bastard disappeared around the corner.

He turned and wasn't at all surprised to see Yvette gone and Armie there.

"She's in the break room," Armie said low. "She walked off like the queen, but she's upset. Makes me want to choke that bastard."

"Yeah, I know, but I'll handle it," Cannon said.

"Anything I can do?"

"Call the Colonial and ask for Heath Nordan. See if you can leave a message for him. I want to make sure that's where he's at."

"Sure thing." Armie kept pace beside him. "I'm betting he's the one who dicked with your tires."

"If it isn't, then I have more than one problem, don't I?" He left Armie at the reception desk to make the call and headed toward the break room.

Stack cut him off. "She okay?"

"She will be." After he reassured her—which he planned to do right now.

Denver blocked his way. "You need anything?"

He shook his head. "Got it covered, thanks."

Miles and Brand crowded in, too. Cannon almost laughed. Yvette had an entire army at her disposal, whether she realized it or not.

"Just keep an eye out," Cannon told them, already knowing they would. They did it for the entire neighborhood.

They'd sure as hell be extra vigilant for one of their own.

And she was. Yvette might not realize it yet, but she'd been accepted into the inner circle, even if that hadn't been her intention.

He found her seated at the table, spine straight, shoulders back, pose as proud as she could make it.

For a few seconds he just stood there looking at her, taking in her features, that long hair, the trim body. In so many ways, more than just the physical, she turned him on.

She hadn't bothered with a drink. Her hands rested, calm and still, on the tabletop, but he saw the pulse beating in her throat, the way she breathed too deeply.

Now that he'd met Heath, he better understood why she thought she had a problem. In a dozen different ways, as soon as humanly possible, he'd show her—again— that she didn't.

Not with him.

"Hey."

At his soft voice, she looked up. Their gazes held. "He's gone?"

"Yeah." Cannon came on in, but he didn't sit. Instead he pulled her up and out of her chair and into his arms.

She resisted. "You asked where he was staying so you could check up on him, didn't you?"

He nodded.

"You won't actually meet with him, will you?"

"I doubt he'll agree to it, but if he does, sure." With one finger, he traced her mouth. "What better way to make things clear to him."

She ducked her head. "We need to talk."

"Okay." He loosened his arms, and when she tipped her face up, he took her mouth, kissing her with all the possessive protectiveness churning inside him.

At first she went still, but when she finally gave in, sinking against him, he held her face and gentled the kiss, then put his forehead to hers.

All the anger he'd held at bay sounded in his tone now. "I wanted to kill him. You know that, right?"

Eyes closed, she swallowed and gave a small nod.

"But I would never deliberately embarrass you. You need to know that, too."

"Thank you." She started to turn away, but he caught her waist and sat her on the table, then flattened his hands at either side of her hips.

"Understand, Yvette. The second I saw you, I knew what you were feeling."

Her green eyes stared into his. "Shame?"

That made him frown. "Worry."

"I was feeling both, actually."

"You hid it well. I'm proud of you."

Now she frowned.

"You can confide in me. Lean on me. You know that, right?"

"I know." Her smile flicked with sadness. "But I don't want to be that person anymore."

"The person who needs me?" Because, damn it, he wanted her to be that and more.

"The girl who burdens you."

He let out a sigh. "Now you're just trying to piss me off." Before she could be offended by that, he kissed her again.

She put a hand to his jaw, gentled him and his anger. "Everyone out there was looking."

"They knew what was going on, yes. That's on Heath, not you."

"I don't want them all thinking I'm pathetic."

He shook his head. She'd been hurt so badly, and no matter how she covered it up, how determined she was to soldier on, the wounds hadn't yet healed. "Don't be silly, okay? No one here is judging you. In fact, any woman in your position would get the same consideration and concern from the guys."

Getting her gumption back, she pushed off the table. *"I don't want it."*

"Really?" He caught her hand and held it. "Fine. You go tell a bunch of fighters that they don't need to notice when some asshole comes in hassling a woman half his size. Go ahead. See the reaction you get."

This time real humor teased her mouth. "Stop it." She dropped against him with a groan. "You know I'm not going back out there yet."

He rubbed her back to soothe her. "In about two minutes you are, because we'll be heading out." This was his world, his family. He wanted her comfortable in it, under any circumstances. He wanted his family to be her family.

"You're still working with the kids," she pointed out. "And you haven't yet showered."

Given the way she cuddled into him, she didn't mind that he was a little sweaty. "Armie's finishing up with the kids and I can shower at home. In fact, I was thinking maybe—"

Armie cleared his throat.

They both turned to the doorway.

Beside Armie was a big guy who topped even Cannon by a few inches. His nose had been broken multiple times, his right ear thickened from too many hits. Both his goatee and his Mohawk needed a good trim.

Yvette eased back, but Cannon put an arm around her, keeping her at his side. "Justice. What's up?" He leaned forward for a handshake.

Grinning, Justice drew him away from Yvette and into a giant bear hug. "Good to see you, Saint." He clapped Cannon hard on the back.

After suffering the embrace, Cannon stepped back and flexed his shoulders. "Damn, man, no reason to break my spine." He drew Yvette forward. "Honey, this is Justice."

She held out her small hand. "A fighter, I take it."

"Aw, bet the ears gave it away, huh?" As he'd done with Cannon, he ignored her hand and hauled her in for a much gentler hug, then kept her pinned to his side with his massive arm over her shoulders. "This is a new addition, ain't it, Saint? Every one better'n the last." He squeezed her. "Don't know how you do it, but I approve, I approve."

Yvette just laughed as she freed herself. "Nice to meet you."

Armie leaned in the door frame. "Justice has some news to share."

"Yeah?" Cannon indicated the chairs. "Want to sit?"

"Actually, I'd rather check out your joint here, if you don't mind."

"Make yourself at home."

Armie choked, but Cannon had no idea why.

With another face-splitting grin, Justice said, "Your boy there is strangling himself, so I may as well tell you."

"I'm listening."

"I'm dropping a weight class. Already got shit set up with the boss, so next go around—" he pointed a finger back and forth between their chests "—will be you and me. Winner gets a title shot. What do you think about that?"

It took Cannon by surprise. Not that he'd be fighting for the title. He'd been expecting that.

But hell, Justice had lost only one fight as a heavyweight, though the man he'd lost to had been one hell of a barrier to the championship, so it made sense to shift gears. "I think you chose a harder path, because we both know I'll take you apart."

"Ho!" Justice laughed out loud at that, making Armie flatten his mouth. "So fucking cocky."

"Language," Cannon cautioned without any heat.

He doffed an imaginary hat. "Apologies, ma'am."

Yvette didn't understand. She looked between them. "You'll be fighting each other?"

"So he says." Cannon knew bluster when he saw it, and Justice might want to look as though he thought it'd be an easy win, but he wasn't a dummy. He'd have his work cut out for him. "How set is it?" he asked Justice.

"Carved in stone. Matchmaker approved. Probably three or four months off, though. You should be getting a call today." Sotto voce, he said in an aside to Yvette, "Hope you don't expect him to stay this pretty, 'cause I plan to mess him up a little."

Tipping her head, she sent her long hair spilling over her shoulder. "You're awfully big. How much will you have to lose?"

"Forty pounds, give or a take a few."

She tipped her head the other way, studying Justice. "Are you as fast as Cannon?"

Justice tugged on one ear. "Probably."

Her slow smile claimed "bullshit," even though Yvette would never say it. "You look like a striker. How's your ground game?"

"Pretty good—"

"Not great, huh?" She made a sound of regret.

Justice's grin went crooked as he slanted a look at Cannon. "Damn, Saint. I like her."

"Meaning he knows his ground game sucks," Cannon said with good-natured ribbing.

"I'm workin' on it. I'm workin' on it." He turned back to Armie. "So, Quick, since you look like the guard dog—"

"Quick?" Yvette raised her brows. "Is that your fight name, Armie?"

The way his ears went red had both Cannon and Justice guffawing.

"It is," Justice confided, "but not because of his quick knockouts."

Cannon gave her a one-armed hug. "It's mostly a joke—"

"*Completely* a joke," Armie protested. "And it's fucking getting old."

"—carried over from his youth when he was a little too quick on the draw with the ladies."

"*One* lady, damn it." Armie threw up his arms. "And I made it up to her later!"

Confused, Yvette looked at each man in turn. "I don't understand."

That only made Justice laugh so hard that he fell against the wall.

Adoring her more by the minute, Cannon leaned down to her ear. "He got off a little too fast—as in, he came before things really even got started."

"Oh."

Armie stared at her. "It was back in high school, for God's sake."

"Ah, Quick, some things are never forgotten." After wiping his eyes, Justice grinned at him. "So am I still welcome to check out the place?"

"Stay as long as you'd like." Armie made a show of indifference. "If Cannon can put up with you, I suppose I can, too."

"There ya go." He turned to Cannon. "Come show me around, Saint."

"I'll do it," Armie said, already knowing Cannon wanted to stay with Yvette.

"Thanks." And then to Justice, Cannon added, "I'll be along soon."

"Got some smoochin' to do, huh? I get it. Can't say as I blame you."

Armie walked off, so Justice hurried to follow along. "Slow down, dawg. Oh, wait, I forgot. You're the speedy one."

What Armie said in return wasn't fit for human ears.

As they disappeared, Cannon realized he was still grinning. Being home always seemed right, but never more so than now, with Yvette here.

"You do enjoy fighting, don't you?"

He pulled her in for a taste, mouth to mouth, tongue making a fast foray. When around her, he couldn't resist. "Love it." But not as much as he loved… No, he couldn't start thinking about her that way. Not yet. Way too damn soon to be rushing her like that. "I also love a challenge."

But, damn it, Yvette was the biggest challenge he'd ever faced. A challenge to his control, his peace of mind. His heart.

Armie poked his head back in. "I gave the big ape over to Stack. Wanted to tell you, I made that call and it checks out."

"Perfect, thanks." Before he could leave again, Cannon said, "Armie?"

"Yeah?"

"Justice is okay. Invite him to hang around and make use of the place, okay?"

"Sure." Armie started off again. "I was already planning to give him a proper welcome."

Cannon laughed, and when Yvette looked at him in confusion, he said, "Armie's going to offer to spar with him."

"That's nuts. Armie's what? Six feet?"

"And one-eighty-five. I know. Big disparity in size. But believe me, he can handle himself. Might as well break Justice in right."

Looking grateful for something else to focus on, Yvette asked, "If Armie's that good, why doesn't he fight for the SBC?"

"He has his reasons, but lack of talent isn't one of them." Cannon leaned a hip on the table. "So. Know what I think we should do?"

"Go home so you can shower?"

The way she said that, her warm gaze skipping down

his body, he knew she hoped to get intimate again. And he was all for that idea. But first… "We need to go see the lieutenant."

CHAPTER SIXTEEN

LIEUTENANT MARGARET PETERSON-RISKE was as stunning as Yvette remembered. A dynamo who exuded confidence, control and femininity. Dash, her very adoring husband, seemed every bit attentive as she remembered, even this many years later.

After Cannon called her, Margaret had insisted they stop by and so here they were, in her home, with her precious little daughter, Bethany, climbing up Cannon and squealing his name.

Cannon scooped up the toddler and held her at eye level. "Hey, Button. Did you miss me?"

She squealed again and smooched his cheek, making Yvette smile.

"Bethany," Margaret said, "this is Cannon's friend Yvette."

"'Vette," Bethany said, eyeing her warily.

Cannon held her close to his chest and smoothed her dark curly hair—hair just like her mother's, though she had her father's dark eyes.

"Hi, Bethany," Yvette said.

When the little girl just scowled at her, Cannon said, "Come on, Button. Be nice."

Instead the little girl hid her face in Cannon's neck while reaching out a hand to Yvette.

Charmed, Yvette took it. "You're very pretty."

"Like Mama," Bethany said.

"Exactly," Dash said. "She listens when it suits her. Again, like her mama."

Margaret slanted him a look. "Hush, Daddy."

Laughing, Cannon kissed the top of Bethany's head. "It's time for your bath, honey. You can visit with Cannon later."

Because she loved her baths even more than Cannon, Bethany went willingly, more or less launching herself from Cannon's arms into her father's. "I want bubbles. And my boat, and SpongeBob, and Barbie, and…"

They disappeared down the hall with Bethany still listing toys. SpongeBob and Barbie—quite the mixed couple.

Margaret seated them at the kitchen table, offered drinks, then got down to business.

Cannon had told her a little about Heath on the phone. It bothered Yvette than she hadn't been the one to make the call, but he knew the lieutenant better than she did.

Still hoping to deal with Heath without causing a lot of fanfare, she was hesitant to get the police involved. But he had been out of control today, and she knew it. That meant he could be a threat to Cannon or the rec center, not just her.

So they'd compromised, and were talking with Margaret outside the station.

But unfortunately, that only meant they'd invaded her free time. Yvette detested the drama. "I'm very sorry to bother you with this, especially at home."

"Nonsense. Cannon has great instincts. If he's concerned, then I'm glad you contacted me." She sat at the table opposite them. "I've thought of you often. It's nice to see you again."

"And you." She sounded genuine enough, so Yvette tried to relax. "Your daughter is precious."

"Yes, she is." Her happiness came through in a serene smile. "Dash is hilarious with her. And the men! As you just saw, she adores Cannon, but also Reese and Logan." She leaned forward. "And, oh, my God, Rowdy. It's a riot how he melts for her."

Yvette couldn't imagine the detectives, much less the big badass Rowdy, playing with a tiny little girl. Of course, it seemed natural enough for Cannon to cuddle her.

"She shies away from women," Cannon said. "But she expects every guy she meets to bend to her will."

"And they do," Margaret told her. "Even Reese's son, Marcus. She treats him like a revered big brother and he falls for it."

Cannon had told her about Marcus being adopted by the detective and his wife after his abusive father went to jail and his mother died from an overdose. Thinking about it now left her in a melancholy mood. She had no business being so weak when a child like Marcus could be so strong.

"So." Margaret sat back. "Your ex came all the way from California just to pester you?"

"I assume so, though he'll probably have an excuse for being here. He travels a lot with his job, so I wouldn't be surprised if he has an arranged reason for being here other than me."

Yvette spent some time answering questions, explaining Heath's job as a sales rep for a drug company, how long she'd known him, when they'd dated, as well as when and why they'd broken up.

"She can show you a picture of him," Cannon said.

Yvette pulled one up on her phone. "I noticed his hair was a little shorter now, but otherwise he looks the same."

"Mind if I send this to myself to have on hand?"

"Of course not." Yvette really hated airing her dirty laundry, but because she and Cannon had already discussed it, and she'd agreed, she shared the rest. "I have emails, texts and Facebook posts from him. Plus my friend says he's posting about me on his wall."

"Mind if I see the messages now?"

Yes, she did mind. No sane person would want to share the ugliness of his rage. But she accepted that the best way to protect everyone involved was to share everything, so she pulled up the messages and handed her phone to Margaret.

Clearly Cannon wanted to read them also, but she didn't offer, and he didn't ask.

Margaret sat in silence, reading, her expression forbidding. When she finished, she handed the phone back to Yvette.

"I know," Yvette said, chatting through her embarrassment. "He's nasty. But is he really—"

"Yes, he is." She asked Cannon, "Have you read any of it?"

He took Yvette's hand, his thumb brushing over her knuckles. "Not much."

"I'm sure it's not the sort of thing any lady wants passed around. Suffice it to say he's plenty twisted and a definite problem. So here's what I want you to do." The lieutenant got a paper and pen from the drawer and made a list. "First, keep your distance from him. You, too, Cannon. Avoid him if you can."

Cannon scowled over that, but Yvette gave him an "I told you so" look.

"You'll need a restraining order. That'll be top of the list on Monday. Unfortunately, it's not valid until he's been served with it. If he's still at the hotel, we'll get it to him. But in the meantime, if you're out alone and he approaches you and won't go away, call someone immediately. Even 911, okay?"

Now she felt alarmed. "You really think it's that bad?"

"I've seen plenty of sick bastards, so why take chances? Second, keep all of the messages he's sent you. Print them out and bring me a copy. Have your friend print off whatever he's posting on his wall. Make sure everything is dated."

With every word she said, Cannon's mood darkened more.

"I know you've been blunt, and that's good. But no more playing nice at all. Don't tell him it's not a good idea to be friends. Tell him you will never again be his friend and you don't want him contacting you for any reason."

Knowing that would only cause him to be more caustic, which would definitely cause a scene, Yvette dreaded it—but she agreed. She wasn't a dummy. The lieutenant knew what she was talking about. She had experience with creeps. Whatever she told Yvette to do, she'd do.

"I know being mean doesn't come naturally to most of us. But you don't want him to misunderstand. He can't think that he might be able to convince you, or that if Cannon was out of the picture you'd be more inclined to hook back up."

Out of the picture? Fear slammed into her. "You don't think he'd—"

Gently, Margaret said, "I don't know what he might do, and neither do you. Given what I've read, he's clearly not right in the head. No sane man says those things about a woman he claims to love."

Cannon pushed away from the table and went to lean on the sink. She rarely saw him angry, but now his entire body emanated menace.

A big breath didn't ease the gripping uneasiness, but Yvette nodded. "Okay. Yes, of course."

"Keep your cell phone on you at all times. Make sure your house is secure."

"We already did that," Cannon said.

Margaret twisted to look up at him. "We?"

"I'm living with her."

Yvette felt her face go hot, but Margaret merely nodded. "Good. You might want to think about getting a dog, too. Something with a big bark." She continued listing her instructions. "When you start working at the shop, avoid any set schedule. Don't leave the house at the same time every day or close up the shop when you're there alone."

Gradually anger overtook every other emotion. How dare Heath do this to her?

"My last suggestion," Margaret said, taking her hand, "is to let me go talk with him. We know where he's at, but we don't know how long he'll be here. What if he stays a week, a month or longer? It never hurts for a stalker to know that the cops are watching."

Cannon turned, his arms crossed over his chest, his eyes narrowed, silently asking her forgiveness.

Yvette read the emotion there, but she didn't understand it.

Until he said to Margaret, "She's concerned about drawing attention again."

Yvette sat a little straighter. "It's fine," she stressed, hoping Cannon would let it go.

He didn't.

"Last time she was here she was in the thick of a macabre investigation with reporters all wanting her story." He walked back over to her, his hand on her shoulder.

"Her face was on the news every hour, so you can understand why she'd rather avoid the hype."

"What those men did," Margaret said, "rocked our entire community. With the investigation and the trial, it was headline news for a very long time."

"People will never forget," Yvette agreed.

"But the real story, the only one that matters, is that we all survived. Regardless of what anyone else thinks, that's what you should remember."

"I understand." She really did. And she was grateful. More than anyone could know. "It's just… I detested being the center of gossip and speculation."

"Anyone would. But I promise, I can be discreet. As long as he doesn't go off the rails, no one will need to know that I went to see him."

"Thank you."

Margaret gave her hand one last squeeze. "I'll take care of it first thing tomorrow."

When the lieutenant stood, so did Yvette.

Cannon tucked her into his side.

Margaret took in his familiar hold and smiled. "You know, as long as you're here, I've been thinking about something else."

Given the tentative way she said that, Cannon lifted a brow. "What's on your mind, Lieutenant?"

"You do so much at the rec center already that I hesitate to bring it up."

"I have plenty of help, so feel free."

"All right." She pushed in her chair, then stood behind it. "Have you ever considered teaching self-defense classes for women?" Rushing on, she added, "There are a lot of women in the neighborhood who would benefit."

And a lot of women, Yvette thought with a grin, who would sign up just to be with the fighters.

First surprised, and then thoughtful, Cannon nodded. "Actually, that's a terrific idea."

"I'd be happy to come in and help you get started."

"Yeah, sure, we could use some direction." His grin went lopsided. "I'm guessing the moves a woman needs to know might differ some from what I do in a competition."

Margaret held up her fist. "Smaller hands, smaller bone structure. Most women won't be able to punch their way out of an attack. But there are ways."

With a feigned wince of pain, Cannon put a hand over his crotch. "Bet I know what you're thinking, too."

She laughed. "There's always that. But other strikes are effective, too. I can demonstrate and you guys can follow through. How's that sound?"

Agreeing, he said, "Let me know when you're ready."

"You're in town for a while?"

Yvette wondered that herself. So far Cannon hadn't said how long he planned to stick around, though she now knew he'd have another fight coming up.

She frowned when he nodded without clarifying just how long "a while" might be.

There was a squeal in the hallway and a second later, a very naked baby came charging around the corner.

Running after her with a towel, his T-shirt and part of his jeans soaked, Dash called, "Bethany Marie Riske."

A cat that Yvette hadn't noticed darted up the hall behind them but scooted under the couch when he realized they had company.

"My puppy cat," Margaret explained. "He's old, blind and he still tries to keep up with Bethany."

"Loves her," Dash said, and he scowled down at his daughter.

She wrinkled her nose, crossed her arms and scowled back.

Grinning, his mood lightened, Cannon scooped her up. "Button, what are you doing streaking around the house?"

"Come take a bath wif me."

"Uh, no. Sorry." He kissed the end of her nose and handed her over to Dash, who wrapped the big fluffy towel around her.

"Little girls shouldn't run off before getting dressed," Dash scolded her. Then he kissed her cheek and her ear and in seconds she was giggling.

Holding her under his arm like a football, he headed back down the hall. Bethany giggled hysterically, and the cat emerged to follow.

Margaret shook her head, but she smiled, too. "Don't leave before she gets her nightgown on. She'll be disappointed if she doesn't get to tell you goodbye."

It took only another two minutes before Bethany, now wearing a long yellow nightgown and dragging a blanket, returned. She crawled up Cannon again, laid her head on his shoulder and looked ready to call it a night.

Slowly, so she wouldn't scare her, Yvette reached out to smooth one corkscrew curl.

"You ready for bed, Button?" Cannon asked softly.

"Mama's gonna read to me."

"Yes, Mama is," Margaret said, and she took her daughter, hugging her close. "Tell Cannon and Yvette goodbye, sweetie."

Around a big yawn, she said, "'Bye, Cannon and 'Vette."

Margaret touched Yvette's arm. "We'll talk again soon. Be careful, okay?"

"Thank you."

Cannon encased Margaret and Bethany both in a hug. "Thanks, Lieutenant."

She patted his chest. "Anytime. You know that." Then, more softly, "Read some of those messages, okay?"

After she walked away, Dash asked, "Get everything squared away?"

"Yes, thank you," Yvette said. "And again, I'm sorry for bothering—"

"No bother," he interrupted. "Margo thrives on this stuff. She's especially sensitive about jackasses bugging women."

"You're a lucky man," Cannon told him.

"And I know it." He walked them to the door, but then stopped Yvette from leaving with a touch to her arm. "Call anytime, okay? I promise you, Margaret would prefer to get woken up than to find out later that something happened. I don't know if she told you, but she feels like we all have a bond, given what we went through together."

Yvette couldn't fathom what she'd done to deserve such wonderful people. They'd all been brave, even heroic, and she'd been...a complete wuss.

Being honest, she said, "This is not how I wanted anyone to see me when I came back."

Dash shook his head. "Know what I see? A woman who should have cracked under the pressure and instead is smart enough to handle things the right way."

"The right way being getting your wife involved?"

Dash grinned. "She's good at what she does."

"Very good." Cannon put an arm around her, drawing her into his side. "She's a hell of an ally to have."

"We all need them," Dash agreed. "Both of you, watch your backs, okay? And if you need anything, let us know."

It wasn't until they were in her car and out of the driveway that Cannon spoke. "You can rely on all of them."

At first Yvette didn't understand. "Who?" Then she caught his meaning. "You're talking about Margaret—"

"And Dash. Rowdy, Avery, Logan, Reese…" Steering with one hand, he wrapped his right hand over her knee. "I've relied on all of them plenty of times, and vice versa."

Never would she go crying to his friends, looking for help. If it came to that she'd go back to California. But she was an optimist, so she had to believe it'd all work out somehow.

Now that he'd sort of brought it up, she turned in her seat and gave way to her curiosity. "When you take those long walks at night with your friends, the pole dancers you talk with, all the business people, it's because you're checking up on your neighborhood."

"Something like that."

"An older couple told me that you ran drug dealers away from their shop."

Modest in the extreme, Cannon lifted a shoulder. "I strongly suggested they move along."

"Right. I'm sure that's all you did. A nice, friendly chat."

He flashed a quick grin. "Before meeting Rowdy and his whole entourage, we made things happen by backing up what we said. And yeah, before you ask, that means I got into a lot of fights. Came to the point where it was easier for the street thugs to avoid us than to engage."

"Sounds dangerous."

"It was a few times." His fingers teased over her knee, then behind it. He blew out a breath. "Long ago, my dad died resisting extortion from a local group."

Yvette's heart sank. "I'm so sorry."

"Like I said, it was long ago."

Covering his hand with hers, knowing there was more, she waited.

"After that, some punks tried to give Merissa a hard time. I decided that wasn't going to happen." His brows pinched together a little as he recalled those long-ago days. Only seconds later, he shook off the mood. "That's when I learned I could fight." He glanced at her with a quick grin. "And that there was room for improvement. I started training, got involved in some small venues and kept up with the neighborhood network."

Yvette laced her fingers with his. "You're pretty amazing. You know that, right?"

He lifted her hand to his mouth to kiss her knuckles. "Not amazing, honey. Just appreciative of what I have and the people I know. Including you. And that brings us full circle."

"Should I be dizzy?"

"If for any reason you can't ever reach me, well, Rowdy is the most honorable tough guy I've ever known, followed closely by the lieutenant."

Laughing at that, Yvette said, "A tough guy, huh?"

"Or just tough. And definitely honorable. Dash and the detectives…they're really good men." He let her go and returned both hands to the steering wheel. "But you can always go to Armie, too, or Denver or Stack or—"

"Wow." Mustering a laugh, Yvette dropped back in her seat. "Are you expecting me to rouse up major chaos at every turn? Because seriously, Cannon, I'm hoping Heath takes off and it all just disappears, in which case, why would I need all this excellent backup?"

"I'm expecting you to be beautiful and hot and to keep me crazy with lust."

Wow again. She had nothing to say to that, except that maybe it'd be better if she appeased his lust. Like... tonight.

"But I'm the cautious sort," he said, "and I believe in being prepared. So humor me, okay?"

It took her a minute to get her thoughts in order, then she leaned in and stroked his shoulder. His body was so incredibly honed. She loved the feel of him under the soft cotton T-shirt. But she loved to touch his hot skin even more, so she slipped her fingers underneath his sleeve.

He went alert in a very masculine way.

"I don't want you to worry, Cannon. I'm not going to let Heath dictate my decisions, but I'm not going to do anything foolish either." He started to say something, but she wasn't done yet. "The thing is, I really don't want this to become your problem. Yes, we're in the same house. And yes, I want..." How to put it? "You." That seemed clear enough. But just to be sure, she added, "In every way."

"Damn, honey." He shifted, straightening one leg, tugging at his jeans.

"I appreciate how you handled Heath today. He took me by surprise and I was embarrassed. But no matter what he said or did, I wouldn't have gone anywhere alone with him. It might have gotten even more embarrassing, but I could have handled it."

That only made Cannon look more determined. "Glad to hear it."

In no way did he sound convinced, and that concerned her. "I hope you listened to what Margaret said. You don't need to seek Heath out. You don't need to defend my honor."

"I don't, huh?"

Now he almost sounded annoyed. She eyed him. "I'm

not saying you have to ignore Heath's insults if we run into him."

"Gee, thanks."

"But you can try letting me deal with him before you get in the middle of it."

He grunted over that.

"Mostly," she said, "I want to thank you."

That got his attention. "For what?"

"For offering to back me up." *Again.* "For caring." God, she hoped he did. "For…everything." *Mostly, for being you.*

He was quiet for a very long time, and that made Yvette even more uncertain about his feelings. Cannon was such a great guy to everyone. He was known for always treating women with respect, even the women he turned down. For as long as she'd known him, he'd been a defender…of everyone.

She knew he cared for her, but then, he cared for a lot of people.

Damn it, she wanted to be special.

Because he was so very special to her.

Finally he said, "I'm going to leave my truck at Rissy's until we get the garage cleaned out. Then we'll both be able to park inside. I don't want to leave it sitting out there like bait."

"That makes sense." Another thought occurred to her. "You spend most of your time in Harmony, Kentucky, right?"

Suspicious, he asked, "Why?"

"You have a house there?"

"Yeah." He glanced at her. "I'll show it to you someday, okay? It's not that long of a drive. Maybe three hours."

Realizing he had an entire life set up elsewhere did a

lot to dampen her mood. Out of necessity, his time here would have to be limited. "I'd like that. Thank you." Going back to her original train of thought, she asked, "Your house has a garage?"

"Three-car, yeah." Again he glanced at her. "And a pool. I'd love to see you in a bikini."

She should have smiled at the wolfish way he said that, but guilt had a stranglehold on her again. "If you weren't here, playing house with me—" most likely because he worried about her being alone "—then your truck would have already been safely locked in a garage instead of—"

"Don't think like that." Frowning again, he worked his jaw. "I'm glad you're here, damn it. Despite everything going on, I want you to be glad, too."

How could he not know? She was so happy to be home. To be with him.

But she'd so badly wanted it to be different.

Because she couldn't do much about Heath right now, or his tires, she adjusted her attitude instead, smiling, leaning toward him to again stroke his hard shoulder. "I am. Very much so."

Briefly, he turned his head to kiss her wrist.

"I'll work on the rest of the boxes first thing tomorrow." She was anxious to see everything she had, and to get the best stuff moved to the shop. Though she loved all the time she spent with Cannon, it was *his* time—his training, his contribution to the rec center, his friends. She wasn't used to being idle for so long. She needed to be busy.

Once she opened the shop, she'd get back in the swing of working. That'd do a lot to help her regain her emotional balance.

"What do you think about a dog?"

"I'm not sure." She'd always wanted one, but her

apartment in California didn't allow pets. And even if it had, her space was too small to fit in an animal.

But a pet…it was such a sign of permanence. Wasn't it? She hedged by saying, "I like animals."

"Me, too. With my travel it hasn't been possible, but you're staying now, right?"

"Yes."

"And the backyard is plenty big enough. I could even put up a fence."

More and more he made plans that seemed so permanent, without ever really telling her his long-term intention. But however life rolled out, she would love having the company of a dog. "Okay."

"Great." Decisive, he said, "How about we visit the shelter the Sunday after I work at Rowdy's?"

Thinking about taking such a big step with him made her nervous, uncertain and utterly euphoric. She started smiling and couldn't stop.

When she looked at Cannon, he was smiling, too.

"Happy?" he asked her.

"Very."

They turned the corner to her house. The last rays of the summer sun splashed brilliant colors over the horizon.

With her focus on Cannon, thinking about so many things, she saw the exact moment he frowned. "What's the matter?"

His hands flexed on the steering wheel. "You know there's something between us, right?"

Since he'd just recently said so, she guessed, "Lust?" And she was only half teasing.

"Hell, yeah. The lust is there in spades. I think about you and I want you. I see you and I salute."

Confused, she repeated, "Salute?"

"My johnson stands up and takes notice."

"Oh." Her gaze automatically went to his lap, and her eyes widened.

"But it's more than that, too."

It was his tone, more than anything, that shot her attention back to his face.

Warmth filled her heart. Recalling how patient he'd been, even when she'd told him about her hang-ups, she bit her lip. "More?"

Looking far too grim, Cannon said, "No matter what, I want you to remember that."

What did he mean? He seemed to want an answer, so she nodded. "All right."

With a demeanor of determination, he pulled into the driveway, turned off the engine and stared at the front door.

Yvette followed his gaze and blanched at what she saw. Fury mixed with defeat.

The spray-painted message destroyed the front door. Bloodred drips trailed down to the small porch.

"Go home, bitch."

Shaking her head, she denied the command.

Someone wanted her to go—when she'd only just decided to stay.

CHAPTER SEVENTEEN

TOGETHER THEY GOT out and moved closer.

Avoiding the paint—still fresh and sticky—Cannon unlocked the front door and helped her inside. "Stay put one second, okay?"

With a nod, she stood there, looking a little numb, a lot defiant.

So proud.

He did a quick surveillance of the house, but everything was in order. He checked on the garage, the small backyard, each window.

When he returned, she had her cell phone in her hand. Without him having to ask, she said, "I was ready to call for backup if we needed it."

"Smart." Wishing he could have shielded her from this, he drifted his thumb over her cheek. "Nothing else seems disturbed, though."

"Good." Moving away, she dropped her purse on the couch and stalked into the kitchen. He heard water running and, bothered by the way she stayed so contained, followed her.

She had a bucket in the sink, filling it with soapy water.

Cannon reached around her, turned off the water, and hugged her up to his chest. "That'll only smear it and make it worse. In this heat, it'll be dry in another half hour. Then I can sand it off."

"The door will be ruined."

"So we'll replace it."

"It's all over the porch, too."

"A power washer will get it off."

Through a strained laugh, she leaned back against him. "Do you have an answer for everything?"

"For chickenshit stuff like this I do." Keeping her close, he turned her in his arms. "You're not going anywhere."

She looked up at him with those big green eyes both sad and sweet, and like every guy everywhere, his reaction was a throbbing boner.

"Promise me," he said.

"I'm not budging." Patting his chest, she moved away. "But I'm not leaving that paint out there for all the neighbors to see either."

"I can cover it up."

"I'm going to take a picture first." Solemn, she reminded him, "Margaret wanted us to document everything."

So she figured it was Heath, too? "All right."

Together they went out front and took care of it.

After reporting the vandalism to Margaret, he sanded off as much of the paint as he could. It looked terrible, but now no one would know what it had said.

Yvette brought out a sheet and tacked it over the front of the door while he had a quick chat with their closest neighbors. Unfortunately, most of them were elderly and hadn't seen anything.

Or they didn't want to get involved.

If any of the neighbors had businesses in the area, he'd have an in. But they were quiet, retired people who wanted to avoid trouble.

Not a problem. He had a network that could cover a

lot of ground. Starting tonight, he'd put as many people on it as he needed to.

"Nothing?" Yvette asked when he rejoined her.

He shook his head. "I should have put a damn security camera here, too."

Though she tried to hide it, he could tell the sick prank had distressed Yvette. "I'm the one who should have realized how far Heath might take it. I just never guessed he'd follow me from California. Why he's suddenly being so persistent, I have no idea."

Cannon knew it was because of him. Heath had probably assumed she'd remain available until he could figure out a way to coax her back to him.

Now, with another man in the picture, he felt threatened.

"We'll both be more careful from now on." He put his arm around her. "Come on."

Once inside he attempted a casual demeanor to conceal his anger. "While I grab a shower, why don't you get something together for us to eat?"

"Got a preference?"

You. No, he shouldn't think that. Especially not with her watching him so expectantly. He'd need to either handle things in the shower—or make it ice-cold. "Something light. Maybe a sandwich?"

"I can handle that." Again she patted his chest, and, damn it, it felt too much like a dismissal. "Fifteen minutes?"

He wasn't a chick. "Make it more like seven."

Unwilling to leave her alone for long, he grabbed clean clothes and rushed through a head-to-toe scrubbing. Even with a quick jerk, he was back out of the shower a minute shy of the designated seven.

He'd taken the sharpest bite off the clawing lust, but hadn't even come close to denting the possessiveness.

Someone, likely Heath, wanted to scare Yvette. Given the man's obsession, he might even want to hurt her.

Wouldn't happen.

One way or another, Cannon knew he had to put an end to the harassment.

She was in her designated spot on the couch, a tray of food on the coffee table. Cannon soaked up every nuance of her mood as he joined her. On top of fixing the food, she'd washed up and changed into a long nightshirt. Now, sitting yoga style on the deep cushions, she pulled her hair over her shoulder and with dexterous speed worked it into a braid. She held a band in her teeth and when she reached the ends of her long hair, she secured it.

Her lashes swept up as she faced him. "I wasn't sure if you wanted chips or pickles. I mean, because of your training."

She had both on the tray, so he grabbed up a pickle slice. "This is good, thanks."

She'd cut the sandwiches into little triangles. Cute. He ate the first one in one bite.

She nibbled on hers, and since she wasn't a picky eater, he took that as a sign she was still troubled.

"Want me to run to the porn shop for a movie?"

The teasing almost got her to smile, but instead she turned it into a "behave" look.

And that made *him* smile. Assuming he'd have to suffer through some sappy drama, he said, "What, then?"

Picking up the remote, she found an old horror movie. "How about this?"

Damn, she made it easy to like her. "Looks good."

They settled in for the duration, and thanks to a lot of

special-effects blood and the gruesome movie monster, she ended up curled against his side.

He wanted her, so damn much, but he didn't know of an easy way to segue from what had happened to seduction.

He was lounged back, legs sprawled, Yvette a warm, soft weight against him, when the movie ended. He started to move—and realized she'd fallen asleep.

Carefully, unwilling to wake her, he eased her down so that her head rested on his thigh. He played his fingers along her braid, then over her shoulder. On her side, she dipped from her shoulders to that small waist, then back up to her rounded hip and down the long length of her slender, shapely legs.

As much as he wanted her naked and under him, he also wanted her to feel secure and safe when with him.

He wanted her to lean on him.

No way in hell would he move.

EVERY TIME SHE looked at Cannon, her temperature spiked.

Partial chagrin, partial desperate need.

She'd fallen asleep on him last night.

The last thing she'd remembered was waiting for him to make a move. But he hadn't. And as much as she hated herself for it, she had to wonder if he'd held back out of consideration for her, maybe thinking she needed more time.

Or because he did.

She'd awakened this morning when he stretched and only then did she realize they were still on the couch. Startled, she'd jerked upright and accidentally head butted him. They'd both groaned, him rubbing his jaw, her rubbing the top of her head.

Cannon always looked drool-worthy, but never more so than in the mornings with beard stubble and dark, rumpled hair and sleep-heavy blue eyes shadowed by long sooty lashes.

When he'd gifted her with that small, sexy smile... Yeah, she'd wanted to demand that he satisfy her. Right there and then.

Instead she'd stayed mute until he'd kissed her softly and headed off to the john.

Remembering, she wanted to groan again.

After that, he'd gotten a call from one of his trainers, a guy named Havoc, who gave him more details on the upcoming fight. She'd made coffee while listening in.

He'd fight again right after Halloween.

That meant he'd have to get back to more rigorous training soon. Full-time. In Kentucky.

Away from her.

And, damn it, she missed him already!

With near desperate urgency, she wanted to take advantage of the time they had left. But right after their jog, he'd put in a call to Armie, telling him about the vandalism, and the next thing she knew the guys were there. Guys, plural. Armie, Stack and Denver. Only Miles and Brand were missing, left behind to run the rec center.

They took turns hugging her, commiserating, offering to break heads for her and inadvertently keeping her from jumping Cannon's very sexy bones.

They were all protective, hilariously so, but after Margaret called to say Heath had apparently already checked out, Cannon turned grim. The lieutenant explained that she'd gone to the hotel first thing that morning, but he was no longer registered there.

Either he'd gone back home, or he'd moved locations. There weren't many places to stay in the small town of Warfield, but just outside their township, in the city limits, there were a variety of hotels to choose from.

If Heath hadn't flown back home, at least he was no longer so close, and that gave her comfort.

To put Cannon more at ease, she called Vanity and requested an update if Heath posted anything on his Facebook. So far, he hadn't.

She could tell it worried Cannon, which in turn made him more demonstrative. He continually touched her, kissed her, watched her.

Now, in the late afternoon, she was still feeling the need.

While Denver and Cannon worked to get the new door installed, Armie and Stack finished loading the last of the boxes from the garage into Cannon's truck. She was just in the way at that point, so she went inside to get more drinks.

With them all helping, the shop was now ready for her to arrange things, the garage was almost empty, the front porch had no signs of paint and…and she felt like crying for no good reason at all. Worry? Relief? A buildup of everything, starting with losing her grandpa and ending with an unknown vandal?

Maybe lack of sexual relief? She blew hair out of her face. Yeah, that could be it, because around Cannon she stayed keyed up.

When Merissa and Cherry dropped in, Yvette heard them before she saw them. Merissa started giving someone directions, and Cherry was flirting, saying those teasing things that seemed to come so naturally to her, but always eluded Yvette.

After adding more ice to the pitcher, she poured herself a tall glass. Working with the guys now had her sweaty, dusty, grimy and far too emotional.

"Hey."

She looked up to see Armie striding in, his countenance grim.

Lowering the glass, she asked, "What's wrong?"

"I was going to ask you the same thing." He stepped around her to refill his own drink, then guzzled it down like a man dying of thirst.

"I would have brought that to you."

"I needed the break." He tugged a cobweb out of her hair. "Why are you hiding in here anyway?"

"I'm not hiding." Not exactly. But to keep him from digging, she lifted a brow and asked, "Why are you in here hiding?"

He started to answer, but clammed up when Merissa walked in, muttering, "Coward."

She, too, went for the iced tea.

Like a deer caught in the headlights, Armie froze, only his eyes moving as he tracked her approach. As soon as she stepped past him, Yvette saw his attention drop southward—to her backside showcased in snug shorts.

His nostrils flared.

Whoa. Did Cannon know his best friend had a major case for his sister? Doubtful.

Armie shoved his glass toward Yvette. "Thanks, doll. Better get back to it." And with that he literally fled the kitchen.

Trying to hide her smile, Yvette said, "So what was that all about?"

To her surprise, Merissa slumped. "He despises me for some reason, though for the life of me, I have no idea why."

Yvette could only stare. Seriously? That was what Merissa thought?

If so, she was even more clueless about guys than Yvette.

"I don't think—"

Cannon stepped in. "You want to ride along to the shop, maybe give some direction on where to put the rest of the boxes? Or do you just want the guys to drop them off and you and I can arrange things when we get a chance?"

"I'll go." She needed more time to get it together anyway. Tonight they were going to Rowdy's bar and would probably be there late.

Meaning she still wouldn't get a chance to explore that exciting intimacy with Cannon. It'd be better if she stayed busy instead of dwelling on missed opportunities.

Merissa said, "Who all's going?"

"Denver will stay and help me finish up the door, but the rest are heading over there."

She finished off her drink. "I'll go along, too, then." Hooking her arm through Yvette's, she said, "Happy to lend a hand."

Cannon caught Yvette before she could leave. His attention took in her disheveled hair, her flushed cheeks. He brushed dust off the end of her nose. "Be careful."

She found it difficult to tease with her awareness of him so keen. "Afraid one of the guys will drop something on me?"

Using utmost care, he smoothed her hair. "Let them do the heavy lifting."

"Hey, I'm not a complete wimp."

"You're not a fighter either." He drew her up and against his chest and his mouth touched hers, featherlight, as stirring as a storm.

When he released her, she touched her lips.

Which prompted him to kiss her again. "We have to

leave for Rowdy's at six." He held her chin up with two fingers beneath, his gaze warm and admiring. "Give yourself plenty of time to do whatever you want to do to get ready."

"You don't want me to go like this?"

Giving a small shake of his head, he whispered, "You'd start a riot."

Now, what did that mean? She was a complete mess and knew it. She wrinkled her nose. "It's going to take me at least an hour, so I won't be gone long."

Still keeping her close, he studied her face, slipped his warm palm around her nape.

Oh, she knew that look....

Sure enough, right there with Merissa protesting, he kissed her again, this time longer and hotter. Just what she didn't need, since they couldn't follow through.

Although she had to admit, she would never turn down the opportunity to taste him.

"PDAs," Merissa griped, "especially in front of your sister, are so very uncool."

Cannon grinned as he let her go. "Around Yvette, I can't help the occasional public display of affection."

"I like her," Merissa said, "so you're forgiven."

Yvette wondered if they both meant it. If Cannon did feel any real affection for her, would Rissy be okay with it?

After Merissa got in the car with Yvette, Armie tried to trade places with Denver. But Cherry had decided to stay behind, so Denver wouldn't budge.

It was all pretty hilarious, and definitely distracting.

At the shop, they all pitched in, and not only did they get the boxes unloaded from the truck, they got many of them emptied into the glass cases and shelves that she'd already arranged around the shop.

Now that she'd scrubbed the floors clean and put out area rugs it all looked amazing, if she did say so herself.

As soon as she got her business license, hopefully within the next two weeks, she'd be able to do a grand opening.

Just as they finished up, she noticed some girls—probably high school age—staring in the big front window. When she looked behind her, Yvette saw both Stack and Armie as the girls probably saw them.

Big, built and shirtless.

She grinned and nudged Merissa.

"What?" Merissa asked as she broke down an empty box.

Yvette nodded at the window.

Snorting a laugh, Merissa also looked at the guys. Or more specifically, at Armie. Unaware of his audience, mostly because he'd been doing his best to ignore Merissa, he reached his arms up, hands locked together and stretched.

Merissa sighed.

The girls outside knocked on the window and waved. When Armie glanced at them, they twittered and flirted and one looked to be adjusting her shirt to show more cleavage.

Smiling crookedly, Armie shook his head, and as he went to look away, his gaze caught on Merissa. The smile faded under a frown.

Merissa tucked her hands under her chin and mocked the girls, giggling as they had, batting her eyelashes, all in all acting foolish.

Yvette and Stack both laughed.

Even Armie cracked a smile.

"Our adoring fan club," Stack said. "Too bad they aren't twenty-one-year-old hotties instead of jailbait."

Yvette remembered a time when *she'd* been jailbait, shamelessly coming on to Cannon.

Dropping the act, crossing her arms and aiming her ire at Armie, Rissy said, "Or what? You'd mosey out there and offer yourself up?"

"Something like that," Armie replied with identical challenge.

Stack raised a hand. "I would, yeah." He glanced again at the girls, a brow lifted in speculation. "Hell, if I knew for certain they were eighteen—"

Gasping, Merissa threw up her hands. "You guys are shameless!"

In an aside to Armie, Stack asked, "Does she believe her brother really is a saint?"

Not wanting to hear about any of Cannon's escapades, Yvette interrupted. "I can't thank all of you enough. Just look at this place now." She turned a circle, giddy with exuberance. "It's almost full and I still have more boxes."

"What else will you need to do?" Stack asked.

"Nothing more today." A glance at the time on her phone told her she needed to get home and get ready.

"Well, if you need me, just let me know."

She smiled at Stack.

"Same here," Armie said.

Marveling at their generosity, Yvette nodded. "You're all...wonderful."

"It's how it works," Armie told her. "Cannon's saved my ass more times than I can count."

"Me, too," Stack said.

"I know about you," Rissy told Stack before she turned to Armie. "What'd he do for you?"

"Not your business, Stretch." He pulled on his shirt. "Let's just say we're family, okay?"

"Not you and me," Rissy said.

He scowled at her. "I was talking about Cannon and me."

"I'm his sister."

"Is that a news flash?"

Speaking over them, Stack said, "They squabble like siblings, don't they?" With an arm around Yvette, he said, "If we're all done here, I need to get back to the rec center."

Armie said, "Merissa is heading that way. She can take you and I'll go with Yvette."

Merissa opened her mouth to argue, but must have changed her mind. "Sure. Come on, Stack. We'll talk. About *things*." She shot a look at Armie so he'd know exactly what she wanted to discuss.

Smirking, Stack murmured, "Oh, the stories I can tell...."

As they disappeared out the door, Yvette expected Armie to blow, but instead he laughed.

"You aren't worried?" Turning out lights, then digging the keys from her purse, Yvette rejoined him.

"No." He took the keys from her and, after they stepped out, locked up everything. "Stack enjoys needling me, but he'd never tell anything he shouldn't. He's as dependable as they come."

"Such a big secret," Yvette mused. "Now I'm dying of curiosity."

Not taking the bait, he opened the truck door for her. "Gotta know, huh?"

"Oh." Surprised at how he'd said that, she shook her head. "No, I was just—" He closed her door and walked around to the driver's side.

"You realize what a great guy Cannon is, right?"

"Absolutely." Reaching out, Yvette put her hand on

his forearm. "But, Armie, really, I wasn't prying. It was a bad joke."

"It's all right." He started the truck, but didn't yet pull away. Staring straight ahead, he said, "I was once accused of something…pretty bad. The sort of thing no up-front guy wants to be accused of."

Feeling his emotional distance, Yvette retreated. "I'm sorry," she said again.

He chewed his lip, then shook his head and put the truck in gear. After a quick glance at the road, he pulled away from the curb. "I hadn't done it, just so you know."

She had no idea what "it" might be, but she nodded. "Okay."

"Cannon knew it, too. No questions asked. No doubt. He believed in me one hundred percent."

Sounded like Cannon. He was a man of very strong convictions, and obviously a great judge of character. "I'm glad he was there for you."

"If he hadn't been… I dunno. It would have gotten pretty ugly. But Cannon did what he always does. He got involved. Found the right people who could clear me, stood up for me even when others didn't." He flexed his shoulders, cracking his neck. "Feel free to ask him about it if you want."

"I don't need to." She could tell it was a very private, still-painful incident for him. "I trust Cannon, and if he trusts you, that's good enough for me."

Armie relaxed enough to wink at her. "See, this is why you fit right in."

Did she? She hoped so. Around Cannon's friends, she felt more at home than she had since moving to California. "The thing is, that's between you and Cannon. It doesn't obligate you to me by extension."

"Sure, it does."

"No—"

"If Rissy needed something, you'd try to help her out, right?"

Without thinking about it, she said, "Of course."

Satisfaction curled his mouth. "Because she's Cannon's baby sis, and you care about Cannon."

God help her, she loved Cannon. Always had and probably always would. There wasn't much she wouldn't do for him.

Clearing the melon-size lump out of her throat, she squeaked, "Yes."

"There you go. Accept the helping hand when any of us offers, okay? We'll be offended otherwise. And seriously, we're all annoying as shit when we're offended."

He spoke of "us" and "we" as if the fighters who utilized the rec center were always of one mind. And maybe, when it came to certain things—like Cannon—they were. She didn't really know what to say, so she said simply, "It's very much appreciated."

"And fun, right? Everyone enjoys hanging out together. It's not as though hanging a door or moving a few boxes takes all that much effort."

"I had fun."

"Good."

He turned down the street toward her house. They saw that the door was up, and it looked terrific. Better than the old door. Probably more secure, as well.

"Dirtbag."

Yvette had been occupied watching Cannon replace tools in the garage, but at that growled sentiment, she looked at Armie. "What?"

"The coward who dicked with your door. I hate that sneaky crap."

She pretty much hated it, too. "It bothers me a lot that

my problems are spilling over and affecting Cannon. If I could, I'd keep him totally uninvolved."

Armie snorted. "Some friendly advice—don't say that to Cannon. No involved guy would want to hear it, but Cannon gets more involved than most."

Knowing he was probably right, she said in a smaller voice, "I only meant uninvolved with the trouble." And before he made her feel even worse, she explained, "I wanted him to see me differently this time."

At that, Armie laughed outright.

Insulted, she narrowed her eyes at him. "Why is that funny?"

"How the hell did you want him to see you? The poor guy is upside down over you." He lifted a brow. "Majorly in lust."

"Armie," she warned.

But he'd already moved on. "He likes you, too, though. Wouldn't have brought you around the rec center otherwise. And clearly he enjoys you. Don't think I've ever seen the guy so touchy-feely, and always smiling." Shaking his head, he asked, "Did you want him to be oblivious?"

"Of course not." She wanted him to be...well, impressed. And didn't that just make her sound shallow?

"Then I'd say he's seeing you exactly as he should." Softening, going more serious, he said, "But, hon, I get what you're saying. You wanted to show him that you were free of the past."

Exactly! "Yes, that's what I meant."

"Only no one ever is. Not me, not Cannon." He glanced at her. "Not you. Some shit digs in, gets under our skin, and while we might get used to it, we can't get rid of it. It takes part in everything we do, every decision we make."

Did Armie's past play into his outrageousness? Most likely. She rubbed a smudge of dirt on her jeans. "The thing is, Cannon got pulled into all my mayhem before I moved away. Then, as soon as I get home, I find out my grandfather has more or less saddled him with me. I was dealing with that, but now Heath is here, causing more trouble." The spot of dirt remained—much like her problems.

"I say you just go with it."

She gave up on her messy clothes and instead stared at Armie. "Go with it how?"

"Stop fighting fate. Stop fighting Cannon."

"I haven't been!"

"Bull. I see it, so I guarantee you that he sees it." He pulled into the driveway, and Cannon started out of the open garage to greet them.

"You're here," Armie added. "Looks to me as if you're staying. So jump in with both feet. Tiptoeing around never got anything accomplished."

She didn't have time to assimilate that before Cannon opened her door, tugged her out and greeted her with his mouth on hers.

"Way to make me feel like a third wheel," Armie complained.

Cannon kept his arm around her waist. "Everyone knows you like things in threes."

"Not when I'm just a bystander." Grinning at Yvette's blush, Armie added, "Got everything moved in and locked up again before we left."

"Great. Drinks are on me tonight."

When they both laughed, Yvette said, "Why is that a joke?"

"Because neither of us will be drinking." He stole another kiss, took her hand and started for the garage.

"I have to show you what we found." He looked back. "Come on, Armie. You'll want to see this, too."

In the middle of the floor was a medium-size safe. Yvette looked up and saw a panel missing in the ceiling. "It was up there?"

"Yeah. Centered on two-by-fours across the rafters. Damn thing weighs around a hundred pounds. We had a heck of a time getting it down."

"We?" Armie asked, walking around the safe.

"Denver helped. It barely fits through the opening, so it was pretty awkward."

"And if you misstepped, you and the safe both would have come through the ceiling."

Yvette knelt down to look at the locks. "Why would Grandpa have that up there?"

"No idea," Cannon said. "But with the double locks, we'll need both the key and the pass code to open it." He crouched down beside her. "You run across anything like that?"

"Not so far, no. But I can keep an eye out."

"Until then, I think I'll bring it inside, just in case he has anything valuable in there. Doubtful, given where he had it stored, but..." Cannon shrugged. "Could be whatever is in there is so important that he didn't want to leave it in the obvious places."

"A mystery." Armie rubbed his hands together. "Now you have me interested."

"Where do you want me to put it?" Cannon asked.

"Our..." She glanced at Armie and amended, "My bedroom, I guess."

Though Armie said nothing at her near slip, he had to pinch his mouth to keep from grinning. "Guess I should get going. I'll see you both at Rowdy's."

After he'd left, Cannon hefted the safe to carry it in,

and Yvette held the door open. He set it inside her closet for safekeeping.

Yvette double-checked the various keys and papers that they'd gotten from Whitaker, but there wasn't anything for the safe. She glanced at the clock and knew she had to hustle to get ready.

Tonight, when they returned from Rowdy's, she'd do a search to see if she could find a way to access the safe.

She watched Cannon peel off his shirt as he headed into the hall shower and decided the safe could wait. As soon as they got home, she'd let him know she was ready. Past ready.

She'd waited long enough.

CHAPTER EIGHTEEN

THE BAR WAS insanely packed. Every table, booth and bar stool was taken with standing room only. Denver, Armie, Stack and a few others had tables toward the back—leaving the up-front tables for Cannon's fans—and luckily they'd saved her a seat.

After seeing her to their table, Cannon cupped her face. "I might be busy for a few hours, but I'll keep checking back here."

For what? If Heath was still around, he couldn't bother her in a place this congested with onlookers. "I'll be fine," she promised him. "Go and have fun."

Customers started chanting his name, leaving him chagrined. He touched her mouth with his fingertips, leaned in for a demonstrative kiss that made it clear they were together, then turned and headed up front.

All along the way, male fans greeted him with fist bumps, high fives and the occasional clap on the shoulder.

Female fans were more outrageous, running their fingers along his shoulders or arm as he passed, blowing him kisses, doing what they could to gain attention.

Totally in his element, Cannon reciprocated to the crowd and mugged for pictures.

Rowdy and his wife, Avery, stayed busy filling drinks from behind the bar, with Ella and two other waitresses wending repeatedly through the crowd with trays.

When Cannon reached the front, Rowdy paused to shake out a Rowdy's bar T-shirt and, with the women wolf whistling and cheering him on, handed it over to Cannon.

Yvette could barely see, but when she heard the new roar, she went on tiptoe to peek.

At ease, Cannon stood there in jeans only.

Her heart tripped, especially when she saw Mary right up front, toasting him with a beer.

He pulled on the black shirt that served as a uniform for the bar and the cheers turned to mournful protests. Grinning, Cannon wagged his finger at the crowd.

Bending to her ear, Armie murmured, "Better get used to it. At a fight preview it'll be even worse. Or an after-party? Forget it. The women try to molest him."

Yvette lightly elbowed him, which only made him laugh.

The night rolled on pleasantly enough. The women who weren't flirting with Cannon flirted with Armie and Denver and Stack.

Armie seemed resistant, which told her he was her watchdog for the night. "Raining on your parade, aren't I?"

"Naw. I needed a break anyway."

She laughed with him.

Cannon came around, bringing her a glass of wine, beer for Denver and Stack, water with lime for Armie.

And again he kissed her. "Having fun?"

"It's terrific," she told him. One hand to his chest, smoothing over the Getting Rowdy logo, she asked, "How are you holding up?"

His hand curled over her nape. He put his mouth to her throat, her jaw, up to her ear, where he whispered, "I miss you."

She felt herself flushing. Everyone looked at them. "You're going to break so many hearts tonight."

His teeth caught her earlobe, his tongue touched and he breathed, "I'm discouraging all the guys who are looking your way."

A surprised laugh burst out, and she hugged him. "Don't be silly."

"Silly, huh?"

"You are the center of attention," she told him. "No one is paying any attention to me."

As if perplexed, he studied her face, his blue eyes dark in the dim light, his lashes leaving exaggerated shadows over his gorgeous face. "Amazing."

"What?"

"You really don't realize." He shook his head, went back to her ear and whispered, "I love your modesty. It's as sexy as the rest of you."

Heart thumping, lips parted, Yvette watched him finish circulating the room.

She jumped when Armie nudged her.

"Penny for your thoughts."

Her face went hot. No way would she tell him how the *L* word had taken out her knees, or how the brief touch of his hot tongue had started a slow burn inappropriate to the situation.

A wicked gleam entered his eyes. "I've heard it all before, you know. Done it, too. You won't shock me."

Mute, she shook her head.

"That good, huh? Damn, girl, you know how to pique the interest. And I'm betting whatever I imagine is going to be more explicit than the truth."

When Denver laughed, they both turned to see Cherry now sitting in his lap. That didn't, however, keep her from enjoying some playful, suggestive banter with all the guys.

Cherry really was a world-class flirt, Yvette thought. Maybe she should take lessons. That way, instead of freezing up when Cannon teased her, she could tease right back.

Another hour passed without Cannon making it back to them. Between serving drinks, he signed autographs and posed with fans. One guy didn't like how his date ogled Cannon. Already drunk and obviously stupid, he tried to challenge him, but Cannon laughed it off, ducking out of reach of a wild haymaker thrown at his face.

Rowdy escorted out both the man and his protesting lady friend.

Not being much of a drinker, Yvette was only on her third—was it her third? anyway, another—glass of wine when she noticed Armie looking beyond her, his interest blatant. Expecting to see Merissa, she followed his gaze and spotted Mindi.

Instead of her business suits, the lawyer's assistant had changed into a sleeveless, body-hugging dress and strappy sandals. Her blond hair hung loose in soft curls. Their gazes met. Yvette wanted to look away, but for some reason couldn't.

After smiling and nodding, Mindi zeroed in on Cannon. Her eyes narrowed with sensual intent, a satisfied smile lifting just the corners of her shiny lips.

Every guy at her table noticed Mindi, so Yvette could only assume that Cannon found her attractive, as well. And why not? Regardless of Mindi's uncharitable personality, Yvette had to admit that Mindi looked amazing.

She now regretted wearing her SBC T-shirt with Cannon on the front over skinny cropped jeans and flat sandals. She'd been thinking only of supporting him, having fun and being comfortable.

She should have worn her own sexy dress, damn it. But…that just wasn't her. And why should she try that hard anyway? She didn't want or need to compete with Mindi. Hadn't she made a promise to herself to be independent and courageous? That included standing up for herself.

She drained the glass, put it on the table and rose from her seat. "I'm going to squeeze up front a little."

One arm around Cherry, Denver toasted her with his beer. "Go get 'em, Yvette."

She glared at Armie. "Why is he drinking if you and Cannon aren't?" Stack had tossed back a couple of long-necks, too, as had most of the men there.

He came to his feet with her. "Cannon rarely does, but he definitely wouldn't while working, right? And since I have a fight in three weeks, I'm the driver stuck with getting the other lushes home safe."

Way to drop a bombshell! She leaned against the table. "You're fighting? Since when?"

He looked self-conscious. "Since…I don't know. A couple of months ago?"

She pushed his shoulder. "Why didn't you say anything?"

"I just did."

"Armie doesn't like any fanfare," Denver offered helpfully.

"Keeps it to himself," Stack added, then made a "shh" sound with his finger to his mouth. "Don't tell. Wouldn't want anyone to notice, you know."

Yvette wondered if that had anything to do with his past. "Where?"

"Where what?"

She crossed her arms and tapped her foot. "Where are you fighting?"

"Just a local venue. No big deal."

Of course it was, more so now that she knew he kept secrets. "I want to watch."

He rolled one shoulder as if it didn't matter, but then rubbed his neck uncomfortably. "Fine. Whatever. Cannon will be there. Grab a ride with him if you want."

"I wasn't asking permission." She softened, patted his chest, then remembered that Mindi was closing in on Cannon. "Later."

He snagged the back of her shirt, bringing her back around.

She was a little more wobbly than she should have been and bounced into him.

He steadied her, then frowned. "Why the rush?"

Smacking his hands away, she glared at him.

Armie just quirked a brow in that "what?" way of his.

So why not tell him? Maybe it was the wine making her feel more open, but she liked Armie, felt comfortable with him as a friend. And he could give great insight on Cannon.

"That blonde you were eyeballing?"

"The chesty one struttin' her stuff?"

She *did* strut, damn her. "Were you eyeballing any others?"

"Pretty much all of them, hon."

That threw her, but only for a second. "She works for the lawyer who handled my grandfather's estate, and she's made it clear she's after Cannon."

With an exaggerated eye roll, Armie took her arm and started with her toward the bar. "Are you drunk?"

"A teeny-tiny bit tipsy." She leaned in to confide, "I never drink."

"No? Seriously?"

Was he being facetious? "Vanity says I can't hold my liquor. She's my friend."

He laughed. "Okay."

"But the wine has nothing to do with it."

"Yeah, it does, because you should know you don't have to worry about—"

She dug in, stalling their progress. "But Mary is here tonight, too!"

"Who?"

"Keep up, will you? She's the woman Cannon was going to sleep with, except I showed up and accidentally derailed his plans." Which she was now glad about. "I'm sure she's hoping to…reconnect."

Armie blew out a breath, and smiled. "Hate to break it to you, honey, but Mary and Mindi will have to wait in line."

They stopped at the front of the crowd, and Yvette found Cannon with a gaggle of ladies hugged up to him for a picture.

More ladies waited, as Armie had said, in a freaking disorganized line.

So many women.

She deflated.

"He doesn't cheat," Armie said into her ear so only she would hear.

She knew that, but she didn't want him to be tempted either, to maybe regret his decision to move in with her.

Watching the indulgent, comfortable way Cannon interacted with the women put her stomach in knots. These ladies were straightforward, without complications; they wanted him, and he could have them. Any one of them would wallow in his attention and in the pleasure they received.

When someone crowded close to her other side, she paid little attention. The place was so jammed that personal space was in short supply.

Then the expensive perfume hit her and she wanted to groan. She swiveled her head around and met Mindi's patronizing smile.

"Hello, Yvette."

Armie glanced at her, too, then away. Maybe, Yvette thought, they could shun her and she'd just go away.

That plan got foiled when Merissa waved to them from across the room. Yvette waved back, but Armie, after a muffled groan, deliberately stepped to her side and boldly ran his gaze over Mindi from the top of her head to her toes and back again to her cleavage. "Mindi, right?" he asked her boobs.

Smile slow and full of pleasure, Mindi nodded. "That's right." And to Yvette, she said, "You've moved on, I see."

Not understanding, Yvette lifted her brows.

"I'm surprised," she murmured, giving Armie a reciprocal study, "since they're so different."

"Oh." She actually believed Yvette would leave Cannon for Armie? Absurd. "No, I'm not… That is…"

"I'm a mutual friend," Armie drawled. "No more."

Hearing that smooth, seductive tone, Yvette slowly pivoted around to look at Armie. Right before her eyes he transformed into a man on the make.

Fascinated, Yvette stood there, her eyes wide. Was this because Mindi turned him on, or because Merissa was watching? She glanced to the side, caught the hurt on Merissa's face.

"I totally get what you're putting out there," Armie murmured, "and I approve."

His seductive words recaptured Yvette's attention.

Mindi preened.

"Tell me you came here alone."

Yvette wanted to gag. Actually, she might have, given how Armie smiled at her and rubbed her shoulder.

Interest quickened Mindi's breath. "I'm alone, yes."

He somehow got between Yvette and Mindi without his movements being noticeable. "You won't leave alone."

"I won't?"

Firm, confident, he stated, "You'll be coming home with me."

"Oh." Hand to her chest, Mindi leaned toward him, then caught herself. "But I came to see Cannon."

"Look at him all you want, honey, I don't mind. But that's as far as it'll go." He touched her collarbone, and both Mindi and Yvette held their breath. But he just drifted his fingers over her shoulder—in a pretense of moving her hair back.

Good Lord. This was worse than watching a porno, because it was up close and personal. Yvette needed to get away from them before she saw more than she wanted to.

"What do you say?" Armie asked her.

Mindi's gaze went from Armie to Yvette and back again. "You've convinced me."

"Was there any doubt?"

So cocky. Yvette shook her head. It was going to take a very strong woman to get Armie in line. And thinking that... She searched for Merissa and finally located her at the table in back with the other fighters. She faced away from Armie.

"There's such a crush up front," Mindi purred. "Would you mind getting me a glass of wine? Then we can get better acquainted."

"Let's seal the deal first." Armie dipped in and took her mouth—not touching her anywhere else—and Mindi sank like a stone. She leaned into him, clutched at his shoulders, went on tiptoe—

Armie eased her away with a smile. "Don't go anywhere, now." As he started off toward the bar, Yvette tried to high-five him.

He laughed, squeezed her hand instead and strode away.

Well, whether he celebrated with her or not, she appreciated how he'd given Mindi a new focus.

A focus that *wasn't* Cannon.

Mindi seemed to be trying to regroup, which Yvette took as a good time to escape.

Until Mindi stalled her by saying, "I wanted to talk to you about Cannon." Nudging Yvette toward a quieter corner, she added, "More specifically, you and Cannon."

"I can't imagine why." They had to step around Cannon's line. He was now serving drinks to ladies who waved their money in the air.

His gaze touched on her and he frowned.

Summoning up her brightest smile, Yvette wiggled her fingers in a wave and did her best to let him know everything was fine. The last thing she wanted to do was put a cloud on his fun.

"So you're still with him?"

She pulled away from Mindi and leaned back on the wall. Not that she needed the support, but she definitely felt the buzz. "How is that any of your business?"

Mindi put on her pitying face. "Oh, honey, how long do you think it can possibly last?"

"I repeat, it's not your concern, Ms. Jarrett."

"It's just that I'd hate to see you hurt again." She smoothed Yvette's arm, sort of petting her with compassion.

Yvette's skin crawled.

"You poor thing, you've already been through so, so much."

The ice going down Yvette's spine did a lot to clear her head. "Everyone eventually loses a family member."

"Yes, but that's not what I'm talking about." Finally withdrawing, Mindi folded her hands together in front of her. She continued with the mask of pity, as if she cared only about protecting Yvette. "Cannon told me everything."

Like a giant fist clenching her heart, pain expanded in Yvette's diaphragm. Pride helped her to keep her tone cool. "Everything?"

Mindi nodded, looked around and pushed closer. "He's a great guy, everyone knows that. But—" she bit her lip with uncharacteristic hesitation "—he's still a guy."

The idea that Cannon might have confided in this woman devastated her—not that she'd ever show it, definitely not to Mindi. Neck stiff, throat tight and eyes burning, she asked, "Your point?"

"I understand you were sweethearts before you moved away?"

Hardly. Cannon had dodged her at every turn. That was, until she'd almost been killed.

"He saved you, I know." Mindi's words were soft and gentle. "He said that because you were so young, you adored him for it."

Each word cut deeper. She'd been infatuated with him long before that. But yes, having him come to her rescue had meant he'd forever stolen her heart.

"Men love being macho," Mindi told her. "A man like Cannon more than most. Now that you're back, he's drawn by all that sweet hero worship."

Yvette wanted to throw up.

Or at least get out of the crowded bar so she could sort through her heartache alone.

With no encouragement from her, Mindi continued, "You have to be realistic, honey. You know he has a life to get back to. A big and very demanding career."

True.

"He lives in Harmony, Kentucky, now."

"I know that." Just as she knew eventually he'd have to return there.

"If you know it, then why are you creating a life here—a life I know you want with Cannon? That's just setting yourself up for heartache."

Unable to help herself, she sought him with her gaze. Cannon sat on a bar stool, laughing with two men, surrounded by more fans, all of them admiring him.

If he knew Mindi was repeating everything to her, he'd come to her rescue. Again.

As Mindi had just explained, he still saw her as that immature, needy girl incapable of caring for herself.

"I know we got off on the wrong foot," Mindi continued. "Mostly because we both want him. The difference is that I'm realistic." She touched Yvette's arm. "And you're not."

She needed to go. She *had* to go. Right now.

She'd ridden there with Cannon, but she wouldn't disturb him. Not for this.

Maybe because she watched him, he looked up and their gazes clashed. Though he smiled at the man talking to him, she still felt his scrutiny. Her stiff lips formed a smile and she managed a nod.

Unfortunately, that only sharpened his attention. He stepped away from the crowd, and Mary blocked him.

It was far too much. Anxiety burned her eyes, left her

pulse tripping. "I'm touched by your concern, Mindi, truly I am. But I can take care of myself."

"That's not what Cannon told me."

She sucked in a breath, leveled by that betrayal.

"He's convinced that you need him. Why do you think he moved in with you?"

"My life is my own. Do me a favor and butt out." Blind with hurt, she looked around, considering her options.

Mary held Cannon's attention.

And now Armie was bearing down on them.

"Goodbye, Mindi."

"You're leaving?" Mindi asked with barely veiled triumph.

Yvette didn't answer.

"You go on, honey." Mindi readjusted the V of her dress over her cleavage. "I'll let Cannon know."

There was nothing Yvette could add to that, so she turned and began pushing her way through the crowd. She heard Denver call out to her. Saw Stack watching her.

They were all worried for her and, damn it, *she did not want that.*

She stepped outside, dragged in a calming breath of evening air and pulled herself together.

She wouldn't leave. If she did, she'd only ruin Cannon's fun. She'd be fleeing, when she'd promised herself she'd never do that again.

Others milled about outside, some drinking, most talking, a few smoking. Traffic went by, headlights bouncing off the surrounding buildings. Across the street, a group of youths laughed too loudly.

Overhead, a million stars and a crescent moon rested against the inky blanket of the night sky.

Yvette looked away from two men who eyed her. Going to the wall nearest the door, she rested back, her palms flat against the rough brick. Five minutes, that was all she needed. Five minutes to clear her head and regain her poise.

Then she'd go back in and show everyone...what? That she wasn't hurt, wasn't affected by Cannon's betrayal?

Yes. She'd be cool and polite and, damn it, she'd laugh and have fun. Or at least pretend to.

Deciding that already made her feel better. She could deal with this, and she would.

Armie shoved the door open, searching.

Yvette said from behind him, "Looking for someone?"

He jerked around, scoured his gaze over her and quickly concealed his anger. "Hi, Yvette."

Smiling, a sincere smile, she said, "Hi, Armie."

"So." He again checked the area. "What are we doing?"

"I was taking a breather away from your date. You were charging out to save me from myself."

"Yeah." He rubbed the back of his neck, a telltale sign of his discomfort. "Figured you were running off."

"Nope." No more running for her. "Just taking a quick break."

"Mindi that tedious?"

"You have no idea."

"Yeah, well. Wasn't planning to talk much with her anyway."

She shook her head at him. "I promise I'll be back in very soon."

With grave suspicion, he asked, "How soon is very soon?"

Her smile widened, morphed into a small laugh. Armie was so funny.

And Cannon... He was the love of her life.

She wouldn't run. Not from him.

Not ever again.

If they had problems to overcome, well, then, she'd been working on problems most of her life. At the very least, they would be friends. But hopefully lovers, too.

"I told myself five minutes. So maybe two or three more?" He opened his mouth and she said, "Alone. Please."

He didn't want to leave her.

"I'm fine, I promise. Please, tell Cannon so he doesn't desert his fans." She touched Armie's wrist. "I'll die if I throw a kink in the works."

"All right." Before he left, he pointed at her. "If you let a bitch like Mindi bother you, I'm going to be very disappointed in you."

Funny Armie.

Wonderful Cannon.

Ohio… Home.

So many thoughts, worries, emotions scurried around her mind. But the most prevalent of all was love. For Cannon.

When Mary stepped out of the bar, Yvette let out a long breath. Maybe she didn't need those three minutes anyway. All she really needed was Cannon.

She pushed away from the wall—and the lamppost sent a long shadow across her path.

With ominous dread, she looked up.

As if genuinely pleased to see her, as though they were old friends who'd just happened to run into each other instead of a stalker finding his prey, Heath smiled down at her. "Yvette."

So he hadn't left after all. Fear tried to intrude, but they were in public. People all around them. Lit buildings. Traffic.

Remembering what Margaret had said, Yvette shook her head. "You shouldn't be here."

"But I am." He moved closer so that she was trapped between the brick wall and his big body.

Anxious about his mood, she tried to push past him.

His smile fading, he blocked her. "Did you think I'd leave without us talking?"

"You checked out of the hotel!"

He searched her face. "How do you know that?" Desperation darkened his eyes; yearning softened his voice. "Did you come looking for me?"

"God, no. I sent a cop to talk to you, to tell you to leave me alone."

A flash of rage mottled his complexion. Bunching up, he leaned down so close she felt his hot breath on her face. "You think I'm a fucking idiot? Is that it?"

His voice was a low hiss, not overly perceptible to the others nearby. "I think you should leave me alone." She again tried to move past him but he caught her arm. It was the same unbreakable, bruising hold he'd used at the rec center. "Stop it!"

"I thought about why your new boyfriend asked where I was staying. I knew what that bastard wanted."

She strained away from the menace of his low tone, his big body. "He wants you to leave me alone, same as I do."

Comprehension had his eyes flinching. "You're drunk."

"I am not." At the moment, she felt plenty clearheaded, and plenty worried. How could she defuse this situation without screaming bloody murder?

His hand tightened even more. "Did that fucker get you drunk?"

"Stop being an idiot!" It was bad enough this had

happened at the rec center. To have it get repeated here, while Cannon entertained his fans—

"I smell it on your breath."

"Get out of my space and you won't." She shoved hard against his chest, but with very little effort he jerked her in close to his body, squeezing her so forcefully she couldn't get breath.

"No," she rasped, the only protest she could manage.

No one intervened. No one said a word.

As he tightened his hold, blackness edged in around her vision. She tried to fight it off, to fight him.

He hushed her, smoothing her hair, whispering, "It's okay, honey, just relax." Her toes barely touched the ground with the way he held her pinned to his side.

To observers, he probably looked like a concerned boyfriend helping a drunken girlfriend home. "We need to talk." He looked over his shoulder as he continued dragging her away. "And it'll best be done in private."

CHAPTER NINETEEN

AFTER RUDELY PUSHING her way to the front, Mary grabbed his arm. "Cannon?"

Not again. He'd just fended her off as politely as he could, but she hadn't been gone two minutes before returning.

He'd already told her there'd be nothing between them. He didn't feel like rehashing it again so soon.

Easily sidestepping her with the way others wanted his attention, he gave her his back.

But she tangled a hand in the back of his waistband and gave a tug. When he looked at her in disbelief, she said, "I'm sorry," then said it again to the young couple he'd been about to serve. "I wouldn't interrupt, except that this is important. At least, I think it is."

Something in her tone gave him pause, and that had him automatically scanning the bar for Yvette.

He didn't see her. Armie had claimed she was only getting air and would be right back in.

But then where was she?

Mary tugged at him again, and when he leaned closer, she whispered, "I just want to help, I promise."

Help with what? He handed the tray over the bar to Rowdy. "I'm taking a break."

"Sure." He skipped his attention to Mary, but didn't comment. "You're long overdue anyway."

"Thanks." Promising he'd be right back, he excused

himself from the crowd. Seeking a modicum of privacy, he pulled Mary slightly away. "All right. What is it?"

"Your... I guess your girlfriend?"

"Yvette?"

As if that confirmed something for her, she let out a disappointed breath. He would have commented on that, but she immediately rallied with determination.

"I saw her outside."

Yeah, he knew that. "She's grabbing some fresh air." Impatience and something more, something turbulent, churned inside him.

"I...I think she needs you."

Needed him because she was upset? Or something more?

Wanting to see for himself, he nodded at Mary. "Thanks." He started away, but again she held on.

"Listen to me, will you?" Aware of the crowd, she lowered her voice. "When I went out, she was there alone. But then some guy got in her space, and I don't know her well, but I do know pushy men. That guy was pushy." Mary lifted her shoulders. "I could tell she didn't like it."

Heath? No, it couldn't be.

Not here, at a crowded public place. Probably just some idiot flirting with her. But, damn it...

Cannon quickly kissed her cheek. "Thanks, honey. Appreciate it." Apprehension pulsed in his temples. He crossed the bar in long strides, wending his way through the patrons with haste, unable to reply to greetings and ignoring questions.

He knew Mary followed him, maybe a few others, too. Damn it, Yvette hated scenes. If he charged out there, half the damn bar would go with him.

He was probably overreacting; he couldn't imagine any guy seeing her and not making a play.

That wasn't reason to go on a rampage.

But his heart beat harder and a dangerous mix of fury and fear stacked up inside him.

He pushed through the doors, quickly scanned the groups of people loitering about. He didn't see her and the panic set in. He turned, searching every dark corner and alley, and finally glanced across the street.

A trio of boys he knew spotted him, and by their expressions alone he knew something wasn't right.

Jogging, he headed toward them. A car horn blared; a driver cursed him.

They didn't greet him as usual, didn't smile at his presence. They were young, but they'd seen enough brutality to recognize it at a gut level.

"Have you seen her?" Cannon asked even before he'd reached them.

"She is with you, then?" one of them asked.

Fuck, fuck, fuck. "Where is she?"

The oldest of boys, probably only sixteen, jerked his head to the side and back.

Cannon peered through the dark between tall buildings to a gravel lot behind them—and saw Heath and Yvette next to a car. Body language said they were both pissed. Heath's voice rose, indistinct but angry.

The kids shuffled restlessly, taught to stay uninvolved, but influenced by Cannon to do just the opposite. It was a daily battle they fought between social apathy and schooled justice. "We were trying to decide if we should come get you—"

Heath opened a car door and Yvette protested. She turned to leave, but Heath grabbed her back.

Every combustible feeling Cannon suffered suddenly ignited, then blew. Forgetting the boys, he took off in a run, rage expanding with his pounding footsteps.

Everything faded from his periphery except for Yvette. Her fear-widened eyes. How she strained away from Heath. The noise her sandals made as they slipped in the gravel.

"Let her go." The lethal order must have given Heath pause, because he hesitated. Yvette almost twisted away, but Heath caught her by the back of her T-shirt. It ripped from the shoulder.

Uncaring who might hear, Cannon told him, "You are so fucking dead."

At that, Heath shoved her to the side and charged.

He had only a second to glance at Yvette, to see she was okay, before Heath was there, right in front of him.

Cannon met him with a fist that knocked his head back. Another to his gut. As Heath reeled back, Cannon kicked his ribs. The hit sounded like a blast, and he knew he'd just broken a rib or two.

On a savage groan, Heath threw his body against Cannon and they both went down.

Not a problem.

Despite the overload of emotion, Cannon moved with precision. Heath thought he had the advantage, being on top. Allowing him to raise up a little, Cannon waited for him to throw a punch, then isolated his arm. Too fast for Heath to see it coming, he used his legs to trap his head and upper body, one leg under Heath's chin, the other across his chest with his arm between. Lifting his hips, he extended Heath's arm until he popped his shoulder.

Then popped it again, ensuring he'd dislocated the joint.

Heath gave a wounded-bear roar. The second Cannon released him, he tried to curl in on himself.

Wasn't happening.

Still driven by fury, Cannon punched his smug face again, heavy punches, right fist, then left, right again—

"Enough." Armie tackled him away from Heath and they both went down on the rough gravel. When Cannon instinctively fought him off, Armie said again, *"Enough."*

Cannon meant what he'd said. He wanted to kill Heath.

Arms locked around Cannon's torso, Armie said in a harsh whisper, "This isn't the audience you want to perform for."

The black cloud dissipated and reality sank in. Familiar faces from the bar circled them, moving in, all talking, taking pictures with their cell phones.

Breathing hard, Cannon easily shrugged Armie off.

Easy only because Armie wasn't fighting him. It was more a matter of keeping him from killing the putz.

"Rowdy called Logan," Armie told him. "Sorry."

"Doesn't matter." His body still singing with the need for violence, he pushed to his feet. The flashes from a dozen camera phones continued to light the night. "Fuck."

"Take a breath," Armie advised.

He tried. But what he felt right then, pure bloodlust, was night and day from a sanctioned fight where he used his cool to win. Different from the defense he offered to the neighborhood businesses to counter bullying thugs. Different from…anything he'd ever known.

This was red-hot, blind and…strangling the fuck out of him.

Sticking close, maybe in case he went after Heath again, Armie said, "She could use a little of that control you're known for."

He'd been avoiding looking at Yvette, only because in that moment he didn't know himself. He'd fought in plenty of competitions. Fought for justice. Fought for friends.

Three years ago, he'd fought twisted fucks who'd tried to rape Yvette, who probably would have killed her. That had been devastating. For her and for him.

But this was so much more personal, because back then she'd been a sweet girl from the neighborhood. Too young. Untouchable.

And now...now *she was his.*

He'd never fought for anything this important.

The second his gaze found her, standing well away from Heath's car, cradling one arm and looking lost on many levels, he had to touch her.

Had to.

He started toward her. To his surprise, she sucked it up, squared her shoulders and came to meet him halfway. When they were close, she bit her lip, undecided.

He made up her mind for her, gathering her close, his arms locking around her, holding her but mindful of her arm.

It took him a bit, but he asked, "You're okay?"

She gave a small, jerky nod. "I'm so sorry."

For only a second more, he kept her against him, absorbing her scent and softness and the steady beating of her heart. But, damn it, she had the means to set him on fire with need, and to piss him off with confusion. Without even trying she left him undone and in pieces.

Another breath helped, one more, and by the third he could grasp sanity again.

"First," he grated, his voice hoarse, "your arm?"

"I'm fine."

His jaw flexed until his temples hurt. "Let me see." He tried to take her arm, but she resisted.

"Cannon." In a hushed, breaking whisper, she told him, "My shirt is ripped," as if she'd committed a sin.

"I'll give you another shirt. Hell, I'll give you fifty fucking shirts." Okay, so maybe sanity wasn't quite attainable just yet. One more deep breath, and more firmly this time, "Let me see your arm."

She ducked her face and managed to hold the pieces of the oversize shirt together while letting him look.

Bruises already purpled her skin, and damn if that didn't throw a match on the smoldering embers of his temper. "I should have broken his leg, too. Or his fucking neck."

"No." Her breath hitched, a little too high and thin. "You shouldn't even be involved in this mess."

It was the wrong thing—the *worst* thing—to say to him.

Stepping away from her seemed his best choice, but he only got two feet before storming back. "I'm involved because *we're* involved."

Eyes widening, lips parting, she stroked him like a mongrel dog. "I know," she said softly, her tone soothing, "and I'm glad."

Glad? She was fucking *glad?*

"But you don't have time for—"

"What? You?"

No answer, just a lot of flinching uncertainty. He wanted to pull back, to be what she so obviously needed right now, but he couldn't.

"Sex?" He tunneled a hand into her hair, anchoring her to him. "A relationship?"

She blinked big, bewildered eyes. "I don't know."

"Well, I do." Still feeling like a stranger in his own skin, he tugged her head back, her face up, until her lips opened for him.

Then he took her mouth. Hard.

She didn't fight him, just gasped in surprise. He sank his tongue in, stealing the sound.

Tasting her.

The wine she'd drunk, her fear.

Her confusion.

Using his free arm to arch her closer, he turned his head, consuming her, relishing her small whimpers, her soft, accepting moan.

Armie clapped him hard on the back, returning him to the here and now. "You might want to put the brakes on that lust, Saint. Looks like you've forgotten, but you're nowhere near a bed."

Jesus.

Cannon freed her mouth, but kept her tucked against his chest. She complied, clinging to him, maybe hiding. Ruthlessly, he crammed back the darkest parts of his rage. "I guess I still have an audience?"

"Most of the women have fainted, but yeah, still there."

Against his chest, he heard Yvette snicker.

No way. He leaned his head back to try to see her, but she squawked and squeezed in close again.

She'd just been through hell. Accosted.

By Heath, and by him.

He rubbed his hands up and down her back. "Are you hysterical?"

Her rude snort surprised him. "Feeling a little faint myself, that's all."

Armie chuckled.

"Don't set me away," she told him when he again tried to see her face. "My shirt is ripped, remember? I'm using you for a shield."

Amazing that she could keep it together given all that

had happened. But the way she kept it together bothered him. She held on to him, she'd kissed him back, but, damn it, he felt…something. Some distance. Some trumped-up facade of self-possession.

For their onlookers?

Or for him?

"Yvette…" The timing sucked, granted. And still he wanted to strip away that cloak of untouchable poise.

She patted him. "We've caused enough of a buzz without me flashing the masses."

And enough of a buzz without him forcing issues better left for privacy. "God, honey, you're destroying me."

She went still at that, so he sighed and figured he'd just have to set her straight as soon as he got her alone. And thinking of that… He turned his head, searching. "Where's Heath?"

Armie looked at where he'd been, but a sea of bodies now filled the space.

"Damn it." Armie stomped off in that direction just as police sirens split the night.

Accompanied by two uniformed officers, Detective Logan Riske made his way through the throng.

It all went downhill from there.

YVETTE FELT LIKE the Pied Piper as they all went back into Rowdy's bar, followed by the customers. Armie had given her his shirt to cover her torn one, but she was still a mess, still the center of whispers and curious stares and speculation. She hated it.

Cannon had asked all the onlookers to back off, and he'd stated there would be no more pictures.

With mumbled apologies, the crowd dispersed.

Even during this new crisis, the respect he got from those around him made her proud.

Rowdy led the way into the break room, pulling out a chair for her at the long table.

Cannon sat beside her. Armie stood off to his side.

Both Detective Riske, who also just happened to be Rowdy's brother-in-law, and Officer Huffer remained standing.

Rowdy set out cups of coffee for everyone, then got an ice pack for her arm.

When she ignored the coffee, Cannon put it in her hand. "Drink some." The idea of consuming anything made her stomach pitch, but he seemed so upset that she agreed just to appease him.

But that, too, had him grinding his teeth.

Her position was so untenable that she wasn't sure what to do or say. She *felt* it, how all the men watched her. Their concern burned her from the inside out, leaving her face hot and her throat tight.

Why had she gone outside?

Mindi. Jealousy and hurt had blunted her better judgment.

Why hadn't she immediately run from Heath?

Arrogance. She'd truly thought, with others around, that she could keep her dignity intact and just walk away.

So, so dumb. And now all this fanfare. Why hadn't she—

"A little more," Cannon said, again pressing the sweetened coffee into her shaking hands.

"Thank you." Feeling like a complete spectacle, she dutifully sipped.

Silence filled the room until Cannon stood and went to Logan. She could hear the hushed voices, but not exactly what was said.

Whatever it was, the room began to empty. On his way

out, Armie squeezed her shoulder, bent to put a kiss to the top of her head.

Rowdy said, "If you need anything, just let me know."

"Thanks." Cannon reclaimed his seat beside her, half-turned toward her. His knee bumped her thigh, his right hand rested on her shoulder.

Officer Huffer said nothing, just carried his coffee and silently left.

With his free hand, Cannon held the ice pack to the darkening bruises from where Heath had gripped her.

She thought of it, how scared she'd been, how stupid she felt now, and tears threatened. Gulping air, she fought them off.

Cannon's big hand opened on her back, gently rubbing.

She hated it, all of it. The careful concern. The worried gazes. The coddling. Why did she have to keep being a victim?

"Tell me what happened," Logan said. "Take your time, and don't leave out any details."

Nodding, she went through the entire story, explaining how Heath had approached, how he'd whisked her away, not stopping until he'd reached his car.

One question after another interrupted the telling.

Yes, she'd tried to leave, but he'd restrained her, pleading with her before going into a rage.

No, no one had seemed to notice or care that he was practically dragging her along. Perhaps they'd thought her drunk. Or just didn't want to get involved.

Yes, he'd tried to put her in his car. That was how her arm got bruised, her shirt ripped.

Everything had happened so fast.

She told them how Armie had checked on her and about her promise to come right back in.

She hadn't known about Mary until Cannon explained how he knew there was a problem, why he'd gone in search of her.

When next Yvette saw her, she'd thank her.

Oh, the irony in that.

Damn it, she would not continue to be this pathetic.

Lifting the foam cup, she finished off the coffee. It wasn't easy, but she forced herself to sit a little straighter, to stop avoiding eye contact.

"Is there anything else?"

"Yeah." Logan propped a hip on the edge of the table. "You okay?"

"Yes, I'm fine." Somehow she would make it so, because sniveling was out of the question. "Thank you for coming out. I'm sorry—"

"None of that." Logan's voice was kind but firm. "Huffer joined in interviewing witnesses. I already put out an ATL."

When she shook her head, not understanding, he clarified, "Attempt to locate."

"Do you think they'll find him?"

"Depends on what he does. We have his car make and model, a good description of him. And Cannon says he's injured."

"Dislocated shoulder," Cannon said without inflection. "Broken nose, hopefully busted ribs."

With a noncommittal sound, Logan drank more coffee. "So he'll need medical care?"

"Probably."

Logan waited, a brow raised.

"I know how to put my shoulder back," Cannon said. "Nose, too. Ribs just need to heal. But he's not me."

Yvette stared at him, horrified. No, Heath wasn't even close to being Cannon. But he was insane.

Logan just rolled with it. "Okay, so we'll alert the major hospitals, but if he goes directly to an urgent care facility…" His shoulder lifted. "The thing with an ATL is that an officer has to actually come across him. He doesn't have a known residence here, we aren't sure where he's been staying, so if he lies low, could be hard to catch up with him."

Cannon watched her. His enigmatic gaze kept her from knowing his thoughts. He was…intense, but with anger? Concern? She just couldn't tell.

Logan wanted her to go through the story again, just to ensure the details stayed the same and she hadn't forgotten anything.

Telling it a second time wasn't any easier.

"It'll take a couple of days for the arrest warrant." With the cup now empty, Logan crushed it and tossed it toward a garbage can. "Did you have an RO against him in California? If so, we need to notify them."

Another blank look from her.

"Restraining order," Logan explained.

"It didn't seem necessary. He…" She hated having to defend herself. "He wasn't like this, that is, this extreme, until after I left. I could just ignore him."

"Not anymore." He looked from her to Cannon and back again. "It's a good idea if you don't stay alone."

Cannon pushed back his chair. "She won't be."

CHAPTER TWENTY

CANNON DIDN'T WANT to leave, not even for a second. But he also refused to leave her unprotected.

They'd only been in the break room for forty-five minutes—less than an hour that had felt like ten as he listened to her quavering voice, saw her shaking hands and witnessed her humiliation.

She didn't understand that no one blamed her. Because she blamed herself.

No one expected her to keep it together either.

But she did.

He followed Logan as far as the door, thanking him again. It was a good thing to be friends with cops.

The bar crowd hadn't thinned out much. Even from the break room he could hear the boisterous laughter and loud talking. Someone played the jukebox; beer bottles clattered. He rubbed the bridge of his nose but quickly made up his mind.

"Stay put a minute."

Twisting around, a little panicked, she asked, "Where are you going?"

"I'm not leaving." Yet. "You'll stay here?"

She looked wounded that he had to ask. "Yes."

Nodding, he left the room to search for Rowdy and found him in the kitchen. "I need a favor."

Drying his hands, Rowdy nodded and stepped aside with him. "You want me to put out some feelers?"

What the cops couldn't find through legal channels, Rowdy could usually manage...the other way.

"Yeah, I do. But I'll also be doing my own thing."

"Neighborhood watch?"

He nodded. "Can you stay with her while I go get Armie? Then I'll just need ten minutes to get things lined up."

"Not a problem." Knowing time was short, Rowdy started off.

Cannon stopped him with a hand on his arm. "She's..." Stoic beyond reason. "This is..."

"I know." He squeezed Cannon's shoulder. "Hustle it up, okay? No matter what she says or does, she needs you a lot more than she needs anything else."

With the red haze of rage still pulsing through his veins, Cannon wondered if that was true. As far as he could tell, Yvette resented needing anyone—him included.

But thinking about that right now was a major distraction from what needed to be done.

He found Armie exactly where he expected him to be: in a huddle with the other guys, making plans. They were outside together, standing far enough away from the cops not to be overheard.

Armie spotted him, looked him over with concern and said quietly, "I got the ball rolling."

"Thanks." Torn between where he wanted to be and what he wanted to do, he clenched and unclenched his fists. "I can't go anywhere tonight—"

"Damn right," Stack agreed, his gaze remarkably steady for someone who'd been drinking. "Stay with her. We'll canvass the usual places."

"And ask the usual questions," Denver added. "Anything concrete turns up, we'll let you know."

"Otherwise, you'll hear from me in the morning." Armie flexed his bare shoulders. "If he's anywhere around here, we'll know."

"I want a second pair of eyes on her." Cannon knew his own considerable ability. He could handle just about any physical confrontation. But if Heath decided to start shooting, well, who the hell knew what could happen? No way did he want her left alone with the bastard.

In this neighborhood there were plenty of young guys looking for a fast buck. He'd invested a lot of time and energy into steering them away from drugs and gangs. The rec center helped a lot with that. Some of them had even gotten legitimate jobs—but not all.

When it suited his purposes, Cannon didn't mind using them. He paid, and it kept them from doing something illegal. He would never hand over front-line protection for Yvette, but as backup? As an extra observer?

A win-win for them both.

"So." Armie shoved his hands into his pockets. "You're still red eyed and looking fierce."

Hands on his hips, head down, Cannon admitted the obvious. "I've never been this…"

"Out of control?"

Cannon closed his eyes, dragged in a deep breath of the thick evening air. "I wanted to kill him."

"Yeah, I was there. Saw it." He nudged Cannon with his shoulder. "But won't it be more fun to have the fuck rot in jail?"

"No."

"Look at it this way," Armie said, never one to quit. "Did you really want Yvette to witness you disemboweling him?"

A reluctant sound, half laugh, half groan, escaped him. "She'd probably act like that was nothing, too."

"Ho. What's this? You wanted her to start bawling and go all hysterical? Because I have to say, I hate that shit."

"Ditto," Stack said.

"Same here," Denver agreed.

He cast his frown around at each of them and realized their evenings had been blown, as well. "Sorry."

"For?" Armie asked.

"You all had hookups and now—"

"Not me," Stack said. "I struck out."

They all looked at Denver, but he shook his head. "No."

"What about Cherry?" Cannon had seen her in his lap and just assumed...

"She flirted with a dozen different guys." Denver looked at Stack. "Including you."

"She was just joking around."

Denver shook his head again and turned to Armie. "I saw you with a top-heavy blonde."

He shrugged. "Either she'll wait or she won't. No biggie." He pointed at Cannon. "But you already got the prize, so why dawdle out here with us? We've got it under wraps."

Cannon locked his hands behind his head and paced in agitation. What did he want?

Yvette, yes. But for how long? Forever?

Probably.

Did he want her to be needy? No. Never that. He loved her strength and independence. But he needed her trust.

He needed her to be herself with him.

"One thing at a time," Armie advised. He leaned in closer so no one else would hear. "And given how you two tongue dueled before the cops showed up, well, I'm thinking she has her own way of coping. Be the hero, man. Get her home and help her cope."

Scrubbing a hand over his face, Cannon laughed again. "Right. Glad I can always count on you to focus on the important things."

"You know it."

Honestly, that was how they dealt, how they kept things in perspective. Regardless of the jokes, he knew Armie would do everything in his power to help, just as Cannon would have done for him. They relied on each other, and had total trust.

Now, if only he could get there with Yvette.

Pulling it together as much as he could, Cannon put in a few calls making arrangements, then asked his own questions of the witnesses. It all came down to the fact that Heath had tried to take her, she'd resisted and the bastard had gotten away.

Less than ten minutes later Cannon stalked back into the break room. Rowdy was just in the process of giving her a fresh ice pack.

She was in the process of telling him she didn't need it.

"We'll take it with us." Now that he'd done as much as he could, he wanted to get her home.

And then he wanted to clear up a few misunderstandings. The sooner the better.

THE MORE SHE thought about it, the more Yvette couldn't believe her own behavior.

Heath had tried to force her into a car.

Cannon had literally mangled him.

And she'd reacted with…lust?

The woman who couldn't have a climax. Or rather, couldn't—until Cannon.

But good God, out in a parking lot with a rapt audience watching, in some cases recording, everything?

Even now, knowing that he only bided his time, that he'd revealed her deepest, darkest hurts to Mindi, she still wanted him.

Desperately.

It made sense. Cannon was a terrific guy, respected by so many. He had a perfect body, honed with strength.

And his face...those electric-blue eyes, thick lashes, sculpted cheekbones and strong jaw.

His sexy smile.

Heat crawled up her neck; she'd totally forgotten herself in that parking lot, all because he'd kissed her without the kid-glove treatment he usually favored.

Thinking about it sent additional warmth throbbing between her legs. And her belly. Her breasts. Deep in her core.

He'd been consumed with need...for her.

Thank God no one had asked her to repeat that part of things. She'd gotten by just saying that Cannon was checking on her and that was how Heath had escaped.

It was over and done with now, so she needed to stop thinking about it. Better to sort out the problems.

How had Heath gotten up and left after that beating? Witnesses said he'd driven away. That he'd looked terrible. That his arm was clearly damaged, his nose twisted. One eye swollen shut. Blood everywhere.

And still he'd fled the scene.

She didn't know where Cannon had gone after leaving her in the break room. He didn't say, and he was so distant right now, she didn't ask.

It had been excruciating, leaving the bar. So many people staring. Nearly all of them strangers.

Thank God Armie had given her his shirt to wear. That at least kept her decently covered, hiding her own ripped shirt. She was also grateful that he'd stopped Cannon from hurting Heath worse. Not that she cared about Heath's injuries, but she didn't want Cannon to have to deal with the aftermath because of her.

She liked everything about Armie—except for his appreciation of Mindi.

She didn't see the attraction. But then, she wasn't male. Men, she found, were difficult to understand.

And thinking of difficult men…she again looked at Cannon. Each lamppost they passed briefly illuminated his profile.

Cannon's knuckles were raw, his gaze still deadly.

Driving in utter silence, he repeatedly flexed his hands on the steering wheel. She didn't know if he did that because of anger or because his hands hurt.

He looked…maybe combustible.

Exhaustion, both emotional and physical, left her too numb to calculate the consequences, but at the edges of her mind, she knew it was bad.

All of it.

Too tired to be discreet, she asked, "Are you mad?"

"Yes." No hesitation.

Wow. She'd never seen him in this mood like this. Usually he was even tempered, calm personified, in ultimate control.

Unsure how to deal with him, she bit her lip, then asked, "At me?"

Frown intensifying, he glanced at her, over her, before giving his attention back to the road.

Before he could answer, her nervous chatter erupted. "Because seriously, you know I wasn't leaving, right? I didn't lie about that. I just wanted a breath of air."

"I would have walked out with you."

At that moment, she hadn't wanted him to. When she thought of him talking with Mindi about her, it left her desolate. But going into all that now would only make a bad night worse.

And besides, she had her pride.

If all he wanted was, as Mindi had said, to finish what they'd started, well, she wanted that, too. Somehow she'd make it be enough, and he'd never know that she still carried her schoolgirl infatuation.

Knowing he waited, she came up with the first excuse she could find without opening another vein. "You had fans lined up to see you."

"I get breaks, too." That icy calm tone was worse than a shout. "Or did you think I needed to cater to the fans for four hours straight?"

She winced; the way he said it, it did sound dumb. "I didn't want to be a bother."

He laughed, but it sure as heck wasn't with humor.

"I know." Losing her own grip a little, she levered around in the seat to glare at him. "I ended up being a bigger bother!"

"Don't put words in my mouth."

She ignored that to stress, "I didn't *know* Heath was still around. I didn't *know* he was idiot enough to try to drag me off with people all around us. Until tonight, he'd always been a pain, but not a total psycho." He'd escalated into the insanely obsessed role so quickly, she needed time to adjust. "I didn't go off with him willingly, you know!"

Unsmiling, his own temper cracking, Cannon growled, "I thought maybe you went to 'avoid a scene.'"

Until now, until he'd said that, she'd never known him to be a jerk. She couldn't get enough air. Voice strained, she told him, "Yes, I hate scenes, all right? I have good reason and you know it!"

His gaze flickered to her again, maybe with remorse, but she couldn't tell for sure.

"When Heath grabbed me, I wanted to scream." She'd wanted to so badly. She clenched her hands to still the trembling. "But he held me so tight." She saw it all again, felt it again and panic bubbled up. Desperately she fought it back. She would not go hysterical on him. "I could barely even breathe," she whispered. "It felt like he was going to break my ribs—"

Fury bunched Cannon's shoulders, tightened his hands and turned his voice into a snarl. *"I should have killed him."*

Oh, wow. Speechless, Yvette watched the working of his jaw, the way his right eye twitched. He was even more volatile than she'd realized.

Nervously twining two fingers in the ends of her hair, she considered him, then came to a decision. If it was Heath, or for that matter any other man, she'd be worried at the level of his rage.

But this was Cannon, and no matter what, she always felt safer with him, never threatened.

She understood that his fury was on her behalf. Putting aside any errors in judgment when it came to Mindi, Yvette knew he cared for her—as he cared for everyone. She couldn't bear seeing him like this.

There were no words to make the situation better. It required more than that.

She knew what she needed.

He was a big, bad fighter, but maybe he needed it, too.

Unhooking her seat belt, she scooted over next to him.

"What are you doing? Get your belt back on."

"No."

His hands tightened on the wheel, squeezing it as if to crack it in half. "Yvette," he warned.

Hugging up to his arm, she sighed at the contact with his warm body. Rock-solid muscles flexed under her hands, more evidence of his anger. "I'm okay," she gently told him.

When Cannon growled, "What if he'd gotten you into his car?"

She could only admit, "I don't know." It had scared her to death, wondering what he'd do.

They would be home in another two or three minutes. She wanted a bowl of cereal, her pj's, Cannon and bed. Not necessarily in that order.

She put her head back against his shoulder. "He kept saying he loved me and just wanted to talk." Needing the contact, she slipped her fingers up under the sleeve of his T-shirt, opening her palm over all that sleek, hot strength. He had the most amazing shoulders and biceps, she wanted to bite him. Lick him.

Kiss him everywhere.

Musing aloud, she said, "Maybe I should try calling him. Let him talk—"

"Hell, no."

"Okay." She squeezed his arm, loving the feel of him despite all that had happened.

Tomorrow she'd bring it up again and suggest they ask Margaret about it. It might be a way to bring Heath out in the open. She could even give the number to one of them to try calling from her phone.

Knowing he lurked around the area, able to spring on her again, scared her more than anything else.

It seemed so quiet, being on the road this time of night with only the occasional car going past. She idly stroked the inside of Cannon's arm, where he was sleek and smooth and hard.

"Don't be mad at me, okay?" She was too tired for that.

"I'm not." He shrugged her off his shoulder, but only so he could put his arm around her. "I'm mad at…a lot of shit. But not you."

"Do you want to tell me?"

"Yeah, I do." He gave her a brief warning squeeze. "We're going to have a nice long talk."

Stifling a groan, she asked, "Not tonight, right?"

"We'll see."

Which as good as meant he planned to talk tonight. Another groan tried to get out, but she swallowed it back. If he needed to talk, she'd talk. Maybe while sitting on his lap.

In her pajamas.

And maybe under those circumstances, she'd be able to avoid the conversation until morning.

A minute later he pulled into the driveway, got out to open the garage door and pulled in to park.

Holding the hem of Armie's oversize shirt, Yvette hopped out on her own. More than anything, she wanted comfort, snuggling. Sex.

She wanted Cannon.

But if he wanted to lecture her instead, he could damn well wait, at least until she'd gotten her cereal.

CANNON WATCHED HER hustle her sexy little ass inside and knew he'd chased her away.

He struggled with his temper, knew it was useless and considered heading straight downstairs to the workout equipment in the basement.

Wouldn't hurt for him to work off some rage before confronting her.

Mad? Hell, *mad* didn't even begin to cover it. He was caught in such a gripping fury it was all he could do not to go out and find trouble. Surely someone somewhere in the neighborhood needed an old-fashioned beatdown. And if it was more than one person, that'd suit him just fine.

Right now he'd relish a brawl.

But he was respected in his self-assigned role as peacekeeper, in large part because he didn't seek trouble.

He just took care of it when it happened.

It'd be unfair to leave Yvette wondering what he had to say, so he got out of the car. The light from his open door spilled out around the concrete floor and pegboard walls—and reflected off the open garage window.

Knowing he'd left it closed and locked, Cannon slowly got out. Something in the air alerted him; he scanned the garage, and then the window.

One pane was missing, broken out, the glass crunching underneath his feet.

Broken so an intruder could reach inside and open the lock.

He searched the interior and noticed only a few displaced items, the garbage can moved, tool drawers open as if someone had been searching.

Vigilant, he went to the window to pull it down— and thanks to a bright moon he saw the shadow move across the lawn.

Someone was still here.

Hoping it'd be Heath, needing it to be that prick, he headed outside to investigate, his stride long and hurried. He'd just passed through the garage door when more glass crashed—inside the house.

Followed by Yvette's screech.

HEART STILL LODGED in her throat, flattened up to the wall, Yvette took in the broken glass glittering over the sink, across the floor. The item that had sailed through the window? There, half under the table…

A fist-size rock.

Cannon shot into the room, heaving like a marauder. His gaze went everywhere in a nanosecond before searching over her body.

"I'm okay," she told him fast, and pointed. "A rock. From outside."

"It didn't hit you? You aren't cut?"

"No. Just…it startled me."

His gaze narrowed on the window, frustration visibly mounted, and he started to bolt out again.

"Wait!"

Gaze locking on hers, he barked, *"What?"*

He really wanted to take someone apart, she could tell. But she didn't want to be left alone.

Using his pause to her advantage, Yvette grabbed his arm. "Don't you dare go out there." She prepared an excuse for why he should stay, but the worry quickly became a reality.

Aghast at the possibility, she whispered, "What if someone is in the house?"

Cannon's eyes flared. "Call 911." He again started to turn away, but thought to add, "Stay in the kitchen."

Hands shaking, she put in the call, then leaned out the kitchen doorway to watch as Cannon went down the hall, this time with more stealth. He checked the basement door, saw it was still locked and continued down to the baths and bedrooms.

When the dispatcher answered, she quickly explained the situation to the very calm lady on the other end of the line.

The dispatcher assured her that an officer was on the way, but wanted Yvette to stay on the phone until he arrived.

Giving a blow-by-blow report of Cannon's progress

through the house—without finding anything—helped her recollect her calm.

When Cannon returned, Yvette explained that he hadn't found anything. Almost at the same time the flashing red-and-blue lights showed out front.

With relief, she dropped back against the wall.

Using his flashlight, the officer walked around the house. Two security lights had been shot out with a BB gun. The officer found BBs on the ground and embedded into the side of the house. He took a report, promised to update Logan and Officer Huffman—and got a picture with Cannon.

Though his patience looked strained, Cannon remained friendly and smiled for the photo.

After the officer left, she cleaned up the glass while Cannon secured the kitchen window, and when that was done, she trailed him to the garage.

"Why don't you go get your shower while I take care of this?"

She hated to admit it, but didn't see an alternative. "I'd rather wait on you."

Cannon paused in the act of closing the garage window. As if her vulnerability shaved off a layer of his rage, his shoulders eased. "All right. I'll only be a minute."

She sat on the hood of her car, knees drawn up, jumping at every sound. When Cannon hammered a plank of wood over the window, she covered her ears and squeezed her eyes shut.

The noise ended, and his arms came around her, his big hands open on her backside. "You okay?"

She wasn't, not by a long shot, but she nodded anyway. "Tired." Forcing her head up, she met his electric-blue eyes, now volatile with indiscernible emotion. "You?"

Calm as you please, he said, "Murderous rage."

For some reason, that made her smile even as her eyes burned. "I'm sorry."

"Come on." He scooped her up against his chest and carried her into the house.

Just for a minute, Yvette thought, as she rested her cheek against his chest. Then she'd get her gumption back and stop letting him pamper her.

"What do you want to do first?" His chin brushed her forehead. "Shower? Eat? Bed?"

You, she answered silently. *I want to do you.* But sadly, he hadn't made that an option. Food no longer appealed, not even a bowl of cold cereal. If she tried to eat she just might barf.

"I'm beat," she said with a trumped-up smile. "I just want to wash my face, brush my teeth and go to bed." *With you hugged tight around me.*

"All right."

She didn't protest when he carried her into the bathroom. And when he stayed so that they brushed their teeth side by side, she was grateful not be alone.

But then he peeled off his clothes while she washed her face—which made her get soap in her eyes because, seriously, how could she not watch?

When she finished, he took her hand and, wearing only snug boxers, walked with her back into the bedroom.

With every step they took, her heart punched harder, making her breathless. Anticipation sizzled along every nerve ending.

She needed this—she needed *him.*

He opened a drawer and got out another SBC shirt, then held it in his fist while facing her. "You're not sleeping in Armie's shirt."

Actually, she'd forgotten she had it on. "Okay." With

Cannon near naked, she didn't need to be convinced.
The idea of being skin to skin with him ramped up her
excitement even more.

Being daring, thrilled with the way he watched her,
she skinned out of her jeans, pulled Armie's shirt off
over her head and then removed the ripped shirt. Seeing the blue of his eyes darken, she reached back for the
closure of her bra.

Cannon made a rough sound of near pain and averted
his gaze.

Voice quavering, she told him, "You can look." She
wanted him to. She wanted him to look and touch and
kiss....

"No." A heavy load of rigidity resettled in his broad
shoulders. "If I do, I won't be able to stop."

Did he not understand how badly she wanted him?
"So let's not stop."

Eyes still averted, he held the shirt out to her. "Take
my word on this, okay? Tonight is not the night."

Ignoring the offered shirt, she moved up against him,
her breasts to his naked back. "Why?"

He stiffened. "Yvette..."

Arms around him, she smoothed her palms over his
chest hair, down those rock-solid abs. He dropped the
shirt and caught her wrists. "You don't know what you're
doing."

"If I'm seducing you, then, yes, I do."

He laughed, the sound strained. "Yeah, you do." Still
clasping her wrists, he drew in a deep breath and turned
to her.

Though she wore only a pale pink thong, his attention
remained stubbornly on her face.

She might have been humiliated over that, even hurt,
except that she knew Cannon was trying to be noble for

her benefit. Tonight had been rough, and he thought she needed time to recoup.

If she wanted Cannon to see her differently, she'd have to be different, too.

Bolder.

She needed to go after what she wanted. *Him.*

Determined to convince him, she snuggled in close.

Her nipples, now stiffened, brushed his abdomen. He groaned and tried to loosen her hold. "You're hurt."

"Only a little."

"You're upset, too."

"I am. And I know I'll feel better if we—"

"What?" With clear reservation, he cupped her face, lifted it so he could nip her bottom lip then soothe it with his tongue. "If I go nuts on you? Because that's where I'm at, baby. No finesse, no patience like I had last time."

"I like the idea of you going nuts." She didn't need patience; she just needed him.

His nostrils flared. His eyes closed. "I'm not a self-ish prick."

"No, you're not. You're sweet—"

He snorted.

"—and hot, and I *need* to be with you."

Resistance crumbling, he breathed harder. "I can't guarantee you'll come—"

Opening her mouth on his chest, she took a soft love bite.

He shuddered. "Because I can't guarantee I'll last long enough."

She cupped his testicles through the soft cotton of his boxers, then wrapped her fingers around his throbbing length. Stroking, squeezing. "So we'll skip sleeping and do it until we get it right."

His erection flexed—and a second later he lifted her

hands away from his body. "You need to hold up a minute."

Stunned that he'd still deny her, Yvette pushed back
to see his face. "I'm beginning to think you're the one
with the problem!"

After running a hand over his face, he nodded.
"Maybe my problem is with you."

The breath left her, the words hurting like a physical
blow. Thinking only of getting away, she turned from
him.

He pulled right back around again. His hands on her
shoulders were tight but not hurtful. Looking as ago-
nized as she felt, he put his forehead to hers. "You don't
trust me, Yvette, and I want you to. I want that so goddamned bad."

Trust him? "Of course I do."

"No, you wear this mask, hiding who you are and
what you feel. How you react to things. You don't trust
me not to judge you. You don't trust me to see the truth
of things."

"What truths?"

"That you're strong and smart and independent. But
shit happens to everyone, and we all have to deal with
it. The thing is, you don't have to deal alone. Not when
I'm here." He gave her a small shake, followed quickly
by a cradling hug. "Even now," he said, his voice raw, "I
can tell something's wrong."

"My ex tried to kidnap me!"

"I know." He stroked her hair, his determination pouring over her. "You're pissed, and a little rattled still.
That's understandable. But that's not what's between
us now."

No, he couldn't possibly read her that easily, know

her that well. "I don't understand you." Suddenly she felt naked and reached for the shirt he'd dropped on the floor.

Cannon stood on it. She tugged, but he didn't move. She was eye level with his lap, him wearing only boxers, her in a thong.

They should be having sex, not arguing. If it was any other man, anyone but Cannon, they would be.

But if it was any other man, she wouldn't want it.

The absurdity of it hit her, and with it a fresh rush of indignation.

Still kneeling before him, she breathed faster...and blurted, "Mindi said you only wanted to finish what we'd started so long ago."

"What are you talking about?"

"Tonight at the bar. Before she hooked up with Armie."

"Mindi and Armie?"

Yvette again yanked at the shirt; he again didn't move. "She said once it's over, you'll be done with me. I don't know how that can be if you refuse to ever *start with me.*"

She gave up trying to get the shirt and straightened again, wrapping her arms around herself to shield her breasts. Her gaze met his and stalled.

His killing expression gave her pause.

Cannon stepped close. Voice low and menacing, he said, "You discussed me with Mindi?"

He was offended? Full of accusation, she went on tiptoes and leaned into his anger. "You did! You told her my entire history!"

"Never happened, and you should know that."

The whispered words, said through his teeth, stole her anger. She dropped back to her heels. "But...then, how?"

"No way for me to know. But Heath was at the bar. There's a damn good chance he talked to her."

All her most prevalent emotions—anger, umbrage, hurt—crashed in on her. "I never told it all to Heath."

"He's here. It's not a secret. If he did any digging—"

"You're probably right."

He took her shoulders again. "Instead of thinking it through, you automatically believed that I'd told her?"

"She led me to believe..." Yvette rubbed her temple. How many ways could she botch things in a twenty-four-hour period? "I'm sorry." When he didn't reply, she added, "For everything."

Hopefully after a few hours' sleep, things would look better, because at that moment, she couldn't imagine them getting any worse.

She stood there, unsure what to do next, dreading making another wrong move.

"You think I want a quick lay?" With heart-stopping tenderness, Cannon stroked over her hair, moved it behind her shoulders so he could better see her breasts. "You think once I get inside you, I'll be done?"

The way he looked at her now... She shook her head. No, she hadn't thought that. Not until Mindi had spelled it out to her. Then it had seemed all too plausible. "Honestly, I don't know what to think anymore."

He lifted her chin. "Guess there's only one way to find out for sure."

The words, combined with that particular heated look, had her pulse leaping. "You won't quit on me this time?"

His mouth quirked at her wording. "I can't." He levered her away so he could look at every inch of her. While consuming her with his gaze, he murmured, "First time will be fast and hard. Second time might be better. I'm still up in the air on that one." He drew her close and playfully bit her lower lip. "The third time, though…for sure, that one will be all for you."

Oh, God, she could hardly wait.

Cannon tumbled her into the bed—and she knew she wouldn't have to.

CHAPTER TWENTY-ONE

WARM SOFTNESS, FIRM breasts, tantalizing dips and hollows and wet kisses—Cannon wanted everything, right now. With Yvette.

He kneed her legs apart and settled over her, his mouth at her throat, his hands frantic on her breasts. The long day, time spent at the bar and then the turmoil afterward, left her skin rich with her intensified scent. He breathed her in and hurt with wanting her.

He enjoyed her gasping breaths, how she arched into him.

How could she think one time would be enough? He'd run the gamut of emotions today, ending with that mind-numbing rage that had thrown him off-kilter.

He'd still been coming down from that, adrenaline surging, doing his best to comfort her, when she'd decided to make everything sexual.

Mouth open on her skin, he gently ate his way down to her breasts, sucked in one tight nipple, nursed her while plucking at the other with his fingertips.

She moaned his name, her hands in his hair holding him closer.

It wasn't enough. Not even close.

Leaving her nipple wet and flushed, he made his way down her torso, teasing her flat belly, her hip bones, inner thigh, then pressing his face against the crotch of her minuscule panties.

Here, her musk was even stronger, drugging him.

His cock throbbed, ached. He'd wanted her forever, denied himself too long. She was already damp, and he tasted her through the panties, pressing with his tongue, lightly biting.

She tried to twist away, but he held her hips steady. She'd been warned, and she wanted this anyway.

"Cannon," she said on a whimper.

Sitting up in a rush, he scooped up her legs with one arm, then stripped the panties down and off. Looking at her tormented him. He made himself hold back, savoring the sight of her completely bare. She shifted her feet, pressed her knees together.

"Cannon?"

Using both hands, he opened her thighs wide. Yvette turned her face into the pillow, her hands at either side of her hips.

Such a perfect offering.

His chest worked like a bellows, the pressure building until he oh-so-carefully parted her vulva to further expose her.

So pink and shiny wet. Her inner lips swollen. Her little clitoris ripe and ready.

Groaning, he leaned down and tasted her deeply, thrusting into her with his tongue. His nostrils filled with her excitement. He sucked and licked and taunted with his teeth.

He tried to fight it off, but with each small sound she made, the pressure built inside him.

Accepting that it was now or never, he twisted away to find a condom, then stood and stripped off his boxers.

Yvette didn't move except to squirm in need. He'd love to hear her come again, to see that unique mix of pain and pleasure on her face.

Doubtful.

With her rapt attention spurring him on, he rolled the condom down his shaft and lowered himself half over her, his hand going immediately between her thighs to stroke two fingers deep.

So ready.

He shifted over her, positioned himself and, teeth locked, began easing into her.

She tipped her head back, offering up her breasts again.

So fucking beautiful. Not quite there, but definitely cued up. Briefly he mouthed one puckered nipple, then the other, playing her with his tongue, leaving them each red and wet. He watched her through a haze of mounting lust and razor-sharp need. Each broken breath she took, each shiver, the flush on her breasts, the silkiness of her inner thighs.

The creamy clench of her body on his cock.

Lowering himself to his forearms, he took her mouth in a deep, hungry kiss.

And pressed into her as deep as he could go.

She gasped, turning her face away, but he recaptured her mouth again, angling his head for a better fit, taking her mouth as he took her body. Hips grinding, need consuming.

On a vibrating cry, she gripped his shoulders, her nails biting in his flesh.

And he loved it.

He wanted to be gentle, but instead he pounded into her, harder and deeper until she lifted her slim legs around him. Digging her heels into the small of his back, she matched his urgent rhythm.

He fought to stall the inevitable.

A losing battle.

Lifting up with a harsh groan, he rocked out his release, only vaguely aware of Yvette watching him, her hands moving gently over his chest and shoulders.

Sucking in air, totally spent, he sank down onto her small giving body, only some of his tension now gone.

Yvette continued to stroke him.

Outwardly, she stayed still and calm, peaceful in the way she put small kisses to his damp skin, how she tunneled her fingers through his hair.

But inside, he felt her still holding him tight. Felt the little ripples of her need. The heat of her skin and the hammering of her heart.

Attempting to clear the fog of pleasure, he drew in a deep breath, but that only tantalized him with the scent of sex hanging in the air.

He had his face in her neck, so he nuzzled against her and felt her tremble.

He'd left her on the brink of release, without taking her over. And still she touched him with affection.

Smiling against her throat, he said, "Told you so."

"Mmm?" She kissed him again.

And damned if he didn't feel her hot little tongue lick over his sweaty shoulder.

Struggling up onto his forearms once more, Cannon looked at her. Her lips were puffy, her hair tangled around her. She had whisker burn on her cheeks and the heavy eyes of a woman in extreme need.

"How do you feel?"

"Better."

The smile tugged at his mouth. "Yeah?"

With a languid nod, she coasted her nails lightly down his pecs. "Throbbing." Back up to his shoulders. "Maybe...coiled."

He gave a slight press against her. "Wet."

"That, too." She shifted. "I wish I could feel you, and only you."

Dangerous. But damn, it turned him on, the idea of taking her bareback, nothing between them.

Her flesh and his.

He bent to her mouth, kissing her idly this time, his tongue playing with hers. "I need to get rid of the rubber." Amid her protests, he rolled off her and stood.

He couldn't have prepared for her impact. He looked at her sprawled on the bed, his for the taking, and it did things to him.

Crazy, possessive things.

Things he realized he'd been feeling even before she'd left for California. Now they were amplified, more tangible because he could touch and taste her.

Fuck her.

Make love to her.

As he stood there looking at her, she shifted her feet restlessly, knotted her hands in the sheet.

He'd thought to spend time bathing her, teasing her, but he couldn't. Ignoring the rubber for the moment, he sat beside her on the bed and cupped a hand between her open thighs.

Her eyes drifted shut and she lifted into him.

Watching her was the most erotic thing he could imagine. Lacking haste, he worked his fingers over her, then one finger in her. She writhed, her hips twisting, her breath coming faster.

Seeing her primed like this stirred him sooner than he would have expected.

He withdrew, only to sink in two fingers, curling them slightly to reach that special spot for her. She followed where he led without inhibition, gasping, rolling her hips, getting so very close but not quite there.

Coming down beside her, propped on one elbow, Cannon kissed her mouth, then her nipples, suckling each in turn until she was mindless with wanting.

Down her belly again.

"Ah, God. Cannon, please."

"We're getting there."

She fisted a hand in his hair, trying to hurry him.

He pulled his fingers free to tease her glistening clit. "Here, baby? Is that what you want?"

For an answer, she purred and widened her thighs more.

He circled, spreading her wetness around that tiny bundle of ultrasensitive nerves, applied careful pressure, gently tugged.

"Cannon, please..."

He pushed his fingers deep again—and drew her into his mouth.

Fingers still working her, he stroked with his tongue, rasping over her, pushing her, and within two minutes she broke. Her moans were loud and real and powerful enough to get him at the starting gate again.

She'd barely settled, her breath still catching, when he rid himself of the spent condom and rolled on another. Giving her no time to prepare, he cupped his hands over her knees, pushed them far back and sank into her.

Her moan was both pleasure and protest.

"You are so fucking wet now." Already the slick friction built. With each deep slide of his cock, she tightened more until they were both caught in the hot clench of powerful release. Neck and back arched, she gave a deep guttural groan, her muscles squeezing like a fist. While coming, he kept his gaze on her, the sight of her heightening his pleasure. Even as she drained him, his body continued to buzz.

Long minutes later, when he finally worked up the energy to lift himself, he found her fast asleep, dead to the world.

The things he felt… They were too unsettling to contemplate after the hellish day, at such a late hour. Unable to help himself, he kissed her again, softly so she wouldn't awaken. Her parted lips. Her throat.

Her now-soft nipples.

She grumbled a protest and shifted, making him smile, a sappy smile that he felt in his heart.

The bruises on her arm wrecked him. He'd rather break a limb than see her marked like that. He kissed those, too, then carefully separated from her, standing beside the bed.

Her legs were still inelegantly sprawled, her tender sex exposed. Using only his fingertips, he touched her.

She mumbled in her sleep and turned to her side, drawing up one leg.

Yeah, he liked that view, as well.

He wanted to touch her again. Hell, he wanted to kiss his way down her spine to that perfect ass. *Later,* he told himself.

Rubbing both hands over his face, he got it together. She didn't need to be molested in her sleep. He pulled back the covers, lifted her up where she belonged and covered her again.

It took him only a minute to clean up, and then he was beside her, turning her toward him and holding her close.

Knowing he'd never let her go.

THROUGH THE INFINITE darkness closing in around her, she saw glittering eyes everywhere, heard the snickers and whispers. Desperate to find the light, she began searching, groping blindly. She smelled kerosene. And death.

Another snicker, followed by a soft laugh. Someone grabbed her wrist, hard fingers squeezing in an iron grip. Another hand on her shoulder. Her neck. She silently fought. But more hands joined the eyes, faces getting closer—

Yvette jerked awake with a start, gasping, her eyes seeking...

"Hey." Cannon was over her, his hand on her cheek. "You okay?" His fingertips touched her cheek, his brows drawn in worry.

Oh, God. Her face was wet. With tears? Humiliation squeezed her heart. "I...I'm fine."

For the longest time he searched her face until she could no longer meet his gaze.

He turned to his back but pulled her up onto his chest, his hands clasping her backside. "You had a nightmare."

Denials came automatically, but remembering his insistence last night that she trust him, she pushed past her reservations. "Yes."

Maybe surprised, he held silent for a moment, then asked, "A bad one?"

"I've had it before." *Often.* "It's...unsettling." She tried not to clutch at him, but the remnants of the dream, the helplessness and incessant fear hung with her.

His hands moved, cuddling her behind. "Want to tell me about it?"

God, no. She shook her head.

He stroked her behind, startling her by teasing along her cleft.

She automatically tried to slide away.

He gripped her cheeks again, resettling her. "I like you right where you are."

She blinked at him, a little more uncertain now that bright morning sunlight flooded the room.

Of course, Cannon didn't have the same reservations.

Looking at her mouth, his hands again palpating her rear, he said, "We never did have that talk last night."

Dazed from the bad dream followed by his bold touch, she struggled to ground herself. "We had amazing sex instead." Yes, if she could just concentrate on that…

"Very amazing."

Levering up on her arms, she got a better look at him. Rumpled inky hair. Burning blue eyes. Those sinfully long lashes.

She couldn't stop the groan of appreciation. Even resting, his biceps looked amazing. And his chest, the crisp hair, that fascinating happy trail…

"What are you thinking?"

"That I want to lick you all over."

An arrested expression held him immobile for only a moment, then he flipped her onto her back and came down over her, pinning her in place. "I'd like that."

She laughed. "Well, I hope so."

"But first we're going to talk."

She groaned again for an entirely different reason.

"None of that." He took her mouth in a barely there kiss. "Do you want to do this here, now, or would you rather hit the john and grab coffee?"

Twisting, she tried to see the clock, but he didn't give her much room for leverage.

"It's nine-thirty."

"Wow." Very late for him. "We slept in."

"It was damn near dawn when I finally let you fall asleep."

Narrowing her eyes, she asked, "So you didn't sleep in, but you stayed here so I could?"

"Yeah." Lazily, he cupped her breast, rolling his thumb over her nipple with single-minded purpose until it drew taut. His eyes narrowed with satisfaction. "I got to look at you. A pretty fair trade."

He'd watched her sleep? Her face warmed, and then she realized… "I fell asleep."

"Yeah."

"I mean…"

"Right after you came." Still moving with an indolent lack of haste, he grazed his teeth over the side of her neck, her shoulder. Down.

She held her breath…and then those same teeth lightly scraped her nipple and the sparking sensation arched her back.

"You are so sexy." His big hand left her breast and instead he held the side of her face. "But we do have to talk."

That had to be a joke. But no. He looked plenty serious. Incredulous, she shoved at his shoulders, but he didn't budge. "Why would you start all that if you didn't plan to—"

"Because you're irresistible." He kissed her forehead. "And I can't stop thinking about all those sexy sounds you made, how you looked and smelled and how it felt to be inside you with you squeezing me so tight."

Instead of pushing him away, her fingers curled against his muscular flesh. *"Cannon."*

"Sex isn't always like that."

What an understatement. "Not for me anyway."

He shook his head. "Not for me either, honey. Maybe you don't realize, but we're good together. Better than good."

It'd be nice to think they had something special going on, because for her it was so much more than physical.

But how could she be sure? "You've always enjoyed sex." He'd told her so.

"True. But with you, it's more." Plumping up her other breast, he brushed his lips over her nipple, making her want so much more. "It'll always be more." He blew gently against her, then met her eyes. "I know it, whether you do or not."

Squirming against him made her very aware of his erection on her belly. Hoping to forestall the inevitable, she twined her arms around his neck and slid her foot up his hairy calf. "We could talk later."

Taking her by surprise, he caught her hands and slowly stretched them up high over her head. He took his time, pinning her legs with one of his.

Excitement shuddered through her. Yes, she could use a quick trip to the bathroom. And she wouldn't mind a quick gargle to ensure she didn't have morning breath. But everything was secondary to how he made her feel right now.

Anticipating what he'd do next, she held her breath and tried not to wiggle.

"Now," he murmured, after a soft suckle of her nipple. "Tell me about your dream."

Wait, what? Experimentally, she tugged at her wrists; he held her secure. Frowning, she shook her head to deny him. "It was dumb."

He shifted both her hands into one of his. "Tell me anyway."

"Why?"

"Because," he said, then gently sucked at her nipple until her breath left her in a vibrating moan. Curling his tongue around her, he tugged free, leaving her nipple achingly taut. He blew against her, then whispered, "I want to know."

"You're diabolical."

"I'm incredibly turned on." His gaze met hers. "And incredibly determined to get you to open up to me."

"If I tell you, are you going to stop teasing me?"

"I'll only stop if you don't."

Well. That was incentive enough to get her talking. "It really is dumb."

"Most dreams seem that way once you're awake. Not so much when they're happening."

True enough. She tried to ignore her embarrassment. "I…I was in the dark." Her face heated. As an adult woman, she shouldn't still be afraid of the dark.

But sometimes she was.

"Go on."

"I couldn't see much but I knew people were watching me." It didn't take a trained shrink to know why she hated to draw attention. "I could hear them in the shadows."

Cannon petted her, over her hair, her jaw, her shoulder. "That sounds pretty awful to me."

It had been. But she knew that Cannon, if ever faced with that situation, dream or reality, would bravely face the darkness. Finally, she admitted the worst part. "I smelled…kerosene, too."

"Damn."

More than most, Cannon understood the significance of that, how she'd been threatened to be burned alive…. The dream, the latent feelings it had invoked, returned, and she started shaking, her breath strained.

He kissed her cheek, maybe to remind her she wasn't alone—maybe just to get her talking again.

"Hands started grabbing me." No matter which way she'd turned, they were there. She looked into his beautiful blue eyes. "I was ready to scream."

Very gently, he asked, "Why didn't you?"

"I woke up."

Quiet, still petting her, now down her side and over her hip then back to her hair again, Cannon soothed her. "All things considered, that's a pretty gruesome nightmare."

All things considered. She swallowed hard and nodded.

"Thank you for telling me."

So kind and understanding. And so brave. Without thinking it through, she said, "I wish I was more like you."

He gave a gruff laugh and bent again to her breast. "I'm eternally grateful that you aren't." Taking the very tip of her nipple into his mouth, he touched his tongue to her.

God, he was good at this. At teasing and revving up the urgency.

She wasn't nearly as good at taking it. Straining in his hold, she shivered. "If you're not going to follow through, then you have to stop that."

To her disappointment, he released her and sat up. "Know what I think we should do?"

Knowing she would never understand him, she shook her head.

"Let's grab a drink, juice for me and coffee for you." He stroked his hand over her belly, between her legs. "We'll let things simmer a bit."

"Simmer?" She was already boiled over, damn him!

"It's hot enough, but anticipation will make it more so. We can shower together. What do you think?"

"You'll have sex with me again?"

He grinned. "Count on it."

She wanted him now, but she also needed to visit the restroom, and brush her hair, and clean her teeth. "I like it. It's a good plan."

Skeptical at her quick agreement, Cannon stood. "We can head to the shelter later today to check out the dogs. And I want to talk to Margaret, make sure she knows everything that's happened."

She took his extended hand and left the bed. "I was thinking it might not be a bad idea to get hold of Vanity, too. She can see if Heath's posting anything online."

"Good idea." He retrieved the SBC shirt from the floor and pulled it over her head, smoothing it into place, then lifting her hair out of the neckline. His gaze warmed. "I like you in my shirt."

Sighing, absorbing the sight of him in the bright morning light, she admitted, "I like you naked."

Without an ounce of modesty, he nodded. "Good to know."

His smile did it for her as much as his amazing body. "But how about jeans until we get back in bed?"

Making a face, she said, "If you must."

As he stepped into the denim—commando—he reminded her of what he wanted. "I think we might get more talking done that way, don't you?" Not bothering to zip or snap the jeans, he put a perfunctory kiss on her forehead. "Do what you need to do and I'll go get the coffee started."

She watched him walk off, anticipation and dread both warring inside her. This morning he had the kid gloves back on, but with an edge. All that teasing had been... She hugged herself. *Delicious.*

Somehow she'd convince him it wasn't necessary to be so careful with her. He didn't need to cater to her psyche, to understand her fears and weaknesses.

Overall, she'd rather he just ignore them.

Maybe once she totally opened up to him, she'd be able to get him to treat her like any other woman.

She'd been private so long, it wouldn't be easy. But she wanted him, all of him, with no holding back.

And with that in mind, she decided just how to make it happen.

CHAPTER TWENTY-TWO

CANNON STOPPED IN the hall bathroom and braced his hands on the edge of the sink. God almighty, she packed a powerful punch to his libido. Walking away from her had almost taken more than he had in him.

He'd meant what he said. The buildup would be mind-blowing. Given how new she was to this, the pleasure part anyway, he wanted to ensure she was as comfortable, as ready, as he could get her.

Last night… He shook his head. He'd been lacking patience and was high on lust. Not the best combo to throw at someone who struggled with reaching the peak.

Not that she'd struggled much with him, but still…

Using cold water, he splashed his face, ignored the morning beard shadow and quickly brushed his teeth. Knowing Yvette would primp a bit, brush her hair and probably put on jeans, he headed toward the kitchen. He'd just gotten to the end of the hall when a very light, tentative knock sounded on the door.

Lifting aside a curtain from the window, he saw Armie standing there. Good. With Armie he wouldn't have to be overly polite. He opened the door for him, saying, "You can't stay long."

A note in his hand, one foot in the doorway, Armie paused. He glanced beyond Cannon and when he didn't see Yvette, he whispered, "Want me to just take off?"

"Nah. Five minutes is fine." Knowing Armie would

follow, he went on into the kitchen. "I wanted to talk to you anyway."

While Cannon filled the carafe in the sink, Armie pulled out the table chair closest to the wall. "This was in your door." He handed him the note.

Cannon turned it over and read, "Rissy was here." He smiled. "She must have come by this morning, assuming I'd still jog."

"But you didn't."

He shook his head. No, he'd stayed put, enjoying how beautiful Yvette looked in peaceful slumber. "I guess when Rissy didn't see the usual lights on inside, she knew we were sleeping in."

Armie sprawled back in the chair, his legs stretched out, at his leisure. "She was probably worried."

"Yeah. I didn't get a chance to talk to her much last night, but I know by now she's heard what happened."

"She took off early," Armie said.

Cannon shot him a look. "Noticed that, did you?"

Shrugging, he slumped a little more.

"I'll give her a call later, maybe take her to lunch. I think some jackass must have hurt her feelings." Cannon measured coffee grains into the basket. "When she came over to tell me she was taking off, she looked... I don't know. Sad."

Armie was so silent that Cannon glanced back at him again.

Clearing his throat, his friend sat a little straighter. "You see her with anyone?"

"No, you?"

Armie shook his head. "I mean, she hung with the guys some, but none of them would do anything to upset her."

"No," he agreed. Everyone liked Rissy, and why not? She was funny and smart and pretty.

Armie sat forward. "You don't think she got involved with that idiot ex of hers again, do you?"

"No way." He turned to face Armie. "She's not a dummy."

"Right." He started to relax again.

Seeing the perfect segue, Cannon said, "But speaking of dumbasses…"

"Were we?"

"What the hell were you doing with Mindi Jarrett?"

"Nothing."

He looked serious, prompting Cannon to snort. "That's a first for you, then." Armie didn't do second dates, unless he got what he wanted and more on the first.

"Well, I'd been planning all kinds of fun shit, but she booked on me."

Heavy unease sank onto Cannon. "She wasn't with you last night?"

"You know she wasn't. Hell, I was out in front of the bar with you, remember?"

He waved that away. "After that, I mean. When Yvette and I left."

Armie started to answer, but he got a text. "Give me a sec." He settled back again, reading the message on his phone.

Knowing it could be anything from business with the rec center, his upcoming fight or a woman, Cannon went back to fixing the coffee. Assuming Armie would want some, too, he got out two mugs and was just pouring it when he felt two small, soft hands come around him, going unerringly to his junk.

That was startling enough, but then he felt naked breasts on his back.

He damn near dropped the carafe, but managed to set it quickly in the sink.

At about the same time, Armie's chair hit the floor. Cannon twisted in time to see Armie turning his back.

Finally realizing they weren't alone, Yvette screeched, jumping behind Cannon.

One palm braced flat on the wall, the other rubbing the back of his neck, Armie said, "Hi, Yvette."

Yvette muttered, "Oh, my God, oh, my God, *oh, my God.*"

"Asshole," Cannon told him while reaching back to her—and realizing she was completely nude. "Keep your nose to the wall!"

"Yeah, sure." Armie's shoulders moved. "Already saw it all anyway."

Cannon snarled. "Shut up, damn it."

He started to snicker.

To Cannon's surprise, Yvette did, too. In between heartfelt "Oh, my God" laments, she groaned and laughed, and even cursed a little.

"Come on." Keeping her tucked behind him, one eye on Armie, he led her back to the hallway. To Armie, he said, "Don't budge! I'll be right back."

"Sure you don't want me to get out of here?"

"Stay." He had a dozen questions for Armie.

Still keeping his gaze averted, Armie saluted him.

Soon as they were out of the kitchen, Cannon pulled Yvette around in front of him so he could shield the back of her.

And what a beautiful backside it was.

She was still giggling, so he gave her a swat on that delectable tush.

She jumped, put both hands there and started roaring with laughter. It got Cannon's mouth twitching, too.

In the bedroom, he closed the door and leaned back on it. Could a man be more divided?

His best friend had just seen Yvette naked.

Yvette had wanted him enough to come to him, in the kitchen, naked.

He wasn't sure what the hell to do.

Arms now around her middle, she dropped to sit on the bed and tried to get a grip on her hilarity.

Damn, she looked beautiful. Her long dark hair hung smooth over her shoulders, around her breasts, playing peekaboo with her pretty pink nipples. The hair between her legs was just as dark, a striking contrast to her pale belly and inner thighs. She looked sweet and soft all over.

Clearly, she'd hoped to get him off track from their talk.

Cannon crossed his arms. "Armie just saw you buck-ass."

"I know." More giggles racked her. "He almost fell out of his chair."

His smile went crooked. "Neither of us is ever going to hear the end of it."

Wiping her eyes, she smiled up at him. "You could have told me we had company."

"I figured you heard us talking."

"I was brushing my teeth and washing and using my blow-dryer to smooth my hair." Her smile teased. "And thinking of everything I wanted to do to you."

He couldn't wait to find out what that might be.

Though she was still pink cheeked over getting caught, she stood, arms at her sides, and let him look at her body. "I was hoping to derail you a bit."

"I know." But he wouldn't let her.

"Want to know how?" She slowly came toward him, that sexy little smile still in place.

"You're naked. You made a grab for my dick." He lifted a brow. "Pretty sure I can guess."

When she reached him, she ran her hands up his body. Sighing brokenly, she whispered, "Last night, the way you were…"

Crazed with lust. "Yeah?"

"I really loved that." She leaned in and kissed his chest. "I was going to make you a deal."

"All right. Let's hear it." Better now, with Armie waiting so he couldn't easily give in. Having a buddy in hearing distance pretty much guaranteed he wouldn't let her twist him around her little finger.

Still kissing him, brushing her nose over his chest hair, lightly touching her tongue to his right nipple, she said, "I'll stop trying to…to be so private—just with you—if you'll stop treating me like fine china." She took a love bite of his pec muscle, then looked up at him with her big green eyes warm and hungry. "How can I get past that scared little girl I used to be if you can't?"

Was that what she thought?

Was that how he'd been?

From down the hallway, Armie yelled, "I was willing to wait for you two to grab a quickie, but if you think I'm hanging around for extended foreplay, forget it."

Smiling, Cannon put his forehead to hers. Unable to stop himself, he ran his hands over her body, down the indent of her waist, over the rise of her hips, back up to cup her breasts. He needed to touch her at least once to carry him over.

"Cannon," she whispered, sounding scandalized. "I'm not going to do anything *now*, not with Armie out there!"

The smile turned into a grin. "I wouldn't ask you to. After he's gone, though…" He drew her up and took her mouth in a deep, tongue-stroking kiss. "Then you can pay up on all these promises you're making." He stepped them both away from the door. "Get dressed, okay?"

She swatted at him. "Now that I know we're not alone, you can count on it!"

He kissed her once more, a firm, smacking kiss, and left her, closing the door behind him.

In the kitchen, Armie leaned against the sink, downing a cup of coffee. As soon as he saw Cannon he started grinning again. "My heart damn near stopped. My eyeballs are still singed."

"Shut up." Giving up on the idea of juice, Cannon poured his own cup of coffee. He'd need the caffeine to clear his head.

"You have my sympathies, dude."

Lost to his meaning, Cannon shot him a look.

Smooth and sultry, Armie crooned, "She is *fine*."

She was, but, damn it, he didn't want to discuss her nude body with anyone. "I told you to shut up."

"And here you are, stuck in the kitchen with me." Only half hiding his amusement, Armie sipped the coffee. "You sure you don't want me to haul ass out of here?"

"No, I don't." Indicating the table, he said, "Take a seat."

Nonchalant, Armie straddled a chair. "Your priorities are dicked, man. I would *sooo* be on that."

"You're pushing your luck."

"Yeah, I meant if you hadn't already locked it up, ya know?" He set the mug aside. "Given she just tried to molest you in the kitchen, I'm guessing things are on track?"

To stop his needling, Cannon sat across from him and gave him a level stare. "So you weren't with Mindi last night?"

Having some sense left in him, Armie let it go and dug his teeth into a new topic. "Fickle bitch was all about it, right up until she wasn't there anymore. Left me without a word."

New suspicions broke up old theories. "Where do you think Heath took off to last night?"

The switch didn't faze him. "My bet is he went straight to a doctor. We both know what a dislocated shoulder feels like. How the miserable fuck drove away…" Armie shook his head. "Not that you or I couldn't, but he's not trained. Big, sure. Looked like he hit the gym often enough. But I doubt he's ever broken anything or been hit like that before. He looked stunned stupid when you hurt him."

Like the gathering of a storm, the tempest twisted through Cannon once more. He rolled his shoulders, fighting off the ugly grip of rage. "You don't think he'd be up to causing more trouble?"

Snorting, Armie said, "Hell, no. If he found someone to put his shoulder back, well, that hurts, too. And if not, he was probably curled up somewhere crying. Why?"

Cannon tipped his head toward the kitchen window. "You're not real observant today, are you?"

"I saw it," he defended. "I just figured you boarded it up to be extra secure, her being so jumpy and all."

Face hot and gaze on her bare feet, Yvette walked in. "I am not jumpy."

She wore a white sundress that hugged her breasts, then hung full from there down to her knees. The material swished around her legs as she came to the table. She looked soft and fucking virginal and he wanted her more than ever.

Smile settling into place, Armie relaxed more in his chair. "Hi, Yvette."

Shoulders curled, her head down so that her hair half hid her, she said, "Be quiet, Armie."

"But we're...butt buddies now, right?"

She groaned.

"Want me to show you my ass, just to make it even?"

She peeked up. "Is that all you saw?"

"Nope."

Groaning, she folded her arms on the tabletop and dropped her head. Face muffled, she asked Cannon, "Can you shut him up?"

"Sure, if that's what you want."

Leaning close to her, Armie said, "He can rip out my tongue, but the image is forever emblazoned on my brain."

Cannon started to intercede, but Yvette beat him to it. She planted a palm in Armie's face and shoved him back. "Brat."

"Hottie."

"Gawd, give it up, Armie." She squared her shoulders in that now familiar way. "We're both adults."

"And we've seen plenty of naked people?"

She drooped again and in a small voice asked, "Did you really see everything?"

Laughing, he took her hand and gave it a squeeze. "Honestly, honey, soon as I realized what I was seeing, I turned so fast I damn near ran into the wall."

"Promise?"

"It's all a blur." Lifting his brows, he added, "A red-hot, sexy-as-hell blur, but still—"

She snatched her hand away. "New topic!" Then to Cannon, "So you think Heath was too hurt to be here breaking windows and scaring me senseless?"

"You weren't senseless," he said absently, distracted by what he'd just witnessed. "You kept a cool head and did exactly what you were supposed to."

"Right after I screamed."

"Yeah, after that. But anyone can get startled."

"Ah, hon." Armie pitched in on the effort of reassuring her. "You were a rock last night after that bozo tried to grab you." He squeezed her shoulder. "Impressed the hell out of me."

Cannon tried to shake it off, but he was completely leveled. Armie, the guy who never got close to *nice* girls, not even if they were attached to another man, had obviously become friends with Yvette. He was completely at ease with her, caring, funny...*himself.*

Incredible.

Oh, sure, Armie could be friendly with anyone. He was nice to Harper, Gage's girlfriend, but Harper was almost like one of the guys. Armie kept his interactions with her superficial. And he was always respectful enough, though distant, with Rissy.

But with Yvette, the nicest of the nice girls, he was the same good friend that Cannon knew so well.

Yvette had done what no other woman could—she'd gotten close to Armie.

Armie scowled. "What?"

He caught himself and shrugged. "Nothing."

"Screw that. You're staring at me like I've grown a second head, dissecting me or something. I want to know why."

"You're not coming on to Yvette."

He flattened back in his seat. "What? Hell, no! I wouldn't." He glanced at Yvette. "No offense."

She smiled at him. "None taken."

"But damn, man, just because she flashed me the goods—"

"Armie!"

"—doesn't mean I'd do the unthinkable!"

"Yeah, that's what I just said." Cannon knew it, 100 percent. He trusted Armie without reservation.

"So...what?" Expression fierce, Armie barked, "Make sense, damn it."

"All right." If he was right, they had a very big problem on their hands. "I don't think Heath was here last night. I think it was Mindi."

Both Yvette and Armie gaped at him.

"I know it sounds nuts, but hear me out." Leaning forward, elbows on the table, Cannon detailed his suspicions, filling Armie in on everything that had happened. "She's been on me hot and heavy, unreasonably so."

"True," Yvette agreed. "But I figured she just wanted you like everyone else does."

Armie had to rub away his smile over that.

"I was really confused when she went after Armie the other night."

"I was relieved," Cannon told her. "Until I found out she wasn't with him after all."

"Agreeing to go home with me meant she wasn't all that dead set on having you," Armie mused aloud. "No broad is that dense to think you'd take second serve."

"Eww." Yvette scowled at him.

"Not directly second," Armie told her with a laugh. "I meant that Cannon doesn't take other men's leavings. If I'd laid hands on her, he never would."

"Enough on Cannon's nitpicky ways," she announced, then turned to Cannon. "So you assumed she was with Armie last night?"

"Yeah, so I never considered her. But maybe when it all went down, she saw her opportunity, knowing we'd be tied up for a while." He nodded at Armie's phone. "I don't suppose that was her texting you?"

"No, just the promoter. They're going to run the show tournament-style."

Yvette didn't understand, so Cannon explained, "He'll fight more than once."

"Long as I keep winning," Armie clarified.

"Like I said. You'll fight more than once." He knew Armie's ability, even if Armie chose to downplay it. "It's done like a wrestling tournament. Winners keep advancing."

Fascinated, Yvette started to ask more questions, but Armie shook that off.

"Just because Mindi wasn't with me last night doesn't mean she ran over here to wreak havoc on your windows."

"No. But I picked up her scent."

Yvette lifted her brows.

Armie guffawed. "Since when are you a bloodhound?"

"Since never. But she wears that damned overpowering perfume."

Yvette slanted him a look. "I think it's actually expensive stuff."

"Whatever. I don't like it." He'd take Yvette's own personal fragrance any day. But thinking about that, about her skin and hair and arousal, would get him in trouble. "I especially dislike how she wears it so thick. Right after I noticed the broken window in the garage, I smelled it, but it didn't register. I was so set on thinking it was Heath that I totally missed the significance."

Yvette suddenly perked up. "Remember when she dropped by? She was awfully nosy about what we had in the boxes."

"I know." Cannon held out his hand, pleased when she put hers in it. Touching her seemed to be a requisite of every circumstance. "I think your grandfather might have had something of hers—maybe something pawned—and she's hoping to get it back."

"The illegal way?" Yvette frowned. "Why not just ask us?"

"Good question," Armie said. He stood. "I know you two were planning to do the nasty and all that—"

"Armie!"

"—but what do you say we take another look at that safe first?"

In a quick about-face, Yvette stopped censuring Armie and jumped to her feet to join him. "It was hidden!" She tugged at Cannon. "I'd almost forgotten about it."

Keeping her hand in his, Cannon again enjoyed their easy camaraderie. "I think we need to figure out what's inside."

"Should I go or stay?" Armie asked.

Remembering their plans, Yvette bit her lip, then deferred to Cannon.

Damn, he wanted her, more now than ever. That she'd gotten Armie to open up made her all the more lovable. Not that she'd needed a lot of help in that department.

The more time he spent with her, the more convinced he was that he'd always loved her. Even back when he'd told himself she was too young. Even when he'd done his best to remember she was a victim. Long before she'd ever gone away.

In so many ways, she'd always appealed to him. When being bold, shy, determined or scared. He'd fought the inevitable for a very long time.

Now that he was done fighting, he wasn't about to let anything happen to her.

"We lost him again," Armie said in an exaggerated stage whisper. "So...I could give you an hour."

Cannon couldn't yet get out the words.

"Two hours?" Armie offered, managing to look impressed.

Shaking his head, Cannon said, "I might need longer than that."

"Damn, man, no reason to show off."

"I was talking about a lifetime."

Armie turned into all smiles.

Cannon waited to see how Yvette would react.

Indulgent, uncaring that Armie stood there on the alert and apparently not scared off by his out-of-the-blue proclamation, she cuddled up to his chest. Maybe she'd misunderstood, or thought he was only caught up in the moment. Maybe she thought he spoke in sexual terms only. But she patted his chest and looked at him with big, understanding green eyes. "We can worry about the safe later if that's what you want."

"Lucky bastard," Armie whispered.

Freed by his own admission, Cannon tipped up her chin and kissed her—but before Armie could sneak away, he ended it. "Let's see if we can find a key and pass code. I want to know what's in that safe."

CHAPTER TWENTY-THREE

YVETTE WENT THROUGH every drawer, then behind the drawers, trying to find the key and pass code. Armie and Cannon checked the top of the buffet and refrigerator, the tall cabinets, each high place that she couldn't reach. They even went back out to the garage and into the attic to see if they'd missed something up there.

The space over the garage was now empty.

Finally Armie said, "What about in your grandpa's bedroom?"

She and Cannon looked at each other.

A little embarrassed by the truth, she shook her head. "Other than when I first moved back in, I haven't been in there." She'd thought about it many times, but the loss was still too painful.

Cannon hugged her. "I haven't been in there either. I only dropped my bags in the spare room."

Dropped his bags...and then had moved into her room with her.

"The room with only a twin bed?" Armie asked, familiar with the layout of the house. "Wasn't that cramped?"

Even before Armie started, Yvette bit her lip and her face heated.

Seeing that, Armie gave a knowing smile. "Ah. Never used that little bed, huh? Nice." He tried to fist bump Yvette, but she refused to play along, swatting at him instead. He managed to turn that into a palm slap, though, and she ended up laughing.

"So, not to be disrespectful or anything, but do you think we could look around? I mean, if I had something private, odds are I'd put it somewhere in my bedroom."

Agreeing, Yvette led the way down the hall. "I don't recall Grandpa ever storing anything business-related in his room before. He always kept paperwork in the hutch and buffet in the dining room. Not that I was ever in his room much, usually just if it was my turn to clean house. Then I'd go in only to dust and vacuum." She pushed the door open and stepped in.

Sunlight poured through the blinds over the window, showing dust motes dancing in the disturbed air. His bed looked the same, the simple chenille spread neatly smoothed over two standard pillows.

Nicks and scratches, earned through years of possession, showed on the dark dresser and chest of drawers. One shallow dish atop a nightstand held loose change and a few old receipts.

Yvette held back. "I'm not sure I feel right going through his things." As Armie had said, personal stuff was stored in a bedroom. She didn't know much about her grandfather's private life; for her, he'd only been a grandfather. But to the rest of the world, he'd still been a man.

Was it possible he'd had a romance or two? She smiled, imagining him with a girlie magazine tucked under the mattress. Or a love letter.

Cannon and Armie both waited for her to decide what she wanted to do. She strolled to a framed photo on the dresser. "This was my grandma. I never really knew her, but I knew that Grandpa never stopped loving her."

Next to that was a smaller framed photo.

Cannon lifted it, smiling. "You?"

"When I first came here." She'd been so young, and so incredibly lost. In the picture, she looked shy and a little scared...but her grandfather had fixed that. He'd loved her, given her a home and a purpose and a place to call her own.

Tucked into the big mirror frame over the dresser were more photos of her. School photos, candid shots, a few of her at the pawnshop.

Emotions morphed into a physical ache, her heart literally hurting. "I miss him so much."

Cannon looped his arms around her from behind and put his chin atop her head. "Want Armie and me to go through his things? Other than looking for a key, we won't intrude."

She gave it some thought, but eventually everything in the room would have to be stored anyway. It was her duty to do it.

She put her hands over his, leaned into him. "Thank you, but I can help."

"All right." He gave her a squeeze and stepped away. "Where should we start?"

Considering it, she glanced over at Armie...and found him studying the bedside lamp. "Armie?"

"Yeah." He grinned. "I vote we start right here." He lifted the old-fashioned two-bulb lamp and showed the key hanging from the pull switch. Beneath the lamp, stuffed up into the brass base, was a small square of paper.

Wow. Could it really be that easy?

Excitement filled the air. They were each supercurious as to what they'd find.

Nudging her forward, Cannon said, "You should do the honors."

Hesitantly, she retrieved the paper, unfolded it with Armie and Cannon looking over her shoulder, and sure enough, the pass code was written in her grandfather's bold script.

Just then, the ringing of Armie's cell phone broke the silence. It startled her enough that Yvette nearly jumped out of her skin.

"Sorry," Armie said and retrieved the phone from his pocket. He answered without checking the caller ID, saying, "Hello?" while watching Cannon unhook the key. "Yeah, this is Armie Jacobson. What can I do for you?"

Whoever greeted him sent his brows climbing high. "Matter of fact, you're in luck, because he's right here." He held out the phone to Cannon. "For you. The dipshit ex."

In counterpart to Armie, Cannon's brows came down in a dark scowl. "How the hell does he have your number?"

"He called the rec center looking for you, and they put him through to me."

Yvette grabbed his wrist before he could take the phone. She put it on speaker and then handed it to him.

Cannon accepted it, saying with a mean inflection, "Heath. How the hell are you?"

Yvette slowly sank down to sit on the side of the bed. Still holding the key, Cannon joined her on one side. Armie sat on the other.

Though her return to Ohio had been filled with turmoil, in that moment she felt such amazing peace. She had so much more than many people ever hoped to get from life. She had a home. She had amazing friends. She'd been loved by her grandfather.

And at least for now, she had Cannon.

Leaning into Armie, she gave him a quick hug. He faltered, then shoulder bumped her in a comfortable way.

Sighing, she settled up against Cannon. He put his arm around her, pulling her closer still.

After what felt like forever, Heath said, "My fucking arm was broke," and he sounded like a petulant boy.

Sandwiched between such awesome men—men of honor and character—how could she help but pity Heath?

Cannon's smile widened. "Not broke, pal. I just dislocated your shoulder."

"Same thing."

"I'm guessing you've never had a broken bone, right? But hey, come on back around and I can show you the difference."

Through strained breathing, Heath said, "I want to talk to Yvette."

"No. Anything else?"

"Someone broke into the house where she's staying."

Her heart jumping into a gallop, Yvette jerked. Cannon squeezed her to keep her quiet.

As if it didn't matter, he asked, "What do you know of that?"

"I know it wasn't me."

Though he'd just come to the same conclusion, Cannon shrugged. "It fits your chickenshit M.O."

"But it wasn't."

"How do you even know where she's staying?"

More breathing. "Soon as I got to town I made it my business to know everything about her." He blurted, "To protect her!"

"From who? You're the one bothering her."

"Obviously I'm not the only one!"

Not the only one—so did that mean Heath would admit he was a problem?

Cannon had his arm hugged around her, his hand at her waist. And now Armie patted her knee.

Did they both think she needed to be cautioned again to be silent?

She let out a slow breath and smiled to let them know she wasn't an idiot.

"Who else is there, Heath?"

"I don't know, that's why I'm warning you."

"Warning *me?*"

"Letting you know, so you can keep her safe!" In a bid to reclaim his temper, he sucked in air, once, twice. "I went by the house just to…check on her."

"Uh-huh."

God, they'd have to let Margaret know. Or maybe she even needed to stay elsewhere for a while.

"Why would I break in?" Heath challenged. And then, voice raised, "I want Yvette, *her,* flesh and blood. Not her stuff."

Cannon pushed to his feet, muscles all along his arms and shoulders now knotted tight. "Come near her again," he stated in a deadly whisper, "and I'll do more than jack up your fucking arm."

The silence stretched out until Yvette thought Heath had hung up.

Cannon, apparently, didn't. "I've reset my own shoulder a few times, Heath. Did you manage it?"

"No, asshole. But I found someone who could."

"Yeah? Did you cry?"

"Fuck you." More evenly now, Heath said, "I'm not the one who broke in. Now, will you protect her or not?"

"Damn straight."

"Good. Then I'll go home. Just…just tell her for me. Tell her that I love her. That I'm sorry. Will you do that?"

Apparently Heath had used up Cannon's goodwill. "I'll tell her you're out of her life for good. How's that?"

Heath screamed, a primal sound of savage frustration that made Yvette tremble and had Armie rearing back.

And then he hung up.

"Holy shit," Armie breathed. "That dude is seriously unhinged."

Dazed, Yvette stood and went to Cannon. He kept his back to her, his shoulders rigid, his big hands squeezed into fists.

Unsure of his mood, she touched his upper arm.

As if that had unleashed him, he pulled her around in front of him, tangled a hand in her hair, and drew her up for a hot, hard, heart-stopping kiss. Almost as soon as he started, he gentled, his hand massaging her scalp.

She understood. Heath had been near the house. He'd watched her, maybe followed her. It made her ill to think about it.

So they needed to think about something else.

Cupping Cannon's face, she eased away. "Let's go open that safe."

A GUN, NOTHING fancy or unusual, just a .38 Smith & Wesson revolver stored inside a padded case. The big question, Cannon knew, was why Tipton had it put away so securely.

Before opening the case, he'd carried it to the kitchen table. Now they all sat around it, cautious, curious.

He thought of the note Tipton had left him. *Selling will require emptying the house—and that will bring about different problems for her.*

Was this the problem Tipton meant?

"Grandpa never took guns at the pawnshop." Beside

him, Yvette shifted. "Do you think he had it locked up because it was used for a crime?"

"That's as good a guess as any." He wanted to check it, see if it was loaded, but on the off chance it had fingerprints on it... The grip was black, the barrel polished. It looked new, not ominous.

No one touched it, just in case.

Armie straddled a chair. "Think we should go see Mindi?"

"I think," Cannon said, "we need to call Logan and Margaret."

From the kitchen doorway, a voice intruded. "That's not necessary."

As one, they turned to see Frank Whitaker standing at attention. Unlike at his office, he had razor-sharp focus now—and a 9 mm Glock. Cannon could see the magazine, and had no doubt it was fully loaded.

As he eased Yvette behind him, he asked, "How'd you get in?"

Whitaker held up a key in his left hand. "Made a copy." In his right hand, he kept the Glock steady. "No need to see Mindi. She's gone."

"Gone where?" Armie asked, taking a step away from Cannon.

"No, don't move." The gun swung back and forth, encompassing them all. After pocketing the key, Frank used his forearm to wipe sweat off his brow. "I don't want to hurt anyone, so please don't force me to do it."

Staying in the door frame, out of reach, gun hand extended, not all that relaxed, Whitaker indicated the table. "Take a seat. All of you."

Cannon pulled out a chair for Yvette—behind him. "What do you want?"

"The case, first of all. Mindi was sure you had it,

and she wouldn't leave well enough alone. I told her it wouldn't matter. I begged her to leave it be. But she wouldn't stop...."

"You didn't hurt her, did you, Whitaker?"

"Hurt Mindi? No, of course not. I love her."

Cannon felt Yvette's hand on his back, reassurance that she was still okay. With everything she'd gone through, no one would blame her if she fell apart right now.

But she didn't. She stayed calm, stroked his shoulder, and he was so damned proud of her.

As long as she stayed safe, tucked behind him, he could handle anything else. "Where is she?"

"She left me."

"Was she ever really with you?" Armie looked him over, from his balding head to his expanding middle. "Dude, seriously?"

"She loved me!"

"That what she told you?"

Damn it, Cannon knew exactly what Armie was doing. Drawing the fire.

Sacrificing himself, if it came to that.

Reclaiming Whitaker's attention, Cannon said, "I knew something was going on between you two."

"Of course you didn't. Mindi told me she was getting closer to you—as a way to locate the gun, of course."

"Doesn't matter," Cannon insisted. "I still knew. I'm guessing anyone who was ever around you two knew it."

"How?" Desperate for a crumb, Whitaker stepped closer. "How did you know?"

"The way she looked at you. It was more familiar than an assistant to a boss."

Softening, Whitaker smiled.

"What's that got to do with any of us?" Armie asked.

"It has nothing to do with you." He addressed Cannon. "But you...you didn't sell everything as you should have." He leaned to the side so he could see Yvette. "And you. I thought for sure you'd head back to California. So many times Tipton wanted you to stay, he told me so, but you never did. And now that he's gone, *now* you decide to settle in?"

"We'll all leave," Cannon offered. "You know I have a house in Kentucky. I was going to ask Yvette to join me there."

Yvette's hand stilled against him.

"I wish that was true." Slowly, Frank shook his head. "But she's reopening the pawnshop, proof that she plans to stay. I knew eventually she'd find the gun. Don't you see, I can't risk having it discovered."

Armie shifted. "How'd Yvette's grandfather get it in the first place?"

Frank looked as if he wanted to shoot Armie right then, but he drew in a deep breath that tested the buttons on his dress shirt, then exhaled it with new calm. "Tipton and I were friends." To Cannon, he said, "I told you that."

"I remember."

He nodded. "After my wife died—"

"After you killed her?"

"Not me!" Whitaker looked alarmed, insulted. He tugged at the collar of his shirt. "I told you, I don't want to hurt anyone."

"Then who?"

"Mindi. She said my wife had to go or we'd never be able to be together." He swallowed audibly. "While I was in court, she...she took some of my wife's things to make it look like a robbery, and then she shot her."

Deadpan, Armie asked, "Ever heard of divorce?"

Whitaker shook his head. "I couldn't, not without

losing half of everything." He swiped the sweat from his temple, his neck.

The man was sweating like a pig, his nervousness climbing the longer he talked.

Maybe because he thought he'd have to eventually kill them all?

"She refused to divorce me without making me pay, and Mindi refused to wait for me to work it out." As if to convince them, Frank said, "I'm not a wealthy man! I've worked damned hard for everything I have, modest as it is. Half would only be... I'd be broke!"

"No way did my grandfather help you cover up a murder."

At the quiet break of her voice, Frank looked past Cannon to Yvette's angry face. "No. He wasn't like that. He was a very good man."

"Yes, he was."

"One thing I don't understand." Cannon again blocked Yvette with his body. "Why the hell didn't you just dump the gun somewhere?"

"Mindi." Looking more miserable by the second, Frank nodded. "As my assistant, but acting on her own, she took a sealed box of my wife's personal possessions to Tipton. She said she told him I was distraught and she was afraid if I got rid of the things, I'd later regret it." He looked up, his eyes red rimmed. "She said it was leverage, that if I ever tried to turn her in for the murder, everyone would know I was involved, too."

Cannon couldn't fathom any man, much less an educated person of some means, being so stupid.

"And you still think you love her?" Armie whistled. "There's no hope for you."

"Armie," Cannon warned. He did not want or need his friend to play the hero.

Tipton didn't seem to hear him anyway. He stared toward them without really seeing. "Not knowing what was inside, Tipton agreed to hold it for me. I was going to get it back, but then he died...."

"He knew," Cannon told him. "He was a good, honest man, and he knew you'd gotten involved in something you shouldn't have. That's why he had the gun—just the gun, Frank, nothing else—hidden in a lockbox up in the garage attic."

Frank denied that. "No, he trusted me."

"'Fraid not, pal." Armie stood. "He was on to you— and who knows who he might have told? We only just found the key and pass code to the safe, but there could be other notes. You should book while you can."

Shit. Cannon tensed, ready to charge the lawyer if it came to that. He wouldn't let Yvette be hurt, but, damn it, he didn't want Armie hurt either.

Alarmed, Whitaker took a step closer. "Was it in the letter he left you?"

"So you stole a key but didn't read the letter?"

"I couldn't." His shoulders slumped and he sank back to lean on a counter. "Tipton had it sealed, so you'd have known...."

Miserable bastard.

"Did he ask you to stay?" Whitaker looked from Cannon to Yvette and back again. "Is that why you're still here? He heaped on the guilt?"

Shit, shit, shit. Cannon said, "I'm here because I want to be," at the same time Yvette asked, "What letter?"

"You should have gone!" Pushing away from the counter in a rush of frustration, Whitaker waved the gun. "It would have solved everything!"

"The pawnshop," Cannon said, thinking back to that

bucket of rags set by the door. "Did you and Mindi try to set that fire to drive us away?"

"I keep telling you!" Totally losing his cool, Whitaker's voice rose to a ridiculously high octave. "It was *Mindi, not me!*"

"Mr. Whitaker." After smoothing her hand over Cannon's back again, Yvette peeked around Cannon. "None of this is your fault."

He was breathing hard, sweat rolling down his jowls. "No, no, it's *not.*"

Voice gentle and calm, Yvette asked, "Do you know where Mindi went?"

"Away." He looked lost, forlorn, and jumped on the chance at an ally. "I don't know where." He dug in his pocket and extended a note in his shaky hand. "She left me this."

Cannon panicked, thinking Yvette would go closer to get the note.

She didn't budge from her seat. "What does it say?" she asked softly.

The note crumpled in his fist. "That she loves me, but she won't go to jail for me."

"And you love her—but there's no reason for you to go to jail either."

Afraid the lawyer might crack at any moment, Cannon stood, keeping in front of Yvette as much as he could. "It's easy enough, Whitaker." Moving slow so he wouldn't provoke a reaction, he closed the case, fastened the lock and held it out. "Take it. No one will ever need to know."

Undecided, Whitaker licked his lips. "I need to think." Raising his gun hand, he used his forearm to push his glasses farther up the bridge of his nose. His gaze locked on Yvette. "I think I should take her with me."

Cannon stared at him, saying with as much finality as he could, "No."

"If she's with me," he reasoned, "neither of you will try to follow. You won't call the cops either. You'll just have to wait until I release her."

His heart thundered. "That is not happening."

Inhaling courage, ignoring Cannon's protest, Whitaker nodded. "I think that's what I'll do." He pointed the gun at Cannon. "Come along, Yvette, or I'll have to shoot him."

Cannon clamped a hand to her, keeping her back. Eyes narrowed. Pulse tripping. "I already told you, she's not going anywhere."

He lifted his chin. "I'll shoot you."

That was preferable to him taking Yvette. "No one dies from one bullet, and you'd better believe I'll fucking take you apart before you get off a second shot."

Whitaker worked his jaw, then transferred his gaze to Armie. "Fine, I'll shoot that one." He locked his jaw, his finger on the trigger—

Arm extended, Yvette stepped to the side. *"Wait."*

Cannon lunged to stay in front of her.

Whitaker switched his aim.

And pandemonium erupted.

Another man crashed into the room, tackling Whitaker hard up against the cabinets so that his spine connected with the hard edge of the countertop. They went down in a twist of arms and legs, shouts and screams.

The gun went off twice, the noise deafening in the small kitchen.

Cannon covered Yvette as best he could while quick stepping her into the dining room and around a divider wall. There was another shot, and Armie barked, *"God-damn it!"*

The acrid scent of gunpowder burned the air.

Fear left Cannon breathless. He grabbed Yvette's shoulders, quickly looked her over, and other than wild eyes, parted lips and a pale face, she looked unhurt.

He turned for the kitchen—and pulled up short at the sight of Armie now holding the gun and still cursing a blue streak. On the seat of his jeans, toward the right side, blood seeped through the torn denim.

The wound didn't look bad; Armie stood straight, not hunched in pain. His gun hand was steady, his feet braced.

"Armie?"

"I'm okay." Without taking his gaze off the two men, he asked, "Yvette?"

In a shaky voice, she said, "I'm fine."

With the worst of the fear over, the cold fury set in. Cannon told Yvette, "Stay put, okay?" and after her nod, he joined his friend.

"Move," Armie told the two men. "Please, make one fucking move."

Heath, his head shaved, his face covered in whiskers and what looked like a stick-on tribal tattoo, lay on his back gasping for breath, his arm held close to his side.

Battered, with blood blooming on his chest, his stomach, his shoulder, Whitaker moaned. His nose was swollen, his glasses gone, his sparse hair sticking out like the fuzzy feathers on a baby bird.

Armie worked his jaw. "Call—" he gestured, undecided "—somebody. Cops, ambulance. Whatever. That one—" he pointed at Whitaker "—got the brunt of it. Not sure he'll make it. And this one—" he toed Heath's thigh, making him moan "—pretty much came to the rescue, but look at the stalkerish bastard, all disguised and shit."

From behind them, Yvette whispered, "I called 911 and Margaret."

Crouching down, Cannon checked each man for weapons. Heath had a brand-new box cutter in one pocket, a bottle of pain pills in the other. He looked pasty with agony, down for the count, but Cannon didn't trust him.

Even when he'd called, claiming he'd go away, he had to have been nearby. Probably surveilling the house.

Waiting for a chance to get Yvette.

"Watch him."

"Gladly."

He turned to Whitaker. The man seemed to be fading fast, the pool of blood expanding around him on the floor, his eyes glazed, unseeing.

Wishing for a way to spare her, Cannon twisted to Yvette.

She stood only partially in the connected dining room, her bottom lip caught in her teeth.

"Did you tell them to bring an ambulance?"

Eyes still round, she nodded. "I…" She pointed to the cabinet. "I could get some towels?"

Tears dampened her eyes, but she didn't let them fall. Amazing. "Yeah, that'd be great." If she was up for helping, then maybe staying busy would make this easier on her. She wasn't a dummy. She, too, had to realize the significance of Heath being here now. But she forged on anyway.

He'd underestimated her so many times. Never again.

Rushing to the cabinet, she kept her attention off Heath and on Whitaker as she dug out a stack of hand towels.

Cannon finished checking over the lawyer. No other weapons, but he took his cell phone and that note from

Mindi. It wasn't signed, but surely they could match her writing.

Heath whispered, "Yvette?"

Face carved of stone, she kept her back to him.

"I'm sorry, baby. For everything."

Cannon saw her bottom lip start to quiver, and he stood to put his arm around her. To Heath, he said, "If you actually have it in you to care, leave her alone."

Heath closed his eyes, gave one short nod—and passed out.

Whitaker made a gurgling sound…that didn't last. Cannon was pretty sure the bastard had just died.

"Here." Armie shoved the gun into Cannon's hand, snatched up one of the dish towels and started off in a hobbling gait.

"What are you doing?"

He paused, head dropped forward, then grunted a laugh. "One of those flying bullets grazed my ass. No, it's not bad, and yes, it hurts like hell. So if you'll excuse me?"

Yvette whipped around. "Armie!"

"No, doll. I was joking about showing you mine just because I saw yours."

She squawked again, now for a different reason. *"Armie."*

Laughing, he told Cannon, "I'd seal the deal on that if I was you." Then he limped on down the hall and slammed the bathroom door.

Seconds later, the police, the ambulance and Lieutenant Margaret Peterson-Riske all showed up.

CHAPTER TWENTY-FOUR

A WEEK LATER, in the middle of the day, with sunshine streaming in through the open bedroom windows, Yvette went to her knees in front of Cannon. Not for the first time.

And he'd ensure it wasn't the last.

So many things he'd thought would level her—the death of Whitaker, the upcoming trial for Heath who, luckily, remained behind bars. Mindi's arrest as she'd tried to leave the state.

Her grandfather's letter—which she'd read at least a dozen times.

But she was far more resilient than he'd ever imagined. And so damned sexy, he wasn't sure how much more he could take. With the threats behind them, she seemed determined to enjoy her newfound sexuality to the fullest.

With him.

That she proved insatiable only made him love her more.

"I hope," she said around nibbles to his hip bone, "you're thinking of me, and only me."

"You, and everything about you." He tunneled his fingers into her long hair, then forced himself to only hold her head loosely, without urging her mouth where he needed it most. This was her turn to do what she wanted, how she wanted.

As long as she only wanted it with him.

With every day that passed, she'd grown bolder in bed—and out of it. Knowing how much Yvette enjoyed sex with him made him feel far more like a stud than kicking ass in the SBC ever had.

"Every time," she whispered, trailing her open hands over his thighs, her open mouth over his abs, "I see this amazing body of yours, I want you."

Since she said that while naked, on her knees in front of him, he couldn't drum up a reply. Hell, it was all he could do to stay standing.

She cupped his balls in one hand, teased her nose over his cock and made a purring sound of pleasure. "It's not just your body, though."

He'd never survive this. "Babe…"

"Shh." She looked up at him, her green eyes big and soft and hungry. "I want you to know that it's you, Cannon. Not just the well-known fighter, not just the great body. It's everything about you. I hear you and I want you. I think of you and I want you. Will it ever end?"

"*No.*" He tightened his fingers in her silky hair, then had to lock his knees to keep from coercing her. A deep breath wouldn't help. He knew that, but tried it anyway. "I told you we're good together."

Her small hand held him snugly. "Mmm," she said by way of acknowledgment—and licked him, from the base of his shaft up to the head.

He shuddered, waiting on pins and needles—and he felt her hot mouth close over him.

He should have been lying down, he realized as he flattened one hand on the wall to brace himself. Gaze smoldering, he watched her work over him, her mouth, her hands…he even felt her nipples on his thighs.

Lost, he put his head back and fought off release. He

wanted to be inside her, and he wanted her with him when he came.

For as long as he could, he enjoyed her attentions—until he knew he wouldn't last a second more.

"Enough." Using her hair like a leash, he eased her away. "That's enough, honey. No more."

She sank back to sit on her heels, licked her lips and gave him a dreamy smile. "Did I do something wrong?"

Scooping her up, Cannon dropped with her sideways on the bed. "When we're naked and you're touching me, nothing you do is wrong, I promise." He kissed her, slipping a hand between her legs, gratified to find her already wet and hot. "You liked doing that to me?"

"I could eat you up," she murmured, and proceeded to nibble on his bottom lip, his chin.

God, she was hot. "Turnabout is fair play." Kissing his way down her body, paying special attention to all her most sensitive places, he moved off the bed and pulled her to the edge of the mattress. "Put your feet on my shoulders."

For a beat of time, she breathed hard, unmoving. He wrapped both hands around her ankles, lifted her feet up and arranged her as he wanted—wide-open and waiting for him.

On a heartfelt groan, she relaxed her legs, and Cannon used his mouth to get her up to speed with him.

When she was close, she tried to twist away, but he held her still.

"No fair," she gasped. "You stopped me."

"Totally different thing, honey." He put his mouth to her again, licking, sucking, pushing her.

"Next time," she moaned, getting closer and closer, "I won't stop either."

Just thinking about it nearly did him in.

Her heels pressed into his shoulders, her legs stiffening, her neck arching, and she cried out, her pleasure firing him even hotter than her words had.

The second she eased he rose over her, hurriedly rolled on a condom and, keeping her legs high, sank into her.

More often than not, the sex was fast and frenzied, but Yvette stayed with him every step of the way. When she came a second time, he joined her, and he wondered how it could be so incredibly perfect.

Over and over again.

The minutes ticked by, but she didn't want him to move away. He relaxed with his face against her neck, thinking of how easily he could have lost her.

And how he'd once let her walk away.

"You still give too much," she sweetly complained while idly stroking his nape.

Not enough, by his calculation. He wanted to give her everything. Sexual pleasure, sure. Security, absolutely.

Also love, marriage. A lifetime.

But he'd mentioned a lifetime once already, and she'd reacted with compassion.

Not exactly the response he'd been hoping for.

Never had he declared himself to a woman. But ever since her return—or really, since she'd first left him—Yvette had kept him in knots.

She talked about the infatuation she'd had as a schoolgirl, the hero worship she'd had for him as her rescuer.

Now she was a mature, independent woman and she wanted him sexually, yet she kept her emotions under wraps.

It constantly chewed on his peace of mind, needing to know if she loved him. Things had progressed at a whirlwind pace—she'd lost her grandfather, moved back home, been through one crisis after another, had her life threatened from multiple sources.

He had to give her time without pressuring her, and he would—as long as she didn't try to leave him again. Because if she did, he'd fight for her this time.

Sliding her fingers into his hair, she kissed his temple. "Be warned."

He lifted up to see her, took in her messy hair and swollen mouth and had to kiss her, and then kiss her again. "Warned about what?"

"From now on, I'm going after what I want."

He searched her face, unsure of her meaning.

Amused by his confusion, she tacked on, "From *you*."

"From me?" She wouldn't have to chase it down—he'd gladly give it.

Nodding slowly, pleasure teasing her lips, she whispered, "From you. Over you and under you. *With* you." She ate him up with her eyes and sighed. "Just wanted you to know."

He started to ask for details, but barking interrupted his intentions.

Warming him with her happiness, she asked, "Ready?"

"No." He rolled to his back, took a second to get his bearings, then sat up and found his boxers.

Giggling, Yvette pulled on a shirt and panties. "At least he waited until we'd finished."

They would *never* finish. More and more, he had the driving urge to tell her so, and the even worse need to hear her admit it.

Oblivious to his stormy thoughts, looking lighthearted and well loved, Yvette went to open the bedroom door.

Muggles, the midsize, muscular mutt they'd adopted the day after Whitaker died and Heath was arrested, came charging in. He acted as if it had been days instead of a few hours since he'd seen them.

According to the shelter, Muggles had been left outside on a chain to guard a trailer. His life hadn't been an easy one, until his owner had been arrested for making meth and Muggles had gone to the shelter, looking for a better—forever—home.

The day they'd met him, Muggles had slobbered a little too much, bounded around with excess energy and loved Yvette on sight.

Every time Cannon petted him, the dog closed his eyes, licked his meaty chops and rumbled like a lion.

He liked that Muggles accompanied Yvette wherever she went, which would include the pawnshop. It'd be ready to open soon, and although—for now—the danger was over, Yvette had been threatened too many times for him to ever take her safety for granted.

Muggles was a complete sweetheart, but also a superior guard dog, which made him perfect. He got along great with the kids at the rec center, loved the other fighters and had a natural tendency to be vigilant.

Cannon had divided sentiments on the pawnshop. It had come together nicely, and Yvette loved it.

Since he loved her, and it made her happy, he wanted it to work. But eventually he'd have to head back to Harmony, Kentucky. Two or three times a year, he'd be there for extended periods to train with his camp.

When he left, he wanted Yvette with him, not tied down with responsibilities.

He watched her say to the dog, "You want to go to the rec center with us? Do you? Do you, boy? Yes, you do. Such a good boy."

Laughing, Cannon touched the top of her head.

Tipping up her chin, she peered at him. "What's so funny?"

"You talking baby talk to Muggles." And the fact that even that turned him on. "Think he'll let us shower together?"

"Of course he will." She held the dog's face. "Muggles is a good boy, aren't you, Muggles?"

Blissful over the attention, Muggles wiggled and jiggled his strong, squat body everywhere. "Keep that up," Cannon warned her, "and he's going to pee on you."

Muggles did follow them into the bathroom, but he rested on the rug outside the tub and snored while they showered. As long as he could be close to Yvette, he was happy.

Since he felt the same, Cannon sympathized.

Within an hour they were on their way to the rec center. Armie's tournament was happening soon, and though he'd ended up with stitches in his butt, it hadn't slowed down his training, or his determination to fight.

"Doubtful," he'd said, "that anyone plans to punch my ass."

Cannon knew better. Armie was as likely to receive a kick there as anywhere, but he also understood Armie's need to push through. Luckily the stitches were out now, and he'd cleared his physical.

"Have I told you lately," Yvette asked, "how much I enjoy being at the rec center, watching you work with Armie and seeing everything you have going on in the community?"

Muggles gave him a look, then went back to staring out the window, his tongue lolling and his tail thumping.

The statement was out of the blue, making Cannon curious, but he said only, "I'm glad." She might not realize it yet, but she fit into every aspect of his world, and he into hers.

As he kept telling her, they were good together.

Maybe it was time to push her a little after all.

They'd get through the rest of today, and then tonight, when they were alone, after he'd given her another screaming climax, he'd tell her that he loved her.

Then they could start working on making a future together.

SWEAT BUILT ON Armie's shoulders as he continued to work the heavy bag.

Cannon stood off to the side, watching and deciding what to have him do next. When his cell rang, he pulled it from his pocket. "Hello?"

"Hey, stud."

Vanity? Yvette's friend now called often enough that he'd come to recognize her husky voice. "What's up, California?"

"Mmm, not much. Eating a banana split."

He smiled. "Is that code for something?" Vanity could be so outrageous, he was never quite sure of the things she said.

"Yeah. A banana, ice cream, whipped cream." She made another "mmm" sound. "And a cherry on top."

"So did you call me just to tell me that?" He turned the phone away from his mouth and told Armie, "Break in two minutes."

Nodding, Armie started kicking and punching harder, making the most of the remaining minutes. Off to the side, he saw Yvette chatting with Harper, Muggles sprawled on his back beside her feet.

"I knew you'd be at the rec center," Vanity said.

"Yvette's here, too. Did you want to talk to her?"

"Did I call her cell?"

"No. You called mine."

"There you go. Must be you I want to talk to, huh?"

Wondering what she wanted, he went over to stand by the reception desk. "So what's up?"

"I agree, Cannon. Let's get right to the point."

Had he been rude? "I didn't mean—"

"Now that the scrote is gone—"

"Scrote?" Cannon asked.

"Yeah, you know, short for *scrotum,* aka Heath."

He laughed outright. "I know what it means, and yeah, Heath is as gone as a man can be and still draw breath."

"Exactly. So anyway, since I don't need to keep tabs on his sorry butt here in Cali—"

"I never meant to saddle you with that."

"It was my pleasure. Now, are you going to let me tell this or not?"

"I am," he promised. "Go ahead."

"I was thinking I'd visit," she blurted.

Worried about her reception? Hell, as Yvette's best friend, he wanted to meet her. Thanks to their phone conversations, he felt as though he already knew her. "You're always welcome." As he looked out the big front window, a flash of long blond hair caught Cannon's attention.

"Yeah? Anytime at all?"

"Absolutely." With a phone to her ear, the blonde paid a cabbie, then threw something in the big trash can out front of the rec center.

Probably another woman signing up for the women's self-defense classes. They'd start right after Armie finished his fight. The promo was out, and already Denver and Stack had offered to lend a hand, which probably accounted for how women had rapidly filled the class roster.

"How about…now?"

Lost in thought, Cannon said, "Sure." Forgetting the woman on the street, he grabbed the water bottle and a towel and headed to Armie. "When does your flight come in? We'll pick you up."

"No need." She cleared her throat. "I'm here."

"Here?"

"Well, behind you, actually."

That was when he realized how quiet the gym had gotten, everyone staring toward the door.

The blonde.

He turned, and sure enough, there she stood. A Barbie look-alike, Yvette had said. He wasn't that familiar with Barbie, but yeah, he saw it.

Wearing a short denim skirt and a white halter, her blond hair hanging to her ass, her long legs tanned and shapely, she put away her phone while taking in the rec center.

The fact that every man there ogled her didn't seem to faze her.

When Yvette squealed, Cannon's first thought was another threat. Then he saw her dashing over to Vanity, saw Vanity do her own girl squeal and run to meet her halfway.

They did a few circles, still making that high-pitched female sound of excitement. Muggles danced around them barking in maniacal delight, though he doubted the dog knew what the fuss was all about.

Cannon smiled and knew it. Then he looked around and saw every other dude smiling, too.

Beside him, still huffing, Armie asked, "Friend of Yvette's, huh?"

"Vanity. She's from California."

"She's ready to start a stampede."

Yeah, true enough. The fighters were all edging closer, ready to claim introductions.

He glanced at Armie. "Not you, though, huh?"

Before replying, Armie finished off the water bottle. "She's a little too much fluff for my tastes."

Though he knew it wasn't what Armie meant, he said, "No tats or piercing?"

"Cotton candy all the way." He clapped Cannon on the back. "You'd better go head off the masses."

Agreeing, Cannon approached with his hand out. "Vanity?"

"Oh, pfft." She pushed his hand aside and gave him a hearty hug. "Oh, my," she said, her hands going over his back and down toward his ass. "Yvette, you're right. Very studly."

He freed himself with a laugh. "Why didn't you tell us you were coming?"

Yvette winced. "Well…" She looked at Vanity, then back to him. "I knew."

Sheepish? What was she up to? If Vanity was here just to help her pack, they could both forget it. Somehow he'd convince Yvette to stay.

Hands on his hips, resistance mounting, he said, "Well, what?"

Rolling her eyes, Yvette took his hand. "It's better discussed in private." And she dragged him off with a lot of fanfare.

Uncaring that everyone watched.

Cannon wasn't sure what to make of that.

Vanity called after them, saying, "Don't worry about me." With purring undertones, she added, "I'm sure I can entertain myself."

That was all the invitation she needed to issue before a half dozen fighters converged on her. Knowing

Armie would oversee things, Cannon went along willingly with Yvette.

In the break room, she turned him loose and, avoiding his gaze, took a seat at the table. Muggles started dancing, wanting her to hold him. She pulled the dog up to her lap.

Cannon didn't sit. He crossed his arms and stared down at her. "What's going on, honey?"

Still not looking at him, she drew a deep breath, blew it out slowly. "I've been thinking about things. About… the future."

No way. He angled his head, watching her warily, arguments already forming for why she should stay. Forever.

With him.

Two fingers in her hair, she whispered, "I've read over my grandfather's letter so many times."

Guilt softened his stance—but only a little. "I'm sorry I kept it from you."

"He asked you to. And I understand why. From the beginning, my only intent in coming home was to take care of things so you wouldn't be bothered by the ways he'd obligated you."

How could she still have things so wrong? "I've never been obligated." Though he'd certainly taken advantage of the gift her grandfather had given him. "I was here for *you*." Always.

A sad smile flickered into place. "I know. Even after everything you'd already done for me, Grandpa sort of tangled you up in that again, too."

"No. I never—"

"For so long now, you've been protecting me."

"Damn right." Because he loved her.

"But…" She lifted her shoulders. "The threats are over now, so you…you don't need to anymore."

Like hell. "What about the trial?" Gathering steam, he reminded her, "You hate being the center of attention."

"I'm getting better at it." She bit her lip, then cleared her throat. "But speaking of that… Everywhere you go, you're the focus, right?"

Was she worried about getting caught in the spotlight? He wouldn't lie to her, but he also didn't want to give her reservations. "A lot of times, away from the fight crowd, no one knows who I am."

"But if a woman accompanied you to a fight—"

"Yeah. Maybe." Fighting the urge to scoop her up and hold her close, he admitted, "The camera might find you occasionally, especially during a title fight."

She smiled. "Which is coming up very soon."

He nodded. Not that he was thinking about that right now with Yvette keeping him guessing. "You shouldn't worry about—"

"Cannon." She looked up at him with pleading eyes. "Just let me say this, okay?"

"Fine." Determination pulsed through his blood. "But you'd better say things I want to hear, honey."

"You don't have to protect me anymore."

Wrong. "I'm always going to want to protect you, because you're important to me."

She breathed faster. "You have so many wonderful fans."

"True." He took a step closer. "But I want *you.*"

Laughter from the outer room drew her attention, and she glanced that way before facing him again. "And so many good friends."

Another step toward her. "They're all blessings." Softer. "I want *you.*"

"You have a busy life, a thriving career, money and—"

"And you. I want *you,* Yvette."

She straightened her shoulders. "Well, I want to make plans."

He opened his mouth to speak, but she didn't give him a chance.

"I want to be with you. And…and I don't want you to go to Harmony without me."

Wow. After so many straight jabs, she blindsided him with that quick combination. "The pawnshop—"

"That's why Vanity is here!" She rushed to her feet, setting a grumbling Muggles aside. "She'll run it for me when I need to be away."

Had she arranged everything? "When you're away with me?"

"Would that be okay?"

Better than okay.

"Because I know this was all sort of forced on you—"

"Not even close." It was past time he set her straight on a few things. "You know I gave Rissy her house, right?"

"Yes. But what does that—"

"And I bought my own house in Harmony. Free and clear."

"Wow." She swallowed. "I didn't realize—"

"I don't need a share of your grandpa's house, or anything from the pawnshop. But I wanted to be with you, so I went along for the ride."

"The ride?"

"Staying at the house with you. Claiming half the pawnshop so you couldn't just sell it off." He touched her chin. "I used the excuse your grandfather gave me to make my move on you."

She sputtered a laugh, saw he was serious, and her

brows went up. "But…I've always been crazy about you. You knew that."

Meaning he didn't need to make moves? He shook his head. "You never wanted to be here, honey. You'd made a life in California. You'd moved on."

Shaking her head, she whispered, "No. I tried, but…" Looking around, she made sure no one was near the door and able to listen in. "You know things didn't…*work* for me, not with anyone else."

"You know why, right?" He waited for her to say they were good together.

But she went one further and took out his knees, saying, *"Because I love you."*

Flattening a hand on the wall to brace himself, Cannon stared at her. She'd pretty much just shouted that at him.

Wincing, Yvette put her shoulders back and said again, more evenly this time, "I love you."

Damn. "Yeah, that'll work."

"What?"

Pure elation put a smile on his face. "Saying things I want to hear."

"Oh." She closed some of the space separating them. Not touching, but near enough that he could kiss her if he chose to.

And he would—as soon as she finished declaring herself.

"You love me?" he prompted, sensing that she wasn't done yet.

"I do," she breathed. "So much."

"And whenever I have to travel, you'll go along?"

"Yes. I mean, that'd require your cooperation, but I'd like to. I can handle the attention." Her face heated. "I mean, the attention from being with you, the famous fighter known as the Saint."

He loved the way her face colored, how she licked her lips.

"That is…" She searched his face. "If you want me there?"

"Hell, yeah, I do."

She expelled an anxious breath.

Laughing, Cannon hauled her into his chest and gave her a quick kiss. "One condition."

"What?"

"After I get through this next fight, you have to marry me."

Eyes wide, she stared at him, her parted lips trembling.

Cannon whispered to her, "Say yes."

"Yes. Yes, yes, *yes*." Throwing her arms around his neck, she kissed him with hunger, with love. "We don't have to wait, you know. I don't need a big wedding."

More laughter came from the gym, followed by the roar of male camaraderie. Grinning, Cannon said, "You might not, but they'll insist."

She sank against him. "Armie will make an incredible best man."

God, he could hardly wait to see Armie's face when told he'd have to wear a tux.

Yvette touched his chest, played her fingers over his collarbone. "You love me, too?"

He groaned. "How can you not know that?"

"I don't know. I've loved you for so long, in so many ways."

"Same here, though I didn't always realize it." Not giving her a chance to deny that, he kissed her forehead, her nose, then her soft parted lips. "I got hooked on that teenage tease, and even when I tried not to notice you, I couldn't help myself. Then, when I saw you threatened, wanting to keep you safe consumed me."

"I didn't know." She put her cheek against his chest. "Or I wouldn't have left."

"You were still so young." He moved his hands over her back. "And I got involved with the SBC."

"The timing was off," she agreed. On a long sigh, she said, "My grandfather was so wise, forcing me back here."

"I'm glad he did, because I have to say, this take-charge attitude of yours is right up a fighter's wheel-house." He tipped her face up. "When need be, I can fight dirty, though usually I just fight for sport. But when it comes to you, I fight to win."

She smiled. "I think I won this time."

Grinning, he hugged her off her feet. "And I remain undefeated."

* * * * *